Dark Instinct

Elite Protectors, Volume 2

Amara Holt

Published by Amara Holt, 2024.

Copyright © 2024 by Amara Holt

All rights reserved.

No part of this book may be reproduced, distributed, or transmitted in any form or by any means, including photocopying, recording, or other electronic or mechanical methods, without the prior written permission of the author, except in the case of brief quotations in book reviews.

This is a work of fiction. Names, characters, places, and incidents are the product of the author's imagination or are used fictitiously. Any resemblance to actual events, organizations, locales, or persons, living or dead is coincidental and is not intended by the authors.

PROLOGUE

Alena

Chicago

Three months ago, my mommy passed away. I counted it carefully on the calendar. Uncle Walt, an old friend of my family, told me she went to live in heaven. I tried not to be sad; after all, he said it was a very beautiful place and that she would always be watching over me. But it was so hard not to cry every day and every night, especially when my tenth birthday came last month.

That time, there was no cake with candles, no balloons, no birthday songs. That time, there was no mommy, and I was very, very sad. I even asked her to come get me; I wanted to live up there in the beautiful heaven with her.

That really upset Daddy. He didn't like it when I cried and always punished me in the attic when it happened. I hated that place with its low walls, dirty windows, and strange smell of sadness. But if I didn't stay there, he would hit me, and I was more afraid of that than being in the attic, which was cold and dark.

Daddy was very angry and very busy. He owned a bar close to our house, and I hardly ever saw him when Mommy was here, which hadn't really changed... until now.

A few days ago, I found out that more people would be living with us. An aunt and her son. I didn't know until that moment that I had an aunt; maybe she was a distant relative. But whoever she was, she was important to Daddy. He never missed work, not ever, not even when Mommy got sick. But this time, the sun was shining in the sky, and

Daddy hadn't left for work yet; he was just waiting for the aunt and her son.

I had always wanted someone to play with and had set aside my best toys for when he arrived. It would be nice not to spend the whole day alone. When the doorbell rang, I jumped off the couch. I was curious and even happy.

"Daddy, they're here! They're here!" I ran to the door, and he came right behind me.

"Be quiet, girl. I told you to stop with that hellish racket." He flung the door open, and a tall, slender woman, very, very beautiful, turned towards him with a wide, bright smile. That must be the aunt.

"Sorry for the delay, dear." She leaned toward my dad and, to my surprise, kissed him. A kiss! Isn't that what aunts are supposed to do?

"At least they arrived," he grumbled, and I stood there behind him, frozen, while I watched him talk to the woman, who seemed cheerful. Then a boy climbed the front stairs, holding a small, colorful suitcase in his hands. He was as cute as the aunt, with smooth, well-groomed hair, just like Mommy used to do mine.

I looked at my reflection in the window glass and shrank a little when I saw the crooked braid I had managed to do in my hair. I wanted to look a bit prettier to welcome them.

"Come on, come on, come in," Daddy ordered, and they soon passed through the door, but they hadn't noticed me yet.

"Well, the house is quite nice." The aunt twirled in the middle of the living room. "It clearly needs some renovation, but it's charming and..." She stopped when she finally realized I was there.

"This is Alena," my dad introduced me with a lackluster wave. "Alena, these are Norah and Caleb." He pointed to the boy who was the same size as me and, incredibly, had the same hair color as mine, which was a copy of Daddy's—wavy golden brown. It was the only thing I had inherited from him.

"Hi, Aunt Norah. Welcome..."

"I'm not your aunt!" the woman shouted so loudly that I jumped in surprise. "Where does this creature live?" She turned to my dad, completely ignoring me.

"Her room is at the end of the hall, upstairs, away from ours. Don't worry, she won't cause any problems. We'll arrange the room so that they can sleep together. It's a big space."

"No way do I want my son to mix with... her." The aunt—wait, I blinked, confused, not knowing what to call her—gave me a strange look that made me afraid.

"I'm a boy; I can't sleep in the same room as her!" Caleb protested, wrinkling his nose.

"We'll figure something out," my dad interrupted, and I didn't understand what he would do. But I was so desperate to have contact with another child, since I had started my school break early due to what happened with Mommy, that I quickly approached the boy.

"Caleb, do you want to see my toys?" I clasped my hands to my chest, anxious, but the boy wrinkled his nose and looked at his mother, who frowned and held him by the shoulder.

"I don't want to see your girl toys; I have my own, and you'd better stay away from them. They're limited edition."

"I don't want to hear anyone fighting," my dad scolded. "Let's get you settled."

That night, all my things were taken to the attic, and according to Daddy, that would be my new room, and even though I was scared, I shouldn't complain.

Days went by, and the aunt, who wasn't really an aunt, started to look more and more like Daddy's new wife. And now I wasn't just afraid of him; that woman terrified me.

I thought I would be happier with her and her son in our house, but Caleb wouldn't let me play with him and always pinched me when he had the chance. His mother, who I now called Mrs. Norah, made chocolate cookies that filled the house with their smell but wouldn't let me eat them because she said I was messy and didn't deserve them. Plus, she constantly yelled at me. I had always been polite and obedient; I didn't like disorder, just like Mommy, and I tried to follow in her footsteps, but the aunt accused me of things I didn't even do. In fact, she always seemed very angry with me.

From time to time, I could hear her and Daddy arguing in the room that used to belong to Mommy, and they said some strange things.

"She was an idiot and still left behind an identical copy. I can't stand looking at her face. How could you have that... that thing with a sick woman? That wasn't the goal."

"I didn't think it would happen, but in the end, we managed, didn't we? I already have access to 30% of the inheritance, and when she turns 21, we can claim the rest. There was no way to stop her from leaving most of it to her daughter."

"Why didn't she ever use some of the money to renovate this tiny house? With such a large sum, she could at least leave behind a bit more comfort for us."

"Sarah never wanted to touch her father's inheritance; she always said it was for her daughter's future. I tried to manipulate her decision and even managed to extract some values, but in the end, I had to be very patient and rely on pure luck. I almost thought I'd have to deal with this myself; I've never seen anyone resist cancer for so long. I think she became more stubborn when she got pregnant. But anyway, now... the business will thrive. I'll keep using the bar as a front; it helps with all the money laundering I do for the Marinos. We'll have to maintain the same facade to avoid drawing attention."

I had no idea what they were talking about, but it made me immensely sad to see that woman sleeping where my mom had just a few months ago. As time passed, everything began to change even more.

I thought things couldn't get worse, but one cloudy morning, Norah grabbed me by the shoulders and stared at me with narrow, irritated eyes:

"Listen, girl, if you want the right to eat my chocolate cookies, you need to contribute. I can't stand seeing you lounging around in this house all day."

"But Caleb is here all day too, and I don't see him doing much other than playing."

"He's very busy studying; he'll be a doctor one day." I looked at the boy, who was doing nothing more than reading his comic books. "As for you, I suggest you start working soon. You can help your father at the bar," she said in a low, dangerous tone that told me if I disagreed, I'd end up getting hit.

So, at 11, I began working in my dad's bar, sweeping the floor as best I could and keeping the chairs and tables in order. Uncle Walt wasn't happy at all and even argued with Daddy; it was quite a scene. But in the end, the only thing that changed was that Uncle started coming to the bar every day and always gave me a coin or two. I began saving everything I earned in a little jar hidden in a hole in the attic near my bed. Maybe one day I would have enough to buy all the chocolate cookies I wanted.

It took me a few more years to understand that, in the end, my dad had a secret family and didn't hesitate to bring his mistress and their son into my mother's house as soon as she passed away. Yet, I could live two lives and never understand why he hated me so much, just like Norah and Caleb did.

CHAPTER ONE

Ghost

10 Years Later

I ran my fingers across the keys of the grand piano that occupied much of my living room. Night was creeping in behind large, gray clouds that stained the sky a deep gray, void of stars.

I plucked a few notes, feeling deep inside that part of my soul was just like that. Without light.

It had been many months since I'd had such a real and deep nightmare as that early morning. I had freed myself from night terrors, but now and then my mind still played tricks on me, and the pain of those memories left me disoriented. Once again, I was there, in front of the piano, a mantra to help me refocus and try to forget, pouring into the music what I couldn't say in words.

I finished the rest of the whiskey I had been drinking and continued to play as if my life depended on it, trying not to return to that moment of that damned nightmare, which had stopped being about me many years ago.

I remembered that at first, all I saw was a scared, small, and very skinny Zion, repeatedly suffering through everything that had marked me the most. But over the years, after finding a safe place with my dad and a family I would do anything to protect, my dreams changed.

I no longer saw myself being tortured repeatedly, no. After discovering what it was like to be truly loved, my nightmares became about my dad and my brothers suffering what I had endured, and that was worse, infinitely worse. There was nothing that rattled me more than imagining people I loved in danger. Reliving those moments transformed me into someone else, someone I didn't even recognize and feared.

I decided to abandon the piano, ready to take a shower and maybe go out to find one of my brothers, but when I stood up, a loud and very familiar roar shook the entire structure of the house, and my heart shot up into my throat.

"Fuck!" The sound of my car's engine roared again. I jumped over the black couch near the piano and grabbed my Smith & Wesson 380 from a drawer in my desk, racing down to the garage.

I narrowed my eyes and aimed, ready for whoever the crazy, stupid, psychotic person was trying to steal my most prized possession. The engine roared once more, almost as if it was calling for me, and I quickened my steps, stopping abruptly when I reached the bottom of the garage ramp and came face to face with two punks I knew very well.

"Get your hands off my Nazca!" I put the gun away, still unsure if I should shoot them in the ass to teach them a lesson.

Wolf, my middle brother, stared at me with his distinctive bicolored eyes—one a clear, bright blue and the other brown like a sunset. He flashed a crooked, mischievous smile, while Snake, our oldest brother, was sitting behind the wheel of my silver BMW Nazca C2, a super sports car that could reach 100 km/h in a mere 4.2 seconds. My German car could go over 300 km/h and was my most cherished child. A child being tortured by Snake's huge feet and all his countless tattoos.

"He's here..." Wolf whispered to the hoodlum next to him.

"Can I know why the hell my house was invaded? Get out before I rip your hands off! How...," I looked from one to the other, "...how did you get in here?"

"You're not the only one who can make a stealthy entrance and scare others." Wolf shrugged, puffing out his chest, proud of himself. I narrowed my eyes. So that's what this was about.

My brothers and I were adopted, and each of us had a story to tell. The truth was we only discovered happiness after being adopted by our dad, the CEO of Holder Security, a company he created to provide bodyguard services in a unique way, which turned out to be very successful, operating throughout the country and in other places around the world.

My dad turned his three children into the main players of the business, making us his greatest examples. But no amount of training could change our origins and the marks our past left, and that was true for me as well. I had developed the ability to become an extremely silent person, not because I wanted to, but because it was part of me, like the countless scars on my body, and very often it caused shocking scares and accidents, with Wolf, Snake, and our dad being the main victims.

My brothers lived their lives just to scare me, according to those two idiots in front of me, and when they succeeded, they'd make me taste my own poison, giving me a huge fright. Considering my heart nearly stopped when I heard my car's engine, one of the most expensive BMWs in the world, they had succeeded... those bastards.

"There's technology capable of duplicating a key from a photo." Snake stepped out of the vehicle, leaned his large body against the hood of my car, and crossed his arms, revealing hands as tattooed as the rest of his body. His very blue eyes sparkled with satisfaction.

I put my hand to my chest, trying not to rip my older brother's head off, and noticed they were both wearing Chicago Cubs shirts, the basketball team they supported. Which meant they were about to go to a game but found time to come mess with me.

"So..." Snake continued, looking at his accomplice with a broad grin, and he raised a hand where a key identical to my house's gate key was hanging. "I made a copy of the gate key."

"And I knew the alarm code," Wolf added, chipping in.

"How the hell did you find out?"

"I thought it would be difficult, but I tried some combinations, and one of them worked perfectly." Wolf smiled calmly, as if discovering my password had been nothing hard. "We've all used Dad's birthday as a password at some point in our lives; you should change it." He laughed, and I held back the urge to jump on his neck.

"It was pretty easy," Snake started. "First, I checked if the porch light was on. You always leave it on when you're home."

"Then we snuck in, grabbed the car key, and voilà!" Wolf opened his arms. "Now tell me, what's it like to get scared out of nowhere? Desperate? Are you sweating?"

"I hope you are; I know this idiot has made me sweat with his sudden appearances."

"Let me get this straight; you broke at least five laws to scare me? And stay away from my Nazca!" I yanked Snake by the arm, and he laughed.

"It was worth it!" Wolf beamed.

"Oh, god, now I'll have to replace everything and remember not to let anyone with a cell phone near my keys..."

"Ah, don't worry; not just anyone can make a copy of these. That technology can only be done by Jasmin's company and..." Wolf elbowed Snake.

"Okay, raise your hands, step away from the car, and get the hell out of here!" I huffed in irritation, shoving both of them by the shoulders after snatching my keys from their hands.

"Not a chance; you're coming with us." Snake halted his steps.

"What?"

"Snake got three tickets to today's Cubs finals at Wrigley Field, and you're going with us."

"I'm not going!"

"Yes, you are; it's the finals, Ghost, the tickets are sold out!" Wolf's eyes widened further, indignant at my refusal.

"How did you get tickets to a game that was already sold out?" I turned to the older one.

"A VIP owed me a favor, you know how it is." Snake raised his thick eyebrows and grinned. He was known for his special contacts and shady VIPs, mostly mobsters.

"Yeah, I know. Half the world owes you something, and I'm seriously worried about whether the other half is still alive." I laughed and threw my hands up. "Fine, I did want to take a spin in my Nazca."

I changed clothes as quickly as I could, putting on a white shirt and khaki shorts. A few minutes later, I was following Wolf's car with Snake beside me in the passenger seat through the streets of Chicago, heading for a night out with those two idiots I called brothers.

"You're still pale," Snake commented as we approached the stadium. "I should have recorded it. Damn, why didn't I think of that?"

"Because I'm the smart one in the family!" I huffed. "I can't believe they touched my steering wheel. Should I go to your apartment and try one of your collection guns, Snake?" The man's eyes widened suddenly.

"You're crazy!"

"Say you doubt it!"

"How old are you again?" He narrowed his eyes, and we ended up laughing at how childish that conversation had become.

I stopped at the stadium entrance, a dark place leading to the parking lot, where Wolf's car was in front of mine, waiting in line to enter. A few fans were scattered around like grains.

"I'll grab the tickets and drinks; see you at the entrance in a few minutes." Snake got out of the car.

"Okay, I'll park and meet you there," I replied, and only then did I realize how happy I was that my brothers were troublesome enough to invade my house for such a silly reason.

Because of them, I had forgotten everything that had happened earlier, and now I felt lighter and more excited, as I always did in the presence of my family, as if seeing them reminded me that they were safe.

I accelerated, stopping again behind Wolf as we entered the parking lot. As usual, people around started staring at my Nazca. Some pointed, others whispered, leaning in to get a better look. It was an amazing machine and drew attention wherever it went.

I turned a corner and was approaching the underground parking entrance, right next to my brother's car, when a scene caught my eye.

On the other side of the entrance courtyard, there was a staircase where some fans who usually wouldn't enter the game were climbing to catch a glimpse of part of the stadium. Near those stairs, there was a small girl wearing a sweatshirt that was way too big for her. The hood covered her face, which was also hidden by a cap. Three men cornered her at the base of the stairs, which was completely empty with the game about to start. They could have been friends having fun, maybe hanging out together, but their body language told me otherwise. Then she slapped one of the guys who tried to touch her and pointed her finger at him, who seemed much bigger next to her, and the bastard grabbed her hand tightly, making her lose her balance. Another one circled around behind her, and I noticed the exact moment when the third pointed his head toward a dark alley nearby.

"What the hell do they think they're doing?" I snarled to myself, furious. My blood began to boil, and I gripped the steering wheel tightly when one of them grabbed her and started dragging her away.

Damn, they were going to hurt her, and the realization made me tremble as that dark feeling ignited in my veins.

What kind of filthy person would harass a woman? What kind of monster did such a thing?

I spun the wheel, slammed my foot on the gas, and drove my car onto the median without thinking, blinded by the urge to run them over. I threw the vehicle at the three of them, who stumbled and scattered. The tallest one, who was holding the girl by the shoulders, threw her to the ground, and she fell with a hoarse whimper. A wave of brown hair spilled from her sweatshirt as she crawled along the ground until her back hit a pillar.

"What the hell is this?" one of them cursed, and I got out of the car. I clenched my fists, crazy and filled with rage, fully aware of what would happen next.

Alena

I had arrived at the entrance of Wrigley Field Stadium just before the end of the afternoon, hoping to see the players' bus. But after hours of waiting, I realized they were probably already inside the stadium. Still, there was a little spot by the wall where a staircase gave me a view of part of the green field and the scoreboard, and just looking at it made me euphoric.

I had never had enough money to buy a ticket to that place, even though it was one of my biggest dreams, so now and then I would escape and take the bus across the city to at least see part of the field.

I had been working at my dad's bar since I was 11 years old, and spending every afternoon and early evening there, where a television only showed baseball games, greatly influenced all that love. However, I earned very little and needed to save up if I wanted to escape that life where my stepmother and her son, who was my brother, only knew how to torment me. So all I managed to buy from my team was the cap I was wearing and a fake baseball bat that I affectionately named Cubs, in honor of my team, which I sometimes used to break up a casual fight at the bar or to kick out some drunk making a fuss.

It was the height of absurdity that my only friend was a piece of wood, but it was my most reliable companion. That night, I decided to spend the only money I had left after my bus fare to buy a blue bracelet with my team's name. I looked at it, hidden under my oversized sweatshirt. It was my newest acquisition, and I was very happy with it, even though it was simple and the plastic material might soon wear off the team's name.

I climbed the steps next to the stadium and stood there for a long time, just watching the stands fill up as night fell and the outside grew emptier and emptier. I didn't have a cell phone, so all I could do was keep an eye on the huge clock on the center of a luxurious building across the street. When I glanced at it, I nearly fell backward upon realizing I had only an hour left to open the bar.

"Shit!" I cursed.

The trip from there to my house would take at least fifty minutes, assuming the bus didn't take too long to arrive. My dad would kill me if I was late to open the bar. I turned to run down the stairs when I saw three men standing at the bottom. All three turned to me, and a strange chill ran through my body at the way they looked at me.

"Hey, cutie!" the tallest one said, and as I reached the bottom of the stairs, inevitably close to them, I caught a strong whiff of alcohol.

"Get out of the way, asshole!" I cursed. The years I had spent alone dealing with clueless men at my dad's bar had taught me that letting them corner me was never the best option.

"Wow, what a foul-mouthed girl." One of them laughed. His yellowed teeth made him look even paler and creepier. "Am I going to have to teach you some manners?" He reached his hand toward me, and I realized with alarm that we were alone. With everyone focused on the stadium entrance, that area was always isolated. I slapped the guy's hand away and pointed my finger at him.

"You better not mess with me, you idiot." I tried to pretend I wasn't trembling from head to toe with pure fear as I glared at him, but to my surprise, the idiot grabbed my hand and pulled me close. My stomach turned at the stench of alcohol and cigarettes that clung to him.

"Show her, Joe." A second man moved closer and nodded toward a dark alley nearby. I immediately picked up on what they wanted to do.

"Get your hands off me!" Panic made me act, and I started struggling against them, which only made them laugh, enjoying my distress.

"I'll show you what I have here," the guy named Joe said, pulling out his junk as if it were valuable. It wasn't, but the thought of what might happen left me weak and defeated.

"If you don't let me go right now, I'll scream. HELP!"

Joe lunged to cover my mouth, but before he could, a loud, thunderous sound tore through the air. I widened my eyes as a car that looked more like a spaceship crashed onto the median, heading straight for us. The men lost their balance, and one of them fell.

"What the hell is this?" Joe howled, jumping and throwing me to the ground. I stumbled and fell.

The vehicle's door opened, and a man stepped out with an energy that felt like it was anchoring me to the ground. His upright posture accentuated the muscles straining against a white shirt. He looked at me, his intense, hard gaze sweeping over my body, making me shiver. Damn, he was beautiful. He looked like a celestial warrior come from the future.

He ignored the idiots around us and turned to me with a calm voice that sent chills down my spine. It felt like the calm before the storm.

"Are you alright, miss?" I tried to answer, but I was trembling so much that all I could do was whimper.

"Who does this punk think he is, rolling up here in that car?" I covered my mouth when I saw the big guy wielding a metal bar. It probably belonged to the gangs that frequently caused trouble after games.

"Please step back so you don't get hurt," the mysterious stranger warned, cracking his neck. He turned to Joe, who was glaring at him, and smiled. Holy shit, he smiled? "I'm really going to enjoy this."

The man with the metal bar lunged, and the stranger dodged with incredible speed, landing a punch to the guy's face, and a chaotic fight broke out. Desperately, I searched for anything I could grab to hit one of those idiots and help the man who had come to my rescue, but there was nothing. I turned to see him skillfully evading the attacks, moving like he was dancing among them, then began kicking and punching in a way that looked like some martial art involving knees, elbows, and everything in between.

"Damn it, Ghost, I left you alone for two minutes!" A tattooed man came running, so big he looked like a bear.

"What the hell is going on?" Another guy joined the fight, making the chaos even worse.

My heart raced with fear and gratitude; only God knows what could have happened if he hadn't shown up, but I couldn't stay. I knew what would happen if I was late, and I desperately wanted to thank the man from the spaceship car. I wanted to hug him and cry with gratitude, but I had to run. That didn't stop the tears from flowing, especially when I got on the bus.

I felt powerless, weak, and alone. Vulnerable in the face of so many dangers. And what distressed me the most was not having had the chance to thank the man who had probably broken those idiots in half. Ghost. I was sure I had heard him called that, just as I would never forget the image of his face—handsome and fierce.

I had never been defended by anyone in my life, and perhaps that was why I was sobbing in the back of a crowded bus, fully aware of the sad ending he had rescued me from.

I closed my eyes and tried to calm down. But all I could see was his face. The feeling of his voice still sent shivers across my skin.

Thank you, stranger. For doing for me what no one has ever done.

CHAPTER TWO

Alena

Somehow, I found the strength to run from the bus stop to Cliff's bar, my dad.

I stopped at the bar's entrance, barely able to breathe. I gasped and leaned my hands on my knees, still absorbed and almost disbelieving of what had just happened.

"You're late again, you incompetent." I jumped in surprise and looked over my shoulder. Caleb was standing behind me, adjusting his backpack, probably just back from college.

"Don't start." I opened the bar door.

I thanked God when I realized my dad wasn't around and entered the bar, which was spacious enough to accommodate several tables and chairs. The windows were dark and prevented sunlight from fully passing through. I hated that, but it was just one of the thousands of complaints I could make about the bar. I loved being a bartender; that was the truth. Mixing drinks and creatively assembling them excited me. The problem wasn't my job, but who I was forced to work for, at least until I turned eighteen.

"Alena, where have you been, you irresponsible girl? It's time to open the bar." I heard a familiar voice echo behind me from the back of the counter, and I turned in surprise to find Norah, my stepmother, who rarely set foot in the bar, looking at me with visible disapproval. She must have come in through the back doors. Our house was in an alley behind the bar, and to make things easier, my dad had opened an exit that led directly to it. "My God, you look terrible. That tangled hair and, ugh, look at those clothes." She shuddered, scrutinizing my body with her eyes. "You look like a beggar!"

Norah's brown hair fell in shiny waves around her face, which was full of plastic surgery, making her nose even more upturned. She definitely came straight from the beauty salon.

I had to admit my stepmother was a beautiful woman, a beauty that cost half of the bar's profits, but there was something in her eyes, brown like her hair, that no amount of beauty could hide: the hatred she felt for me.

That woman hated me.

"What are you doing here, Norah? Bored? I arrived exactly when the bar was supposed to open, not a minute more or less. Now, if you'll excuse me, I'm going to start working." She shot me a glare.

My life was shit, yes, but I had learned that lowering my head wouldn't improve it at all.

"What a sassy girl!" she hissed. "You should be focused on working since you only have a place to live thanks to this." She threatened over her shoulder, and I tried to do what I knew best: ignore her. "Your father doesn't want a lazy daughter sucking him dry."

How could she have the nerve to say that? I never understood why my dad hated me so much and treated me like a stranger, but I realized I was a burden when he left me with Norah and Caleb, his secret family that also hated me, inside the house that once belonged to my mother. Since then, I spent every day feeling unwanted. I had the right to live there, but I was the only one treated like an intruder.

I turned to her, hot with anger, and only then realized she was standing near the cash register. I could bet she had pocketed half the cash there without even notifying anyone. I had found myself in tough situations because of Norah's withdrawals without notice.

"He doesn't need me to suck anything he has. He already has you for that. Please, write down the amount this time," I muttered, organizing the glasses on the table.

"What did you say?"

"Write down the amount this time!" I repeated, louder.

She glared at me, fury bubbling in her eyes, but the bar door swung open abruptly, preventing her from pouring more venom on me. I widened my eyes when my dad stormed past her.

"Oh, dear, you have to see how rude Alena has been to me," Norah whined, but my dad pushed her aside as she approached him.

"Shut the hell up," he shouted, and I shrank back behind the counter. He could switch from silence to rage easily, but the bulging eyes and trembling hands were something new, making him even more frightening.

The only thing my dad and I had in common was our golden-brown hair, just like Caleb's, who was also frozen in the corner of the bar with our mother. My dad had dark green eyes that were profoundly shadowy, his face lined with deep creases, and he was strong, medium height, but could intimidate even bigger men. And he rarely appeared at the bar, which couldn't mean anything good.

I watched him as he crossed the bar just to peek through the door that led to our house. He looked anxious, his face more troubled than usual, murmuring incoherent whispers.

"Norah, Caleb, I want you both to stay home today," he ordered suddenly, and I widened my eyes, alert.

"What do you mean, dear? I have a dinner date with my friends and—"

"Cancel it, damn it, and obey me. Are you deaf?" He yelled, making both Norah and me jump.

"Alright," she agreed, pulling Caleb closer to her.

"And what about me, Dad? Do you want me to stay home too?" I was scared, trembling from head to toe, and barely knew why.

"No, the bar needs to stay open. Everything has to seem normal."

"How?" He reached me in just a few steps and grabbed my arm, shaking me like a piece of paper.

"You better take care of this shit, do you hear me? Do you hear me?" He gritted his teeth in anger, and I held my breath, trying to keep my feelings in check. I hadn't cried because of those three in years; I wasn't going to start now.

"I heard," I forced myself to whisper, and he released me.

"I won't be going home today," he informed Norah, and left the bar before my stepmother had a chance to question him, which I doubted she would do.

I leaned against the counter to steady my trembling legs and caught a glimpse through the darkened windows as my dad met with two very strange guys across the street, always looking side to side as if expecting to be caught off guard at any moment. A shiver ran down my spine. My dad always met with people who gave me the creeps.

"Son, it's still too early to drink," Norah scolded in a sickly sweet tone, pulling me back to reality.

"Don't start, Mom. It's not for me; it's for some friends from college." Caleb ran his hands through his hair and turned to me. Only then did I see he had grabbed a brand-new bottle of whiskey, one of the most expensive. "You better not tell him about this." He narrowed his greenish eyes.

"You can bet that'll be the first thing I say when he gets back. If you want to cover your friends' expenses, you better have the money for it. If a bottle goes missing from the bar, it'll be my fault, and I'm not taking responsibility for your losses."

"You little whore, useless!" He lunged at me. I reached for my Cubs bat in two quick steps and raised it. I was exhausted from the feeling that that day had been hell on earth, and after everything, I wasn't going to run in fear from my idiot brother.

"You better think twice if you don't want me to hit your knee or maybe between your legs... My aim is perfect, you know that." I stared him down, ready to react.

Caleb had been incredibly cruel to me in the past, and the memories still frightened me, but I forced myself to use them against him, and today I didn't feel so defenseless. Over time, I learned to defend myself, especially when my dad decided it was time to fire the helpers who used to stay with me at the bar so I could take over.

Since I was young, there had always been an adult in charge at the establishment since my dad owned the bar but never stayed there. However, I soon found myself forced to deal with out-of-control drunks and men with ulterior motives on my own, so it was either learn to defend myself or end up getting hurt in some way. There was no other option.

"Cliff won't care that you took a bottle, son. Leave that wild girl alone." Norah waved her hand dismissively and pulled her son by the arm. "And tell me, how was class?"

"It was normal, as always, Mom." He was still glaring at me when he answered her. "You know how it is, unbearable lectures about business, professors who won't stop talking. All that crap."

"When you graduate, you'll thank yourself for the opportunities you'll have. It's a great university; now come have a hot chocolate, I want to know more." She flattered her son and turned to me. "Work properly, girl. And you better stop answering me back and threatening my son for no reason, understood?" she shouted, and I knew by her tone that she was already plotting a way to make me pay for having talked back.

"She never learns to do things right."

"She's a loser!" I heard the comments muffled by laughter as they walked away.

Norah constantly annoyed me, but at that moment, I was even angrier to see how little Caleb valued the opportunity that had practically fallen into his lap.

Caleb lived the life I once dreamed of for myself, but he didn't appreciate anything. Watching him skip class or badmouth the university made me mad, even though I tried not to care. After all, I wanted to study business and one day have the chance to open my own place, maybe even a PUB?

I could have gone to the same university as Caleb; however, with all the work I was already doing at the bar and the house cleaning that was also my responsibility, I had very little time to study and ended up not getting the scholarship. According to my dad, there weren't enough funds to pay for two universities, and Caleb was a better and more guaranteed investment than I was.

There was no place for my future in that family, and that was one of the reasons I had been saving money since I was very young. It didn't matter if I ever got to study business; I wanted to get out of that house and rent a place where I could sleep in peace, find a job where they respected employees' working hours, and above all, be happy, far from all of them. My 21st birthday was coming up in just two weeks, and I would finally be free... finally.

I went to the back of the bar, where a tall shelf housed various bottles and drinks available for customers, and I grabbed a half-full bottle of whiskey. It wasn't the best brand; after all, if my dad caught me drinking one of his precious expensive whiskeys, he would probably kill me. And if I wanted to escape from there, I needed to stay alive, right? But I didn't need to be completely sober.

I poured some of the amber liquid into a short glass and downed the bitter drink in one go. I closed my eyes for a moment and tried to calm myself. I had learned to drink whiskey at a very young age, maybe around 15 or 16. It was illegal for a minor to drink, but it was also illegal for a minor to work in a bar, especially alone. Since we were breaking rules, I might as well have them work in my favor for once.

"Fuck it!" I cursed and prepared for work, pushing all the pain and sadness under an emotional rug.

I didn't need a father who didn't want to be my father, much less a family that didn't like me.

I OPENED THE BAR AND began to welcome customers. The place wasn't very busy, and being small, dark, and right next to an alley where shady business often took place, few men were interested in coming in, and rarely did a woman pass through the door—when they did, they were always accompanied.

My clientele consisted of a few young, lively men looking for distraction, some drunks who usually vomited on my clean floor. There were also men who had been betrayed, abandoned, or kicked out of their homes, constantly huddling in the darkest corner of the bar, hardly speaking, and lastly, those who enjoyed a good whiskey paired with a game of poker.

I tried to distract myself while serving them, making quick and flashy drinks as usual, but whenever my mind found a moment, my thoughts flew back to the mysterious man who had saved me earlier.

Ghost...

I was very curious about why they called him that. He was so handsome and moved with such a firm, quick grace that he reminded me of those special agents we see in movies.

"Where are those thoughts wandering off to, little Alena?" The comment made me blink twice until I found Uncle Walt sitting in front of me, on one of his daily visits.

The tall man with dyed black hair and a gentle gaze seemed to be around 60 years old, but he was as strong as an ox and as gentle as a koala. I had to admit that his large almond-shaped eyes and round ears reminded me of the small animal.

"It's nothing, Uncle Walt." I grabbed my uncle's favorite rum along with a glass and slid down the bar toward him. "It's so good to see you. Has your wife recovered from the flu?"

"She's tougher than a whale in the icebergs." The man laughed at his own metaphor, which I didn't even understand.

"Tell her I said hi." Uncle Walt had been frequenting my dad's bar since I was just a little girl, and before that, he was a great friend of my mother's.

Years passed, and he changed very little. Uncle Walt was as youthful as his wife, who was a bit younger than him. A handsome and kind man, and I held him in high esteem as part of my family, even though we didn't share the same blood.

I spent the rest of the night chatting with my uncle. He usually distracted me from the endless hours in that place, and when I realized it, dawn had arrived and the bar was empty. I prepared to close the doors, my body limp with exhaustion.

"Where's your dad?" Walt asked as he was about to leave. He was the last customer still in the bar.

"I don't know; I guess he's not coming today."

"Lock the door when I pass by, okay? It's not good luck to be alone in this place." I laughed at my uncle's saying and hugged him.

I did as he asked and locked the door as soon as he left. I took off the apron I wore to keep my sweatshirt clean, feeling exhausted to the bones, and all I wanted at that moment was a long, hot shower and to collapse into bed, in my little space in the attic.

I dragged my feet to the compact two-story house on the street behind the bar and climbed the entrance steps. I went to the security hiding place, a broken corner under the living room window, where my stepmother hid a spare key. Since I always came home late, she didn't like me knocking on the door and waking her up, nor did she like the idea of leaving a key available for me. So, I poked the little hole and quickly realized the key wasn't there.

"Oh, damn it!" I pressed my eyes shut with my fingers, already knowing what might have happened.

So that was her way of punishing me?

Norah didn't give me a copy of the key because one of her ways to punish me was forcing me to sleep in the bar when she was upset.

I exhaled in exasperation and knocked on the door a few times, hoping someone might open it for me. I stood there for a few minutes, in shock that she still resorted to that form of punishment every time I answered her in a way she didn't like.

I shivered when a gust of cold wind hit me. I looked at the empty street and remembered the men who had surrounded me at the stadium. What if some nut like them found me here?

The thought terrified me, and I ran back to the bar, where I had hidden a thin blue mattress to stave off the night's cold, along with a blanket and a pillow.

"Damn it, no hot shower tonight," I muttered, grabbed a speaker, and flopped down on the mattress.

I was too irritated to sleep and too tired to stay awake. Once again, I wanted to cry. I swallowed that feeling that felt like it was tearing my heart apart and decided to put on one of my favorite songs, the one that renewed my hopes, in an attempt to calm down.

Singing was one of my favorite pastimes, and I always did it when I felt sad or down. That particular song told the story of a young woman who set out to find herself and bravely moved forward despite her fears.

When she felt scared, she looked to the sky and sang, but unlike me, this girl had someone by her side, someone who became her beacon. And, as the hopeless romantic I was, I spent a lot of time dreaming of a prince who would rescue me from that hell. That night, my prince had a face. Painfully beautiful and very dark, but with a hint of kindness and protection that touched my heart.

I pressed play, and the song "Flashlight" started playing. Every cell in my body reacted to Jessie J's striking voice, and I began to hum softly.

"I see the shadows under the mountain
I'm not afraid when the rain won't stop
Because you light my way
I'm trapped in the dark, but you are my lantern
You help me get through the night"

I closed my eyes for a moment, feeling the end of the song once again, and when the sound stopped, I heard a noise outside the bar, coming from the alley.

"Dad?" I called, turning off the music. I listened to see if I could hear anything else, but a strange silence hung in the air.

It was the kind of silence that makes you suspicious. I ran my fingers around my new Chicago Cubs bracelet and snapped it on my wrist, creating a little pop almost unconsciously, as if I needed to break that deafening silence.

"I'm hearing things..." I whispered to myself, and just as I was about to lie down again, a male voice said:

"You better open this fast, or I'll slice it right here," someone threatened in a low, menacing voice.

I jumped up and ran to the back of the bar where my bat was. I crouched down with it in my hands. My heart raced, but maybe it was just some troublemakers fighting in the street. It wasn't unusual to see a brawl in the alleys of Chicago. Now and then, there was always some commotion in that area, and I, not being crazy, had no intention of getting involved in a gang fight or whatever, so I planned to stay quiet inside. As long as I was in the bar, I would be safe.

That's what I thought until I heard strange voices approaching, and suddenly, the door burst open, and my dad stumbled in, being pushed by a very, very large man.

"No, sir, I beg you, I swear I'll make it up to you."

"You should have thought about that before losing the boss's cargo."

I widened my eyes when I saw that mountain of muscle raise his fist high and slam it down with devastating fury, hitting my dad square in the face. He groaned loudly and fell to the floor of the bar.

My heart thudded in my chest in a desperate rhythm, and I didn't even think. When I saw the man lift his hand again, I rushed toward them, raised my bat, and did what I knew best. I delivered a solid hit to the bastard's knee, who howled and staggered sideways.

"Get your hands off him, you filthy scumbag!" I ground my teeth, furious. Cliff could be an idiot, but he was my dad, and I wouldn't let anyone lay hands on him.

My dad's eyes widened, and he looked at me breathlessly, leaning against the pillar to stand. I pointed the bat at the man, who swore a stream of curses.

"Get out of here, or I'll call the cops!" I threatened, fully aware that I didn't even have a phone to follow through on my threat. Only then did I notice the hooded figure watching the scene with a charming smile partially hidden.

"I think it's best you drop that, little lady." His calm, peaceful voice almost made me jump in fear.

I looked at the man wearing a hood, sunglasses, and a black hoodie. He was tall, but I was sure I could hit him too. However, there was something in his hand that terrified me far more than all that camouflage he wore. A damn gun.

"Dad..." I whispered when I saw the dark object and desperately tried to control the tremor in my legs.

The guy smiled, and the only thing I could see beyond his perfect smile was a tuft of his bright copper-colored hair. The big guy I hit in the knee tried to reach for me, and in his stumbling, he knocked into the armed man, causing his sunglasses to fall along with part of the hood. I froze at the sight of penetrating blue eyes; his hair, as I had imagined, was a vibrant copper. He looked like a cherub, so perfect, but his essence was terrifying.

"Who are you?"

"She saw me," he growled to his accomplice, who groaned even louder and turned to me.

"Stupid girl, you just made things worse, you idiot!" My dad got up, cursed at me, and spat a mouthful of blood. He was probably just angry for me putting myself in danger along with him, but how could I abandon him? Above all, we were family!

"Don't worry, boss. I'll chop this bitch into a thousand pieces and..."

"Calm down, she hasn't done much more than give you a knee injury, has she?" The redhead continued in a serene, calm voice, as if he were sailing in calm waters while I felt surrounded by sharks.

"That bitch must have broken one of my knees. It hurts like hell." The big guy staggered unsteadily, and only then did I notice he was holding a metal bar.

Oh, great! What was happening in the world that I ran into a nut with a metal bar and another with a gun, all in the same day?

"I'm going to finish her." I barely had time to think and raised my bat in shock when I noticed he was coming toward me.

"Don't you dare touch her," the hooded man threatened, confusing me with his calm, slow tone, like a snake waiting to strike. The big guy froze instantly, almost like a marionette.

"But boss..."

"Sir, listen to me!" my dad interrupted, desperate. "We'll have a new shipment next month; I'll be able to recover some of the money. I promise to pay back with interest." I looked at my dad, who didn't even meet the redhead's gaze, as if he were a god.

"Do you think you could pay me back for the cargo you lost? Do you know how hard it was to gather those women? You had one job... just one—" he growled. "Keep the exchange safe. You wouldn't be able to pay me even a third of what they were worth, even if I sold your organs."

"Please, don't kill me. I can get more girls. I swear. Please, give me more time." He knelt before the man, making me raise my eyebrows, completely lost in this conversation.

"Cliff, Cliff..." He ignored my dad's desperation and walked toward me. "Looks like you have much more than you've been telling me." He raised his index finger and tried to touch my face. I jumped back in fright to the opposite side, pointing my bat, fully aware that he was armed.

"How could I have never seen you before? A beauty like this wouldn't escape my notice." He tried to approach again, but I kept my baseball bat pointed at him.

"Don't touch me, and get out of here!" I shouted, nervous and unsure of what to do.

"I like her." He turned to my dad and completely ignored me. "I'll give you one chance to redeem yourself, Cliff. You better make the most of it."

"Whatever you want, sir, whatever you want."

"I'll take this one here, in place of the five you lost."

"What?" I widened my eyes when he pointed at me. "What is he talking about, Dad?" I looked at Cliff, who wiped the blood from his mouth and stared at the man as if considering an irresistible offer.

"Come on, Cliff. This is how we do it in Italy. We collect our debts, and she has already seen me anyway, so there's not much to do."

"Are you telling me you would write off the loss of the five girls?" my dad asked seriously.

"What are you talking about?" I exploded, trembling to my bones. "Why the hell is this man here, in the middle of our bar with a damn gun in his hands? And what girls are you talking about, Dad?" My throat went dry from the fear of the answer.

"Drop that." My dad pointed to my bat.

"No way." I looked from him to the gun the redhead held, feeling my heart pounding against my chest.

"Drop that shit!" My dad yanked my bat hard, and I stumbled trying to hold on to it. "What are you going to do with her?" He turned to the strange guy, who appraised me from head to toe.

"What do you mean by what he's going to do with me?"

"Nothing bad. You know I don't mistreat mine." He waved a hand toward the big guy, and in an instant, he grabbed me by the arms.

"Let me go!" I screamed and struggled. "Dad, what's happening? DAD!" I called at the top of my lungs, but he didn't even look in my direction.

"Cliff, you know there's no going back, right?" Scott pointed my dad's gun at me. "If you bring me trouble because of her... I'll go back to the original plan of spilling your guts in this horrid bar. Now get out of here, and we won't see each other again until I need you."

I exhaled desperately when I saw my dad turn his back on me without even looking at me again, leaving me there in the hands of those two strange men.

"Dad. DAD! Don't leave me here, Dad. Please, Dad! I'm your daughter," I shouted louder and louder until I tasted blood in my throat and shook against that massive body behind me. "DAD!" But it was all in vain.

"You can scream; he won't come back. He knows very well what's good for him, but you..." The big guy started to tighten his grip on me.

"Tape her mouth with something and let's get the hell out of here before anyone notices," the redhead ordered, turning his back, and pure terror gripped me.

I had rarely allowed myself to cry, but when I saw my dad leaving through the other door, not caring about what would happen to me from then on, thick tears streamed down my face. I held my breath, overcome with panic when the man covered my mouth with his hand, and without thinking, I threw my head back, feeling intense pain as I struck the center of his face. I bit his hand immediately afterward.

"BITCH!" he roared, and I ran, air not entering my lungs. Terror nearly froze my legs, but if I wanted to escape, I knew I had to scream for help.

"She's going to be trouble; I'm going to enjoy this," I heard the redhead laughing, standing in the main entrance of the bar. My God, this had to be a nightmare.

"HELP! HELP!" All I had left was to run to the door my dad had exited through, and that's what I did, running nonstop, screaming as loud as I could.

I heard heavy footsteps behind me and was almost at the door when I felt a searing pain in my head, terrible and so unbearable that I wished I would die just for it to stop hurting. Suddenly, everything fell into the deepest darkness, as if death itself had finally embraced me.

And then, I was sentenced to hell by the man I called Dad.

CHAPTER THREE

Ghost

20 Days Later

Where could she have gone? The question lingered in my thoughts every now and then whenever I remembered the girl at the stadium. We almost ended that day at the police station, but luckily we managed to ensure that only the three harassers faced the officer after a stop at the hospital.

I looked for her right after the chaos, but I couldn't find her anywhere. It was as if she had vanished from the face of the earth, and since then, I couldn't stop wondering how she was, if she was scared or traumatized in some way. I hadn't seen her face, only part of her mouth and her long hair, enough for me to imagine her in a thousand different ways in my mind.

I turned off the shower and stepped out, still thinking about her. I pushed those thoughts aside and started getting ready for work. My dad had called me early and was waiting for me in his office, which meant I had no time to waste.

I entered the room, which, like my brothers', had dark, sophisticated furniture. We had inherited a certain imbalance from my father when it came to dark colors for decorating spaces.

I opened the closet, choosing one of the many black suits I had, and tossed one onto the bed. I walked past the large mirror in the middle of the room and stopped when my eyes caught sight of the scars that traced down my neck, filled my chest, and especially concentrated on my back.

Some were wide, deep, and intense, running down the sides where the skin was more sensitive. Other smaller marks crossed over them, turning everything into a vast and grotesque map.

I shook my head and looked away. Sometimes, seeing my reflection felt like peeking into the past.

THE HOLDER SECURITY building loomed like a skyscraper in the middle of Chicago, glinting in the cold fog of that winter morning. The morning rush created a cacophony of blaring horns, raised voices, and revving engines, and all I wanted was to park my black Nissan Sentra, which, unlike my BMW Nazca, was used only for work.

I crossed the entrance hall of Holder Security after leaving my car in the underground parking and was warmly greeted by one of the young men who was increasingly standing out in the place.

"Mr. Holder!" he greeted cheerfully. "Great to see you, I hope you have an excellent day."

"Thank you, Anthony." I smiled and received greetings from the other employees until I reached the elevator, mentally thanking myself for being alone inside that metal box, as it was becoming increasingly difficult to maintain my good humor after yet another night of strange nightmares.

I exited the elevator when I arrived on the 14th floor, where the presidential office was located, and walked down the dim corridor, which had only one fixed light where the secretary's desk was, while the rest lit up as I moved down the hall.

Emma, my dad's secretary, was standing with her back to me, focused on one of the drawers of the cabinet. I stepped a little closer to greet her.

"Good morning, Emma!"

"AHHHHHHHHHHHHHHHHHHHHHHHHHHH!" she let out a loud scream and scattered the papers she was holding everywhere.

"It's me! Emma, it's me!" — I waved my arms in front of my face, protecting myself from whatever she might throw in my direction. After the variety of things my sister-in-law Jasmin, Wolf's girlfriend, had attacked me with, including a legendary incident involving a frying pan, I was forced to become a more cautious man.

"M-Mr. Holder!" She gasped and placed her hands on her chest just as the door to the presidential office swung open with a loud bang.

"What the hell is going on here?" My dad walked past her with wide gray eyes, similar to the ones poor Emma was currently staring at me with.

"I-I didn't hear you come in!" She took a deep breath again, and her mouth, which was now white as a sheet of paper, started to gain color. I pressed my lips together, a mix of amusement and concern that only irritated my dad further.

"Ghost, how many times have I told you to stomp your feet, boy?" My dad placed his hands on his hips and a genuine smile formed on my lips as I remembered all the times he had made that same request throughout my life.

"You know it's stronger than me." I shrugged, ignoring the truth behind those words. "I apologize for the scare, Emma. I promise that the next time I need to come to the office, I'll bring a sound system with me and..."

"Zion" he reprimanded and called me by name.

"Not here anymore who spoke." I waved a hand at my dad's stern face. "But that would be a reasonable option. A little music? No?" He grabbed my shoulder and guided me into his office.

"A little music... tsk!" He walked, grumbling, without letting go of me. "Come on, we have work to do, and poor Emma needs to recover from the scare."

"I'd like to emphasize how very sorry I am, Miss Emma" I said loudly just before passing through the large wooden door of the presidential office.

"Hurry up, kid!" my dad called, and I entered his office right after.

The dark room seemed much larger than it really was, and with every step I took inside, the smell of Cohiba Behike became more evident in the air. One of my dad's favorite cigars, used only in very specific situations.

When he was about to kill one of us.

"Tell me, Dad, what did Wolf do this time?" I walked to the desk at the back of the office and poured two shots of whiskey into clear glass glasses. "I assume you lit this cigar for a reason." I handed him one of the glasses. His gray eyes met mine for a second and I knew something was wrong by the intensity with which he stared at me. "Did something happen, Dad?"

"Besides almost losing my secretary today? Nothing too serious" he joked, making me relax for a moment.

A mere moment that didn't allow me to see where that conversation was headed.

"Sit down, son. I have a very important job to offer you."

"If you remember, Dad, the Sheikh's birthday is coming up. Wolf has made it clear that he won't step foot in that palace anymore, and I think it's safer for anyone if it's done this way, so it's better to send me in his place, although after what he pulled a few weeks ago, he well deserves to be sent to Arabia in a suitcase."

"Did he pull something?" My dad sipped the whiskey.

"Nothing much." If you don't count that those two vandals had broken into my house and messed up my precious car. "In general, your sons live on a tightrope between being an honorable citizen or a shameless criminal." I wrinkled my nose, still indignant. "I think you should know."

"And you think I don't know? Are you aware of how many times I've had to explain to the police chief that Snake was one of ours?" He laughed and finished his drink in one go. "Well, leaving those boys aside..." I couldn't help but let out a brief smile. My dad still treated us like children. I found it amazing. If I ever became a father, which would truly be a worldwide phenomenon, I believe I would understand his way of treating us as if we were still 10 years old, oscillating between needing a hug or a loving punishment. "This is a case that needs one of my three best men. More than that greedy eating idiot Sheikh deserves." He waved the glass in front of his face and turned his attention back to me.

"I'm curious. Who is the man who managed to outdo one of your most expensive clients?"

"His name is Scott Walker, he's the CEO of Biogen Tec. A large biotechnology company that works on various social projects, one of which brought him considerable fame in the field. You may have heard of him."

"I vaguely remember that name."

"They have several projects, and young Walker is involved in all the philanthropic resources that the company employs."

"Interesting. They seem like good people."

"And they are. Walker investigates and provides free treatment for children with rare diseases. He alone has managed to raise enough funds to help people who couldn't afford the treatment, but it seems that this kindness doesn't please everyone. For some reason, they want the guy dead and tried to kill him on his last trip, and now he needs to change routes. His father, who lives in the country he frequently travels to, is very worried and ended up contacting us."

"And what will the job be? I need the VIP file, possible enemies, and all the bureaucracy you already know. Besides knowing the destination we'll have to travel to."

"Well, the destination." He paused for a moment and took a deep breath, which only made me more worried. "I want you to know, son, that if one of your brothers were available, I wouldn't put him on this case." He breathed heavily. "I raised my eyebrows and set the glass I was holding on my dad's desk, puzzled by the direction of that conversation and how it was becoming more of an apology request than a mission. When my dad revealed the place to which he would send me, everything made sense. "I need you to take Scott safely to Italy. Calabria, to be more specific."

"Italy?" I jumped up as if I had sat on a needle, and my dad did the same. "It's been a while since my last mission in that region. You know I'm not a fan of the country."

"Ghost, more than anyone, I know your fear of that place, but I can't disregard your fluency in the language."

"I'm fluent in three other languages; how about sending me to Russia? It's an option." I grabbed my glass again and downed the rest of the whiskey in one go, regretting having dedicated so much to that language, just to communicate with someone who turned out to be fluent in other languages—the language of betrayal.

"You know it's not that simple." He stepped closer to me. "No one, not even Wolf, has control over an overseas mission as well as you do." He placed a hand on my shoulder. "It will be for a very short period, three days at most. All you have to do is take him to Calabria and bring him back breathing."

"A very simple task, right?" I scoffed and looked away. "It seems I've angered some divine entity in past lives."

"Are you sure you're okay, son?" He pursed his lips, confused for a moment. I raised my eyes to meet the light gray, inquisitive gaze of my father. "Did you sleep well?"

There was the question I had heard my whole life, and as always, my old man was scrutinizing every inch of my face, searching for something out of place. Something he probably sensed the moment I walked through that door.

Despite what Wolf and Snake might think, I firmly believed that of the three of us, I was the one who had caused the most trouble for old Reid Holder during childhood. Even though Wolf occasionally ran away and Snake got into fights daily wherever he went. Wherever he went, REALLY. My older brother even fought with a priest, God help us. But I, on the other hand, deprived my father of years of peaceful sleep, and that still reflected in how he behaved around me. Always on guard, always waiting for the moment the darkness would swallow me again so he could try to save me.

"Yes, Dad, I'm fine," I lied, flashing my best smile. "I'm still thinking about poor Emma."

"You're going to end up getting me sued for attempted murder, Zion. What if that woman had a heart attack?" He laughed and turned to a beige folder positioned on the desk. "I'm sorry I have to make you go back there."

"Don't worry." I took the folder from his hands. "I'm angry at whoever dubbed Verona the city of love. City of horns would suit it much better, don't you think?"

"What I think is that you have a strange and funny way of dealing with your problems, son." My old man shook his head and pointed to the folder. "He leaves today in the late afternoon, be ready." He handed me the file. "Don't forget to take the travel kit for overseas trips."

I started flipping through the young man's history and noted that the attack he suffered occurred when he stepped foot in the United States. Scott was shot by an unknown man who was subdued by the young man's security, who apparently only survived due to the shooter's extraordinarily poor aim, who was arrested by the authorities.

"Considering the attack Walker suffered, my attention should be directed to the entry and exit of our country," I commented more to myself. "However, it's always good to have a plan B in any situation. Can you tell me if Wolf still has a hideout in the Calabria region? He had excellent contacts there a while back."

"If there's still a hideout, I can't say, but Wolf keeps trustworthy contacts wherever he goes, so I believe if you need anything, it'll be easy to get, but be careful, Ghost" he warned me as I stood up and adjusted my suit. "You'll be out of our country. I'm counting on you to be responsible."

"And when haven't I been?" He opened his mouth to start talking. "Don't answer, Dad, that was a hypothetical question." He laughed and extended his hand for me to shake. I held on tightly, and he quickly pulled me into a hug.

A hug I didn't even know I needed so much.

"You're my most sensible son, so I ask you for the heart of this old father of yours, bring the VIP back safely and don't dare get hurt on the way." He squeezed me a little tighter in the hug. Or was it me who was squeezing him desperately? "Are you sure you're okay?" he questioned when I let go and forced myself to put a smile back on my face.

"Why wouldn't I be?"

I ARRIVED AT THE WALKER family mansion at the scheduled time, and as expected, there was a whole entourage at Scott Walker's disposal right at the entrance.

I spent much of the afternoon analyzing the VIP's profile, who, by the way, was four years younger than me.

I had to admit, I was impressed. I couldn't understand why anyone would try to assassinate young Walker, not given the illustrious and generous things he did. The guy only did good, but apparently, someone didn't think so.

The thought intrigued me so much that I began researching more about the man who tried to kill him. I was astonished when I found no news about him.

"How does someone attempt to kill a CEO like him and nothing gets reported?" I whispered, staring at my phone.

"Sir?" The driver I had hired to take me to the VIP's house inquired, suspiciously, as he parked right next to the mansion.

"It's nothing." I grabbed my carry-on bag, which contained just enough for three days, along with my backup weapon, and got out of the car.

I slammed the door and was about to turn off my phone when a post from a small BLOG appeared at the end of my search.

Who tried to assassinate the people's CEO, Scott Walker?
Understand the case...

I started reading the article casually. There was a report from a woman who claimed to have seen everything, filled with many superfluous questions that caught my attention. According to Lady News, the blog owner and a science and philanthropic enthusiast, the young man had been surrounded by his bodyguards when the shooting started, and she, who immediately threw herself to the ground like everyone else waiting at the airport, could only hear a few things.

She unfolded a long paragraph of various questions that arose after the fact, which, according to her, seconds later seemed as if it had never happened.

"It was strange. *The way no one talked about the attack. They tried to assassinate someone in the middle of a crowded airport, and no one says anything? Who was the shooter who was never seen again? Why would anyone want to kill such a good man? Besides that, I suspect that the two knew each other, because the shooter kept repeating the same phrase:*

The blame is yours!

What blame, my friends? The gossip in me hasn't slept well since then."

I raised my eyebrows at that information, absorbing every word. I put my phone away and headed toward the entrance of the grand mansion, which seemed to be under 24-hour surveillance.

"Good afternoon, I come on behalf of Holder Security," I introduced myself and handed over the necessary documentation.

"Ghost, right?" A tall, bearded man wanted to confirm from behind the gate. "So you're the one who's going to protect the boss?" He scanned me from head to toe and opened a strangely aggressive smile, full of teeth, that looked more like a snarl than a greeting. "You're the so-called specialist?" he laughed.

For some reason, the comment felt like an affront, especially since that man had more of a criminal posture than a professional bodyguard. But with Snake as my brother, who was I to judge anyone's appearance, right?

"And you are?"

"Doesn't matter," he said quickly and looked at one of the cameras. "That's your cue, you can go in. The boss is already by the vehicles." He opened a rusty iron gate.

I spotted the VIP from afar. He was waiting next to a black vehicle, dressed in an elegant gray suit. His very red hair was unmistakable, as vibrant as sunlight.

"Mr. Walker."

"Ghost, right?"

"Yes, which vehicle is prepared for your departure?"

"This one, but you don't need to check anything; my men already did." He barely took his eyes off the phone screen while speaking. "This is Sergei, our driver." Walker waved toward the man standing in front of the vehicle.

"Good afternoon." The guy was as big as a bear, and I almost choked when I heard the sound of his voice, which was strange, high-pitched, and nasal, like an animal in distress.

"And this is Angelo; both will travel with us." He pointed to another man who was in the car behind.

"Great, I'll test the communication, and we can leave shortly."

I grabbed the radio communicator and connected to the frequency Walker instructed, so I could have contact only with the two bodyguards traveling with us, besides the VIP and me.

"Let's get going. I'm eager to reach Calabria."

I nodded, and after some instructions, we followed in eight identical black armored cars.

"You have a well-known name, Ghost," Walker commented on the way to the airport. "Your family has become important and very influential in the business. I heard that the death threats your clients face decrease considerably once they know they're being protected by someone from Holder Security. That's what motivated my father to hire you."

"We do our job with excellence," I admitted.

"And as one of the heirs to the place, I imagine you're highly sought after."

"I won't use false modesty, Mr. Walker. Both my brothers and I are a reference for the quality of Holder."

"Of course." He glanced at me for a brief moment. His very intense blue eyes narrowed. "I expect only two things on this trip: protection and discretion. Can I count on you?"

"Without a doubt."

"Then we will get along very well."

I tuned into the channel where all eight vehicles would have access and relayed an action plan that would allow us to pass safely through the airport with the VIP, especially since that was where Walker had been attacked; the chances of a new attempt were immense. I positioned each of the security personnel as we disembarked at the airport and turned to Walker.

"Stay close to me, got it? The two will be by your side, and I'll be right behind. Under no circumstances should you stray." We formed a triangle around him, protecting all sides with extra reinforcements.

We crossed the place smoothly without any interventions. We entered the boarding corridor, where only Sergei, Angelo, and I would provide protection for the VIP. The first big guy stood to the left, while Angelo, who had shoulders as broad as Sergei's but didn't resemble a serial killer, maintained his position to the right, and I stayed behind.

Walker began walking, his eyes glued to his phone the entire time, and I didn't know how he was able to walk and type simultaneously. It was as if he had eyes on his feet, because he didn't even stumble. However, out of nowhere, the young man stopped, glanced at the two bodyguards beside him, and then looked over his shoulder.

"HOLY SHIT!" he shouted when he saw me standing just inches away. "You scared me! I thought you got left behind."

"Well, Mr. Walker, you paid me to watch over you. Where else would I be?" I smiled, directing him back toward the airplane entrance.

"I didn't hear you walking behind me; I thought you got lost."

"I don't hear you either, sir, and that bothers me quite a bit," Sergei whispered, sounding like a car crash with that strange voice of his.

"That's why they call me Ghost; now we'd better hurry if we want to board this plane."

"Where did you learn that?" Angelo inquired.

"I believe it's a factory defect," I replied and guided the VIP to our seats on the plane, in a private cabin.

I could have enjoyed the silence of the flight to rest and prepare for landing if it weren't for Sergei and Angelo's curiosity, which made me spend the entire damn flight trying to explain that there wasn't a technique for walking silently. At least I didn't want to share what curse had left me this way, and by the time we landed at Lamezia Terme International Airport in Calabria, I was almost voiceless.

"Sooner or later, you'll have to tell me this secret," Sergei, the bear, insisted excitedly as we escorted Walker out of the arrivals area, where a few men were waiting for us.

"Sergei, I need to keep the VIP intact, and this mission will be quite difficult if my neurons explode. So how about we drop the subject?"

"But you don't make noise when..."

"Sergei, we're in a hurry," Walker snapped.

"Yes, sir." Sergei grabbed the young man's suitcase.

"Welcome back, sir!" A short, stout man with a fine, lengthy mustache approached us speaking in Italian, accompanied by three other men who, unlike him, looked like grim wardrobes.

"How are my things, Stefano?" Walker barely waited for the man to get close before asking. Whatever the topic was, it seemed important and urgent.

"All under control. Your visit is already scheduled, just waiting for you to arrive. We followed the usual rules," he informed succinctly and calmly, until he noticed my presence. "Who is he?" he questioned, narrowing his eyes.

"One of my new bodyguards."

"Is he American? I told your father that he didn't need to worry about your security. We've already taken all necessary precautions, and that will never happen again. There's no reason to trust an American in a suit over..."

"Ghost, this is Stefano. He's the... business manager for my father here in Italy, and this, Stefano, is the bodyguard responsible for my return to the U.S. He is also fluent in your language and understands everything you say." Strangely, that seemed like a warning.

Ah, how interesting... I thought as I watched Stefano turn as red as a pepper. His nose swelled briefly, indeed something quite strange. I had never seen a nose inflate from what seemed like anger, just as I had never seen anyone get irritated because their boss had a new bodyguard. I tried to ignore my sixth sense that told me something was off and smiled at the little grumpy man.

"It's a pleasure to work with the Walker family."

"Walker?" he growled quietly, turning a little redder. "Just what I needed."

"Is there a problem with the VIP's last name?" I questioned, addressing no one in particular, but it was Walker who responded.

"It's nothing. It's just that here I'm known by my father's last name, that's all," he explained, and I nodded, ignoring the explicit anger on Stefano's face.

"Hello, sir!" A woman passed by us, greeting Scott. Then another one.

With each step we took outside the airport, more people greeted Walker as if their lives depended on it. Apparently, he was better known in Calabria than in Chicago, the city he chose to set up the family's research lab.

The cold breeze of Calabria touched my face and sent shivers down my spine. I guided the young man toward where a new convoy of cars was waiting for us.

"Ghost." Scott turned his face toward me before we reached one of the vehicles. "Today you'll meet most of my family. My father still lives here, and it might seem strange how they live, so I ask that you don't interfere in anything. Just enjoy the next three days, and before you know it, we'll be back on that plane."

"Walker, I don't care at all what your family does or doesn't do. I'm here solely to keep you safe." He smiled, and we entered one of the vehicles.

The streets of Calabria were narrow, with few exceptions. The shiny black cars contrasted directly with the place's simple and rustic beauty. Something that caught my attention was that, even with the windows closed, some people waved a timid greeting toward the passing cars as if wanting to show some kind of respect.

We drove around the city for quite some time until we reached a small, high, and completely empty hill; there were no houses nearby except for the gigantic dark-walled castle perched on the slope, offering a breathtaking view of an open and endless sea.

"Is that the Walker family house?" I stared at the castle as we approached. Large wrought-iron gates blocked the entrance, and the thick walls surrounding it seemed impenetrable. Not to mention the multitude of armed men guarding the area.

"Don't say that, American. Not here. You should refer to them as famiglia Marino, understood?" Sergei, who had been silent until now, decided to speak up.

"Sergei, he won't be here long enough to need to learn anything, so just inform the others, okay?" Walker ordered.

"I need to know everything that could put your life at risk, and looking at the number of armed men you have here, I'd say I really need to know what's going on." I narrowed my eyes. "I'm here for your protection, Walker; every secret could cost you your life."

"I think it's clear that I don't need your protection here, right?" He looked at the men guarding the entrances to the castle like they were guard dogs. "But it wouldn't hurt you to understand a bit about the life they lead in this place. As you know, my business is in the United States, and there I've always used the surname Walker, which belonged to my late mother. But my father isn't American. His surname is Marino and it has a lot of significance in the Calabria region."

"It's better to avoid the Walker surname, Ghost. The famiglia might not like it, and if that happens, you won't have time to teach me your secret." Sergei resumed the conversation about walking silently, and I nearly lost my mind just imagining spending three days with him hovering over me, but there was something much more important here. Something I should genuinely be concerned about.

The famiglia?

I raised my eyebrows as we entered the mansion atop the hill, and with each step deeper into the place, things became clearer. The steel gates closed behind us, and a whole new world opened up before my eyes when a burly man with strikingly light eyes, similar to those of his son, appeared on the staircase, causing quite a commotion around me.

"Don Gava!" Sergei greeted respectfully, which confirmed my suspicions.

The father of the famous Scott Walker was a Don of a Calabrian mafia. How wonderful!

Alena

"I see the shadows beneath the mountain
I'm not afraid when the rain doesn't stop
Because you light my way

I curled up under the moldy, somewhat damp blankets, humming the only refrain I could remember, desperate to hear some sound, even if it was my weary voice echoing against the walls of that room.

Room... the word almost made me laugh. That could never be called a room. It was a dungeon, a prison. So cold it made my bones ache. I wrapped my legs with my arms, trying to warm myself somehow, and tightly pulled the tattered and somewhat ripped hoodie I had been wearing since I arrived, which was starting to fall apart. The perpetually damp weather had made the fabric weak, just like me.

I blew on my hands and stared at the closed iron door. I had no idea what lay beyond it, but it was surely better than what existed inside. I glanced around the gray, muddy room, the walls stained up to a certain height, as if one day this place had been flooded by a river. The dirt seemed ingrained in every inch, from the walls to the bedding, which I could bet had never been changed and smelled horribly of mold. In the corner next to the bed, there was a small pipe that ran water 24 hours a day, draining into a small hole that served as my toilet. I had even gotten to the point of wondering if there was a way to escape through that pipe, but after days of searching for a way out, or any hope of leaving there alive, my faith began to wane.

I shivered, and my legs hurt even more from the cold. The wounds were taking time to heal, and I could still see the bruises he had left on my body the last time he was here. Two deeper cuts were almost closed, but the pain of the memory was still fresh.

My stomach churned with hunger, and I stared at the tiny hole near the ceiling. A beam of light shone through it, and I could only imagine whether it was day or night. If it was bright like a flashlight, it was daytime, but now, the light had gone out, meaning night had arrived, and I still hadn't eaten anything.

Usually, a very large man, with a horrendous scar running across his face and almost splitting it in half, would push a plate of slop through the opening under the door, with a strong and strange taste, but it served to alleviate the hunger that hurt so much. I remembered in the early days struggling to endure the sour smell of the food, but after a while, and countless times of vomiting, even that became normal. Though terribly bad, it was a way to keep me alive, but that day I hadn't eaten anything at all.

My hands began to shake with the weight of it all. There were only two things I knew about that place. Scott was the name of the man who came to visit me every week; I had heard someone call him that from outside once, and whenever he was about to arrive, they deprived me of any food.

Perhaps they wanted to leave me even weaker, even more susceptible. As if my loose clothing wasn't a sign of how much weight I had lost since waking up there; I could barely stand for long without feeling dizzy, but if there was something I was not willing to do, it was to give in. He would never get what he wanted from me, and I would fight to the end of my life to show him that.

I knew I needed to resist; I felt the urge to fight in my cells, to want to regain control over my life, but I had no idea if I would truly be strong enough for that.

CHAPTER FOUR

Ghost

"I heard they sent one of the best men from Holder Security. Welcome to my home, Ghost." Don Gava approached me confidently, while more than twenty pairs of eyes scrutinized us, most armed to the teeth.

I noticed from his tone when he said my name—firm and threatening—that he wanted to make it clear to whom I should be loyal here, as if the bizarre tattoo above his eye wasn't terrifying enough. The man had several of them along his arm, and not all seemed to have been done conventionally.

"I appreciate the hospitality, Don Gava, but I must emphasize that I am not here for leisure. I came for the protection of Mr. Scott." I avoided the VIP's American surname. In cases like this, any conflict between the parties should be avoided, and I would act as I had been trained, using impartiality. "It will be as if I am not even here."

"I'm glad to know of your discretion. And you, couldn't wait until next semester to return? You know it's not the best time." He completely ignored me afterward and turned his attention to his son, who I only then noticed had tucked his phone into his pocket for the first time.

"You know I can't. I'm going to change clothes, have them prepare everything," he warned and disappeared with his father into the mansion.

"I'll show you where your quarters are." Sergei guided me through the entrance of the castle, which had at least six stories of thick stone walls. This made its interior cold and dark.

I was surprised to see a constant and lively movement inside the house. There were women, men, and even some boys, arranging everything with surprising speed.

"The Don throws a party whenever his son comes to visit, which has lately been weekly visits," Sergei tried to explain. "You'll enjoy it; there are plenty of beautiful women and the best wine you've ever tasted."

"I appreciate the invitation, but I'll pass. I intend to store my bag and find Scott." He turned toward a staircase, and we ascended in silence. Something unusual for Sergei, who, by all indications, couldn't keep his mouth shut.

He stopped at the end of a long corridor, which, like the rest of the house, was dark and very cold, and opened one of the many side doors.

"Here is your room."

"Thank you." I was already stepping into the room when the man's firm voice reached me. "Listen, Ghost, there is no safer place for Mr. Scott in the world than here, so if he tells you to stay away, just do it. You'd better worry when we return to the United States. Calabria is Don Gava's domain, and he is like a god here. No one would dare lay a finger on the boss."

"I'm here to ensure that this truth becomes law. Still, thank you for the advice, even if it sounds more like a threat."

"You know best." He turned his back and left, leaving me even more intrigued.

After unpacking, I roamed the mansion, scouting, and, to my dismay, Walker had disappeared. I asked two security guards where the guy might have gone, and received intimidating looks and unintelligible grumbles in response. One of them, a guy named Roberto, had a thick scar running down the middle of his face and seemed even more irritated by my insistence on finding the guy.

"Great, I lost the VIP!" I muttered quietly, a few hours after an exhausting search.

The party had already started, and I was watching everything from the second floor of the castle. There was plenty of extravagance in every corner of the place, hosting about fifty people dressed in elegant, flashy attire, with almost that many staff members rushing back and forth.

A band ruled the space, playing a melodious and captivating live song, and half the guests were eager to dance, while the other half enjoyed wandering along the long table made of pure wood, laden with countless variations of Italian food and desserts that were replenished from time to time.

Don Gava hardly appeared, but when he did, he resembled a famous politician, surrounded by women who made their interest in the mobster clear, emanating power down to his bones, attracting the attention of several men wanting to seem interesting in Gava Marino's eyes. I pressed my lips together, bothered by the fact that my father had no idea the VIP belonged to that family; after all, if he had known, at least he would have warned me. But apparently, the famous Scott Walker wanted at all costs to hide his mafia origins.

I continued watching the Don for a long time until the cold blue eyes of the man fixed on me. I nodded in acknowledgment, and he raised the champagne glass he was holding, a broad smile plastered on his face.

"What is a handsome man doing standing in a dark corner in the middle of a party?" A very sweet voice called out in a delicate accent. I turned and found a woman with long, wavy hair, wearing a red dress that accentuated her curves, holding a champagne glass raised in my direction. "Can I get your attention for a moment?" She bit her full lips.

"I'm sorry, but I think that will be impossible. I'm here for work," I declined and was about to pass her when the woman touched my arm.

"Mr. Scott told me you were off tonight."

"Did you see him anywhere?" I narrowed my eyes, beginning to suspect he had sent that woman over to get rid of me, which would be a huge waste of time.

"Only when I arrived at the party and asked about you. I know every face in the area, and I must say, yours is a sight for sore eyes. I have a line of companions waiting for a chance to spend a night with me, but I'm willing to leave them all waiting for a moment alone with you." She winked, throwing all her charm at me, and I had to admit she was a beautiful and very attractive woman, but my attention at that moment was dedicated to my runaway VIP.

"Well, I guess the lucky ones in your line got lucky today. Excuse me." I turned my back and left as quickly as possible.

I passed by people dancing, drinking, kissing... almost having sex in the corner of the hallway, while others laughed loudly and drank more and more. However, that catastrophic atmosphere disguised as joy made me uncomfortable. I tried to avoid Italy at all costs, precisely because I had frequented it too much at one time in my life. There was a memory stuck in my mind that every part of that country made me recall. From the language to the accent, the perfumes, the Italian food, the always impeccable wine. Everything, absolutely everything reminded me of her and the past I had tried to leave buried in Italy, but now I was there, and there was no escaping that wretched nostalgia.

Don Gava's mansion didn't make my life any easier. That place radiated such a heavy energy that I was already feeling suffocated, but I had to keep my mind neutral; after all, we never, under any circumstances, got involved in our clients' personal lives, just as we could never allow our personal problems to interfere with our work.

Wolf was the only rebellious sheep who went against the commandments of our father and Holder Security, and I was too happy about the outcome of his story with Jasmin, but that would never apply to me, so the best thing to do was find my VIP and make sure he was okay.

I roamed the empty corridors looking for any sign of where the young man might have hidden, and after a long time listening to the shrill laughter of the Don's guests, I was about to give up when I saw an unmistakable head of red hair turning one of the countless corridors in the place. I followed to the spot where I had seen him pass. He was alone and wearing the same clothes as when he arrived. Scott started walking quickly, and before I could catch up to him, he turned into a small entrance at the end of the hallway and disappeared.

I walked as fast as I could. If that slick guy made me run around that damn castle again chasing after that skinny neck, I'd end up strangling him myself.

I arrived at the spot where I lost sight of him and found a small, narrow door almost the same color as the walls, which were a muddy brown, cold and dark. I pushed the wood, and it opened easily, revealing an even narrower and steeper staircase that spiraled down to an unknown destination.

I weighed my options: climb that staircase wherever it led and find the VIP, or leave him to his own devices and risk that idiot breaking his neck on those steps?

I exhaled, exasperated, and narrowed my eyes, remembering what he had told me when I arrived.

"*You just need to protect me on American soil. Here, do whatever you want, just don't stay behind me.*"

Now and then, we encountered VIPs like that. They thought a bodyguard's job was selective, that they could choose where and when we should work. What they didn't know was that there was not a minute of rest when we took the job until it was done. It was a life that depended entirely on our protection, and I couldn't allow any loopholes for something to go wrong. My mission there was to protect Walker's little neck, whether he wanted it or not.

I began to descend the staircase, which was slippery besides everything else, and I had to visualize all the good things that guy did to keep from abandoning him right then and there.

"Sick kids... he helps sick kids," I muttered as I descended the last treacherous step.

I looked around and raised my eyebrows as I realized where I was.

"What place is this?" I whispered, staring at a dirt corridor that looked more like an underground tunnel, where some yellowish lights indicated a sinister path.

I followed the tunnel, which was very cold and damp, until I found a fork. One path was lit by the dim yellow light that made the place look like a horror movie set, while the second option was a completely dark path.

I glanced back and forth, feeling like I was in a damn labyrinth, but I decided to go where the lights were on; after all, in horror movies, everyone who chose the dark path ended up dead. Idiot people!

I walked down the corridor, and when I turned a corner, I came face to face with something that made me even more uneasy.

My eyes scanned the area where several very old wooden doors were lined up next to each other, as if they were dungeons hidden beneath the castle. A shiver ran through my body.

What the hell are they doing down here? What kind of place was this?

I took a few more steps, trying to hear something, and it wasn't long before I found my lost sheep. Scott was standing in front of one of the doors, his gaze glazed and fixed, not wavering. His hands were clenched into fists, as if he were anxious about something. A small, strange smile stretched across his lips, and I continued to approach, intrigued by it all.

He reached for the door latch and was about to open it when he looked to the side and saw me.

Alena

I RUBBED MY ARMS WITH my hands in an attempt to alleviate the wind that was coming through the small holes in the room. The damp walls made the intense cold inside that prison even worse. I shivered and kept my eyes closed, feeling too weak to even open them, wishing, even if just for a moment, that I could fall into a deep sleep, something I had concluded had become impossible since the day I woke up there.

I exhaled, disoriented, and to my pure horror, I heard footsteps in the corridor.

An unprecedented anguish took hold of me. I dug my nails into the mattress, and my eyes filled with tears I struggled to hold back. I had promised myself I wouldn't give him the pleasure of seeing me cry, and until then, I had succeeded, but fear, even though I wanted to hide it as deeply as possible, crept into my chest, and I could hardly breathe.

I looked at my dirty hands, as well as my feet, and pulled my long, filthy hair in front of me. The memory of what he did to me the last time he was here hit me with full force. I thought it would never stop, that he would kill me, and in the moment of pain, part of my subconscious wished he would indeed kill me. It would be the end of my torment once and for all, but unlike what I imagined, I survived.

I could still taste blood in my mouth when that bastard whispered in my ear:

"When I return, you will be tamed, even if I have to cut you into pieces to do it."

My breath began to quicken with the memory. My head felt full of water, mixed with a hunger so deep it made me feel excruciatingly nauseous. I placed my hand on my chest, overwhelmed by the sadness that emerged amid the fear and incapacity I felt. He entered there, hurt me in various ways, as if he were my owner, as if my body belonged to him, and the only thing I could do was try to protect myself.

But how long would I have the strength to fight?

The footsteps approached and stopped in front of the door.

It was him!

I knew it; I could feel it!

I stood up unsteadily and leaned against the corner of the wall at the back of the room. There he couldn't catch me by surprise, and he would have to face me directly. I clenched my fists and prepared for another battle that might cost me my life. I ignored the tears of despair streaming down my face and waited.

He fiddled with the lock, and for a moment, I felt my heart stop. I raised my fists, ready to retaliate as best I could, and suddenly, I heard his repugnant voice scream, startled.

"Shit, Ghost!" he cursed. "I didn't hear you come in. What are you doing here?" I recognized the voice that haunted my nightmares.

My God, it was really him. I sniffled, weak, preparing for the worst. There was no way out; for days, I had lost hope of leaving that place alive.

"I think I ended up getting lost in the endless corridors of this place. Is this a labyrinth?" someone said. I didn't recognize that voice, but I could be sure of one thing.

Everyone there was the same.

Everyone there was a monster!

CHAPTER FIVE

Ghost

Scott seemed much more nervous than he would like to admit. His blue eyes were wide, and his body assumed an immediate defensive posture. This only piqued my curiosity further. What was behind that door that made him act so evasively?

"Shit, Ghost!" He jumped. "I didn't hear you come in. What are you doing here?"

"I think I ended up getting lost in the endless corridors of this place. Is this a labyrinth?" I tried to sound indifferent.

"You shouldn't be here," he said, grumpy. "There's a party going on upstairs, and you're wasting your time chasing after me." He grabbed my shoulder and guided me away from the door. "Think about it, Ghost, how many times have you had to look after someone at such a prestigious party where you could have been invited instead of being the bodyguard? Countless women are waiting to experience your American charm."

"Oh, my dear..." I brushed off his hand, uncomfortable with the touch on my shoulder. "I'm not known for swapping my profession for fleeting pleasures. I came here to keep you safe, and I'll follow you through this entire castle if necessary. I have a reputation to uphold, and keeping you alive is part of it." I scanned the corridor that looked more like a dark, damp, endless tunnel. "What is this place? Is it a dungeon?" I glanced again at the wooden doors, and a tightness in my chest made me uneasy. What the hell was behind those doors?

"It's a museum." Scott smiled, softening, and began walking toward the steep, slippery staircase we had come down. "Our house is historic, and as you can see, this place is older than you can imagine." He approached one of the doors and opened it, showing me its interior. "I have no idea what has happened down here, but I have one certainty." He flashed a mocking smile on his fair face. "It must have been memorable." He pointed to some dark stains on the stone walls.

It was a prison.

The realization took my breath away for a moment. That cursed place was a dungeon. I could feel the malice seeping through the cold, dirty walls, and the old tremor that occasionally threatened to drive me insane began to take over my body.

"What do they use this place for nowadays?" I could hardly recognize my voice, which emerged low, cold, instinctive.

"Well, Ghost, what do you think we do here?" Scott laughed. "Like I said, it's just a museum. Now and then, I bring a girlfriend here to impress her and maybe even scare her? It's an infallible tactic; they get scared and cling to me." Another awkward laugh. "Now, let's go. Maybe you'll find someone who can take that strange, almost murderous expression off your face," he joked.

"Alright." I put my hands behind my back, trying to hide the tremor at being in that place and the strange, bitter memories it awakened in my mind. "Your guests are waiting for you; it's better not to keep them waiting."

"Sì!" he replied in Italian before heading back up the stairs to the party.

I spent the next few hours watching every move Scott made at the party. He drank, danced with one or two girls, smiled at some colleagues, and then his gaze would drift for a brief moment before he started his act all over again.

He was uneasy, just like I was. I could sense that something was wrong, something out of place, and even though I felt compelled to find out what it was, I knew it wasn't my business. Still, I wondered why the hell they kept that dungeon intact like that? Even though it looked very old and somewhat decrepit, it was clear that someone maintained it in considerably stable conditions. The lights under the doors were new, with no burned-out bulbs. Not to mention the door hinges, which instead of being rusty and falling apart, gleamed in the light, indicating they were new. How was that possible?

I didn't know, and even though I tried with all my might to stop thinking about that damned place, I couldn't. I had spent time in a dungeon like that before, and even being so new, it was terrifying enough to be etched in my memory.

"Maybe that's why..." I whispered to myself, realizing I was probably seeing things that weren't there because of my past traumas.

"But you promised!" A man questioned Scott at the corner of the party, and I quickly assessed his body language.

He was irritated, gesticulating wildly, and his clothes weren't suited for the party; they belonged to someone who had worked all day and was anxious to get home and rest. His Italian accent was thick, too strong. Maybe he didn't live in the Calabria region and probably crashed the party.

I quickly approached since none of the other bodyguards were near Scott and remained by his side without him even noticing.

"You said that when you returned to Italy, you would tell me where you sent her. I've paid everything I owe, tell me. Where is my sister?" The man grabbed the lapel of Scott's pressed shirt.

"Keep your hands off, sir," I threatened, ready to remove the man from the party against his will if necessary.

"Oh, shit!" Scott jumped in place, while the man in front of him widened his eyes, startled by my presence. "Are you always like this? Silent as a cat?" Scott put his hand on his chest and waved his fingers at another bodyguard who came rushing toward him. "Escort Mr. Alex out of here. And you'd better be satisfied with leaving on your own, my dear." He slapped the man's shoulder as he was dragged away by the guard, shouting a string of curses in so many dialects that I got lost.

"Is everything okay?" I pointed to the man who was still flailing toward the exit.

"It's fine. It's normal to see some scenes around here. They're annoying but harmless." He shrugged, watching the path the man was taken. "Alex had a debt with my family and pawned one of his assets. He's a poor guy; he's lucky my father lets him live." He flipped a champagne glass and rolled his eyes, bored. That figure was so discrepant from the image everyone portrayed of him in newspapers and on the internet that I began to wonder how much of it was real. Did he also act in his father's business?

"I see." I didn't understand a damn thing. "And why was he looking for his sister with you?"

"Because he's a lunatic." He laughed, but I noticed the exact moment his gaze faltered. "Well, the party is over," he announced suddenly and loudly, receiving a chorus of dissatisfaction from the select elite present. "Don't cry; there's more tomorrow," he shouted, already heading up the stairs to the second floor. I started to follow him, but Scott turned to me as we reached the bottom of the stairs. "My room is right there." He pointed to one of the doors in the right-hand corridor. "I'm going to retire. No need to tail me. I'll see you tomorrow, Ghost."

"If that's what you want." I nodded, aware that he wouldn't back down.

Scott gave a brief, funny bow and turned down the corridor, disappearing moments later.

I leaned against one of the pillars, which were very white, just like the diagonal stairs that led down to the hall, now beginning to empty. I felt restless, maybe even anxious, and started walking through the corridors of the place, suppressing the absurd and somewhat masochistic desire to return to that strange dungeon.

I passed through the two main corridors as the night spread and even counted how many doors were in each. Eight doors in the corridor where Scott's room was, and another eight in the next corridor. I was surprised when I turned one of them and discovered another corridor to the left, this one with a total of twelve doors. One of them was open, and even though I shouldn't, I peeked through the crack. I was surprised to find a library.

Sleeping would certainly not be an option, but maybe I would find a book that could hold my attention for the next few hours?

I looked down the corridor and didn't see a soul wandering around, and from there, I had a good view of Scott's room, which would greatly help me keep that irresponsible neck of his intact.

I entered the library, which, like the rest of the house, had a genuine smell of seawater. There was a small lamp on a very wide table, which alleviated some of the darkness in the room. I was surprised by the number of shelves packed with books and felt a bit excited.

I approached the table, where some papers were cluttered, and noticed that one of them had been left half-open, as if someone had forgotten it there. I touched the paper, a dark ivory tone, and opened it, finding the strangest map I had ever seen on the face of the earth.

I examined the drawings closely. The circle of each line resembled a floor plan. Was it the mansion's floor plan?

I unfolded the paper more and noticed a reference in the center, as if it represented the entrance hall. Above it was a floor. I counted the number of rooms, and the description matched the number I had counted earlier. So it really was the house's floor plan.

I studied the map for a while longer and was surprised by the labyrinth it seemed to indicate existed. Just below the first floor, there was a depression and a tiny access point that led down to another long corridor, forming a cluster of ten rooms. I began to wonder if that depression was the steep staircase that had led me to the dungeon.

"So there are ten cells..." I whispered to the darkness and continued analyzing the map, but a curious detail caught my attention.

The floors didn't end at the dungeon; on the contrary, the map indicated a point further down, through the other passage, in the opposite direction. Probably the one without light, and that was where the labyrinth began. Left, left, right, left, left, right. The path was repeated four times and ended right there.

"What a strange place." I observed the paper shimmering under the lamp's light.

Could it be that underground place still existed? What would the age of that map be, and where would the labyrinth end?

Many questions formed in my mind. The way it maintained a pattern of two lefts for a right seemed fascinating. It must have been a way for the Marino family's ancestors to remember the path. Both for going and coming back.

I was pulled from my curious musings when I heard heavy footsteps in the corridor. I closed the map, leaving it exactly as it was. I moved away and approached the door, ready to leave the library when a strange conversation caught my attention.

"A brand new shipment arrived in the United States this week; did you hear?" one of the guards commented to someone, who soon replied, making me recognize his goose-like voice.

"Are they of good quality?" Sergei responded.

"Definitely. I saw the photos with my own eyes. They came from Mexico. Top quality. Brand new and hot." He emitted a rough sound that seemed like a stifled laugh, and I narrowed my eyes, trying to understand what the hell they were talking about. "They'll arrive around the end of the month, stay at the boss's headquarters until the order is given for them to come here. I hope they don't take too long, or I'll have to settle for the one from the basement. It's been a while since we got one of our own."

"Are you crazy?" the goose replied, alarmed. "He'll kill us if we touch her. It's his product, you know that. And speaking of him..." The man's voice trailed off but soon returned reinvigorated. "Good evening, sir!" he greeted in a solemn voice.

"Where is Ghost?" That was the first question Scott asked, which put me on high alert. Wasn't that idiot supposed to be sleeping?

"We haven't seen him, sir. Maybe he got distracted with one of the guests?"

"That would be too good to be true. That idiot doesn't leave my side." I pursed my lips at the audacity. The urge to step out of my hiding place grew stronger, but I waited to see where that conversation would lead. "He must be wandering around the mansion." He exhaled forcefully. "Roberto, find him and keep an eye on him. Make sure he doesn't dare go down those stairs again, and if he resists, show him your best manners."

"Yes, sir," the man replied enthusiastically, and I had to admit I would love to see that bodyguard try to stop me, but I needed to focus on other facts besides wanting to strangle those three.

Why did Scott want me away from the dungeon?

"Sergei, come with me. I need you to stand guard; I'm going to visit her." His voice sounded malicious, and both guards laughed.

"Is today the day you get what you want, sir?" the giant goose asked, excited.

"I hope so; my patience is wearing thin. Let's go."

I heard the footsteps start to fade down the corridor and peeked through the door just in time to see Scott, completely dressed in black, wearing a luxurious silk robe and holding a huge whip.

"What the hell..." The question died in my mouth, and several pieces of that puzzle began to hover in my mind.

"I hope they don't take too long, or I'll have to settle for the one from the basement. It's been a while since we got one of our own."

The phrase echoed in my subconscious, and I left my hiding place just in time to see Scott and his bodyguard disappear through the passage leading to the basement.

"It's none of your business," I whispered. "You have nothing to do with this, Ghost." I spent the next few minutes trying to convince myself to stay quiet, but there was something in the air, something too strange to ignore, and even though I didn't know what it was, my senses were alerting me and preparing me for the worst.

I may seem like the most proper among my brothers, but there was a dark side to my soul, a side I fought every day to keep hidden beneath a careful facade of self-control.

All that place, from the mansion to the bodyguards, especially the dungeon, had sharpened part of the dark side I struggled to contain. Knowing that there was something in that basement that Scott didn't want me to see only fueled my desire to find out what it was. I decided to tread as discreetly as possible the path that would lead me to the basement, driven by an insane and inexplicable impulse.

I was going to find out what he was hiding down there, whatever it was.

CHAPTER SIX

Alena

By that point, I no longer felt hunger, but a certain dizziness overwhelmed me. However, every fiber of my body seemed to awaken when the sound of footsteps reached my ears.

He's back!

I stood up too quickly, tangling myself in the blanket, and the whole floor began to move. My vision was filled with countless black dots, and my hands began to tingle. I stumbled to the wall, unable to see anything, and leaned against it, blinking desperately to regain my sight. He couldn't catch me off guard; it would be too easy, and if there was one thing I would never allow, it was for him to turn me into his property.

The sound of the latch being dragged made me tremble from head to toe. I swallowed the tears that seemed to tighten my throat and prepared myself when I saw the dark wood being pushed open calmly and the man stepping through with a black bucket. I raised my face, ready to look into his eyes.

The bastard closed the door behind him and held the bucket firmly between his fingers.

"Look at that, my little dove is standing!" the bastard said with a wide grin.

His blue eyes shone as he approached. He was a man who must have had success with women, those who were not his victims. After all, he possessed an intense and striking beauty, matched only by the wickedness in every inch of his body.

"You're quite resilient; many others didn't make it past a month." A month? Just a month? I had the feeling I had been trapped between those walls for at least a year, given the agony and despair I felt day after day. "I brought an old acquaintance." He raised his hand, and I sucked in my breath hard when I noticed he was holding the whip with a metal tip.

I swallowed hard, remembering the excruciating pain that object caused, and I needed to gather all the strength I had to remain standing before him. I thought about throwing myself on the ground and begging him not to hit me, but I knew that wouldn't do any good, so I gritted my teeth; if that bastard really believed I would give in, he was sorely mistaken, and I had been trapped there for far too long to make a decision.

I would leave that place lifeless, but I would take him with me if I could. I forced a smile that confused him for a moment.

"You won't find it funny when I break you, Dove." He raised the bucket and threw whatever was inside it at me.

I screamed as the painfully cold water hit me all at once, and then he unraveled the whip.

"I'll keep my promise. I'll break you until you allow me to possess you. You are mine, Dove; it's my right." He moved closer, keeping me on alert. "And when I'm done with you, you'll be begging me to fuck you, you whore." There was his true allure.

That man didn't want to rape me; he wanted me to surrender to him, he wanted to dominate me, and he would torture me until I accepted him without fighting, without resisting. His pleasure was to subjugate me, but there was something in my chest, something I didn't know, an overwhelming desire to fight and show that I was my own master, and that cursed man had lost against that feeling.

I wasn't born to be dominated. And it was this certainty that gave me the strength to keep fighting.

"I'll die before I let you touch me. I'll never give you that pleasure." His eyes sparkled with hatred, and he lunged at me with all the fury he possessed.

I screamed in pain as his hand grabbed my long hair and yanked it hard.

"Oh, Dove, do I need to teach you another lesson?" I thrashed, roaring like a wild animal when he tried to restrain my hands. I knew what he intended to do: to tie me up and beat me with that damned whip.

No! I couldn't allow it; I had to resist.

He easily locked one of my hands.

God, please, no.

I fought against him as he pulled my hair tighter. I managed to kick his leg and leaped over him at the first opportunity, running toward the door. My God, just the hope of reaching it filled my lungs with life. A hope that vanished as soon as he grabbed my neck from behind, throwing me to the ground with force.

My head spun, and for a moment, I thought I wouldn't be able to move with the excruciating pain that prevented me from opening my eyes for a moment, but I gathered all the strength I had left and crawled to the wall, facing him in the eyes. The bastard looked at the whip and crouched down before me.

"You're pretty strong for such a little woman." He laughed and raised his hand toward my face. "You've got grit, I like that, Dove, but I'm getting a bit tired." When I saw his hand approaching, I didn't think twice; I grabbed his arm and bit down hard, until I felt my own jaw crack and the taste of blood, his blood, spread in my mouth. "You little bitch!" He fell back onto his butt and grabbed the stream of blood now running from his forearm.

I lunged at him, trying to reach the whip, but it didn't take a second for him to regain his balance and stand before me. The blow I received next made me scream sharply and loudly, the tears I tried so hard to hold back streamed down my face as the pain spread over every inch of my skin.

"Why don't you just give in?" He raised the whip once more, and I howled again as the metal tip pierced the skin of my leg. "Just give in, Dove. It's hard for me, you know? To hurt such delicate and perfect skin." And once again, I was lashed. My voice had already faded; the pain was so intense I couldn't make a sound. "Although if you gave in..." He grabbed my hair.

"Let me go!" I breathed, weak, and he tossed me like a crumpled piece of paper onto the bed.

"If you gave in, it wouldn't be any fun, would it?"

And he raised his hand with the whip, which soon cut through the air and my skin once more.

Ghost

I DESCENDED SLOWLY along the path I had found earlier. It was funny how I was treading the same square meters as before, but now they had a different hue. Perhaps it was the certainty of being where they didn't want me to be. Breaking rules was, indeed, interesting. Maybe that was why Snake held such disdain for them.

I smiled at the joke and continued walking cautiously.

I descended the first staircase and noticed there was an iron door close to the entrance of the lower floor, one I hadn't noticed the first time I traced that path, nor on the map I spent a long hour observing. There was a gap open, and I leaned toward it, pushing the door a bit wider. I squinted at the sight of several black cars parked outside in the courtyard we had arrived at. It seemed like an emergency exit within that expanse of impenetrable walls.

I mentally noted the information and continued down the stairs. At the bottom, there was a small, very old iron door in a rusty brown color. I opened it and faced the stairs again, which, by the way, seemed designed to make it difficult for anyone to descend them. They were so steep that I could easily roll down.

I closed the door behind me, and before I began to descend, I felt compelled to check my weapon. Perhaps my dear VIP would try to kill me after that little adventure.

"At least there's no clause preventing me from killing a VIP who's trying to kill me," I whispered to myself, finding it amusing.

The smell of mold mixed with earth filled my nostrils as I approached the first basement. I walked down the dimly lit corridor, and it wasn't long before I reached a fork that divided into a dark corridor and a lit one. I recalled the directions on the map and took the risk of stepping into the darkness. In the distance, I could hear a strange sound bouncing off the walls.

I took another step into the dark, curious, and widened my eyes as I noticed some little lights flickering ahead. As I entered the tunnel, the vibrant sound grew louder. It sounded like flowing, living water.

Was it an exit to the sea? Did that second labyrinth lead to the ocean? What sense did that make?

I couldn't complete the thought because a piercing sound cut through the night, freezing me in place as I drew my weapon instantly. I hurried back to the fork and stopped again, aiming at the empty corridor. I turned my attention to any noise and heard faint, choked sounds. My breath hitched.

I took another step and was met with complete silence, which was soon broken by the shrill ring of my cellphone. I hit my hand hard against my pocket, and the ringing stopped, but the call didn't. I pulled out the phone I had brought exclusively for the mission in Italy, operational in the country, and saw Snake's name flashing on the screen.

I turned it off and switched it to silent. Before I could put the phone away, Snake called again. Something he rarely did.

Something had happened. I answered the phone without diverting my attention from the empty corridor.

"What's the surname of the family you're staying with the VIP?" His voice was crackling due to signal interference, probably because I was underground, but I could still hear the mix of aggression and concern in his tone, typical of Snake.

"I'm sorry to say this isn't a good time to build a family tree, brother," I whispered. "I'll call you back."

"Ghost, you took Walker as a VIP, but that little shit doesn't use the same name in Italy. By accident, I got the information about your VIP today; I knew you were going to Italy, but I had no idea who your ward would be. Pay attention; it's important. What name have you heard around?" The urgency in his voice made me think twice before hanging up.

"Why does it matter?"

"Because you might be in the wrong place, brother."

"I'm at Don Gava's mansion, the famiglia Marino," I replied. "Do you recognize that name? They fit the style you like; you should see what a strange bunch..."

"Get out of there. NOW!" he shouted so loud it almost made me deaf.

"Come on, man, have you been drinking? What the hell are you talking about? Why would I abandon the VIP?"

"Brother, the Marinos are targets for all the mafias in Italy. They work with something dirty. Something you can't handle, and for God's sake, I've always suspected that Walker had some ties to mafia business in Italy. If I had known that idiot would come looking for us and that he was Gava's son, I would have never allowed our father to accept..."

I pulled the phone away from my ear as another strange sound echoed down the corridor.

"Get back now; it doesn't matter what they think or say. Just get out of there immediately!"

"I don't know what your freakout is about, brother, but I'm a big guy, don't you think? I know how to handle any problem, and I really need to check something now. I'll call you back later."

"No, you don't know," he shouted back. "Damn it, Ghost, they're involved in trafficking."

"Half of your VIPs are too. Don't be a hypocrite."

"They traffic something none of my clients would accept, brother." He raised his voice. "Damn it, Ghost, they traffic people."

"What?" My voice came out as a whisper.

"Get out of there now!"

They're trafficking people!

I lowered the phone, Snake's voice shouting my name felt like part of a distant dream. I hung up and put the phone back in my pocket, feeling my mind shut down for a moment.

The secret passages, the organized and lit cells, the maps, and the obsession with the surname, everything. Now it all fell into place.

A piercing and desperate scream sliced through the air, so agonizing that I could feel the pain through that sound, which sent me further into a frenzy. All the numbness in my body began to yield to the memories of everything I had gone through. The agonizing pain, the scars that would never leave my body, the fear, and then everything again. In an infinite loop. I touched the scar on my neck and shuddered at how much of me was slipping away each time I inhaled the fetid air of that dungeon. How much I was yielding to my other self. That which transformed me into something I didn't know.

Into a monster.

Snake tried to warn me, but it was too late.

I followed the sound, which grew louder and more intense. As I drew closer, I could identify the screams. It was a woman's, and with each new wail, I felt a rational part of me die, leaving me blind.

I dodged down the corridor and found Sergei standing near one of the steel doors. He was smiling and watching whatever was happening through a crack in the door.

Human trafficking.

The phrase echoed in my subconscious, and without realizing how, I got close enough to the man to be behind him.

Another scream, now weaker, escaped through the door, and I was so close that I could feel the shimmering, impactful energy he left in the air. A trace of pain.

I raised my weapon and struck Sergei's head hard before he could even notice my presence. His large body fell backward, and I caught him carefully to avoid making any noise. But before I stood up, I delivered two more blows that would keep him incapacitated for a good while, damn goose.

I straightened my posture, possessed by a wild instinct that was blinding me, and looked through the crack where Sergei had peered just seconds before. The scene I saw behind that door took away any trace of humanity that still remained in my body. My world tilted when I saw a young woman being ruthlessly whipped by the sadist I was supposed to protect.

I kicked the door down, aware that it would be the first time in Holder Security's history that a bodyguard turned against his VIP, and it was a point of no return that I was more than willing to cross. I was going to kill him, and I wouldn't regret it at all.

Alena

THE THOUGHT WANDERED through my confused mind. The intense pain was the only thing keeping me lucid, but even that I was losing, like grains of sand slipping through my fingers. I tried to resist as much as I could, tried to stay strong, but I couldn't.

I closed my eyes as he raised his hand once more, waiting for the pain that didn't come. A sound from outside distracted him from me, and then the wooden door burst open violently.

"Ghost?" He stopped with the whip in the air when a tall man stepped through the door. My blurry vision prevented me from seeing him clearly, but the fear that he was there to hurt me made more tears stream down my face. "What the hell are you doing here?" he shouted between gasps of air. "Get out now. That's an order. You shouldn't be here, you bastard."

I dragged myself to the corner of the room and huddled there as I saw the stranger ignore that order, but instead, he tilted his head to the side, as if assessing the scene before him with a coldness so lethal that it made me swallow hard.

"Leave, or I'll make you..." Suddenly, my aggressor's eyes fixed on something outside that door. "Sergei! What did you do to..."

He didn't have time to finish the sentence. The shadowy man lunged at him with full force. He grabbed his whip with one hand and his neck with the other. Scott looked infinitely smaller beside him.

"You like this, don't you?" The unknown man smiled, making every inch of my body tremble with fear. There wasn't a trace of emotion, neither good nor bad, just a blank and very cruel expression.

"Don't make this mistake, Ghost. My family owns half of Calabria; you won't be able to leave here alive, but if you stop this now and let me go..." A hiss cut through the air as the whip cracked hard, striking the face of the man who had been assaulting me just moments before.

I held my breath at the scream of pain that filled the small room. The stranger he called Ghost shoved Scott into one of the corners near the door and raised the whip again, hitting him several times in succession with the instrument. I could see drops of blood flying everywhere with each new strike, just as it had happened to me minutes before. Scott tried to fight back but could barely move, as the man easily restrained him. Soon after, he dropped the whip on the floor and leaped onto the bastard with a chilling fury.

Each blow left a dry sound of breaking things in the air, and he continued. Hitting without stopping. Blind, bloodthirsty, violent, relentless. Without changing his sober and calm demeanor.

I wanted to flee, I wished I could run toward the open door, but I knew I couldn't. I was injured, weak, and so cold that I could hardly feel my fingers. I could only stay there, and despite not feeling a shred of pity for what was happening to Scott, I feared I would be the next one to be massacred like that...

"My God!" I groaned softly.

There were no words to describe it!

And for some reason, I couldn't look away. But God, how I wished to.

Then, suddenly, he stopped and stared at the inert, bloodied body before him. Scott's robe, now open, clearly left a strong and intense trail of blood. Was he dead? A mix of feelings hit me; I wished like never before that he had died, even though I risked falling into the hands of someone much worse.

I jumped in place when the man moved, but he didn't even glance in my direction. On the contrary, he walked out the door, and for a moment, I thought he wouldn't return, but the stranger came back dragging a large man dressed in black. He was unconscious, or dead; I couldn't tell. I was shocked by the mechanical way he dragged him, as if he were used to it.

What did that mean? What was he doing there?

Ghost continued with his serious expression, as if in a trance, and after tossing the big guy into the small room, he searched the man's pocket until he found a cellphone and threw it outside the cell. I shuddered at the sound of the device breaking somewhere, and he leaned against the wall right after, staring at a fixed point in front of him for a moment. It didn't take long for his dark eyes to turn toward me, sweeping my body part by part until they stopped at the blue bracelet on my arm. That seemed to mean something to him as he stared at it intently.

I sniffed; it would probably be my turn now, and I knew I had no strength left to fight. His eyes remained locked on mine, and even though at that moment they were just a blur to me, I continued to stare back.

"Don't be afraid of me," he said terribly calmly, extending his hand toward me. "I'll get you out of here safely, I promise." More tears rolled down my face, and I stared for too long at his bloodied hand, extended, waiting for me.

What kind of malicious game was this? Who was this man, and why did he want to help me? Was he lying or telling the truth? I couldn't know, but what choice did I have? I preferred death to spending another minute in that place, and if he was capable of doing that to the man who kept me here, they must be enemies. I couldn't know.

"I'm sorry, miss, but we don't have time." He kept his hand extended, and only then did I notice the tremor in his fingers.

There was no choice; it was him or certain death. I reached out my hand and touched his, trembling. He pressed his warm palm against mine, and the firm security of his touch made me exhale the breath I had been holding tightly in my lungs.

I tried to stand, but the only thing I managed was to sway to the side, and the stranger quickly wrapped one of his arms around my waist. I tried to pull away as he locked my leg with the other arm, but I was too weak to make any movement.

"I won't hurt you; I just intend to get you out of here as quickly as possible, okay?" he repeated patiently, and his voice didn't convey even a hint of the intense fury he had walked in with just minutes before. "I'm going to lift you in my arms; hold on to me."

I felt my body being hoisted, and he soon pressed me against his chest and began walking quickly. We left the room, and he closed the door right behind us, trapping the two men inside the small room.

"This will give us a little more time." The light in the corridor was bright compared to the dim lighting I was used to, and I shut my eyes against the sting it caused. "I hope you like adventures, miss, because we're about to embark on one of the big ones."

CHAPTER SEVEN

Ghost

Fuck! Fuck! Fuck!

I began to calm down as I walked, needing to think about what I would do from there on. I was aware of what I had done; even though I felt completely out of control, I understood the consequences I would have to face, and not for a moment could I regret them. How could I have acted differently?

The moment I looked through that door wouldn't leave my mind. She was being beaten, and when I walked in, I already knew I was willing to kill him. Everything happened so fast, and it took me a while to regain control of my own mind. That was when I truly saw her.

A small young woman, badly hurt, trembling in the corner of the dungeon. The look she gave me when I approached would likely haunt my nights from then on. It was the exact moment when her hope died completely, as if she felt her time had come, and part of my heart felt like it was ripped away upon recognizing that feeling. Something I had lived with for a very, very long time.

Snake was right; human trafficking was something I didn't know how to handle. It was my biggest trigger, the only thing that turned me into a version of myself that I didn't know and sometimes even feared. But there, running through the corridors with that small, light young woman trembling in my arms, completely hurt, I couldn't feel an ounce of regret. In fact, the feeling that burned in my heart was quite different. I wanted to explode every damn resident of that place.

I nestled her cold body against mine. She was very wet, and looking at the bucket I had briefly seen in the corner of the cell, I deduced that he had probably soaked her on purpose in that freezing winter. He was a sadistic son of a bitch.

She shivered with every step I took, and I could feel her discomfort with my touch, but we had no time for more explanations. I needed to reach the exit as quickly as possible to try to warm her up somehow.

I ran with the young woman in my arms and couldn't wield the gun in that position, so all I could do was be as silent as possible and go unnoticed—something I had a vast experience in.

I cautiously looked at the next corridor that would lead me to the steep staircase that would get us out of there and saw no one along the way. I lowered my eyes to her and noticed the excruciating silence in which the young woman kept herself. I feared I wouldn't be able to get her out in time.

"It's going to be okay," I whispered, unsure of that.

I continued speaking to her in English from the moment I saw the unmistakable Chicago Cubs bracelet on her wrist, one of the most famous baseball teams in Chicago, which was an alarming coincidence. Maybe that girl was American; maybe she lived in the same city as I did—there was no way to know.

At that moment, none of that mattered; I was more worried about climbing that devil's staircase without making any noise. Keeping silent would give us an advantage, and it was only for that reason that I didn't put a bullet in the heads of those two idiots, because it would wake up the whole house and we would lose the element of surprise.

I began to ascend the steps, balancing her in my arms. She squirmed a bit, and a low moan escaped her lips.

"Please, don't move, miss," I whispered close to her ear. "Or we'll both fall." She seemed to understand, as I felt her body tense slightly and remain still.

I climbed step by step, with calm and precision, and only realized I was holding my breath when we reached the top of the staircase.

I opened a crack in the door and saw through the long corridor two guards talking in the distance, Roberto and Angelo. I cursed under my breath. There was no way to cross that passage directly, but...

"The emergency exit!" I opened my eyes wider as I remembered it. It was in the door next door, and it wouldn't be hard to get through if those two idiots didn't turn our way. "Okay, now I need you to remain completely silent. We're counting on that to reach the exit, alright?" She didn't respond, nor did I expect her to.

I carefully opened the door, keeping my eyes on the two hulks at the far end of the corridor. I had to concentrate on all the experience I had in walking silently because if they heard any noise and looked back, everything would be lost. I walked slowly, one step after the other, my breath almost nonexistent, so great was my concentration. I reached the door I had found earlier that led to a garage and opened it slowly; I could only breathe once I passed through it.

Several black cars were arranged in the small courtyard, and I chose the one closest to the exit, a very thick iron gate that seemed impenetrable. I began to wonder if I could knock down the gate with the car, but first, I needed to break into one of the vehicles.

"One madness at a time," I said to myself.

I thought I would have to struggle to unlock the car door with the young woman in my arms, but when I forced the handle, I realized, to my luck, that the car was open.

I opened the door and placed her on the passenger seat. I immediately took off my jacket and wrapped her shivering, icy body in it. I scanned her delicate face for a moment, and the expression of pain she maintained drove me crazy. Bloodstains dotted her face, and part of her clothing was torn, revealing more red marks. She was all bruised, and that must have hurt like hell—all because of that piece of shit. An overwhelming urge to go back there and ensure he was truly dead made me clench my fists tightly, but I knew all too well that if I did that, the chance of that girl leaving there alive would come to an end.

I fastened the seatbelt around her and closed the door. I ran around the car, and when I was getting close to the driver's seat, a man appeared to my right.

"What's going on here? Is the boss leaving?" I froze when I recognized Stefano and his dog-like mustache. I had noticed that when we met at the airport, he didn't seem like a bodyguard; he looked more like Don Gava's consiglieri or something like that.

"Yes, and you know how he hates to wait, right? Do you have the gate control?" I tried to maintain my composure, and for a moment, the man bought my story and pulled out the gate control, but he sensed something was wrong as soon as he looked at my blood-covered hands.

"But what...?"

"Ketchup! Never knew how to eat civilized." I stepped closer to him, and he frowned, confused by the warm smile I gave. It didn't take long before he reached for the gun at his waist, but I was faster and struck him with an elbow from above, making him stagger; however, he swayed but didn't fall. "You're resilient, huh?" I punched Stefano, who staggered, and I locked in a chokehold around his neck. My fingers burned more than usual; I probably sprained my hand after what happened in the dungeon. "You should have accepted the ketchup story." I squeezed and released him on the ground, unconscious. I grabbed the control right after.

I took the man's gun and kept it with me; two guns were better than one, and I had no idea what we would face when exiting that gate—actually, I had no idea where we should go.

I got into the car and closed the door, glancing at the young woman who was trembling uncontrollably and keeping her eyes closed. I turned on the car heater to the maximum and activated the gate control. I floored it through the narrow streets of Calabria, aimless, directionless.

My bag with some clothes and my passport was left at the mansion, which left me with only my wallet, my gun, and my phone. I grabbed the device and called the only person I knew I could rely on if I needed a safe place in that hell.

"Zion?" Wolf's worried voice came through on the other end.

"Hello, brother!"

"Is something wrong?"

"Oh yes, definitely." I took a sharp turn, and the car screeched. I mentally thanked the gods that it was still early morning. There wasn't a soul in sight, and they wouldn't notice our hasty presence. "Do you still have that hideout in the Calabria area?"

"I do. I'll send you the location of the keys. But why do you need it? Did something happen to the VIP?"

"Well, if he survived, he's going to be a bit pissed at me because I stole something that shouldn't belong to him." I thought the bastard might have survived, but only because I regained my senses before I killed him with my own hands.

Even though he deserved to die, I couldn't do it in front of her. I glanced at the young woman making low, painful sounds that seemed to strike directly at my heart.

"What? What crazy story is this, brother? You... stole from the VIP?" Wolf's high-pitched voice almost made me laugh.

"Yes."

"For my holy patience, Ghost, what the hell did you steal from that man?"

"A prisoner. Isn't that exciting?" I took another turn, lost in the maze of identical streets filled with houses.

"A PRISONER?"

"Yes. I don't have time to explain right now, brother, but it would be a huge help if you could give me the address of where you hid the key."

"Yes, yes, of course!" I activated my phone's GPS, ready to receive the address, and set the route to the location he provided. "Go to this place; there will be a newsstand where my trusted contact keeps it. Knock on the side of the stand, and he'll take care of you. Say my name."

"Alright."

"What car are you using?"

"One I stole from the parking lot of those lunatics."

"Don't you dare go get the key with the same car, you hear me? Switch vehicles immediately; they can track you. — Ah, the older brothers..."

"Sure, brother, don't worry."

"Damn it, Ghost, how can I not worry? Just trust my contact; tell him to provide food and everything you need for the hideout. He'll know what to do. The place is well-maintained and should have almost everything you need there."

"Thank you, Wolf. I need to go now; wait for my contact."

"Wait, Ghost..." I hung up before the conversation could drag on. Wolf would end up crashing in Calabria if we continued and he understood the real situation I had gotten myself into, which he would indeed find out soon. Just a call from Snake, and it was likely that the whole Holder would invade Italy.

I did as he instructed and stopped the car as soon as I found an appropriate vehicle. I parked in a desolate, dark street and got out, panting, when I spotted a simple two-door blue car with dark windows.

I approached it and forced the door open with my knife. I then ran back to the vehicle where the young woman was. I opened the car door and unbuckled the seatbelt around her, but when I tried to lean close to her, the girl jumped in the seat like a scared cat and stared at me in terror. Her very large eyes had a shade unlike anything I had ever seen. They were cinnamon-colored with a very bright, intense golden iris, but they were filled with so much fear that a sharp pain shot through my chest.

"Calm down, it's me. I'm going to take you to another vehicle," I warned, but I noticed how she clung to the seat in resistance. I crouched down to be beside her and began to speak softly. "Listen, miss, I don't know if you understand what I'm saying." I glanced again at the bracelet on her wrist, the only indication that maybe, just maybe, she could be American, but there was no time to test other languages. "But if we don't get out of here now, we'll be easy prey for those bastards." She closed her eyes and relented.

I lifted her into my arms. Her face fell against my chest, and I held her tightly as I ran as fast as I could to the second vehicle.

I carefully placed her in the passenger seat, and she began to tremble more. I accelerated, aware that even time was against us, and drove as fast as I could to the address Wolf had provided.

It didn't take long to find a small newsstand with a semi-open door at the end of a street. I parked beside the stand and got out with my gun drawn. I had to be prepared.

I knocked three times on the metal and the door of the stand opened immediately, revealing a short, young, skinny guy with an elongated nose and small, narrow eyes looking at me.

"I came in the name of Wolf," I said, cautiously observing the two entrances of the street. "I need to pick up a key."

"And who are you?" he asked in Italian, eyeing me suspiciously, but I could hear the American accent in his words.

"I'm his brother."

"Prove it. Which one?"

"Ghost." How did he know Wolf had two brothers? Were they friends or something? "And you're not Italian, so you can speak to me in your mother tongue."

"How did you find out?" he started speaking in English. "What the hell, if you're Ghost, then you have the scars. I want to see them." He raised his thin, long nose in my direction.

"Why the hell would I show you that, and how do you know about them?" I stepped back from the newsstand, my eyes wide.

"You don't really expect me to hand over the key to the first idiot who shows up here in the name of Wolf, do you? There are two brothers; one has the tattoos, the reference is the snakes, the other has the scars, and only those two brothers, along with Wolf himself, can access the key, so show me the damn scars or kill me trying to find the damn key. You decide."

"You have quite a mouth, don't you?" I pulled down part of my dress shirt and turned my neck enough to give him a glimpse of the horror stretched across my back. His small eyes widened, curious and attentive. "This is the most you'll see of me, sir. So it's best not to take too long, or this street will soon become a war zone."

"Sir," he repeated the honorific. "I like you." He turned inside the stand and grabbed a book, opening it carefully. In the last pages was a key, and in another book, there was a small piece of paper wrapped up.

"Here you go. The key, the address, and the phone number of a security contact who is close to this city. Pentedattilo is a ghost town, sir. You'll know you've arrived when you see a pile of stones that forms five fingers. There won't be anyone there; the only one who will come to you is this contact."

"That's exactly what we need right now."

"I'll let him know you'll be arriving soon, and he will visit you as soon as you settle in and provide everything you need to stay hidden. Food, weapons, missile launchers..."

"Missile launchers?" I widened my eyes, considering the offer.

"Just kidding... or not. You'll only know if you need one."

"Thanks, I guess." I ran to the car right after and sped away as fast as I could, desperate to get us to the hideout quickly.

I looked at the young woman beside me every second that passed. Huddled and too small, too hurt. She continued to fight with every breath and even tried to move; she didn't seem willing to give in or give up, and that was good. I could see the effort she was making to stay sane amid everything, but from the excessive tremors in her limbs, she wouldn't endure that cold much longer.

I activated my phone's GPS once more and navigated through the narrow, empty streets of the city. The yellowish lights created a shadowy path, but I tried to cling to it to disguise the darkness and fear that were starting to overwhelm my heart.

I glanced at the girl once more, and the question I refused to pay attention to continued to surround me, like the oxygen in my lungs, insisting with each breath I took of the cold night air.

What if she doesn't survive?

The thought was about to throw me back into darkness, and every time I thought of it, every time the hypothesis crossed my mind, I felt an urgency as strong as life itself to return to that damned place and make each of those bastards pay.

"Get a grip... now!" I whispered to myself, trying to calm down as I noticed the tremor in my hands increasing.

For many years, I had managed to stay sane against those impulses that used to turn me into another man, but today... seeing what that bastard was doing to her ripped away all the self-control I once had. But now, if I didn't focus my attention on our path, it was likely we would both end up dead before dawn.

I exhaled slowly and returned my gaze to the streets of that place, dedicating all my attention to the mission of reaching the hideout. I drove for what felt like an eternity, and after a long while, we entered a highway that wound around a mountain along the Calabrian coast, where a gigantic sea silently accompanied our despair. I accelerated through the curves until I spotted in the distance a large pile of stones that curiously formed the shape of a hand with five fingers.

That was it!

I drove into the narrow stone streets. There was no light in that place except for the headlights of the stolen car, and through them, I could see some small houses along the way. Many of them only had two or three walls standing, but some were still in good condition, and it wasn't long before the GPS indicated that we were close to the hideout. A certain relief filled me.

The location was situated at a high point on the hill, behind several abandoned houses that concealed it while also providing a privileged view of the road.

That village was filled with crumbling houses, with brown brick walls stacked side by side. It was clear that the city was abandoned, but soon I found a house different from the others, with reinforced walls, a medieval appearance just like the pillars around it, and it didn't seem abandoned like the rest. I parked the car near the building, taking care to hide it between two semi-destroyed houses.

"We've arrived!" I got out of the vehicle, euphoric, looking over my shoulder to ensure there was no one watching us, and I was happy to confirm that we were indeed the only humans around. "Miss, we're going to have to..." I opened the passenger door and stopped when I saw that she looked even paler now. The young woman was shaking so much that her teeth were chattering uncontrollably, and she was gasping for air.

I touched her neck with my fingers, and my suspicion was confirmed. Her pulse was rapid, combined with her extreme paleness, cold skin, and the tremors in her hands... she was suffering from hypothermia.

I lifted her into my arms and had the impression that my heart had stopped. No... not just my heart; it was as if the whole world had come to a halt while I ran with her toward a destination as uncertain as her own survival. I jumped down a few steps, too disoriented to think. I opened the door without letting her go for even a second and locked it as soon as we passed through, blindly running through the dark rooms of the place until I found a generator next to a small bathroom. I turned it on, and in the next moment, all the lights in the rooms came on.

I entered the bathroom where there was a dark bathtub surrounded by a faded, flowery plastic curtain that looked very ugly. I turned the shower knob, and a spark of hope hit me when steaming water began to flow from it.

I didn't even think. I stepped into the bathtub with the young woman in my arms. I removed the coat from her shoulders and tossed it aside, wrapping her in my arms and holding her under the stream of hot water, silently pleading for it to work.

"Please, respond!" I asked quietly, like a prayer, as I held her under the hot water that poured down in thick jets, cleaning the young woman's face and arms.

She had black hair, as dark as her eyebrows, flowing long down below her waist, and it was stained with traces of dirt. I caressed the strands as the water touched our bodies, washing away some of the blood, dirt, and all the grime from our skin.

I pressed her against me a little tighter, trying to warm her quickly, only then realizing how truly small she was. Her body fit against mine delicately, and I wet my hand, gently cleaning her face. I noticed her thick eyelashes on her marked face; her full lips parted slowly in search of air, as if merely breathing caused her some kind of pain. I clenched my jaw at the sight of the abrasions beneath the dirt, and that killed me a little more.

"Hey," I called when I saw her move her fingertips. "Miss?" She jumped into my lap, her huge eyes wide with fear, and she froze in my arms. "Calm down," I whispered into her hair. "I'm trying to help you; no harm will come to you," I promised, but I noticed she still resisted, as if my touch frightened her, and the thought of what she might be thinking about me worried me. I needed to get out of there; I needed to distance myself from her, even though my whole body was pleading otherwise.

I didn't want to leave her alone for even a minute, but if I wanted to earn her trust, that was exactly what I had to do.

"I'm going to step out, but please stay and warm up." I immediately got out of the bathtub and saw her shrink back into the corner under the shower.

She stared at her hands, her eyes moving from one to the other as if trying to fit a piece into a puzzle. The young woman remained there, paralyzed, looking at the same spot for far too long while the dirty water flowed down the bathtub.

I looked around, noticing for the first time anything inside that hideout. The bathroom was small, without a mirror or window, but it was well-organized, despite looking like someone had died in that decrepit bathtub.

I opened the gray cabinet beneath the sink and was extremely happy when I found dry towels inside. I was so absorbed by adrenaline that I didn't feel cold, but she... I turned to the girl, who continued staring into the distance, now with her hands in her lap. I needed to warm her up.

Her lips were trembling, and I knew that somewhere in that hideout there would be clothes... black ones, most likely. Wolf had an obsession with them.

"Miss..." I lowered myself next to the bathtub, and it was enough for her to gasp and curl up even more in fear. Fear of me, fear of everything that had been done to her. "My God." I ran my hands over my eyes. How was I going to help her without scaring her? I lowered my voice and began to speak more calmly. "You need to warm up." I pointed to the towel and gestured with my hands, since I didn't know if she understood my language. "We need to get rid of these wet clothes. Can you understand?" She didn't move, just continued staring at her own feet in the bathtub.

"I'm going to turn off the water and look for clothes for you. Can you dry yourself?" I extended the towel, and slowly she raised her gaze, which once again seemed to shoot me down with that intense and rare golden hue. I had never seen a color like that. It looked like a mix of cinnamon, amber, ochre, and different shades of gold and tawny.

Her gaze locked onto mine, and for a moment, I couldn't do anything but drown in the most beautiful and unique eyes I had ever seen.

She stared at the towel and raised her hand with difficulty; it seemed she understood what I had said, but her arm fell back into the bathtub before she could reach it. She looked at the towel again, and her lips trembled more. A deep sob rose in her throat, and the young woman began to cry, shaking her head in refusal. She was too weak to even hold such a light fabric.

A painful knot closed around my throat at the sight of her crying like that. Seeing the suffering in the sounds she made made me bring my hand to my chest, trying to contain the pain that arose there.

How could they do that? How could they have the audacity? Audacity? No, because a brave man would never do something like that. Only cowards could commit such cruelty.

When I realized it, I had already stepped back into the bathtub. I turned off the shower, knelt in front of her, and cautiously passed the towel over her trembling shoulders.

"It's going to be okay." I kept looking into her eyes, wishing more than anything that I could wipe away the sad and terrified expression trapped on her delicate face. "Trust me; I will protect you. They will never lay a hand on you again," I promised, and I lowered my eyes to the towel. "Let me help you. We need to get these wet clothes off and warm you up." By some divine miracle, she didn't pull away when I moved closer. "I'll hold you in my arms and take you to one of the rooms," I warned, and that's exactly what I did.

I lifted her from the bathtub against my chest. The house was rustic, with a large stone pillar dividing the center, where a fireplace would be very useful as soon as I managed to dry that girl. The place was small and cozy. There were three entrances on the lower floor: one led to the bathroom, another to the kitchen, and the third to the bedroom, but none had doors other than the bathroom's.

A staircase rose up the side of the hideout, leading to a small second floor, where there was an open little hallway from which one could see the entire interior of the hideout and a narrow iron door. That was probably a special room, and I could swear that Wolf had turned that place into a panic room, but I would have to check another time.

I entered the bedroom, which had a wooden double bed, a small dresser, and three chairs that looked like they were about to fall apart from being so old.

"Can you stay sitting?" I asked, but she didn't answer, so I had no choice but to lean her against the headboard of the bed.

I placed her on the mattress, which was covered with a brown blanket, and helped her recline. I turned to the dresser and nearly shouted with happiness when I opened one of the drawers and found a pile of black clothes that Wolf used to keep in his hideouts, along with a small first-aid kit.

"This will do!" I placed the kit on the bed and picked out a warm shirt and adjustable pants. They would probably fit like a balloon on that small girl, but there weren't many options. I also grabbed one of the underwear that was there and unconsciously wondered if Wolf ever stopped to think that maybe one day a woman would need to hide in that place. "Now I'm going to help you get out of those wet clothes." She shrank back when I reached for the towel, and even though she was weak, she tried to resist. "We need to do this, or you'll get sick if you stay in those damp clothes. Don't worry; I won't see anything, and the towel will ensure that, okay?" She didn't move or try to jump to the other side of the bed, so I figured it was fine.

I stretched the towel covering from her chest down to her hips and began to chatter as I removed each piece of clothing from the young woman, ensuring the towel stayed in place throughout the process.

"You're going to be alright; it may not seem like it, but I know what I'm doing." I had always been a good liar. "I'm a bodyguard, and keeping people alive is my job. I even had a hamster once; I took really good care of him until..." I stopped when I remembered the fate of poor Mr. Rupert. "Well, never mind, you don't want to hear about my hamster." I carefully removed her pants, and all the lightness I had tried to maintain in my voice to calm her dissipated the moment I saw the number of bruises and marks on her legs. I clenched my jaw, trying with all my might to look away, but I couldn't. There were numerous small cuts, probably made by that damned whip. Some of the more recent ones were still bleeding, while others were deeper and in the process of healing. "I'm going to... clean the wounds," I said with difficulty.

I opened the first-aid kit and began cleaning each one. I could feel her effort not to pull her leg away at times due to the discomfort. When I finished with her legs, my jaw was sore from the pressure I had put on it, trying to control the anger that began to take over me every time I recalled how she got those injuries.

I couldn't freak out there; she needed me. She needed my best version, and that's what I would give her. My best.

I touched her hand to clean it and found it strange when she didn't offer any resistance. I looked at her, and she kept her eyes closed, a troubled expression on her face. A small crease formed between her dark eyebrows.

"Miss?" I called, fearing she had fainted. I brought my fingers to her neck to feel her pulse, and I heard her sigh heavily at the touch.

She fell asleep!

No, she didn't just sleep; she passed out!

Her delicate fingers stretched between my hands, and I looked down at them. The skin on her knuckles was almost raw, probably from the strength she used to try to defend herself. I closed my eyes and took a deep breath, aware of what she would still have to face.

They broke her. And if there was one thing I understood about that, it was that she would never be able to put all her pieces back together again. Not even time would make her forget what happened here, and every once in a while, the glue would come loose, and the pieces would fall apart. She would be like me—a patched-up person completely marked by human trafficking.

"I'm so sorry this happened to you." Once again, that damned knot closed my throat, and I spent the next hour there, repeating that phrase like a mantra, cleaning each of the wounds they had inflicted on her, feeling as if it were on my own skin. After dressing her carefully and laying her on the bed, I tucked the covers around the young woman, who, even in sleep, still wore a disoriented expression.

I felt her pain; I knew how terrible it was—pulsating and constant—but those who had done this to her had no idea. They couldn't imagine how many times she would wake in the night screaming, fearing she was back in the dungeon. They had no idea that she would probably never let anyone get close to her again; they didn't have the slightest clue, but I wanted so much to show them what it was like.

I ran my hands through the young stranger's dark, damp, tangled hair and heard her sigh at the brief touch.

"They will pay. One way or another, I'll make them pay," I whispered, allowing the version of me that I had fought so hard to control to come to the surface.

Being the Ghost everyone knew wouldn't be enough to get her out of there safely. I needed to be the Zion I had tried to bury many years ago.

CHAPTER EIGHT

Ghost

I changed out of my soaked clothes and put on a set similar to hers: a warm, discreet black sweatshirt. Then I went to check the house to see how safe we were. All the windows were secured with thick iron bars, and inside, there was a wooden window that blocked any light from coming through, which would keep us hidden in the ghost town, making us just another dim little house in the middle of nowhere. The front door was surrounded by semi-automatic locks that I hadn't even noticed when I arrived carrying her. There were eight in total. Just activating one would lock them all simultaneously.

I lit the fireplace in the living room, which would probably warm the entire house since it was quite small, and I climbed the stairs to discover what was on the second floor, in that room behind the iron door. I wasn't surprised when I found a rustic, Italian-style panic room. The walls and ceiling were reinforced with steel plates and bars. There were canned food, water, cookies, and a bulletproof vest.

I picked it up and thought about putting it on her as soon as she opened her eyes, but I paused to consider if that was the best choice at the moment and didn't take long to put it back on the iron table. She had already been through so much that it would be too much to stuff her into a vest now. But surely, when we left that hideout, she would have to wear it, even if I had to strap her into it.

I looked around the room a bit more and found a large black box under the table, where more first-aid supplies were stored. I pulled out the heavy box, and a growing sense of happiness washed over me when I opened it.

"It's good to see you," I said to the five guns laid out inside. Two Smith & Wesson pistols similar to mine, a .38 caliber revolver, and a Magnum, a very powerful weapon, each with two magazines. "What kind of trouble were you expecting here, brother?" The question danced on my lips, and as if sensing I was talking about one of them, I felt my phone vibrate.

I picked up the device and saw Snake's name flashing insistently on the screen. I closed the panic room and leaned against the wall of the open corridor on the second floor, where I had a full view of the small hideout.

"Hello, brother, how are you?"

"How's it going?" he roared on the other end of the line. "Zion, I thought you were dead by now. I've been trying to call you for hours, and it kept going straight to voicemail. Do you have any idea how lost we are here without knowing a damn thing, fucking hell? I didn't survive all these damn years to die of a heart attack because of you."

"I miss you too, Snake, but I fear the signal here is unstable, especially in a ghost town," I joked, trying not to reveal all the worry that was overwhelming me. "I'm sorry for not being able to communicate earlier; I was busy escaping from some psychotic killers."

"Did he make it to the hideout?" I heard Wolf's excited voice in the background, and the thought that they might have my father made me swallow hard. Imagining how worried he would be and how much he might risk to resolve the situation made me even more desperate.

"Snake..."

"Where are you, Ghost? We're coming to get you right now."

"Snake..."

"We'll bring weapons! Weapons... Wolf, do you have those explosives you mentioned the other day? Maybe the Jasmine project?"

"We'll take everything we have. Some men and Shaw too. A little faith will help us," Wolf shot back, mentioning one of the bodyguards who had become a great friend and was now part of the Holder Security team, with his unshakeable humor and faith. "We're going to Calabria and..."

"Cedric!" I roared, finally letting my true state show. Pure rage and worry. "I want you to listen carefully."

"The call is on speaker," Snake didn't contest; I rarely called him by name, and he knew that couldn't mean anything good.

"Is my father with you?"

"No, he doesn't know yet. We preferred to know where you were first before saying anything."

"Great, don't tell him anything for now, but I need you to stay alert for any retaliation that that bastard Walker's family might attempt against any of you in the United States."

"Brother..." Snake laughed, as if I had just told a joke. "They wouldn't be crazy enough to try to approach any of us."

"Not at all; our biggest concern is your protection, Ghost," Wolf confirmed, and I had to take a deep breath to convey the part they didn't yet know about rescuing that young woman.

"You don't know everything that happened. They might have a motive to want revenge."

"What do you mean by that, brother?" Snake inquired.

"I lost control down there." The silence that followed made it clear they understood what I was talking about. "When I went down to the basement, I found a fucking dungeon—I started to tell them what I had seen and heard, but nothing I said could explain the musty smell permeating the air mixed with a funeral-like scent of death. It was as if pain infiltrated our nostrils and showed us the worst side of humanity. That's what I felt when I stepped into that damned place. "And when I saw her," I continued, "it was like going back to my childhood." Only now I was no longer a defenseless child.

"Did he survive?" Snake's voice came through restrained, as if he were trying to control the anger he felt.

"I don't know. I couldn't shoot that bastard in the head because it would attract the attention of the entire house, and we wouldn't have been able to get out if that happened, but when I saw him last, he looked more dead than alive. And if that's true, I doubt Don Gava will let the death of his only son go unpunished."

"We'll be ready, brother," Snake said. "I've been researching this mafia. You won't be safe while you're stepping in Calabria. You can't trust anyone, only Wolf's contact. The people here are extremely loyal to the Marinos. From what I found out, they have a stronghold over the region, and it's not through benevolence and protection. They control everything in the worst way possible: through fear." I clenched my jaw. "If a person has a debt with the Marinos, they simply collect by taking one of their family members. Usually a woman, who is never seen again. There's not a single resident who would go against the Marinos' principles; after all, they know what can happen." I recalled the guy who was looking for his sister at the Marino party, and now everything made sense. They had definitely kidnapped the girl to settle some debt. "It seems many families have lost someone to this mafia, so our best chance is to go to Calabria to bring you back."

"No. If you come here, you'll be out of your protection zone. You'll just put yourself in the crossfire along with me," I asserted, pressing my eyes with my fingertips.

"And isn't that what brothers are for? We arrived at dawn," Wolf declared.

"Brother, I know how much you want to help, but if you come, we'll attract too much attention, and we'll spark a war in the middle of this place. I would put her at even greater risk. I need an escape route to get out of Calabria."

"And what's your plan, Zion? Do you intend to flee Italy with this girl? Do you even know where she came from?" Snake questioned.

"I have no idea. She wears a bracelet with the name of her baseball team, the Chicago Cubs, but there's no way to know if she's really American, and to make it easier, she hasn't said a word so far. I don't even know if she's capable of speaking. I also can't guarantee a detailed plan. I only have one certainty so far."

"And what is it?"

"That she'll go wherever I go. I won't leave her alone until she's safe."

"He's going to give us a heart attack." I heard Wolf mutter.

"In that case, I have an idea of how to get him out of there. Wait for a call, and if you don't want us waking up in Calabria, you'd better figure out how to answer it."

"Thank you, brother," I said, grateful for everything they were doing for me and everything I knew they were capable of doing.

"You'll soon receive a visit. It's a small, very red-haired young man, just like Walker's scrotum. He's my most reliable contact after the guy who gave you the key; he will bring everything you ask for and need. Just let him know." Wolf barely closed his mouth when a loud knock echoed through the house.

"I think he's already here," I commented, drawing my gun, preparing in case I was mistaken. "I'm going to hang up, but remember, don't say anything to our father for now."

"Then it's better to come back alive and whole, Ghost," Wolf threatened. "Otherwise, the Holder family will disappear."

"He'll definitely kill us all," Snake whispered. "Take care, brother. And stay in the hideout until my next call."

I hung up the phone and kept the gun at the ready as I descended the wooden stairs. I passed by the bedroom and peeked inside to check if the young woman was still sleeping, and I could only breathe normally when I saw her curled up under the blankets.

I walked to the door and noticed that, in addition to all the locks, there was also a tiny hole where I could see who was outside. I peered through the hole and caught a glimpse of a very small guy carrying a large bag.

"Who are you?" I decided to ask, even though I knew the answer. I needed to confirm if this was Wolf's helper.

"My name is Brian; I'm Mr. Wolf's contact. I came to bring supplies."

"Wait a minute, and you'd better not try anything funny; if you know my brother, you know how prepared I am for anything."

"Not at all, sir." I found it strange how he spoke fluent, impeccable English, as if he were not Italian but American, like the other guy.

I unlocked one of the locks, which caused all the others to open as well, and I peered through a crack in the door, keeping the gun aimed at the visitor, who looked even smaller from the front. The young man was skinny with an angular face, wearing discreet, warm khaki clothes, along with a beret that, combined with the early morning and the darkness of the small ghost town, obscured most of his face, leaving only a few wavy, bright red strands visible.

"Hello, sir! You must be the youngest, right?" He broke into a huge smile, raised the large bag in his small hands, and brought it closer to the door.

"How does everyone know I'm the youngest? I could just as well be the oldest," I questioned, a mix of curiosity and anger, and the boy laughed.

"It's just that according to Mr. Wolf, if I found the older brother, I would suddenly want to run away and hide."

"And what about the younger one? What did he say?" I cursed my curiosity given the risks we were running. But what could I do? I was just very curious.

"That I wouldn't hear you coming." He widened his smile, as if that made sense. "I think it's better if I come in, sir, to avoid someone seeing the light escaping from the open door. It may seem like little, but in a ghost town, any light is a beacon." Only then did I notice a very small logo on the front of the large bag. It must have been where the boy worked. "I left a phone number attached to the bag. Call me whenever you want, for whatever you need."

"Why are you helping us? What contract does my brother have with you?"

"What I have with your brother goes far beyond any contract. I owe my life to Mr. Wolf. He gave me a fresh start with my husband, the one who provided the keys for you, and I swore to repay him with whatever he needed," he replied with genuine joy. "I'm happy to have the chance to do something useful, and oh, there are some painkillers in there too; they might be useful."

"Thank you; they will definitely be useful, and thank your husband for me again." He pushed the bag closer to me and stepped back. The boy seemed to read the doubts in my mind as if they were written right on my forehead.

"Don't forget to call me." He pointed to the paper stuck to the large bag and ran down the stairs.

I locked the door and took the bag, which was much heavier than I had imagined, to the small kitchen, which contained nothing more than an old brown refrigerator that was unplugged, a cabinet of the same color and perhaps even older, a half-decrepit black stove, and a sink that looked as inviting as the bathtub.

"Well, let's see what we have here." I opened the large bag and was shocked to find a grocery order made and packed with great care.

There was a bit of everything. Painkillers, as he had said, coffee from a brand I had never seen in my life, teas of various flavors, everything needed to make pasta with sauce, seasonings, and... I stopped taking out the groceries when a hollow sound broke the silence of the early morning.

"Eggs!" I let out a breath, exasperated when I saw two of them broken and smearing everything in their path.

I tried to imagine what that girl would like to eat when she woke up, but considering our effective, if not disastrous, communication, even if she were here, standing in front of me, I wouldn't be able to get a word out of her.

And just thinking about her filled me with an overwhelming urge to return to the bedroom, and before I knew it, I was entering the room darkened by the wooden windows.

She was still sleeping deeply. Her slightly parted lips inhaled and exhaled calmly. Her once damp hair was now a bit tangled in the pillow. I approached slowly, as if each step weighed a ton.

I stopped when I reached her side and studied her face, which held a firm crease between her well-defined, arched eyebrows. I brushed aside a strand of hair from her face and held my breath when one of the many bruises on her body became more visible. It was the same mark on both sides of her face. Perhaps he had hit her with a blunt object, or maybe she had injured herself while trying to escape. There were so many "maybes" that I began to wonder if I would ever know more about that girl than just empty doubts. Would I ever find out what truly happened to her?

I exhaled sharply and stepped back. I needed to get that girl out of there safely. Even though I didn't know what happened, even if she never spoke a word to me, I would ensure she was free to do as she pleased with her life, but before anything, she needed to eat.

I spent the rest of the night organizing the weapons and decided to prepare a breakfast of scrambled eggs and hot coffee when a weak winter sun rose on the horizon. If there was anything that could bring people closer, it was food, and at least in that, I was good.

I arranged breakfast on an improvised tray and walked to the bedroom, balancing it carefully. I entered the room and raised my eyebrows when I saw that she was not in bed. I scanned the dark room and saw a shadow huddled in the corner near the window. I approached the switch and turned on the light.

"Good morning, miss..."

"AHHHHHHHHHHHHHHHHHHHHHHHHHHH!" A shrill scream echoed through the room.

"Ow!" I cursed as something flew toward me, and I had to use all my motor skills to dodge without spilling the tray of coffee on myself.

The young woman, however, seemed to be more frightened than I was, and after throwing the first thing she found at me, she jumped and lost her balance, falling onto an old wooden chair that shattered into several pieces.

She crashed to the floor and quickly reached for one of the sharp, broken pieces of the chair, aiming it at me as if I were a lion and she the tamer. My heart, which felt like it had gained the power of Wolf's idiot motorcycle, was now racing at 300 kilometers per hour.

"I'm sorry, I'm sorry!" I rushed to say and placed the tray on the bed. I caught a glimpse of the object she had thrown at me: a small metal bowl that had probably been abandoned on the floor for who knows how long. "I'm really sorry for the sudden entrance; I thought you were still sleeping." I tried to explain, even though she might not understand a word I was saying. "Please, drop that wood; you might hurt yourself. Look, I just brought coffee." I pointed to the tray left on the bed and noticed the exact moment when her extremely bright eyes found it.

She pressed her lips together and didn't let go of her makeshift weapon.

"Well, at least we made discoveries in this little moment of surprises, right? Can you speak, or... scream? Now I just have to figure out what language you speak." I stepped closer to the bed and pushed the tray nearer to her. The young woman shrank even more against the wall when she realized we were closer, so I returned to the entrance of the room. "Come on, eat. You must be hungry."

I moved away so she would feel more comfortable, leaning against the door frame and watching her divert her eyes from me to the coffee on the bed like a wild animal afraid of a trap. She swallowed hard, some of her dark hair falling across her face, hiding her expression, but I could guarantee she was indeed hungry, and it didn't take long for her to give in. Slowly, the little warrior began to walk toward the coffee, but her eyes were fixed on me, just as she kept the old, sharp piece of wood in her hands.

"Don't worry, I won't come closer; I just want you to eat," I repeated, gesturing with my hands, hoping she would understand.

She continued, one step at a time, keeping her wary eyes locked on mine, like a lion about to pounce at the slightest movement. She looked at the plate on the bed and suddenly dashed toward it as if her life depended on it, grabbing it with both hands and returning to the corner of the room. The young woman huddled against the wall with the plate propped against her legs and began to eat quickly. Very quickly. As if she hadn't eaten in ages.

I couldn't explain the violent, pulsing pain that ignited in my chest at the sight of her eating in such a desperate manner, as if at any moment someone would rip the plate from her hands.

"I don't think breakfast is going anywhere." I tried to muster a smile, but I had never had so much trouble pretending anything in my life. "Eat slowly, miss, or you'll end up making yourself sick."

She didn't listen to me, as I had imagined. She continued eating quickly, keeping the makeshift stake of wood by her side, as if it would guarantee her safety.

I clenched my fists until I felt my knuckles burn. Seeing her was like taking a peek into the past that I had tried so hard to forget. I could imagine the hunger she was experiencing; after all, I had felt the same when I lived on the streets. Even though I was too young, there were scenes I could never forget, even after all these years.

Once, I was so hungry that I felt dizzy, I wasn't seeing straight and asked a woman who had just ordered two hamburgers with fries for food at a fast-food joint—one for her and one for her daughter, who must have been about the same age as me at the time, just over 9 years old. She didn't like the request, felt bothered, and complained to the owner, who came after me in a rage. He threw me into an alley next to the restaurant, and that was the day I learned a valuable lesson.

I was alone in the world. With no one to help me, having hope in people who had more than I did to offer was the biggest foolishness I could commit, but getting beaten by a fast-food owner was nothing compared to what happened to me later.

There was absolutely nothing worse than being kidnapped and sold like an object and feeling your life slipping away into the hands of people who only wanted to do you harm. That kind of thing could destroy the most precious thing we had to survive: hope.

I looked once more at the young woman who was finishing her meal. There wasn't a part of her body that wasn't injured in some way. The fingers she used to grip the spoon tightly were scraped, her face bore large bruises just like the rest of her body, and her legs—God, her legs were completely wounded.

Almost without realizing it, I brought my hand to the base of my neck, caressing the thick scars on the back of it, and a bitter certainty settled in my throat.

Evil leaves marks.

CHAPTER NINE

Ghost

I spent the next few minutes leaning against that door, a mix of despair and fascination as I watched her finish her meal. Her cautious gaze occasionally met mine, and when she finished, she left the plate on a small table in the corner of the room and climbed onto the bed, burrowing under the covers while still holding the sharp piece of wood.

"You don't need to hold onto that thing. You might end up getting a—" I hadn't even finished the sentence when she sucked in a breath sharply and released the wood, closing her eyes briefly as pain crossed her face. "Splinter in your hand!" I added, letting out my breath while the little warrior glared at me with a deadly look that made it clear she wouldn't allow me to come closer.

She pressed her hand against her chest but kept the wooden shard by her side. She was in pain, but still preferred to have something to throw at my head if necessary.

"I didn't take you out of there to hurt you." I took a step toward her, and as I approached, her eyes widened even more. "Calm down, little Saiyan; I just want to see what your faithful protector did to your hand." I pointed to the piece of wood with my nose and raised my own hand, indicating hers. "Can you understand what I'm saying?" I tried again in English, and when she continued to stare at me as if I had suddenly turned into a unicorn right before her eyes, I began testing some of the languages I knew. "What's your name?" I asked in Italian, Spanish, and in a rough Russian.

I tried everything, even sign language that I knew briefly, but nothing worked. She still glared at me with an angry, distrustful pout that, for my personal hell, became cuter by the minute as she held her injured hand. Another wounded place among so many on her body.

I took a deep breath and placed my hands on my hips, feeling like a complete failure. The frustration was so intense that it felt like I was trying to carry water in a sieve. I ran my hands over my eyes and crossed my arms.

"What good is speaking so many languages if I can't speak yours?" I forced a weak smile. She narrowed her eyes, and though she wanted to hide it, I could see the trace of pain that passed over her face. "Wait here a moment." I went up the stairs to the panic room and returned with another first-aid kit in hand, which was much more complete than the one I had found in the room when we arrived.

The young woman's eyes widened in surprise when she saw what I was holding, which seemed to mix anxiety and fear.

"You already have injuries for a lifetime." I approached the bed and saw her shrink back even further under the covers, but the fact that she hadn't run and hidden in the corner of the room was already an improvement.

I lowered my eyes to the box in my hands, unable to acknowledge the fact I had just spoken. After all, it was enough to look at her to understand what I meant. It was hard to find a part of her pale skin that wasn't injured in some way.

"Let me help you get that splinter out of your hand." I indicated my own hand while speaking. "You'll need it without any infection if you want to get out of here alive." She pressed her lips together and looked again at the first-aid kit.

I didn't know if she understood what I said, but her hard expression began to soften, and I took the chance to move closer, explaining each step I would take to avoid scaring her.

"I'm going to sit on the bed, okay? I need to get closer to remove this." I saw her eyes widen as I got nearer. I sat on the bed beside her. Her arms and shoulders were tense. She was making a tremendous effort not to flee from me. "Can I see your hand?" I extended my palm toward her.

The young woman stared at my open hand for a while, probably pondering whether or not to trust me. I watched closely as something seemed to hurt even more, and she let out a sound of pain.

"Trust me, miss." I looked into her deep golden eyes for a moment and felt trapped there, in those bright irises. I had to blink to pull away from those two beams of intense light. "Let me see how it is, please. I can't stand seeing you in more pain than you've already suffered," I whispered, and before I realized it, I had already spoken.

My chest was tight, and my heart raced faster with concern.

She pulled her hand from her chest and looked at it for a moment, her eyes closing briefly. She exhaled deeply and then extended it toward me, opening her eyes again and keeping all her focus on me.

"I'm going to touch it. I promise I'll be quick." I opened my hand and gently touched hers; it was clear from her pained face how terrified she was of the simple mention of touch, and I could feel her body tremble as soon as our fingers met. "Let me see what happened here." I opened her small trembling hand between mine and was surprised by the large size of the splinter that had pierced her skin. "Shit!" I cursed and rummaged through the first-aid kit, pulling out a pair of tweezers. "I'm going to take it out; it will be quick. Hang in there; I know you can do it." I raised my gaze to meet hers. I knew she probably didn't understand anything I was saying, but still, the words kept spilling from my mouth.

She watched me carefully, the fear etched in her beautiful irises was palpable, but somehow she found a way to trust me, and I couldn't risk losing that small connection. So, I carefully guided the tweezers and in seconds, I pulled out the large piece of splinter and heard a soft groan from her.

"Done, the worst is over." I cleaned the area and placed a band-aid on the side of her hand where the cut had occurred.

As soon as I finished, she pulled her hand away and shrank back under the covers again.

"What do you say we put that medieval weapon aside?" I pointed to the broken piece of chair and reached for the wood. "Since you're not trying to stab my throat with your teeth, I think you understood what I said."

I stood up and gathered the piece of wood along with the others that were scattered from the broken chair. I was just about to leave the room with all the pieces in my arms when an urge to look into those rebellious eyes one more time overwhelmed me. I turned to her, who was now watching me with a mix of insecurity and curiosity.

"There's a fireplace here in the living room; if you want to stay close to it, just say so. Or better..." I laughed when I realized how comical that was. It was clear she wouldn't say anything. "Just step out of the room. The bathroom is right next door. The place isn't very big, so..." I waved my hand as I realized I didn't quite know what to say and left feeling more lost than when I entered.

I went up to the panic room on the second floor, my thoughts tormented. Had she understood at least a little of what I said?

"How am I going to help her if I can't communicate with her?" I pressed my eyes with my hands and took a deep breath, feeling more lost than ever, but there was so much stuck in my throat.

I couldn't judge the fear written in that girl's eyes. Beyond everything she had been through, there was still a fact that I had been willing to ignore until now. She saw what I am capable of; she witnessed my worst side, and thinking that she was afraid of me left me devastated, but she had reasons to feel that way, and that was a truth I couldn't contest.

I spent the next few hours gathering in a small bag everything we could take with us when the moment came. I climbed up and down those small stairs more times than I could count, and I swore to myself that all this hustle was just to prepare us for something inevitable—our escape. But deep down, I knew I didn't want free time to think about her and everything that had happened.

However, the more I tried to ignore the presence of the mysterious young woman in the room below, the more her bright, intense eyes peeked into the darkness of my mind. The delicate, fine features of her face, the long black hair that transformed her into an Amazon—each detail kept swirling in my mind.

I climbed the stairs once more, looking for the vest I intended to leave visible for when we were ready to leave the hideout, and it took me a moment to realize I was being watched.

When I reached the second floor, I looked toward the young woman's room, as I had done all three hundred times I had climbed those damned wooden steps, and to my surprise, there she was, watching me from the entrance of the room like a mailman checking for a dog ready to attack his heels. Her dark hair hung somewhat tangled down her back, and she hid her hands inside the sweatshirt, which was indeed much too big for her. I couldn't help but smile as I noticed she was standing.

I paused what I was doing and leaned against the wooden railing of the corridor on the second floor. She kept her wary eyes on me for a moment longer, then her attention drifted away. She scanned the hideout with her eyes and began to walk when she found the bathroom. I raised my eyebrows as I noticed she was limping, and all the brief happiness at seeing her react faded away, replaced by pure rage.

Before I knew it, I was gripping the railing as if my life depended on it. It didn't take long for her to come out of the bathroom, which thankfully had no mirror. I imagined it would be very difficult for her to see herself in that state, and I mentally thanked God that I had only seen one in the panic room.

I stood there watching her return to the room. She continued, step by step, and stopped just by the door, raising her eyes in my direction. Her large eyes gazed at me with more softness this time, igniting a spark of hope in my chest. She pressed her lips together as if she wanted to say something but remained silent and then disappeared into the room shortly after.

Perhaps that was the best time to explain my behavior in the dungeon or at least try to.

I went to the kitchen and prepared a quick juice to help her hydrate. When I approached the entrance of the room, I decided to knock twice on the round wooden frame to announce my presence and avoid startling her again.

I entered the room next and found her on the bed, watching me cautiously. Soon her eyes scanned what I was holding.

"Hello." I tightened my lips into what I hoped was a smile and raised the glass in her direction. "I brought you some juice. It will help you hydrate, will you accept?" To my complete surprise, she looked from the glass to me and nodded. "You understood!" I almost shouted. An unknown euphoria surged in my chest. Maybe she wouldn't speak, or didn't want to talk, but she certainly understood me.

I approached her carefully and handed her the glass. I waited calmly as the young woman gulped down the drink in one go and pulled one of the deteriorating chairs closer to sit down without alarming her.

When she finished, she placed the glass on the small table beside her and wiped her mouth with the back of her sweatshirt. I lowered my eyes to her face, and once again, the bruises there made my stomach churn.

"You..." I tried to start speaking, but it was hard to think when I remembered the state I had found her in. "Your leg... where does it hurt? I saw you limping when you left the room; is it one of the injuries?" She shook her head in refusal, and a mix of joy and despair filled me. I was truly happy to make some progress in our communication, but that wasn't enough to quell all the anger I felt for everything that was happening. "Can you show me where it hurts?" She shrank back for a moment, as if considering the idea, and looked at my hands with a distrustful gaze that revealed all the internal struggle she was facing.

"You're wondering whether or not to trust me, aren't you?" She swallowed hard and clutched the blankets with her hands. "That's a tough question, and often we make the wrong choice, but I can assure you that my only interest is in helping you. I've made some good enemies for that purpose, and I don't regret it. I can promise you won't regret choosing to trust me either," I pleaded, looking into her golden, intense eyes that captured my attention more and more.

She pulled the covers away with a crease between her eyebrows, touched the edge of the black pants she was wearing, and rolled them up to her knee, revealing a huge bruise on the side of her leg that hadn't been there when we arrived.

"Can I get closer to take a better look?" I said, and I saw her confirm, nodding. I observed the skin tone displaying a light golden hue, but it was completely marked and a bit swollen. "I need to touch it. I think I know what it is, but it would be good to confirm." She nodded, and I reached my hand toward her leg. Her body stiffened as I grazed my fingers over her skin, and I saw all the effort she was making not to jump up and flee from me in the compressed eyes and the firm crease between her eyebrows. "I'll be quick."

I quickly analyzed her leg, and as expected, I confirmed the tight muscle, which was causing her difficulty in moving the limb. I withdrew my hand from her leg, and she pulled the covers back at that instant.

"It's a bruise. Probably caused by trauma to the area." I let out my breath, furious, and ran my hands through my hair, which by now was completely disheveled. "The most effective treatment would be ice and an anti-inflammatory ointment. Unfortunately, we don't have either of those here, but I'll try to arrange for it with our security contact." She bit her thick lips as she processed what I had just said. "I'll be back in a moment; I'll ask them to at least bring ice; that will help reduce the pain and allow you to walk—or run," I wanted to add, given our uncertain destination.

I left the room and called Wolf's contact to request the missing items. The young man claimed it would be safe to bring the ice early in the evening when darkness would grant us more discretion. I ended the call and returned to the young woman's room, where she was motionless, staring at the chair I had occupied minutes before as if it were about to come to life.

"He'll bring the ice early in the evening," I informed her as I sat back down in the chair, taking care that it wouldn't break.

I took a deep breath and looked at her. Only then did I realize she was now watching me, caution evident in every breath she took, yet still, a mix of suspicion and curiosity filled her gaze.

What was she seeing?

That question took me back to the dungeon. They say the first impression you have of a person is the one that counts, the one that sticks. It was like that with my brothers. Snake was never well-regarded, poor guy. He usually instilled fear in men and a mix of panic and fierce attraction in women with his bad-boy demeanor. Wolf, on the other hand, also made quite an impression, especially because of his two-colored eyes, but I... unlike my brothers, was exactly the opposite. I always had the gift of going unnoticed. Except with her.

The first contact that young woman had with me was disastrous, deplorable. She saw in me something that no one ever saw, something I fought to hide away in my heart. She, trapped there for who knows how long, suffering all kinds of torture—mental and physical—had to trust a man as aggressive as the monsters who imprisoned her.

I needed to tell her that was an isolated incident. She had to know that she wasn't escaping with a psychotic madman.

"Miss," I began to speak, looking at my own hands for a moment. It took me a while to lift my gaze back to her. I felt ashamed, above all. It was hard to talk about it, about losing my self-control and all the trauma that led me here. But I needed to; we needed to. "When you saw me for the first time... what I did to Walker, well, I wanted to apologize for you witnessing that. Unfortunately, I'm not good enough to say I regret it, but I didn't want you to see that scene. It wasn't my best version." An agonizing knot formed in my throat as I realized how much I wanted her to believe that. "In fact, I have triggers."

I averted my gaze from hers for a moment, trying to tell a stranger what I had taken years to say to my own father.

"I'm adopted, just like my brothers, but until I found a family that truly cared for me, I went through things I still can't forget. Things that can still turn me into something different." I pressed my eyes with my hands, unsure of how to continue. "I was a homeless child and never knew my parents. I was raised by a woman who said she was a friend of my mother's, who took pity on me. She also lived on the streets, and we weren't close or anything. She just made sure I didn't die. I ended up learning a few things, and when she saw I was old enough to fend for myself, she left too." I shrugged, not wanting to share that I spent weeks waiting for her to return. "Living on the street was very hard, especially for a child, but I managed to get by."

I still remembered vividly the cold nights, the hunger, the longing for something I didn't even know what was, and the desire to feel important in someone's life. That was my greatest dream—to be loved. To know that someone would be willing to take care of me. To give me medicine when I got sick, to tell me stories so I could sleep, to hold me. I remembered asking for those things at Christmas events where a Santa

Claus would hand out gifts to homeless children. And it was after one of those events that everything happened.

"One day, after participating in a community event, I returned to under the northern bridge of the city, where several homeless inhabitants slept. It was one of the warmest places in the city. We stayed there until the shelters opened to protect us from the winter cold. When I got to the bridge that night, I noticed it was empty. The shelters had opened earlier, and I was the only one left behind." I looked at her and noticed her attention was fixed on every one of my words, motivating me to continue. "I knew where the shelter was, so I grabbed my gift, a little car I had just received, and headed there, but before I arrived, a car stopped next to me, and a man came at me with everything." She gasped sharply, her large eyes widening as she understood. "He knocked me out with one blow, and when I woke up, I was trapped in a strange room that smelled of old, damp wood. There was a camera recording me, and I had no idea what was happening. I thought the worst part was being trapped in that place for days, without seeing anyone, without eating or drinking anything. But hell was waiting for me somewhere else." I forced a smile that didn't reach my eyes as I recalled the devilish, painful memory. "I was kidnapped and sold on the Deep Web, which is one of the layers of the web where people commit all sorts of criminal acts." She brought her hand to her mouth as I maintained my focus on her eyes, clinging to the warm, intense spark they emitted to finish telling that story.

"I was sold to a couple who lived on a farm in the middle of nowhere," I summarized, not wanting to detail the absurd things that happened there. "I never saw anyone in the area during the time I was there," I admitted. "There were other trafficked children like me. Some older, others even younger. I remember that when I got there and saw the house and the couple who welcomed me with what I thought was genuine affection, for a moment I believed I had arrived in paradise, but it didn't take ten minutes for me to discover the truth. We lived trapped inside the mansion and couldn't make noise at all. I was bought by a couple of siblings who lived like husband and wife and were sadists who punished us for the slightest sound. The rule was very simple: if we remained in extreme silence, we had access to food, clothes, baths, and dry beds.

As a reward, but if we made noise... whatever it was—walking with heels clicking, running, dropping a single button on the floor, sneezing, coughing, crying, waking up screaming from a nightmare at night, everything, absolutely everything resulted in punishment." My hands began to tremble, and the movement didn't go unnoticed by the young woman, who lowered her eyes to them as I clenched them into fists. "They did terrible things..." I pressed my lips tightly as I recalled the punishment cage.

That's what they called the damp cell to which we were taken every time we slipped up. It was in the basement of the house, right below the huge room where a wall held a photo of every child who had passed through there, including mine. There must have been about twenty photos, but there were no more than five children there. This made our fate in the hands of those demons all too obvious. I remembered my first nightmare in that place; I woke up screaming, and the woman who forced me to call her mother grabbed me by the ears, dragging me to the basement. It was the first time I had been there, but I never forgot the smell of damp mold and earth that permeated the place. She stripped me of my clothes and locked me in the cell, facing away from her. I was whipped there until I passed out, but she waited for me to wake up to start again, always saying she needed to teach me, that one day I would thank her.

It wasn't the only time I went down to the basement. They branded us with a whip that had iron tips, cut us, and tortured us day after day. Most of the time on our backs, always preventing us from seeing what they were doing. They wanted us to feel fear, pain, uncertainty, panic.

I touched the collar of my sweatshirt and pulled it down, turning a bit to the side so she could see the beginning of my torment. The marks that penetrated my skin and destroyed my soul. She traced my neck with her gaze, and her eyes widened as she noticed the large scars there.

"I have so many of them that it's impossible to count." I released my shirt and exhaled loudly. "Over time, I learned to move in silence. If we didn't make any sound, they wouldn't punish us." She raised her eyes until they met mine.

"Is that why I can't hear you walking around the house?" Her melodious voice seemed to fill the small room.

"You can talk!" I widened my eyes.

"Y-yes." She clutched the covers in her hands, her cheeks turning a very red and lovely shade. "I'm sorry I didn't say it earlier."

"No! Don't be sorry; you just needed time to trust me and feel comfortable enough to talk," I said, half euphoric, with a weak smile that even made my jaw hurt. I was so happy that the story for a moment slipped from my mind. "And yes, that's why you can't hear me. I'm known as Ghost, but my name is Zion."

"How did you manage to get out of there?" she asked softly, wary, but her voice had a sweet tone like honey, and I couldn't help but admire her.

"The FBI found us some time later, but unfortunately, it was too late for two other kids who were with me." I fell silent for a moment, recalling the night Ratinho was brutally murdered.

That was his nickname because the boy was very small and could steal with ease. Once, he assured us he could steal the keys and get us out of there. He was caught in the act and sentenced to death by those psychopaths in the basement. We spent hours listening to him scream until he was gone. But I wouldn't tell her about that. She didn't need to know the horrific details of that horror movie I called my past.

"Afterward, I was taken to the hospital with the survivors, where I was hospitalized due to severe anemia. From there, I went to the orphanage, and after a while, I was adopted." I rubbed my eyes. "My story found a happy ending, but it left many physical and emotional scars. My biggest trigger is facing the same situation I went through. The same one I found you in." She twisted her hands together and bit her lip; only then did I notice her eyes were glistening. "I had no idea that idiot Scott was capable of such cruelty. I found you in that place by chance. I'm sorry you went through this. I also wish I could have prevented you from witnessing my worst side."

"Your worst side is still better than anything I've experienced in that place." She sniffled. "Thank you for getting me out of there. You saved my life." She brought her hand to her eyes and wiped away a treacherous tear that insisted on falling.

"Don't cry," I pleaded, anxious. "I'm sorry for sharing this heavy story, but I needed you to understand who I am to try to help you. If anyone understands what you went through, it's me. I just need you to trust me to get you out of here."

"And what if they catch you too?" I smiled at her concern.

"Don't worry, I'll take you to a safe place, but for that, I need you to tell me something about yourself," I began to probe her. "I'm from Chicago, and that bracelet you're wearing belongs to a baseball team from my city. I imagine you might live there." I continued and saw her lower her eyes to the bracelet as if she had just remembered it. "Can you tell me where you came from and how that man got his hands on you?"

She looked at me confused, as if she suddenly got lost in her own thoughts. The urge to help her hit hard in my chest, making my heart race. She was already talking, and apparently, I had gained a bit of her trust. We had made so much progress to go back now.

"Well, then how about we start with a simple question? Can you tell me your name?" She stared at me, a little wrinkle forming in the middle of her forehead.

"I don't know; I don't remember anything."

I raised my eyebrows, suddenly feeling the ground shake beneath my feet.

"What?"

CHAPTER TEN

Alena

The mysterious stranger stared at me as if horns had sprouted from my head. His serious face looked lost, and once again, I found myself observing him. I tried to find in his eyes the lack of humanity I had seen in the dungeon, but there was nothing but kindness and confusion. Still, a strange feeling washed over me as I looked at him, as if I knew him from somewhere.

Zion, the silent man who saved me, was tall with broad shoulders that shaped his always upright silhouette, as if he were ready for any misfortune at any moment. His brown eyes were slightly narrow, and his square jaw, well-defined by a stubbly beard, matched his mysterious demeanor. It was something I was still trying to process. His hair was as dark as mine and was disheveled after all the madness we had been through.

"What do you mean by 'you don't remember'?" he asked, leaning briefly in my direction.

"I only remember waking up in that place," I revealed with sorrow, sighing deeply, which caused a sharp pain in my lower back, another spot where that bastard had struck me. "As soon as I opened my eyes, I felt a strong pain in my head, and the first people I saw were Scott and a strange man who said he was a doctor. He examined me, but I have no idea what he said." I touched the back of my neck, where for days I felt such intense pain that I feared my head would explode at any moment, and I pressed my lips together at the painful memory. "I think they just wanted me alive, regardless of what it took."

"Does it still hurt?" He stood up and moved toward me. Instantly, I recoiled and held my breath, shrinking against the headboard, and he stopped where he was.

"Calm down, I'm not going to get close," he said patiently, and I closed my eyes tightly, embarrassed.

"I'm sorry," I said, pressing my eyes with my fingers.

I couldn't help the panic and despair that consumed me at the thought of anyone touching me. It was like going back to the dungeon, with that bastard trying to break me every second.

"I understand your fear," he said gently, "but I'm very concerned. Do you have any idea what might have happened to cause you to lose your memory besides the pain? Have you heard anyone talking about anything?"

"Absolutely nothing," I confessed. "I have no idea even where in the world we are. I couldn't understand a single word from the people I encountered along the way." I exhaled, frustrated. "All I know is... I don't know."

"Almost a philosopher," he joked, but I didn't understand, and soon he began to laugh. "There's a philosopher named Socrates, who once said, 'I know that I know nothing,' which indicates that it's wise to recognize the extent of our own ignorance."

"He seems intelligent." I pursed my lips. "I think I've become the very embodiment of ignorance. I also have no idea why I'm wearing this bracelet." I raised my arm to show him the small blue plastic bracelet that had accompanied me through that torment.

"You're in Calabria, Italy."

"Italy?"

"Yes, but don't worry. We'll find out who you are and how you lost your memory, little Sayajin." He had such deep confidence that he almost convinced me. "My priority is to keep you safe and get you out of here. We'll solve one problem at a time." He flashed a cold smile that seemed more like a disguise in light of what I had said.

I couldn't judge him. He was helping a stranger who didn't even know her own name, let alone why she was trapped in that place. I had nothing to offer him.

"We'll stay in this hideout for a short time. I'm waiting for orders to take the next steps safely. Until then, try to rest and avoid moving your leg until the ice arrives, so it doesn't get worse." He stood tall, casting his shadow over me. His strong arms pressed against the black shirt he wore, identical to mine. "Do you want to eat something else? I can prepare something quick."

"Thank you, I'm satisfied," I replied, feeling my face burn as I remembered how I had reacted the first time he brought me food. The embarrassment made me shut my eyes tightly.

"What's wrong? Are you in pain? Where?" He fired several questions at once, and when I opened my eyes, I noticed how hard he was trying not to get close to me, and that realization filled me with relief. Apparently, he wouldn't force me into anything.

"No, it's not that. It's just that... I'm embarrassed about how I acted when you brought the coffee. I'm not like that, but I was so hungry that I acted like an animal." I lifted my eyes to him and found his two brown stones scanning every part of my face.

An intense glimmer passed through them, and for a moment I saw his face harden, but the next second, he softened his expression. However, I noticed there was something there, something hidden away that he didn't want me to see.

"I won't let you go without anything," he said seriously. "Ask me for whatever you need, understood? I'll bring you a painkiller right away; it will help you rest better."

"Yes." I nodded and spoke again as he was moving toward the door. "Sir, what is Sayajin? You've called me that twice now." He turned around again, this time with a genuine smile that spread across his tired, marked face, making his eyes even more slanted.

"It's a race of warriors. And you don't have to call me sir; I'm the Ghost, remember?" He winked at me and left right after, leaving me completely confused.

Ghost... it was clear that I remembered. How could I forget a man like that? Silent, fast, lethal, and... protective.

"And now?" I whispered to myself.

What would I do? Should I blindly trust that stranger? He was risking everything to get me out of there, but how could I force my mind to forget everything that happened? What if he deceived me again?

I took the painkiller he brought, and my head spun the instant I was alone again, with more and more questions arising endlessly. I wanted to believe in him. Hearing about his past lifted a weight from my chest that I had been carrying since the day I woke up in the dungeon. There was another person in the world who had lived what I had. He knew what it was like... the pain, the fear. He knew, he felt.

I might want to fight with all my strength, but there was a bond connecting me to him. I had nothing, no one until the Ghost saved me. He meant much more to me than I would like to admit.

✷

THE DARK, SEALED WINDOWS prevented me from knowing whether it was still day or night. The cold in the hideout began to increase, and I hid my hands under the blanket. It might already be night. I felt so tired, but for some reason, I couldn't sleep. I was afraid it was all a dream. I was terrified of waking up again in the dungeon, at the mercy of that cruel man.

A soft knock caught my attention, and when I looked up, there was Ghost again, with a brief smile and a platter in his hands.

"I brought your dinner and the ice, along with a spray of dubious origin, but my contact swore it would be useful for bruises. Shall we find out? The worst that can happen is it doesn't work." I almost smiled at his enthusiasm.

He set the platter on the table beside me and took a plate with a pasta dish that looked delicious. Pure gratitude hit me. I hadn't known what it was like to eat something tasty, warm, and revitalizing since I woke up in that place without remembering anything. It felt so good not to be feeling cold, hungry, and even scared anymore. Too good to be true.

"What's wrong? Did I do something wrong?" He leaned closer to me, and before I knew it, his hand was near my face, but he curled his fingers back before he could actually touch me, and only then did I realize a solitary tear had trickled down my cheek.

"It's nothing," I lied, brushing my hands over my face, trying to suppress the urge to run to the other side of the bed at his presence so close to me. Maybe I had shown something, because he quickly stood up, directing all his attention to the ice pack he had brought. "I'm just happy to eat something good and warm." He turned to me and looked deep into my eyes. The world paused for a moment, with only the wind breaking the silence.

"How long did you go without eating in that place?" he asked seriously and intently, as if he wanted to mentally note every word I would say.

"I'm not sure, because at times it felt like the night would never end, but whenever he came to see me, they left me without food for a long time, and..." A sob caught in my throat as I recalled what happened afterward.

"Stop, little one. I'm sorry I brought this up; you don't need to tell me anything, especially not to relive it. Just eat, okay?" His deep, firm voice was so comforting, so warm that the sharp pain that started to swell in my chest began to ease as his eyes remained locked on mine, as if caressing my broken soul. I could see through his gaze the calmness and compassion he held for me, but the knuckles of his fingers were white from the strength with which he clenched his fist, and it occurred to me that it must be hard for him to relive all of that as well.

"May I?" He pointed to my leg under the covers and handed me the plate. "Can I apply the ice pack while you eat?"

There was care and concern in his question and above all, respect for what I was feeling, and for the first time, I felt an urge to let him touch me, even though the idea of that touch lingering scared me; it would be okay if he just stayed there, applying ice to my leg.

"I-I think you can," I assured, uncertain.

I feared that when he touched me, all those feelings would rush back. The sense of despair mixed with pure agony and the foreboding that, at some point, that touch would bring me pain. It was what made me want to run and hide under the bed. Something I couldn't even explain, let alone control.

"Don't worry," he said, pulling back the covers. "I'll be very careful, and I'll let you know all my movements." He tried to reassure me, but I felt my body tense as he rolled up my pant leg, exposing the bruises and wounded skin of my leg. "It'll be okay," he whispered, turning to grab the ice pack.

Then, with extreme care, he caressed the sore, hard muscle with the tips of his fingers and placed the ice pack over it.

"You'll feel a chill, but I'll move it from time to time so I don't hurt you more, okay?"

"Uh-huh," I agreed, unable to move or even take a forkful of the pasta. Then he slowly pressed the ice pack against my skin. I held my breath as the cold sensation spread through my calf.

"How are you feeling? Does it hurt?" he asked suddenly.

"A little, but I feel some relief."

"That's great. You're very strong, little one." A smile involuntarily lifted my lips at the affectionate strength with which he said that, and only then was I able to take my first bite of the pasta, which was divine.

I spent the next few minutes eating while watching Ghost place the ice on my leg and then take it off after a while, only to put it back again, patiently. He held a small towel in his hands that he used to dry the trail left by the melted water, and it was there, close to him, that I could see where the scars began. Just below his hairline. One of them encroached upon part of his neck, thin but striking.

What had you had to face?

"All done. Now I'm going to apply the spray, and I believe you'll feel much better by tomorrow. Apply it again before you sleep, okay?" he instructed, standing up and taking the now-empty plate from my hands. "Rest; tomorrow we'll have a long day. If you need me for anything, just call. I'll sleep right here in the living room."

"Thank you, s-sir..." I cleared my throat. "Ghost."

"You're welcome, little one."

He left the room right after, and I knew I wouldn't see him until dawn. I snuggled into bed, feeling the painful throb that had been bothering me for hours lessen considerably. It had worked, and I owed it all to him. The silent stranger who chose to protect me.

✳

I TRIED TO SLEEP AFTER applying the spray again, but I couldn't. The bed, though a bit uncomfortable, was infinitely better than the one I had been forced to sleep in for all those days. In fact, the real reason sleep had escaped me was fear. Just closing my eyes brought back memories of Scott's voice ordering me to yield, swearing that I would be his sooner or later, and that thought alone made me lose my breath and swallow painful sobs.

That's how I spent long hours staring at the ceiling of that place, tossing and turning in bed, searching for any semblance of peace, but I couldn't find it. I was dead tired, yet I still couldn't close my eyes, and it was at that moment that a strange sound caught my attention.

The noise started low but constant, growing louder until it resembled someone groaning and murmuring. I lifted my head, trying to imagine what it could be. All I could remember was Ghost telling me he would sleep in the living room, from where the sounds were coming.

I got up too quickly, feeling my leg throb in the sudden movement, but I didn't care. I limped slowly toward the sound until I reached the living room. There was nothing but a fireplace crackling as the wood burned. I was startled when another groan echoed through the air and froze upon finding Ghost, so tall and muscular, curled up on the sofa. He was trembling, and his hair was plastered to his forehead with sweat. I placed my hand over my chest as a painful sensation surged there upon realizing that the sounds were coming from him, groaning unintelligible things and seeming to suffer greatly.

I stepped a little closer, desperate and unsure of what to do. His face wore an expression of pain, creasing his damp forehead and destabilizing me. He was having a terrible nightmare; I needed to wake him up.

"Ghost," I called softly, but it had no effect, so I tried again, a bit louder, but nothing. He continued to tremble and seemed to be suffering so much that my own eyes were brimming with tears when I decided to touch him and shake him. "Ghost, wake up!" I shouted.

He opened his eyes wide and grabbed me tightly, his strong fingers closing around my arms, and it was my turn to shake from head to toe.

I was startled and pulled back. I escaped his hands and curled up in the corner of the wall, my chest rising and falling sharply as I tried to catch my breath. He blinked, confused, breathing in gasps. His expression was troubled, and it took him a moment to realize where he was.

"You," he whispered when his eyes fell on me. I could still feel the strength of his fingers on my arms, and even knowing it wasn't meant to harm, I was terrified. "Shit!" he muttered low, as if speaking to himself, and ran his hands through his hair, hiding his face. "I'm sorry, I... had a nightmare," he admitted, hiding his trembling hands in his jacket. I edged away, still feeling my legs wobble until I reached the opposite side of the sofa; otherwise, I would have collapsed to the floor. "I'm sorry, I shouldn't have touched you; I'm just not used to being caught off guard; I'm usually the one who does that," he confessed, his lost eyes focused on me without really seeing me. "It's been a long time since I've slept near anyone. You must have been scared by..." He stopped talking, visibly disoriented. "I didn't mean to frighten you." His moist eyes lifted, and the wall I had just erected began to dissolve as I saw so many feelings in him that I recognized in myself.

Fear, apprehension, terror, uncertainty. It was all there. He was fighting a similar battle to mine; that was the truth. We were two unfortunate souls trying to survive in a cruel world.

"It's okay," I tried to reassure him. "I just don't like being touched," I admitted. "Every touch makes me remember, even if I don't want to, his blows." I lowered my eyes to my lap and stared at my own hands, and when I returned my gaze to him, Ghost was watching me intently, a sorrowful expression on his face.

"Did I hurt you in some way?" he asked sincerely, the concern evident in his voice.

"No, not at all; I was just startled," I said quickly, and I saw him exhale sharply and lean back against the sofa. "What was the nightmare about?"

"About the past," he revealed, his voice still trembling. He opened his eyes and stared at the ceiling, getting lost in thought. "After everything that happened in my childhood, I started suffering from night terrors."

"What's that?"

"It's a sleep disorder. It basically consists of unconscious panic attacks. The person lives the dream as if it were real and endless. They scream, cry, make a commotion that can wake half a city, but usually wake up without remembering anything. There's not a single spark of what happened, except for the physical and emotional pain, which makes us feel that something is lurking in the dark, waiting to swallow us whole."

"How terrible!" I gasped, shocked and afraid that I might suffer from that someday too.

"It took me years to get rid of this disorder. My episodes would wake my father and brothers every night. I can't imagine what they went through since I joined the family, but they never abandoned me. Their support helped me overcome it, but I still have nightmares, and sometimes they become too real. Especially when I have triggers." He took his hands out of his pockets to rub his eyes, and I noticed the trembling had lessened considerably. "My brothers know how much this situation affects me, so they're doing everything they can to get us away soon. I can't, I just can't control myself. That side of me you saw when I found you is something I try to eradicate with all my strength. I have no pride in remembering what I'm capable of." He looked at me then, and only fear and insecurity were etched in his slanted eyes watching me.

"You know, when I saw you entering that cell like that, I was terrified just because I thought I could be next, but now, there's no better memory than seeing you beating that bastard." Ghost broke into a slow, weary smile. "I also have nightmares," I admitted for the first time, and his attention focused on me. "Some are strange; they seem like fragments, like a puzzle with distorted images and shapes, and sometimes I don't know if I'm awake or asleep. Right now, for example, I don't know if I'm dreaming or if I'm still alive." I tried to smile but only managed a grimace. He sat down, increasingly attentive to what I was saying. "I don't want to sleep. I'm afraid of waking up in that cell, trapped. To be honest,

I'm afraid of everything, and not remembering my past terrifies me even more. The worst part is that I don't even know who I am. All I've ever seen of myself is this part of my hair, and it doesn't seem like much." My lips trembled as I grabbed a thick strand of my dark, tangled hair.

"You never had a chance to look in the mirror." That wasn't a question; it sounded more like an affirmation from someone who had an idea.

"No. If you don't tell me what I look like, I'll keep on not knowing, and it just heightens the feeling that I'm living in a parallel reality. Can you tell me something? Can you guarantee that this isn't a dream?" A certain shame washed over me; it sounded so silly to say those words out loud, but it was true; I was so, so afraid that all of this was just a dream.

"Take this." He extended his hand toward me and held it out there. I looked at him, confused. "You'll feel better if it's you who touches me. It all depends on you. Hold it and let go whenever you want," he assured. I stared at the open hand reaching out to me. "Trust me, you have control, give it a try." I bit my lip, unsure, but there wasn't much that could go wrong if I touched him there, was there? I hoped not.

I raised my hand, fearful. I touched my index finger to his and stroked his cold skin until I gathered the courage to hold it with all my fingers. Ghost allowed me to intertwine our fingers, maintaining only the necessary strength for them to fit together.

"You can pull away at any moment," he whispered, and I kept my eyes fixed on our intertwined hands. "Now, close your eyes."

"Close my eyes?" I widened them even more, making him laugh.

"Yes, just for a bit. We need to inhibit some senses to better feel others." I found myself closing my eyes and ignoring the nagging feeling in my chest telling me to do the opposite. "Now, take a deep breath and forget the sound of the wind outside, forget everything, and focus only on your breathing." I felt Ghost guide my index finger to his pulse, and I almost cracked my eyes open, not out of fear, but pure curiosity. "Breathe and stop peeking," he teased me in a playful tone. "Now feel. Your skin against mine, my pulse in your fingers. Listen to my voice, feel my presence." I took a deep breath and tried to follow his instructions. "Are you feeling it?"

All my subconscious was fighting to make me open my eyes and run far away, but I wanted so much to discover whatever Ghost wanted to show me that I stayed there, trying, against all odds. And it didn't take long for the subtle thumps of his pulse to touch the tips of my fingers.

"Yes!" I replied ecstatically. "I can feel it." I smiled at the prospect.

"This is real, little one. I am real," he assured softly, sending a tingle up my neck. "You have very black, long hair like a sacred veil. Your skin is light, a soft honey, as if it has been touched by the sun itself. Your large eyes have irises of a golden hue I've never seen before, sprinkled with little brown flecks. Beautiful, intense. You have a turned-up nose, thick and heavy lashes, arched eyebrows that raise at the slightest sign of danger, and a mouth that is... um..." he coughed.

"What about my mouth?" I opened my eyes.

"I-it's there. It's a mouth, right? What else is there to say about a mouth?" He cleared his throat, leaving me confused. "What I mean by all this is that we are real." Ghost's gaze traveled down my face with a different, intense expression. "This..." He pointed to our joined hands. "Is a safe harbor, okay? Whenever you feel lost or think you are dreaming, hold my hand. You will always be free to take it out of this clasp whenever you want, but you will always find it here, waiting for you."

"Thank you," I said with difficulty. The emotion that overwhelmed me felt like it was suffocating me, as if that handshake had suddenly transformed into a strong, reassuring embrace.

"I'm no poet; I couldn't describe you as you deserve. So, I can show you, if you want."

"How?"

"There's a mirror upstairs. I can bring it, but with one condition." His face took on a serious, concentrated expression. I tightened my grip on his hand, unsure of what that meant.

"What's the condition?"

"That you won't be scared of the bruises on your face. They will disappear in a few days, I promise."

"Okay. I won't be scared." He brushed his thumb over my hand in a nearly imperceptible caress.

"I'll be right back." I realized he was waiting for me to let go of my hand before getting up, and when I did, I couldn't hold back the question that slipped out before he started up the stairs.

"How did you learn this? About the hand?" Controlling my movements had really made me feel more secure.

"It was a technique my father used with me for a long time until I could truly trust him. I'm glad it helped." He rushed up the stairs and returned minutes later with a medium-sized mirror in his hands.

He placed the object against the wall in front of me, then covered it with his body. I got up from the sofa, my anticipation and fear of what I would see mixing together.

There was no worse feeling than not knowing who you were. Which world you belonged to, or if anyone was concerned about you. Worse than that was not even being able to imagine what your own appearance would be like.

I approached the mirror, and Ghost stepped aside. I gasped as soon as my eyes met those of the girl on the other side of the reflection.

Is that me?

The question died on my lips before I could speak. I brought the tips of my fingers to my face, which felt so strange to me. Ghost was right; huge bruises marked both sides of my face, marks that would frighten anyone, but I was so shocked to see myself for the first time that I couldn't look away, and my eyes were indeed large.

My hair was in pure disarray, rebellious strands going in all directions, but it fell long down my back. Most of my body was hidden behind that loose clothing, but I could tell I was much shorter than Ghost. My face was thin, my nose also turned up as he had said. My eyes were drawn to the full mouth I saw in the mirror, with a small arch forming a heart. It was a normal mouth, at least. The way he spoke made me fear what I would see. But there it was, that reflection... that was me.

Tears filled my eyes. Joy, satisfaction, and a hint of pleasure enveloped me.

"She's quite beautiful, even with those marks." I brought my hand to my face and touched one of the bruises that stained my skin.

"You are beautiful," Ghost breathed beside me. A weak smile lifted my lips, and I couldn't contain it. I was too happy to have discovered what I looked like.

"Thank you for this." I pointed at the mirror and turned back to face myself, trying to memorize every little detail.

"I'm going to take you out of this country and prove to you that this isn't a dream." Our eyes met through the reflection in the mirror, and there was so much determination in his voice, so much certainty in his deep brown eyes, that a flame ignited in my chest, consuming me. For the first time since waking up in that dungeon, I felt a glimmer of hope.

I spent a long time there, in front of the mirror, while Ghost watched me carefully from the sofa in that room, which was much warmer than the bedroom thanks to the fireplace. And with the presence of the silent man, it felt much less lonely too. I sat on the opposite side of the sofa, still exhilarated by what had happened.

"How do you feel now?" His firm voice broke the silence of the night, rising above the crackling wood that burned slowly.

"I don't know how to put it into words." I smiled. "My heart is racing. I'm happy, euphoric, but I still feel the fear pulsing in every muscle," I admitted, confused.

"It's like that at first. Our mind gets disturbed, lost." He leaned forward. His black shirt was pressed by his solid torso, revealing muscles I hadn't noticed before. "I also didn't know the difference between reality and nightmare. It was my father who guided me onto the right path."

"How did he choose you?" Suddenly, I felt an overwhelming need to learn more about that man. To know what his past was like, to understand everything he had been through. Ghost carried so much of me within him.

"Well, the time in the orphanage wasn't easy, but compared to everything I had lived through, it was like being in an amusement park... without the fun." I laughed.

"Sorry. That just sounded funny." I tried to press my lips together to contain my smile.

"I like seeing you smile as much as I like hearing you talk." I laughed again at the memory of Ghost's wide eyes when he heard me speak for the first time. "I'm someone who prefers to find humor in every situation; I think humor can make everything better, but when you're a child abandoned to your own fate, it's hard to think that way." He returned to his story, and I opened my eyes wider, paying attention to every word. "I was very afraid of everything and everyone. I lived hidden, sometimes for two or three days. The nuns at the orphanage went crazy looking for me, and over time, the other kids began to see my behavior as something they should challenge. They formed groups with the goal of discovering where my hiding place was. They only managed to find me in one of them."

"And what did they do?" I leaned toward him, fearing what else might have happened to him.

"Nothing but turn me over to the head nun; they just wanted to find me. That was their main objective, but seeing that many people after me only terrified me more," he confessed. "That was when the night terrors began, and I started waking everyone in my dormitory. It was then that I went from a mere game of hide-and-seek to being a punching bag for the older boys who were awakened at night by my screams." He broke into a sad, firm smile that made me shudder.

It was only then that I realized I had dug my nails into the edge of the sofa. A painful knot formed in the middle of my throat.

"After a lot of complaining, they put me to sleep in a makeshift little room at the end of the hallway, where the brooms used to be. I was terrified of that place; it was dirty, damp, and the foul smell reminded me of the cells from the house I had been rescued from. Still, they locked me in there every night. So, I began to hide in the late afternoon until one day, I managed to conceal myself under a large wooden box near the entrance parking lot. I spent the night there, and early in the morning, I was awakened by the sound of a vehicle stopping nearby. A man had come to the orphanage, which was quite rare. Instantly, I heard the voices of the boys who used to beat me, humming my name as they searched for me. I knew what would happen if they found me, and I didn't think twice. I left my hiding spot and saw the man by the car talking on his phone, distracted, with the car door wide open. It was the first time

I used silence to my advantage outside captivity. I slipped behind him unnoticed and hid in the back seat."

"Oh my God!" I gasped at the bravery of Ghost, so young. "And then? What happened?"

"I stayed hidden there, waiting for him to return. I intended to escape at the first opportunity, and when he came back, he started the car without realizing I was there. It took him a few minutes to notice a child was hiding there, but when he did, he began to laugh. I've never forgotten that moment." His eyes lost focus, staring at a fixed point in the fireplace, and a slow smile lifted the corner of his lips. "He was fascinated that I had managed to get in there without him noticing. He stopped the car, asked my name, and all I did was ignore him. He said we needed to go back to the orphanage, and I was terrified. I tried to get out of the car, but he wouldn't let me. He said I shouldn't be afraid, that he had come looking for a son, and apparently, it wasn't him who chose me; it was I who chose him." I blinked, moved by the story. Maybe there was still love in this cruel world. "He adopted me that day. He gave me a home, a place to return to, a safe harbor." He slid down the sofa to sit beside me and extended his hand, placing it open over his own leg.

I looked at the inviting palm and remembered the sensation that surged through my chest when I touched it, as if I had found a rock to lean on. Instinctively, I guided my hand until our fingers were once again intertwined, connected by a bond I knew I could break because Ghost was introducing me to something I couldn't remember ever having: freedom. The warmth of his palm seemed to warm my heart.

"I will do for you what he did for me. I won't leave you alone until you can reclaim your life." My eyes locked onto his, which gently caressed my hand.

"Thank you." I leaned my head back on the sofa, feeling my eyes grow heavy as if they weighed two tons, and I stared at our joined hands. I began to wonder how such a simple touch could be so comforting. "When I was in that cell..." I opened my mouth in a slow yawn. "I dreamed every day of the moment someone would take me away from there. An angel, perhaps." I took a deep breath, the drowsiness enveloping my body. "I'm happy that this angel is you."

I didn't hear his response. I simply surrendered to the comforting darkness that surrounded me, without letting go of the hand that kept me warm.

CHAPTER ELEVEN

Ghost

She slept sitting up, and there was no more beautiful sight than seeing her there, eyes closed, thick lips slightly parted, and her hand relaxedly joined with mine. This meant she was starting to trust me, and I felt like a lucky bastard for it.

I'm happy that this angel is you...

I smiled, remembering what she had said just moments before she drifted off completely, and I lowered my eyes to her face, observing her more closely. Beneath the bruises that troubled me constantly, there was a young woman of extraordinary beauty. Delicate, lovely. Looking at her was like gazing directly at a star; I had never seen a woman of such sublime beauty.

I had no idea what they had done to her in that place, and just the thought made me feel sick. I wanted to be the guardian angel who would safely take her away from there; I wanted to save her more than anything in this life, and I couldn't even entertain the thought of failing.

"I won't allow anyone to dare touch you again, little one," I declared, knowing I would have to fight to get out of that place, but willing to do whatever it took to keep her safe.

I tried to lean her body back so she could lie down on the sofa in front of the fireplace and keep her warm, but just as I was about to pull away, she unconsciously hooked her free hand into my shirt and tumbled over onto me, snuggling into my lap and curling up on the sofa into a very cute little ball.

I caressed her hair, sliding my fingers through the strands, unable to wake her to move her, and I reclined my own body on the sofa while feeling her rhythmic breathing make her chest rise and fall. The warmth of her body against mine sparked a strange tingling in my chest. She was light as a feather, but in my bold heart, her presence felt like a massive weight.

Midnight fell upon us, and after spending hours watching her and trying to imagine her past, what she liked, and what she did before ending up in that place, I eventually fell asleep right there with her in my lap.

I woke up to my phone vibrating like crazy on the table in the living room. The young woman still slept in my lap, and I used all my cunning, which really made me feel like a lizard, to get off the sofa without waking her. I managed to disentangle myself and rearranged her, covering her better with the blanket.

I reached for my phone and only then saw that I had five missed calls— from Snake, Wolf, and even Jasmin.

It was impossible to control the smile that spread across my face at the thought of my sister-in-law, Wolf's girlfriend, an adventurous woman always looking for trouble. I glanced at the young woman on the sofa and wished Jasmin could meet her. It would be good for her to have the confident and daring presence of my sister-in-law, someone to talk to and confide in. After everything Jasmin had gone through, she would surely help calm her.

I exhaled forcefully and made my way up to the panic room, where the signal seemed to be better due to its height. I called Snake, who answered and spent a good five minutes cursing me for not answering sooner.

"Brother, I know you want to kill me..."

"Kill you? No! I'm going to rip each one of your limbs off, you damn bastard. How many times do you want us to think you're dead?"

"Let me talk to that bastard!" I heard Wolf roar from the other side, and I couldn't help but burst into sudden laughter.

"Snake, I apologize. It wasn't intentional." He cursed a few more times and then calmed down. "We're safe here, we haven't had any problems, and I've managed to get closer to the girl. She's trusting me more and more."

"At least that's progress. Where is she from?"

"She doesn't know."

"What do you mean she doesn't know? Was she kidnapped as a child?"

"Unfortunately, she doesn't remember anything. Just waking up in the dungeon with a severe headache. I don't know if she lost her memory on the way, or if her brain shut down due to everything she was going through." My voice dropped as I tried to control the fury that burned within me every time I thought about that.

"Oh, damn it!"

"What is it?" I heard Wolf question.

"I'm putting it on speaker." And he did, repeating what I had just said to Wolf.

"What the hell!" was the response from my brother with the two-colored eyes.

"Listen, Snake, I need you to check something," I said. "When I was at the Marino mansion, I overheard a disturbing conversation that didn't make sense until I found this girl."

"What did you hear?" he asked.

"A conversation between two bodyguards. One of them told the other that a new shipment had arrived in the United States and was in the possession of the boss," I informed. "So far, so good. But then he said they were young and... hot. Colombians or something like that."

"Shit, it's getting worse," Wolf retorted.

"They were talking about women," Snake concluded.

"Yes. I want you to find out where these women are. Ask the CIA for help, Snake. Agent Petrova has always been willing to help you, and she also has good contacts in the FBI; they'll be interested in the case."

"Always is a strong word. What we have is nothing more than a favor exchange. That woman doesn't hate me any more than I hate her," he huffed. "But it's for a good cause, so you can count on us."

"See if there are warehouses registered under Walker's or Marino's name. Look near the coast. Something tells me they plan to take them away by sea."

"You know that if we find them, it's going to blow up, right? Our father will know immediately, and Walker's name will be on the most wanted list in the country, which will be great," Wolf said. "But it could have repercussions all over Calabria and affect you."

"So be it." I breathed heavily. "It's what has to be done. I don't know if Walker survived, and it's quite possible he didn't, but if otherwise, if we blow the captivity, he'll be exposed, and given all the fame he's achieved, the case will spread quickly, and the entire Marino family scheme will collapse."

"It's not like we don't enjoy a bit of chaos, right?" Snake laughed. "We'll find them, Ghost. And we'll figure out a way for you to get out of there."

"I'm looking forward to hearing from you, brother."

"I made contact with the Don of the Sicilian mafia."

"Ah, excellent contacts, by the way," I joked, making him laugh along with me.

"Where you are is the territory of the Marino family. As I said, they keep all the citizens under a cruel power, and when they aren't obeyed or need to collect a debt, they kidnap family members who are never seen again, and there's no one to turn to. This trick isn't looked upon favorably by members of other mafias in the region. The *famiglias* value honor, respect, and family above all else. It's dishonorable to traffic people; it's cruel. They are under the radar of several mafias, one of which is Don Matteo's, from the Vitale family. It was thanks to the contacts I've had with him throughout my life that I learned the story about the Marino family, which hasn't been challenged in years. Their hideout is a fortress, impossible to penetrate. But the advantage is that the enemy of my enemy..."

"Is my friend," I completed.

"Exactly. Besides, Don Matteo is a good friend of mine." *Tell me something new...* I thought, but I preferred to save my brother's dubious friendships for a future discussion. "The Don will shelter you as if you were part of his own family. You'll be safe when you reach him, and from there, you can go back to Chicago."

"And here, the deal is with us. We'll wait for you with all the firepower at our disposal," Wolf added.

"Great! And where do I find Don Matteo?"

"The problem is exactly that, getting there. You're in Pentedattilo, which would be a short trip, about an hour. But the easiest route is also the most obvious. So, we've created a longer detour that's much safer. You need to drive to the coast until you reach a border point where the Marino family has no control but has access. From there, you'll take a boat that will take you to Sicily and that's it. Don Gava won't be able to get his hands on you within Don Matteo's territory."

"By the route we calculated," Wolf continued with the plan, "you'll spend two days driving and a few hours by boat. My contact will have a safer car available for you than the one you stole, so you'll pass even more unnoticed. So it's simple: go as quickly as possible to the location we indicate and leave Italy as soon as you meet with the Don of the Vitale family, understood?"

"Is this Don really trustworthy, Snake?"

"Of course! I wouldn't recommend someone I didn't trust with my own life. Honor means a lot among mafia members, brother," he emphasized. "Don Matteo is a just man, but dangerous, and he has serious problems with the Marino family. Plus, he owes me a bit more than just his head, so trust me, Matteo will take risks for you."

"Okay, let's put the plan into action," I agreed and moved closer to the railing on the second floor. I looked at the young woman lying deeply asleep on the sofa, hoping that this would work out.

"I'll send the address now. Get everything ready and get out of there as quickly as possible."

"Snake, if my father finds out, tell him I'm safe with your friend. I don't want to worry him, and don't forget there must be a shipment of women from all over Latin America waiting to be rescued; we can't stay idle."

I hung up after confirming a few more details with my brother and placed my hands on the wooden railing of the second floor, watching the girl curled up under the blankets in peaceful calm. I wished that calm would never end, but I knew our world was about to be turned upside down once again, and my only certainty was that I would put myself at the front lines of that war to protect her, no matter the cost.

Alena

"LITTLE ONE?" A LOVING voice called from a distance. The word danced in my ears. I liked the feeling it brought to my chest. "It's time to wake up." I blinked as the sound became more intense and found a familiar pair of eyes watching me with a small smile on his firm lips.

I took a deep breath, too relaxed to even move. I had no memory of ever waking up so comfortably warm, despite the pain spreading with every deeper breath I took.

"Hi," I whispered, hoarsely.

Ghost was crouched right in front of me. His long, toned arms were carefully propped on the sofa to avoid touching me. His dark hair fell over his intense eyes and was slightly tousled, as if he had tried to arrange it somehow. The stubble on his face gave him the rugged expression of a warrior, highlighting the square jaw of someone who knew a thing or two about the world. He looked different. It was impossible to ignore his presence before me. He embraced me without touching, only with his gaze.

"Buon giorno, piccola guerriera!" His voice came out melodious, and God, I had no idea what he had said, but the language seemed made for him. I had heard him speak it before, but no one danced with words like Ghost. It was as if he could reach into a heart just by whispering them.

"What did you say?" I asked.

"Good morning, little warrior," he repeated, holding a cheerful smile. "Did you have a good night's sleep?"

"The best I remember." I tried to sit up, but the simple movement triggered a series of painful points across my skin, and I couldn't suppress the muffled groan that escaped my lips.

"Take it easy." He rushed toward me but stopped just before touching me. His dark, bright eyes fixed on my face, and a crease of concern appeared between his brows. "Are you in a lot of pain?" he asked quietly, his eyes scanning my body as if trying to see each of my injuries.

"Don't worry, I'll manage," I tried to respond optimistically, but the reality was that I had no choice. I couldn't fail under any circumstances. I needed to endure to survive, and complaining wouldn't help me at all. "Oh, damn it, I took the spot where you were sleeping."

"That sofa was definitely made for someone your size, so you did me a favor." He stood up, maintaining a thoughtful expression.

I propped myself on my elbows, holding my breath as a sudden sharp pain shot up my leg, and only then did I notice a tray with breakfast resting on a small table in the corner of the room.

"I'm glad you're well-rested." He leaned over the tray and fished out a small envelope with his fingers. He tore it open carefully and took out a pill. Grabbing a glass of water, he handed it to me. "Take this; it'll help with the pain." He handed me the medicine.

"Thank you." I swallowed the pill with a bit of water.

"We'll leave after breakfast," he announced next.

"Where are we going?"

"I'll explain everything once you've eaten some protein." He stood up from the sofa and touched the blanket covering me. "May I? I'll help you get up. If you don't exert yourself too much, you'll recover faster." I nodded in agreement and watched as he pulled the blanket off with exaggerated caution.

Ghost extended his hand toward me as soon as he removed the blanket, and I found myself staring at the man before me. His muscles looked solid, and his movements were very strong. My eyes traced the exposed skin on his neck and stopped when I found the scars marking him. I sighed, recalling the story he had told. I raised my hand to him, aware that this man had known hell, just like I had, and I felt a slight tingling rise up my arm as his hand enveloped mine, as if he could hold all my pain with just one touch.

"You can lean on me if you want." He leaned closer, and until that moment, I had felt victorious for allowing him to touch my hand without panicking, but all that tranquility faded when I felt his other hand support the base of my back.

Suddenly, the touch became too intense, too firm, and like a quick flash, I was thrown back into that cursed dungeon. The memory of that monster's aggressive touch hit me full force, and I jerked to the side, startled. My feet got tangled in the blanket, and I was thrown to the other side of the small sofa, nearly falling face-first to the ground.

"Miss!" he said loudly and tried to catch me again, probably afraid I would fall to the floor.

"No, please," I spoke through clenched teeth, raising both hands in front of my face. A sudden tremor hit me just as a sharp pang pierced my battered body. "No... touch... me... please." I gasped for breath and raised my eyes.

Ghost stood there with his arms open, as if ready to come to my rescue at any moment, and a lingering discomfort filled my chest. I knew he was trying to help me, but I couldn't control that feeling when he touched me.

"I-I'm sorry. I can't control it."

"I apologize; I shouldn't have gotten so close." A furrow of concern appeared between the thick, firm eyebrows of the man, and I noticed he was analyzing me once more. A second later, he extended his hand toward me, palm up. "How about this? Can you hold my hand like before? I won't touch you in any other way." Why did that phrase sound so poignant and sad?

I didn't know, but I stared at the open palm and tried to remember how good it felt to hold it the night before, how that brief touch had managed to ground me in reality, and I raised my hand, fitting it into his.

His fingers intertwined with mine, and carefully, he helped me to my feet. For a moment, the pain was so intense that I had to lean against the sofa and close my eyes to stay upright. Apparently, all my muscles had been affected in some way.

"Breathe deeply, little one. You can do it," he whispered beside me, and despite the confidence his voice projected, I caught a strange note in it. As if, somehow, he too was feeling my pain.

Ghost supported me for a few more minutes as my body began to wake up and understand that it needed to work, pain or not. And so I dragged myself to the bathroom and washed my face. I returned to the small room a few minutes later, where a hot cup of coffee, fresh toast covered with something red that looked delicious, and scrambled eggs awaited me.

I served myself and sat on the sofa under Ghost's watchful gaze. A sigh escaped my lips as I bit into the toast and took a sip of coffee.

"Strawberries..." The word came to my lips, and I widened my eyes at the sweet flavor. It was so delicious, this warm food, so fresh. I savored each bite as if there were no tomorrow.

Ghost smiled and nodded in confirmation, but he only spoke again after a while.

"We're going to the house of a Don, a friend of my family." He began to explain while patiently sipping his coffee, his attention fixed on each of my movements. "There's a car waiting for us outside. We'll be traveling for almost two days in it, stopping only for essentials, and then we'll get on a boat heading to Sicily, where he lives." I paused with a piece of toast halfway to my mouth. A sense of danger infiltrated my veins, and a superhuman fear gripped me.

"Is it safe?" I asked, putting the toast back on the plate.

"I'd be lying if I said yes, *mia cara*." He sipped his coffee, as if contemplating what to say next. "We'll have to cross a region where we're sought after more than gold. We'll face various risks from here to there, but I need you to trust me above all. We'll face them, and we will win. Is that okay?"

"Yes, I trust you," I admitted for the first time. "But how can you be sure we'll win?"

"My brothers and I have a very clear idea of the troubles we can withstand. It's almost a motto..." He smiled, and his eyes drifted to the coffee cup in front of him, as if he were recalling something good. "You should never enter a battle believing you can lose. The option must be considered, but not embraced. Only those who enter to win are victors. And I will do everything to keep you safe; you have my word, miss." He looked into my eyes once more, and a wave of feelings rushed up my neck, warming my cheeks as I noticed his observant gaze dancing over my face. "You'll discover that a Holder never breaks his promises."

WE HAD OUR BREAKFAST, and soon after, we started packing some things to take on the journey that would decide our future. I noticed Ghost was wearing a black Velcro strap secured to his left leg, over his matching pants.

"What is that?" I asked while closing one of the bags he had given me, which contained some blankets to protect us from the cold on the road.

"It's a holster." He turned his leg toward me, pointing to a small gun tucked inside the holster. I pursed my lips, eyeing it warily. "We need them..." he lifted a small bag he was carrying and opened it, revealing four more guns inside. "Many of them."

"My God!" I widened my eyes as he pulled out two more and put on a new type of holster that crossed over his arms like a backpack, placing one gun on each side. He then grabbed something from the table that looked like a vest, but without sleeves.

"This is for you." He shook the object and came toward me. "Please take off your sweater. It'll just be for a moment."

"Am I getting a weapon too? Maybe this is a good time to mention that I don't even know how to hold one. I might have held one once, but, as you know, I can't remember my own name; God, how am I supposed to shoot a gun? You need to teach me!" I babbled on without realizing Ghost was watching me with a smile barely contained on his lips.

"Don't worry; I intend to keep you away from the weapons. This is just a vest. It's meant to protect you from any shots."

"Oh!" I gave a forced smile, not at all happy about the possibility of being shot.

"We'll put it under your sweater, alright?" I agreed, even though I felt my whole body start to tremble at the thought of putting ourselves in danger again.

I knew I had to get out of there, and worse... I felt like we didn't have much time left before someone from that family reached us, but I feared even more facing that bastard who had locked me in that place. He filled me with fear and a terror that bordered on phobia.

I lifted the sweater cautiously, trying not to think of him. The movement sent a pang of pain through my limbs, and a groan escaped my lips as I pulled the fabric over my head.

"Done," I announced, left with only the shirt Ghost had given me the night we arrived.

I looked up at him, who was staring at me strangely as he surveyed every part of my exposed skin. His eyes lingered on my right arm, and I glanced to see what had captured his attention. There was a large purple mark, almost black, marring the skin on my arm, and the injuries extended with small abrasions, some cuts, and large bruises.

"It's n-nothing," I stammered when I met the deep intensity of his gaze, trying to reassure him. I had noticed how his face darkened every time he saw one of my injuries, and it left me distressed. Distressed for myself, but even more so for him.

"Does it hurt?" he whispered, and suddenly a delicious smell filled my senses. Something reminiscent of cleanliness and a cloudy morning. Cold and warmth, the joy of discovering something new, and the sadness of saying goodbye to someone. How could a smell carry so many sensations? I leaned in, trying to absorb more of that aroma and opened my eyes wider when I realized it was coming from him.

"No. Not right now. Just when I move too quickly," I tried to answer, but my thoughts drifted as he lifted his fingers and stopped just inches from the skin on my arm, without actually touching it, and he lowered them until they connected with my hand—the only place he knew was safe—sending a shiver down my spine.

"It hurts me," he said, staring at my hands. "I'll make sure they pay for what they did to you." His voice dropped low, becoming dangerous.

"I don't want you to do anything that puts you in danger too." The phrase slipped out before I could contain it, and I was startled by how true that statement felt. "I also want to be able to defend myself, and since I don't know how to use a gun, maybe you can give me a knife. I would have loved to have one in that prison. I'm sure I could hit someone."

Ghost then lifted his eyes, and a slow, lazy smile spread across his lips.

"How about we keep the dangerous weapons under my care for now? I don't want you to get hurt or get scared of me and accidentally stab me; I've seen you're good at throwing things. Now, raise your arms, please," he said casually, and my face burned even more, recalling the previous day.

"It's a risk to consider since you're silently unbearable," he laughed, and that sound was so delightful it made me smile too.

I did as he asked and felt him slide the vest over my head, which, by the way, weighed much more than I could have imagined.

"I'll gather everything that can help us in some way, and we'll leave in ten minutes." He fastened the vest over my chest, filling me with a terrifying courage that bordered on nonexistence.

It would be a dangerous path, and I knew all too well that a million things could go wrong, but what kind of coward would I be if I didn't fight with all my strength? That's exactly what I had done every day during my captivity. I fought, and I wouldn't give up now that I had someone by my side willing to risk his life to get me out of there. I owed that to myself and to my guardian angel who was hiding more weapons in his clothes.

Ghost was a warrior angel, and I was liking that more and more.

"ALL SET!" HE ANNOUNCED a few minutes later, holding two bags. "Stay here; I'll check the exit and come back to get you. Keep the door locked and only open it when you hear my voice, understood?"

"Yes," I agreed quickly and loudly.

"Very good, *soldier*!" For some reason, he laughed and headed toward the exit, drawing the gun from his waistband. He peered through the small opening in the door and opened it, letting a sliver of light illuminate the space.

I couldn't help but notice how comfortable he seemed in that position, as if he had been born to carry a weapon and protect people. My admiration for the unknown man who saved me was beginning to grow; I felt so grateful for everything he was doing that I had no idea how

I would thank him. It felt like a dream, an opportunity to be free again, given by a stranger who took my problems upon himself.

"Lock it for a moment," he requested and closed the door behind him. I ran to it and did as he instructed, waiting anxiously for the moment I would hear his voice, which didn't take long to happen.

As always, I didn't hear him approach the door. There was something truly fantastic about the way this man moved. The entire floor of the hideout was wooden, and the old house made the boards creak with the slightest touch. How on earth did he manage to move around in silence?

"It's me; you can open up. We're ready to go." I immediately unlocked the door, and he stretched out his hand toward me.

I touched his fingers and fit my hand there, seeking his heartbeat that brought me back to reality, seeking his shelter.

The bright daylight fell upon my eyes like embers from a hot fire, and instinctively, I covered them with my arms.

"Damn, I completely forgot you were stuck in the basement for who knows how long without seeing the light." He focused on me, hurriedly removed his own jacket, and placed the fabric over my head. "There you go; open your eyes slowly. I covered your face so you can adjust gradually." I did as he said, and at first, I felt a stinging pain deep in my eyes, as if someone had thrown a jar of pepper in them, but as I struggled to keep them open, the sting gave way to pure surprise.

A weak sun, of a faded yellow, bathed a decaying city, with old walls and crumbling buildings in ruins. Far in the background, behind the city, there was a vast, endless sea where small waves shimmered in the bright blue, adorned by a mountain on its side that seemed to greet me with a large open hand. The conflicting display of scenery made a smile bloom on my lips.

"We're in Pentedattilo, a ghost town. It was abandoned a long time ago due to the natural disasters that frequently occurred here at certain times of the year," he explained without dropping the shirt, which had become a shield against the intense light.

I took a step toward that vastness, but a sting in my leg made me slow down.

"Do you think you can lean on me?" He offered his arm, and the first feeling that reached me was to pull away. It took me a few seconds to consider the offer, and he noticed. "In that case... hold my hand and try to use it for support, what do you think? Come on, I won't bite. At least not in this crummy country." He extended his hand and flashed a huge smile, revealing perfectly aligned white teeth.

"You don't like it here?" I grasped his hand.

"Italy? Not at all." He supported me as best he could, helping me down each of the wooden steps from the hideout while maintaining a proud gaze and keeping the gun fixed in his free hand. "I lost something very valuable under Italian soil, and although this country isn't to blame, I can't help but associate it with my fateful tragedy."

"What did you lose here?" We finished descending the steps, and he completely removed the shirt that was now sliding down my shoulders. The weak sun immediately touched my skin, and I smiled at the tingling sensation it caused. A languid, delightful warmth.

"I'll tell my story another time." He halted his steps while I still held his hand as if my life depended on it. "How are you feeling?"

"I don't remember ever feeling the sun like this," I said, closing my eyes and surrendering for a moment to that incredible sensation. I couldn't even believe I was feeling the breeze of the wind playing with my hair, tossing it in every direction.

"You'll be able to feel the sun as often as you want when you're in a safe place," he said softly behind me. "Will you come with me?" I opened my eyes and nodded in agreement, but he suddenly froze, staring at something on my face, as if I had suddenly sprouted two more mouths. "What is it?" I asked, startled, bringing my fingers to my cheek.

"Your eyes." He stopped in front of me as if observing something very surreal.

"What about them?"

"They're..." He paused and shook his head. "How in God's name can someone have eyes that color? They're like liquid fire. They seem to ignite right in front of me." He blinked and smiled. "Your irises are even clearer in the daylight. Sorry to startle you; I just... was caught off guard. I didn't imagine they could be even more..." He stopped at the end of the sentence, leaving the unspoken word hanging in the air, and I took a deep breath, unsure how to handle the warmth and firmness of his gaze on mine.

"More what?" He opened his lips, but before he could say anything, his eyes fell on my mouth, and a second later, he shook his head as if dismissing an unwanted thought.

"It's nothing; we have to go." He extended his hand for me to hold again, and I fit my palm into his, which was much larger than mine, feeling the security in the firmness of his touch that, while gentle, seemed capable of protecting me from the entire world, reminding me that this was real. *He was real.*

I walked slowly over the uneven ground. My leg was much better than the night before, but I still carried the sensation of having been hit by a truck. Every knot in my body ached, and it was incredible how Ghost seemed to know that, even though I avoided complaining. He always stayed close to me. I felt his protective energy drawing nearer each time my leg threatened to give way.

We walked together until we reached a black two-door car with dark windows. He opened the door for me to get in and only released my hand when I sat in the seat next to the driver. He walked around the vehicle, and I held back a laugh when I noticed how the car seemed to shrink in size when Ghost took the wheel with his long legs and striking arms.

"Listen, little one..." His eyes searched mine. "I would like to believe that we will reach Don Matteo without any hindrance, but if I did, I would be a fool and be going against my own instincts." He winked and pursed his lips; the prominent jaw gave him the exuberant appearance of a prince. "There's not a moment that goes by when I'm not expecting the worst, and this awareness has helped me greatly in every situation where I needed to protect a VIP."

"VIP?" I interrupted, confused.

"They are the people who hire a bodyguard like me. That's what we call them. In this case, you are now my VIP, and I will protect you using the same techniques I use in my day-to-day work."

"And what are those?" I asked, a mix of excitement and fear bubbling up.

"First, I need you to place all your trust in me," he began to explain. "I know it won't be easy, but you must remember that together we will succeed, but apart, our chances dwindle significantly." I nodded, attentive. "Secondly, if we are intercepted outside the car, I want you to stay by my side, no matter what is happening, keep your head down and follow my instructions. Another thing I need you to be aware of is two emergency signals. In some cases, the bodyguard must deal with danger close to the VIP and away from himself. For example, a thug taking the VIP hostage. While the police are being alerted, the bodyguard may need to save the client with just one movement: stop and go."

"How?"

"See this." He clenched his fist. "This signal means stop. That is to remain absolutely still, like a statue, even if I have to shoot in your direction, understood? If I make this signal, it means you need to stay absolutely still and trust me, okay?"

"Understood. If you close your fist, I become a statue."

"Exactly." He laughed. "And if I open it like this, you need to run or duck."

He spent the next few minutes outlining possible situations and guiding me on how to act in each of them. They all seemed extremely dangerous and surreal.

"Got it?"

"I think so." I opened my eyes wider, anxious. "So, if a war breaks out, I should cling to your leg?" He let out a loud laugh that filled the car.

"It's almost that. Now, there's just one detail left." He turned toward me and suddenly leaned in. I gasped sharply when I saw him loom over me, covering my body with his. "I'm just going to fasten your seatbelt," he warned, already over me, and I was flooded once again by his striking presence. "There we go. Ready to go?"

"Do we have any options?" I tried to smile.

"This is our best alternative," he assured, his eyes brightening as daylight seeped through the windshield. "Don't be afraid."

"I won't be," I blatantly lied. "I'll do everything I can to get us out of here and not get in your way. Even if I can't remember my last name to present it as proof of my character, I can promise you I will never break a promise made to you. Never!" I declared, certain that I owed that man much more than I could ever repay in two lifetimes.

"You're a remarkable woman, little one." He flashed a side smile, different from any I had seen before. That one, in particular, sent a shiver down my arms. "Whatever your name is, it must be as beautiful as you." I bit my lips and hid a smile.

I had no idea what hell awaited us outside the hideout, but I was grateful to have an angel fighting by my side.

CHAPTER TWELVE

Ghost

It was incredible the control a man could have in the face of adversity. An adversity that stood at least one meter sixty tall, with the sweetest smile I had ever seen and eyes that could definitely scramble my thoughts. Yes... my adversity had no name, but it was messing with my senses.

I was still absorbed by the color her eyes took on in the sunlight, just as much as by the scorching heat that permeated my chest when I approached her. What the hell was that?

I must be going crazy. If there was anyone I would never allow myself to see in another light, it would be her. First of all, I had no right. She was confused, didn't even know who she was or the feelings consuming her. Secondly... damn, I couldn't!

There was still the trauma that compelled her to accept any touch. I could tell she was gradually trusting me more, which was incredibly difficult after everything she had been through, and I would never take advantage of that trust. She believed my word, and I would do what I knew best: protect the girl until she was safe. Maybe I could find her family, maybe there was someone else. Someone who could touch those full, shaped lips that formed an accentuated arc, which looked so sweet on her beautiful, delicate face.

I accelerated down the road, suddenly gripping the leather steering wheel between my fingers. The idea bothered me, but it was the fate of that young woman, and I should feel happy if she were to reunite with her loved ones. Whoever they were. I huffed, unable to be more altruistic than that.

"Ghost?" she called me, her round eyes filled with concern, and only then did I realize she was staring at the road as if a band of demons was dancing right in front of me. "Are you okay?"

"Oh... yes! Just focused on the road." I tried to smile. "According to my brother, this is the longest route, but it's also the safest. We won't encounter anything for many hours. I brought some canned food in case you get hungry and some water; it's in the back seat and will help until we find a safe place to spend the night." She nodded in agreement and turned back to look out the window.

She seemed enchanted by the scenery rushing past, with rolling green hills and rocky outcrops that appeared to be stacked by hand, each landscape enhanced by the vast sea along the coast.

She began to hum something softly, distracted. It didn't even seem like she realized she was doing it.

"What song is that?" I asked, shifting my focus back to the road.

"It's just a snippet; I can't remember the rest of the song. Still, this little refrain was the only thing that calmed me when I woke up in that place." She sighed deeply and started tapping her fingers on the edge of the door, her big eyes staring at the horizon. "I tried for days to remember the rest, but I couldn't. I still feel frustrated about it. It's like I'm always adrift. Always waiting to remember something I lost." She shrugged, unaware of the depth of that situation. Remembering that snippet was already a connection to the past she had forgotten; even if small, it could transform into something bigger and help her remember everything.

"Can you sing for me?" I asked.

"No! That would be humiliating." She looked at me with a wrinkle between her raised eyebrows and a little pout that was, for God's sake, too cute. "I may not have memory, but I still have dignity," she said seriously, making me laugh.

"I'm passionate about music," I revealed suddenly. "It was one of the many hobbies my father introduced me to since I couldn't latch onto anything." I told her, trying to make her feel more at ease. "While my brother Christopher showed a natural talent for target shooting and my older brother Cedric was almost a boxer from a young age... I didn't identify with anything other than hiding around the house, and after trying every possible option, my father was nearly ready to give up until one day I found an old piano in one of the houses my father intended to buy."

"You're a musician too?" She opened a sincere smile full of hope. She seemed to like the topic.

"No, I would never risk performing like that. I enjoy playing. Piano, mainly, but I play other instruments like guitar, too... But besides enjoying playing, I love appreciating the sound each instrument makes." I glanced at her and noticed her attention was fixed on me. "I would love to hear the snippet you were humming. We don't have a radio in this car. I'd be very happy to listen to anything that helps pass the time."

"You might regret it. And if you laugh, I'll have to throw myself out of this car from embarrassment." I laughed. "Look, you're already laughing!" She pointed at me accusingly, but with a slight sparkle of amusement in her eyes.

"I promise this time was a different case. Please, save me from this boredom."

"Alright, but you asked for it." She straightened her body. "It's just a refrain, which I repeat endlessly with the feeling that it's incomplete like the rest of my memories, but it makes me so happy that I feel good repeating it. It goes like this..."

Then she began to hum, very softly, not looking in my direction out of sheer embarrassment. Her voice came out like a caress amidst the turmoil, the blessed light at the end of the tunnel. My heart missed a beat with the impact I felt as I was reached by that delicious tone, perfect, delicate yet firm at the same time. I almost had to stop the car, the shock overwhelming me.

"And that's it... it's just the part I remember."

"I'm amazed."

"Was it that bad?" She curled up in her seat.

"Bad?" I exhaled sharply. "I fear I'm carrying a musical revelation with me. You have a surreal voice, it's so beautiful."

"How can you say that if you only heard me sing a small snippet?"

"Exactly because of that. Your voice is sensational even in small doses; just imagine when you remember the rest of the lyrics? Speaking of which," I shot back, excited, "I know that song. I just don't know how to sing it, but I'll find a way for you to hear it."

"Really? Is that possible?" The joy that blossomed on her battered little face tugged at my heart.

"Yes, little one. Everything will be possible. Whatever you want." I found myself making promises I prayed to God I could keep, but how could I do any differently? She was a little angel who had only known pain until now; I needed to bring a bit of joy into her life.

I spent the next few hours with my mind stuck on that enchanting sound. On those full lips humming, in the exotic, vibrant eyes of the young woman beside me. I tried to think of anything else, anything at all, even the stones that scraped the wheels of the car and disappeared into the piles of dirt surrounding us, but with every second, it became harder to ignore the subtle, constant beat of my heart when I thought of her.

I needed to reach our destination soon, or I would go completely mad.

The sun that had previously wrapped us in weak waves of heat gave way to a cloudy, dark sky, heralding the onset of a storm, which began to worry me. The minimal, if not nearly nonexistent, lighting in that region of Calabria would complicate our journey, especially if we encountered a downpour.

I accelerated the car a bit more. If I could gain some time, we would leave the coast and enter the side of the city, where we would be safer regarding the weather. But there was another danger that wouldn't cease until we reached Sicily, and it was thinking of that that made my heart leap when I spotted a car coming in the opposite direction.

"Oh my God," she whispered upon noticing the vehicle and shrank back as we approached it. I brought my hand to the gun strapped to my waist and prepared myself.

"Don't worry; it might just be a local passing by." I tried to calm her, but my gravelly voice wouldn't fool even a child.

For a moment, my mind was taken to a future where those bastards managed to get their hands on her again. Just the thought terrified me, and I had to dig my fingers into the steering wheel to try to stay sane.

No, I wouldn't allow it.

I kept my eyes trained on the vehicle, which now up close looked old, with parts of the paint scraped off, as if it had collided with something. I almost sighed in relief when I saw an elderly couple driving it. A woman with white hair was telling something to her husband, keeping a big smile on her wrinkled face, while the man, struggling to focus on the road, seemed to agree without truly hearing anything.

"It's just a couple," I said in a whisper, glancing at her for a brief moment. The young woman released a breath and relaxed into her seat.

"I thought it would be easier," she commented, turning her face to the window where some raindrops were starting to cling to the glass.

"The journey?"

"No, facing any of them," she admitted, looking at her own hands that were resting in her lap. "I swore that if I saw any of the men who locked me in that place, I wouldn't think twice before going after them and maybe, with a little luck, gouging out someone's eye."

"Violent... I like that." She flashed a smile that didn't reach her eyes.

"But just the thought of any of them being in that car made me lose control of my actions. I could only feel an absurd fear." She shook her head and buried her face in her hands.

The rain, which had previously left only a few streaks on the glass, was now pouring down heavily, creating a loud noise. The road, which hugged the edges of rocky and sandy cliffs, began to receive a bit of dirt that soiled the asphalt, turning everything into a great muddy mess. "How will I survive if I can't even defend myself?" She took a deep breath once, then twice. I noticed the effort to stay calm was slipping between her fingers, and she looked on the verge of a panic attack.

"That's why I'm here, little one..." I began to speak in an attempt to distract her. "Being a bodyguard means being responsible for someone's safety. My job is to protect, embrace, and be responsible for your well-being. You don't have to feel obligated to face anything; this is my job."

"You can't face them for me."

"But I will. I specialize in doing what they don't expect from me." She lifted her eyes, glistening with the tears she was holding back. I nodded, giving her a side smile, and extended my hand to her. "Your fear is real, but so am I. Remember that?" Her lips trembled, and she grabbed my hand tightly, as if it were a lifeline. I swallowed hard, hating to see her so broken, wishing more than anything to destroy every bastard who caused that. "Everything will be alright." I stroked her hand with my fingertips and continued the journey, plunging deeper into a stealthy and aggressive storm.

We reached a steep incline. The winds hit us hard, and the car's brakes didn't seem to handle the watery, slippery road. I feared for a moment, but soon I spotted the end of the hill, which descended into a straight and completely empty avenue. I took the opportunity to release the brakes a bit and descend more lightly. That helped, but upon reaching the bottom of the slope, I heard the sound of something popping, and the car began to skid. The young woman clung to the seat with all her strength as I tried to maintain control of the vehicle until we finally stopped.

"Damn!" I cursed, unbuckling my seatbelt.

"What are you going to do?" she asked, her eyes slightly wider.

"I need to check if we've got a flat tire." I opened the door, and when I looked back at her, I saw pure terror etched on her face. "I need your help."

"W-what should I do?" she said, uncertain.

"I want you to sing that song until I get back." She widened her eyes, confused. "Can you do that for me?"

"I think so."

"That would be great. I'll be right back."

I stepped out of the car, and a million fine, cold droplets hit me like a flurry of needles thrown by the fierce wind. I checked the tires after confirming we were alone in the middle of nowhere and returned to the car a few minutes later. I paused before opening the door. There was a low, constant murmur coming from inside. She was singing. I smiled, happy to realize that the little one had followed my advice.

"What was that?" She nearly jumped in her seat when I entered the vehicle.

"Looks like we almost got a flat. One tire is low and needs to be inflated if we want to continue our trip. I have to find a gas station in the area. God help us." I started the engine and resumed our journey, now at an even slower speed. The low tire made the car shake, which worried me; if we needed to flee, we'd be in a tight spot.

"We'll make it," she said optimistically, clenching her fist. "We have to make it." Her golden eyes met mine, as clear as the raindrops hitting the glass. The bright irises were filled with fear, but still, she was trying to stay brave.

"That's the only certainty I have." At least that was what I wanted to believe.

Fortunately, we entered a straight highway with few pressure points that could cause a flat tire, and after a few kilometers, I spotted a gas station resembling an abandoned structure. The grimy walls were far from inviting, much like the convenience store, which I feared was a front for organ sales. There was no one in sight, which would be perfect for us.

"I'll fill up and inflate the tires. We'll get out of here right after. Stay in the vehicle and don't let anyone see you, okay?" I warned. "I might slip by unnoticed, but you..." I glanced at the young woman curled up in the passenger seat, still wounded and marked, yet exuding a rare, spectacular beauty. "They might suspect something. Cover yourself with the hood; I won't take long." I was absolutely certain that the moment anyone laid eyes on her, we'd have trouble.

"I'll wait right here," she confirmed.

I looked around to ensure no one saw us and reached the pump on the side of the gas station, feeling a mix of apprehension and agility. The tension energized me, and I kept brushing my hand against the gun at my waist, preparing for the worst.

I crouched to inflate the tires and noticed a gray car parked on the opposite side of where we were, obscured by a broken and abandoned soda machine. That worried me; we weren't alone.

I repeated the process with the other three tires, ensuring no unforeseen events would delay our trip, and when I was at the fourth tire, the low sound of the bells under the convenience store door echoed through the empty space. I squinted and straightened my posture, glancing in the direction of the sound. The sight froze me from head to toe.

Two guys emerged from the small store, conversing in an extremely low tone in front of the establishment. One of them, a tall man with broad shoulders, was chewing on a toothpick between his gold-studded teeth, while the other, slightly shorter, scanned the horizon as if searching for something or someone. The hand resting on his hip revealed a very familiar bulge. He was armed, and as much as I didn't remember those faces, deep down I felt they were men from the Marino family. And if there was something I never fought against, it was my own instincts.

I calmly pulled the pump away from the tire, trying not to draw attention, but I noticed the whispers had grown louder, and when I turned to the car, I saw the two men staring at me, analyzing me as if they were trying to recognize an old friend, with one crucial difference: if they recognized me, they wouldn't come running for a hug.

I gave a nod, maintaining a normalcy that bordered on madness, and approached the vehicle. I opened the door just as the gold-toothed guy took a step toward me. That was when my little passenger decided to give some sign of life. A very inopportune moment, I must admit.

"Ghost, can you open this for me?" she asked, handing me a can of food with her big, innocent eyes that didn't foresee the danger so close. "I just can't..."

"Hey!" the big guy shouted as soon as they realized I wasn't alone, already coming our way in an attempt to intercept the vehicle and probably check if we were who they were looking for. The young woman froze, holding the can inches from her face.

"I think your snack will have to wait a bit," I warned, leaping into the car, starting the engine, and speeding away, tires screeching.

I heard the men cursing loudly in their native language and accelerated even more, returning to the completely empty highway engulfed by the darkness of the storm, which seemed to grow denser.

"Oh my God, they're coming!" She looked back. I glanced in the rearview mirror just in time to see them getting into their own vehicle and speeding after us. "They're really coming." She started to panic.

"Hold on to your seatbelt and follow exactly what I say. It's going to be alright." I tried to calm her, which only made her whimper softly and shrink into her seat. "Do you trust me?"

"With my life, I'd say." She looked at me with wide eyes, which almost made me smile amid the panic.

I slammed my foot on the accelerator and noticed in the rearview mirror that they were closing in. I pulled out my gun and positioned it on my lap. According to the GPS, there was a sharp turn ahead; I needed to keep my distance from them until then, where they wouldn't be able to match my speed. At least that was the plan, but if there was one thing that could always change, it was that damn fate, and when I heard the sound of the first shot echoing beneath the storm's roar, I knew that this fight wouldn't be easy and that I needed to react accordingly.

Then the shooting began.

Alena

MY FINGERS WERE NUMB, but I still kept them dug into the passenger seat as if my life depended on it, and I well knew it was true. If I moved, I would end up dead. The feeling that death was whispering words in my ear intensified when I heard the first gunshot. I screamed, startled, and looked at Ghost. His posture had completely changed, as if a switch had flipped, transforming him into someone else.

His pupils were dilated, and his eyes were fixed and narrow, like a wild animal stalking its prey, moving so quickly and precisely that I could feel he was calculating something.

The vehicle behind us was already very close. A man leaned out of the passenger window and aimed at our car mercilessly.

I sucked in a sharp breath and nearly choked when another shot rang out behind us. I whimpered when Ghost had the brilliant idea to roll down his window. That terrified me; he would be even more vulnerable to the car behind us, which was closing in fast.

"They're going to catch us," I said in a whisper, every muscle in my body tensed, and the pain it caused didn't compare to the panic. I could barely breathe.

Ghost raised his gun, as serious as a commander in front of an army, glanced in the rearview mirror, and leaned out the window, shooting back. Up close, the sound was painfully louder, like thunder crashing right beside me. The response was immediate, and we were hit by more gunfire.

"If they had any doubts about us being who they're looking for, they don't anymore," he said, tense. "We need to get rid of them before they alert the others."

"When you say we need to get rid of them..."

"I have to... take them out of our way." He hesitated, and I knew what he meant. Ghost had to kill them, or they would kill us.

He accelerated and gripped the gun again, shooting blindly while trying to gain distance as he stared at the GPS like the solution would appear there. The thugs then, to my surprise, abandoned the attempt to flank us through Ghost's open window. Their speed dropped just long enough to approach us from the opposite side.

On MY side.

"Shit! They're going to try to hit you. They must suspect you're unarmed."

"Maybe it would be a good time to start trying. AHHHHHH!" I screamed as I felt the impact of their car against ours.

The vehicle jolted, the sound of metal scraping against metal produced a deafening screech. We were thrown to the side of the road; Ghost struggled to regain control of the car, the continuous sound of tires skidding and gunfire pierced my soul. I was so terrified that I almost forgot how to breathe.

"Just a bit more..." I heard him whisper, accelerating while focused on the GPS.

I stared at the small map stuck to the dashboard and realized we were on a straight highway, but that wouldn't last long. There was a curve ahead, and we were heading towards it as fast as a bullet.

"Ghost..." I whimpered. "There's a curve. A very, very close curve."

"I know. I'm waiting for it," he said, focused on the road, and in the next instant, we were hit again.

"Are we going to make it through at this speed?" I shouted.

"No. That's the point."

"Oh my God, do you have a plan?" I clung even tighter to the seat and felt the upholstery give under my nails.

"I do, it's nothing great, but considering the wise philosophy of *Fast and Furious*, '50% of something is better than 100% of nothing.'"

"We're going to die!" I hissed, in shock as I saw the curve approaching, quick and full of rocks.

Ghost reached for a lever and pulled the backrest of my seat, making it fall backward. I fell onto the seat.

"GET DOWN!" he shouted suddenly, and I didn't even think to argue.

Everything that happened after that passed like a movie before my eyes, fast, fervent, and extremely frightening.

Ghost, unlike anything I had imagined, suddenly slammed his foot on the brake. A loud noise echoed in the air, and the car swayed, trying to stop on the wet road. I widened my eyes when I saw him raise his arm and point the gun at my window, his eyes darkening and a grim expression taking over every inch of his face just moments before he started firing without stopping.

I closed my eyes and stifled the scream that reached my lips as countless shards of glass shattered and fell onto me. The sound thundered in my ears and felt like the beginning of the end of the world. Everything happened simultaneously, creating a destructive cacophony.

The tires skidded, the men began shouting in that strange dialect under a rain of bullets that seemed endless, and as if it couldn't get worse, Ghost pulled the handbrake and everything started to spin. The car spun, spun, and then I heard a loud, crashing sound. It took me a moment to realize I was holding my breath. An accident had happened, and by some miracle, it wasn't our car.

"Shit!" Ghost cursed and slammed his hand on the steering wheel, resting his face on it for a moment between bursts of breath. "We made it." He straightened up and threw his body back against the seat, exhaling forcefully and running a hand over his face, visibly relieved.

I tried to think rationally, but was hindered by the feeling of being turned inside out. I couldn't control myself. I unbuckled my seatbelt and jerked my body up, opened the door, and fell to my knees on the damp ground. I emptied everything in my stomach, gasping for air. I heard the door opening, and soon Ghost was beside me, holding my shoulders.

"N-no..." I tried to stammer and ask him to back away as another wave of nausea hit me. "D-don't look..." And there went the rest of my breakfast.

Ghost's strong hands gently gathered my hair, and he placed his palm on my forehead.

"Breathe slowly, little one." I felt his voice seep into my pores and closed my eyes. I tried to focus on it. "That's it, breathe. The worst is over. You're safe now. That's it... very good." I inhaled deeply, clinging to the warmth and firmness of his hand on my forehead. "They're done," he assured me, and for another minute or two, we remained there under a steady, but now lighter rain. The cold wind refreshed my body and eased the nausea I felt. Gradually, I managed to open my eyes again.

I found Ghost's eyes watching me. The brown pupils, as intense as a deep lake, were dilated, alert, but there was a sea of worry behind them. I blinked and realized, after all that madness, that he was truly willing to go to any lengths to protect me. The gratitude that embraced me at that moment formed a painful knot in my throat.

"T-thank you!" I stammered, trembling.

"Are you okay? You didn't get hurt, right?" His eyes traveled down my body, analyzing every part.

"No, nothing happened. Actually..." I took a deep breath, "I'm shocked I didn't collapse."

"I told you..." He shrugged as if I had confirmed something obvious.

"How?"

"I said you were brave. I rarely misjudge someone. Now we need to get out of here, little one." I took his hand and stood up, God knows how, considering my legs felt like they were about to melt.

Ghost cleared the seat as best he could, sweeping away the shattered glass so I could sit. I glanced at a cloud of dark smoke at the corner of the steep curve ahead of us, where the car that had been chasing us just moments before now lay on its roof, beginning to catch fire.

I couldn't tear my eyes away as we passed them. Even though the smoke prevented me from seeing them, I knew they were dead, and that realization generated a mix of relief and fear. The reality of it all was horrifying.

We continued our journey, now with one less window, which made the ride a bit colder, but bearable. I tried not to speak, as I didn't know if I could utter a complete sentence without breaking down completely. The tremors gave way to a vague distraction, as if my mind suddenly started to swim in a dark sea. I glanced out of the corner of my eye at Ghost, who maintained an upright posture, his attentive eyes focused on the road ahead, and his clenched jaw told me that maybe I wasn't the only one still absorbing what had happened, but when he noticed I was watching him, a quick smile lifted the corner of his lips.

"How are you feeling?" he asked lightly, as if his own worries had evaporated.

"I don't know." I tried to return the smile, but the worried expression that took over his face made me realize I had failed miserably. "It feels like I just came out of a blender; I can barely believe we're alive, and that's terrifying."

"It's okay to feel fear," he commented, and when I looked at the road, I noticed we were approaching a village. "I myself am still in disbelief that I spun the car in the middle of an armed chase. I wish Snake could see this," he whispered the last part as if he were talking to himself.

"I think fear doesn't even come close to what I'm feeling." I shrank back as we came across the first traffic signal at the entrance of the small town.

An elderly lady was patiently waiting for the light to change. She seemed distracted, balancing an umbrella with one hand and some bags with the other, until we stopped beside her. Her dark blue eyes began to widen as she noticed the state of our car, which by that point looked like a Swiss cheese with a shattered window.

I shrank under her startled gaze, and Zion let out a low, melancholy laugh as the woman stumbled across the street.

"Maybe it'll be a bit hard to pass through the town without being noticed, huh?"

CHAPTER THIRTEEN

Alena

We stopped as night fell at a motel away from the city. The place was not very inviting, with some broken windows where the glass had been replaced with rough wooden planks, deep cracks in the walls, and some clothes that seemed to have been abandoned on the balconies of the two-story building.

"Is this where we're going to spend the night?" I questioned, unsure.

"Yes, but keep in mind that this motel may look bad at first glance, and, well..." He paused and wrinkled his nose. "Actually, it is bad." He sighed. "We'll be lucky if we find hot water, but it's a two-star motel where they don't ask many questions. They probably won't ask for identification." He turned to me and touched the hood of my sweatshirt, carefully pulling it over my head. His eyes looked deeper from the many hours of driving non-stop. "We'll rest a bit and leave before dawn."

I nodded, agreeing, and stared at the dark sky fighting to reveal a few stars among the thick clouds. It had stopped raining, but the damp, cold weather remained intact, making everything feel a little sadder and more frightening.

"Shall we?" He opened the car door for me to get out.

I looked at our vehicle, which was full of dents and had been carefully parked in the last spot in the garage, the one closest to the street, which, due to the low ceiling of the place, would hide some of the damage that could raise suspicion.

A shiver ran through my body as I remembered what we had experienced hours earlier, while Ghost checked the gun magazine beside me as casually as if he were tying his shoelaces.

"Little one, I want you to stay behind me and keep your face as covered as possible. Is that okay?" He leaned in and pulled my hood tighter on both sides. I lifted my face and found his energetic, intense eyes probing me.

His dilated pupils were alert. His face looked harsher as the stubble accentuated, which did nothing to diminish the extraordinary beauty of the man, who seemed to grow more handsome by the moment. From his firm, expressive lips to his thick, well-groomed eyebrows. The challenging gaze, the stubborn, confident voice, and the smile... how could someone have been born with a smile capable of setting an entire village on fire?

He opened a slow, sideways smile, and I had the impression that fire was approaching me at a surprising speed.

"Why are you looking at me like that?" He widened his smile, but his gaze was confused, even worried.

Good question... why the hell was I staring at him like that?

A strange sound broke the silence between us, and I almost died of embarrassment when I realized it was my stomach, ready to start a rebellion.

"We'd better get inside. I'll look for something decent to eat, other than canned food, before you bite my arm."

"What an exaggeration!" I turned my face, mortified, and followed him to the entrance of the place.

"Remember to do everything I say," he warned, and my whole body stiffened as I recalled what happened the last time he said that.

"I hope I don't get stuck in a car that's being targeted by armed crazies again." I rubbed my face, exasperated, which curiously earned a brief laugh from Ghost.

We entered the motel, which was as strange inside as it was outside. The two floors were surrounded by iron bars that resembled a prison, where piles and piles of clothes were scattered. The smell of the place was putrid. It seemed like no one had cleaned it for a long time, but in the end, that didn't matter; I wasn't there for a vacation.

I kept walking, so close to him that I could easily be mistaken for his shadow.

Ghost approached a table where a pile of papers accompanied a white plate full of food scraps, where a medium-height man with a sour expression was intently watching something on a very small TV. His eyebrows were enormous, gigantic, and joined in the middle of his forehead, making everything seem like one piece. Quite scary.

I remained silent and watched my bodyguard talk to the man in that unfamiliar language, while using his body as a shield to keep me away from the attention of the guy, who didn't seem too pleased to have his attention diverted from whatever he was watching on that TV.

Ghost was so adept at the language that I could easily believe it was his mother tongue. He conversed calmly and assertively, as if he were in his own home.

I was jolted from my reverie when the attendant suddenly said something and stood up, trying to look at me, but Ghost positioned himself protectively in front of me, opened his wallet, and pulled out several bills. For the first time, I saw the man with the thick eyebrows genuinely smile upon receiving the money and handing a key to him. I imagined that must have been a sum much larger than he usually earned for a stay, and I felt bad for not knowing if I would ever be able to repay that amount to Ghost.

"Let's go." He touched my hand and guided me up the stairs of the place, his eyes scanning from corner to corner, and I didn't miss the hand resting on his waist, ready to draw his gun at the slightest sign of danger.

We hurried up the stairs and I was truly relieved that the room was a bit more comforting than the reception and the facade of the place.

The walls were a dry yellowish color, slightly faded. There was a small television on a piece of furniture, a little door on the side that probably led to the bathroom, and one bed... a single double bed with neatly arranged sheets and two pillows on it. Ghost rummaged through the place as if searching for something and even checked the bathroom.

"There's hot water!" he revealed, excited. "Take a shower while I make sure we're safe in this place." He continued to rummage through the room, and the thought of stepping under warm water made me shudder with pleasure.

"That would be a dream," I said softly.

Ghost smiled.

"I checked the windows and bathroom fixtures. I also left some things for you on the sink; if you need anything else, just ask me. I'll check the rest while you shower, take your time, little one." I nodded in agreement.

I entered the bathroom, which was small but quite clean, and came face to face with a mirror above the sink. I looked at my reflection once more and narrowed my eyes at the sight that was still strange to me. The girl staring back was a stranger, with long, tangled hair, eyes marked by deep dark circles, and several small bruises on her face; she looked tired, maybe even a little weak. But there was a sparkle in those golden eyes, and I recognized it. It was the will to live and be free that she and I shared. Even though I didn't remember her, I knew we were one and that our main goal was, above all, to survive.

I opened a slow smile when I found everything Ghost had set aside for me to take a shower in front of the mirror. There, in a small pile, was a white towel, a small bottle of shampoo, another of conditioner, soap, and disposable toothbrushes.

"A toothbrush." I nearly jumped for joy.

There hadn't been many ways to brush my teeth in that dungeon, and after throwing everything up at our last stop, I was desperate to taste toothpaste.

I stepped into the cramped shower with all the hygiene items and turned on the faucet. The hot water cascaded down, covering my whole body, from my damaged hair to the tips of my toes. I ignored the sting I felt when the water touched some of my wounds, closed my eyes, and tipped my head forward, feeling the weight of the world on my shoulders. My mind began to wander, as it always did when I found myself in complete silence. I tried once again to remember anything that had happened before that damn place, but instead of recovering an old memory, a new one infiltrated my mind.

Suddenly, the hot water, the steam, the feeling of getting rid of the cold... everything, absolutely everything made me recall the moment Ghost entered the bathtub with me back at the hideout. He had hugged me, I was sure, and even though fear had blinded me at that moment,

I still remembered his strong arms encircling me protectively, his steady breath brushing against my ears, and the softly whispered words seeking to calm me.

I opened my eyes and placed a hand on my heart. There it was again, the incessant and painful throbbing as I remembered him. I exhaled loudly, fearing whatever that feeling was, while secretly wishing that at some point, I would be able to accept that embrace again.

I finished my shower with a fear pulsing through my blood. What if I could never let anyone touch me again?

The possibility terrified me, and a mix of fear and anger filled my heart. I knew who was to blame; I knew that bastard had managed to break me somehow, but deep down, I felt that if there was anyone capable of helping me pick up each of my pieces, it was the man in the room next door. The silent stranger who continued to fight to protect me without even knowing who I was and asking nothing in return.

Ghost, who bore as many scars as I did, and was the only one capable of getting close to me and quickening my heart.

✷

WHEN I CAME OUT OF the bathroom, Ghost was waiting for me with two bowls of steaming hot soup.

"I don't know the source of this soup, but it looks tasty. Come on, eat while it's hot."

I sat next to him and tasted the soup under his watchful gaze. I moaned as the hot broth slid down my throat and a warmth blossomed in my stomach.

"It's delicious!"

"What amazing news." I smiled, watching him taste his own soup as if he were about to swallow a furball.

"You don't believe me? It's really good."

"It's not that I doubt your palate; it's just that... well, it looks a bit poisonous!" He wrinkled his nose at the soup, which was dark and had some suspicious white specks floating in it.

"I think anything for me ends up being a feast." I smiled and shrugged, returning to my soup. I took a while to realize he was watching me with a sorrowful expression. "What's wrong?"

"It's nothing." He exhaled. "I just sometimes wonder how, after everything, you still find the strength to smile. You have my admiration, miss." He sipped the soup while I sat there like a statue, paralyzed by his words, with the spoon just inches from my mouth. "Hmm, it doesn't taste like death." He looked at me with wide-eyed surprise and made me laugh.

We finished the soup, and Ghost returned to his mission of monitoring the room, now checking the exit through the window. He opened it and poked his head outside, letting a gust of cold wind pass through.

"Shouldn't you take the opportunity to shower too?" My face flushed as the question slipped from my lips, but it wasn't fair that only I got to enjoy a hot, relaxing shower.

"I can't." He ran his hands through his hair. "I'll just splash some water on my face. It's dangerous to leave you here alone and unprotected. The time it would take me to get out of the bathroom if something happened... it could be too late."

"That's not right!" I dropped the brush onto the bed. "I assure you I can manage for a few minutes; we're safe here, right?"

"A bodyguard doesn't work with that perspective of safety. We're always expecting the worst; it's the safest way, and don't worry, I'm used to it. I'm your bodyguard now; you come first, always." He smiled and entered the bathroom, making sure to leave the door open. I heard the sound of the faucet running, and I stood up, bothered, and ended up dropping the TV remote.

Like everything in my life, I couldn't remember the last time I had watched anything, and the curiosity about what might be on pushed me to turn it on.

What the hell was I thinking...

The TV screen lit up as soon as I pressed one of the buttons, and my eyes nearly popped out of my head when a couple appeared before me. The woman was on all fours, her legs wide open, while a huge man, in every sense of the word, was going deep inside her. The loud, intense moans quickly filled the room.

"Oh my God! Oh my God!" I started pressing all the buttons, trying to turn it off, but nothing worked, and now he was shoving it into another hole, dear God! I panicked; had the remote died? This couldn't be happening. "Damn it!"

"What..."

"OH SHIT!" Ghost appeared right next to me, and I was so startled that I threw the remote at him and jumped onto the bed to the sound of "Ahhhhhh, ohhhhh" coming from the couple.

"Why do they always have such precise aim?" he grumbled, bringing his hand to his face where the remote had hit him squarely.

"I don't know how to stop this thing!" I yelled, nervous.

He went to the TV and pulled the cord from behind it, and the pornographic scene ended. I grabbed the pillow and buried my face in it, wishing deeply to evaporate.

"Looks like the channels here are something else." His voice was contained, and I could swear he was holding back laughter.

I lowered the pillow and saw him covering his mouth with his hand.

"This isn't funny." He couldn't hold back anymore and started to laugh, pressing his eyes with his fingertips, and even I had to laugh at that ridiculous situation.

Ghost

PRICELESS!

The word perfectly summed up the expression frozen on that girl's face, and I had to use all my self-control not to burst out laughing every five minutes.

I leaned against the window, recalling the exact moment I entered the room and saw her there, desperately pressing all the buttons on the remote while a couple was having anal sex on the motel's TV. I shook my head.

I never imagined I would soon be hit squarely by a flying remote, but not even that could erase from my mind the memory of my little protector's face, completely red. I looked over my shoulder just to see that she still had her eyes wide open.

"What are you looking at out there?" She tried to change the subject.

"An escape route," I said, excited, and turned my attention back to the steep iron stairs leading to the parking lot below. All the rooms on the second floor had one. "A bit deadly, but still an escape route." I looked back at her.

"Great, it's good to have a plan." She tangled her fingers in the large black hoodie she was wearing, her eyes glued to the bed as she twisted her lips, restless. "This is where they do that, isn't it?" She blurted out, as if she had been holding the question for a long time, pointing at the TV. Her cheeks took on a much redder hue, making her infinitely cuter.

"Well..." I approached her and leaned against the small table next to the bed. "It's what some people do when they stay here." Suddenly, her face started to turn pale. "But don't worry, the place is always well sanitized." I hoped I was right about that place. "And it's not just for that that people come here."

"Not?" She leaned her body towards me, curious.

"They also host all kinds of fugitives and good girls at throwing things." I glanced at the remote, and she bit her lips.

"I'm sorry about that; I didn't know you were right next to me."

"I guess I really will need to stamp my feet, right?" She laughed and cautiously lay back on the pillow, as if being careful could erase the things that poor pillow had been through. Her long, wet hair spread out, marking the light sheet.

I narrowed my eyes and went to the bathroom. I rummaged around until I found what I was looking for and returned to the room shortly after.

"Sit for a moment." She obeyed, and a little wrinkle of concern formed between her eyebrows when she saw what I had in my hands.

"What is that?"

"A hairdryer, probably from the Mesozoic era, but it will do. Your hair is too wet; you'll end up getting sick." I plugged the device into a socket near the bed. "Turn around, please." I picked up the brush she had been using a few minutes earlier and noticed she was still looking at me with a worried expression. "Don't worry; I'm not going to touch anything but your hair." She nodded and then turned around. I turned on the hairdryer and started drying her hair slowly.

The strands flew everywhere in a constant back-and-forth, the sweet smell of conditioner filled the room, engulfing my senses. I slid the soft strands through my fingers and noticed they became lighter as I dried them. Everything was under control until I brushed through a tangled piece of hair and accidentally pulled on it.

"Ouch!" she moaned and laughed at the same time.

"Sorry!" I tried to detangle the stubborn tuft. "I've never done this before."

"It's okay; I have too much hair; I won't miss a few strands." We laughed together, and I continued drying her hair, enjoying the lightness of the strands sliding through my fingers like grains of sand slipping away. They were soft, long, and voluminous. I could hold them for all the time in the world, and for a moment, I wondered what it would be like to pull on them, perhaps doing exactly what we had seen on that TV.

"Damn!" I cursed and almost threw the hairdryer across the room when I realized where my thoughts had gone.

"What's wrong?"

"Nothing. Your hair is beautiful, that's all." It wasn't a lie, after all.

I put away the hairdryer, taking a moment or two to compose myself, and sat in front of her on the bed, trying to push away that last thought at all costs, but as soon as I looked at her, I groaned in indignation. The girl became more beautiful with every moment, and her dry, full hair framed her delicate face poetically.

"Thank you!" she said, her voice choked with emotion as she ran her hand through her hair.

"You don't have to flatter me..."

"I really do. I need it very much." Her eyes sparkled with what I thought were tears, and she gave a soft sniff.

"Why are you crying?" An uncomfortable tightness spread through my chest. Seeing her cry became one of the things I hated most in the world.

"It's not from sadness." She wiped the tear that had rolled down with the back of her hand. "I'm just grateful for everything you're doing for me. This kindness, it's not something I'm used to."

"I believe you don't remember all the kindness you must have received once, little one." I longed to wrap her in my arms, but I knew I couldn't, so I settled for just stroking her hand with mine. "In any case, I would do it all again if I needed to."

She bit her full lips and hid a smile behind them.

"What will happen when we get out of here?" She blinked, suddenly more serious.

"Out of Italy?"

"Yes."

"First, you'll meet my family. Then we'll see what to do."

"And what if they don't like me?"

"Impossible." I crossed my arms. "I can affirm that I liked you the minute I saw you. At least in the minute I felt rationally in control of my own emotions. My father will feel the same way. He would agree with everything I'm doing, perhaps not without a little complaining, but he would understand. I could only have a dignified life because he helped me when I didn't even believe I could. My father is that kind of man, who takes in anyone who needs it."

"It must be nice to have a family, or at least remember one."

"It's incredible. Even more so when we know what it is *not* to have a family," I confessed, crossing my hands in my lap. "When it's like that, we end up valuing everything more intensely. It's easier to get used to it when you're born into a loving family. It's easy to fight with relatives, wish not to see them for months, ignore worried calls from a mother asking if you did well on your first day of school, argue with your dad because you want to stay out later from a party... all of that is normal routine for normal people, but we are not normal people," I whispered the last part and raised my eyes to hers, which were listening attentively.

"What do you mean by that?"

"From my experience, every detail of my relationship with my father and my brothers was as important as the air I breathed. Every call, every scolding, every punishment, absolutely everything was essential." My eyes drifted down to the dark floor of the room for a moment, as memories brought me a sense of joy. "At first, when I got used to having a family, I felt a surreal fear, as if at any moment it could be taken away from me, and if there was a greater fear than that, I was unaware of it. It took me a long time to understand that my family was permanent, and that is, most of the time, the situation for people like us. Those who are born with everything are used to having everything, but those who experience the other side of the story think differently. It's as if life gave me a second chance to be happy."

"No one should have taken your first chance," she said softly, almost as if thinking out loud, and her large, shining eyes landed on one of my hands.

The little one slowly raised her fingers, fearful, finding the thin scar on the inside of my wrist and then stopped just millimeters from touching it.

"You can touch it if you want," I allowed.

She turned my hand between hers, which were much smaller than mine. Her eyes swept over every bit of skin, and she did the same with her fingers, trailing down the center of my palm until grazing the sensitive inside of my wrist, caressing the scar with her fingertips in a gentle back and forth that made me hold my breath for a moment. I swallowed hard; never had such a simple and subtle movement triggered such an overwhelmingly delightful sensation.

"You're so strong and determined that sometimes I forget you have worse marks than mine."

Her unpretentious and innocent touch took on incendiary shapes. The sudden silence was broken only by the sounds of our irregular breaths, and I could swear my heart was beating in my ears, and if I could hear it, maybe she could too.

"They run down the entire length of my back," I reminded her. "It's not pretty, but it means I survived; soon you'll think the same of the marks that remain as reminders." I pulled her touch away and intertwined her hand with mine in a firm grip that I prayed to God would be enough to drive away the insane and completely unreasonable thoughts now permeating my mind. "And one day, they stop hurting."

"Promise?" Her eyes widened a little more, sparkling like a starry night.

"I promise, little one." I raised a finger and almost touched her face but withdrew before doing so. I knew exactly what her limit was, and I wouldn't cross it. "You, like me, will need help to heal. Therapy, maybe a long vacation, and friends."

"And what if in my world, in my real life, I can't have any of that?" The fear that overflowed from her eyes consumed me.

"If your world prevents you, you'll live in mine. It's a pretty simple solution, actually." I opened a side smile, realizing how wonderful that option seemed to me. She let out a shaky laugh as if I had said something completely absurd.

"Ghost, I can't..."

"I'm your protector, little one," I cut her off. "And I will continue to be, even after we cross much of the ocean. None of this will change; I don't want you to worry about the after. There's something more important you need right now."

"What?" She straightened her posture, and I couldn't help but notice the grimace of pain that crossed her face and the breath she released.

"You need to rest." I made a mock bow toward the bed. "Lie down on this suspiciously sourced bed and try to sleep, okay?"

"And you? You need to sleep too."

"Don't worry about me; I'll organize the weapons and..."

"You can take this side of the bed." She grabbed one of the pillows and curled up on the right side of the bed, leaving the left side for me.

I looked at the mattress as if it were spewing water in all directions; that wasn't a good idea, not after realizing that every second next to that woman only served to make me more aware of how attractive she was.

"I think I'll only be able to sleep if I know you're nearby." She bit her lips, and her face flushed a lovely shade of red. That had become my favorite color.

"Are you sure?" I wanted to confirm, secretly hoping she would kick me out.

"Yes."

God help me... I prayed as I turned off the main lights, leaving only a dim, yellow light from the lamp. I placed the gun on the counter, lay down beside her, and pulled the blanket over us.

"Can I hold your hand?" she asked, and I offered mine instantly, happy to gain a bit more of her trust.

She intertwined her hand with mine, delicate and eager at the same time, and that touch... oh, that touch. It felt like it could hold my heart between her fingers and calm its beats. I focused on her soft skin, the steady pulse, the warmth radiating. In that moment, I felt like I was sinking into quicksand. I was being pulled toward her.

Our gazes met, and I found myself lost in the vastness of her energetic, incandescent pupils. The reflection of the lamp light sparkled in her eyes, and the more I observed it, the more certain I was that I was in the presence of a thousand constellations.

"What are you looking at?" she breathed, and the warm air of her breath touched my face, leaving me dazed. I had never wanted to touch someone so much who I shouldn't.

"The stars in your eyes," I revealed.

"How?"

"Outside, the sky is cloudy, yet despite this, even if we can't see them, the stars are up there, shining day and night, without stopping. I think some of them have made their home in your eyes; each little dot scattered across your irises seems to twinkle in the light. I fear I'm too enchanted to look away, I'm sorry." She opened her lips in a perfect O that highlighted the allure of her mouth. "Your name should be that. Star, the one who brings me hope."

"You think I can bring hope to someone?" she said, disbelieving and shy.

"That's all I've felt since I met you." She surrounded my hand with both of hers, and I continued, revealing even more than I intended, but for some reason, while staring into those unique eyes, I felt unable to stay silent. "The first moment I saw you, I clung to the hope that you were still alive, then that you would survive until I could get you out of here. Since then, all I can have is the hope of being enough to save you, little one. You've become my star, and I won't accept any ending for this story other than a happy one," I whispered, embraced by a genuine, profound, and desperate feeling to make each of those words a reality. "You need a name after all. Can I call you that from now on?"

"Star..." she tested the name, and I noticed her voice was choked. "It's perfect." Again, that urge to hug her and protect her in my arms almost suffocated me, but I had to settle for the warm smile that graced her lips before she closed her eyes and unconsciously brought my hand close to her face.

Ah, my Star... what should I do with this persistent feeling and all the desire that seems to consume me more each time? I closed my eyes and swallowed hard. Now she had a name, and it was already tattooed in one of the most dangerous places that could exist. My heart, which at that moment beat fast and restless.

CHAPTER FOURTEEN

Star

A loud and tempestuous sound rumbled through the early morning, tearing me from a calm, dreamless sleep. I opened my eyes, startled, and stifled a scream, gasping from the shock.

"What was that?" I asked, feeling dizzy from being woken so suddenly. Ghost, unlike me, sprang from the bed like a cat, grabbed his weapon, and dashed to the door of our room.

A colossal uproar echoed through the motel walls. The sound of splintering wood, shattering glass, and increasingly loud, frantic voices filled the place.

"I think we have company." He cracked the door open and quickly shut it again. "Yeah... we have company. Lots of company!" He sprinted across the room and peered out the window.

"W-what if it's not them?" I asked, getting out of bed with impressive speed.

"There are armed men everywhere on the first floor, and they were about to head up to the second. I don't think all that racket is the guests giving them a warm welcome. They're breaking everything in their path looking for something we both know what it is. It's them, Star." It was the first time he actually called me by my new name, but all the charm faded when more sounds of things breaking echoed through the night.

"What are we going to do?" My teeth began to chatter from nerves, and I stifled a scream when I heard what sounded like a door being kicked right next to us.

Ghost moved quickly around the room, dragging the bed until it was pressed against the door. Then he came to me and intertwined his fingers with mine.

"We're going out the window. There's a ladder on the side that will take us to the parking lot. We have to go now."

"Okay, fine. We can do this." I held his hands with both of mine and repeated that little phrase two more times, as if constant affirmation would make it true.

We ran to the window, and he opened it, helping me swing my legs through. I leaned on his arm to descend and winced when a sharp pain shot through my calf, trying to ignore it. I didn't have time to feel anything that wouldn't help me get out of there fast.

I jumped through the window, and soon Ghost did the same, until we were facing each other. I stared at the steep iron ladder, a cold knot in my stomach.

"Just go down slowly, one foot after the other." Ghost barely finished speaking when the door to our room took a hard hit, then another, and another. They would get in soon, so there was no option. I needed to descend, even if it meant rolling.

"WE FOUND THEM!" someone shouted, and I couldn't even muster the courage to look; I just threw myself down the ladder, grabbing on as best I could.

The sound of gunfire exploded close to me, and something told me it was Ghost covering us. I started sliding down the rungs, banging my shin against a metal edge, the pain so sharp I gritted my teeth, but I couldn't stop.

"I've got you, you bitch!" I froze at the bottom of the ladder, recognizing the voice that bellowed from our room's window. I looked up, and there he was.

Scott stared at us with a gaze that transcended madness. His once-impeccable face was twisted. His nose was so crooked, accentuating his swollen jaw, and one eye was so bruised it seemed to have vanished. He gave me a sinister grin that made me hold my breath, frozen before that monster.

"Star!" Ghost pulled me to the side of the ladder, forcing me to move, since my legs wouldn't obey. "I need you to listen, okay?" He alternated between speaking and firing at the men, keeping them from coming down the same ladder we were using. "Our car is five meters away, but it's five meters in the open. I'll cover you, and I want you to run like there's no tomorrow. Those are their cars." He pointed to three vehicles, two black and one navy blue. "We'll use them as shields."

I remembered the madness we faced to escape alive from an encounter with one of those bastards; what would happen if all three came after us?

I took a deep breath, trying to find the courage to do what I was thinking. If I didn't slow them down, it would be our end anyway.

"Give me the knife." I turned abruptly to Ghost, who was waiting for the enemy's gunfire to cease before countering.

"What?"

"The knife!" I shouted, extending my hand. "The one you refused to let me have. I know you hid it in your boot. Hurry, Ghost..."

"What are you..."

"Just give me that damn knife!" He blinked, dazed, but reached down to his heel, pulling the object out and handing it to me with clear hesitation in his brown eyes. "I'm going to slash their tires. That way they can't come after us." He widened his eyes as he realized what I planned to do.

"Listen, kid, I'd rather you run and stay safe, not..."

"Our chances will be nearly zero if they catch us, look at how many men and that lunatic..." I could barely formulate the sentences.

"You're right, but I want you to use the cars as cover and slash the tires on the right." I nodded in agreement. "Let's cross over, and please, be careful with that knife."

Ghost waited one more second, listening intently to the gunfire, and suddenly, we plunged into the middle of the shooting.

"There's no use running, it's the end for you," Scott roared from the second floor as soon as he saw us, using the window ledge as a shield. The bullets struck the iron edges of the ladder, ricocheting with a sound reminiscent of clinking silverware.

I ran with my heart in my throat, fearing that at any moment I would be hit by one of those shots, barely able to breathe as I neared the car belonging to those men. I raised the knife from the Swiss army knife and plunged it into both tires on the right side while Ghost covered us. I did the same with all three cars.

"I did it!" I shouted when I finished and noticed the number of men shooting at us from the second-floor window had decreased, which could only mean one thing... they were all heading down to the garage.

"Let's go, quick!" Ghost switched out the magazine of his weapon with impressive speed and grabbed my hand.

We reached the car, and I opened the passenger door, throwing myself inside, and Ghost did the same. He started the engine and accelerated away from the main exit. If we passed by there, we would definitely be shot at, which, to be terrifyingly honest, was already happening. I saw in the rearview mirror one of Scott's henchmen reach the cars and only then realize the tires had been slashed.

"Damn it, call for backup!" the guy cursed, and Ghost peeled out, tires screeching, into the cold night. It didn't take long for us to lose them, and only then did it start to sink in.

I dug my nails into the seat, trembling from head to toe. Ghost began talking non-stop, I knew he was surprised by what I had done to the tires, but his voice suddenly started to fade. I took a deep breath, but for some reason, the oxygen wasn't filling my lungs. I began to gasp, choking.

"Star?"

"He's alive." It was the only thing I could say.

Ghost

I DROVE AS FAST AS I could without skidding off the slopes to my right or rolling the car in the dense forest to my left. I knew I couldn't stay on the road for long, or we would be easily found. So, I studied the map and found an uncertain path through the woods, but it was our best chance.

The rain intensified as we left the road and entered a dark, bumpy dirt path, with not a single light except for the car's headlights. Thick, tall bushes obscured the view of the highway, but I needed to be alert for any holes that might appear in front of us.

I glanced at Star, who was very quiet. Her wide eyes were fixed on the dashboard, and her fingers dug into the seat, which wasn't a good sign. We moved deeper into the woods until we found a suitable place to park, and a terrifyingly silent darkness engulfed us as soon as I turned off the headlights.

I let my head fall back against the seat for a brief moment and inhaled deeply, flooding my lungs with oxygen. The adrenaline still pulsed in my veins; my whole body was alert, and I knew I would remain that way until dawn.

"They won't take long to find other cars to come after us, so our best chance is to stay off the roads for the night. I doubt they'll think we know any other route. We'll be lucky if they pass by us and continue searching ahead. That way, they'll never find us." I turned to her; she still wore a distant expression, as if only her body were present and her mind was elsewhere. "Star?" I leaned into her space, examining her face closely. Her eyes were frozen on a fixed point. "Are you listening?"

"He's going to..." she whispered so quietly that I doubted she had said anything at all.

"What?" I leaned in closer.

"He's going to find me," she suddenly screamed, making me jump in my seat from the shock. "He's going to... he will succeed." She began to cry, but it wasn't normal crying; it was fear. It was pure, devastating panic. Tears streamed down her face in thick layers, and she began to thrash around.

"He's not going to lay a hand on you..."

"YES! He will catch me. I-I will go back there... no, no, no." She choked on her words and began to struggle, gasping uncontrollably, and then she jumped into the back seat.

The whole scene unfolded quickly. In an instant, we were parked in that woods, and the next moment, it felt like my heart was being torn apart, piece by piece.

A little piece vanished at the sight of her shoulders shaking repeatedly; another piece disintegrated when I noticed her wide eyes and the deepest fear etched in her cinnamon-colored irises. Her breath hitched, and all I wanted at that moment was to be able to hold her pain in my hands and take it for myself.

I leaped over the seats behind her without thinking. Star was thrashing and screaming, repeating the same phrases. She buried her hands in her hair, still shaking violently, and curled up in the seat, unable to stop moving, like a wild animal cornered by a hunter. A loud, convulsive cry echoed through the woods, and I held my breath.

"Star..." I tried to hold her, but she pushed my hands away with force. I couldn't allow her to thrash around like that, so there was no choice. I'd rather she hated me for touching her than let her hurt herself in front of my eyes.

I pulled her body against mine and wrapped my arms around her. She squirmed, trying to break free from the embrace, but I held her tight.

"Star, I'm here. Listen to my voice, little one. I'm right here and I'm not going anywhere. Remember?" I whispered in her hair, and she continued to push me away, sobbing uncontrollably as she struggled, out of control. The sounds she made were so heavy with pain and despair that I felt my own eyes burn.

I didn't give up, nor did I even consider letting her go, and the more I held her, the clearer it became to me that this was the right thing to do, this was the place I wanted her most. I wanted Star safe in my arms, even if it brought her dangerously close to my heart, which was pounding wildly.

"I'm here for you, little one." She sobbed loudly, and her shoulders shook.

Star stopped pushing me away, and the hands that had been trying to separate us now clutched my shirt tightly, as if I had become the only thing she found to breathe.

My little one buried her face in the curve of my neck, and what started as a low cry turned into a roar of pain. I wrapped my arms around her waist, pulling her closer to me and onto my lap. She cried and trembled nonstop, the pain in each sound she emitted was so deep it burned in my bones.

I didn't know what to do; I didn't know how to take away that suffering that seemed to invade her soul. All I could do was hold her in my arms, gently stroking her hair.

I buried my face in her dark hair, which smelled sweet and clean from shampoo, and spent a long time with her there. Her hitching breath brushed against my neck, and she sobbed. I tightened my grip on her, almost instinctively, and ran my hands down her back, soothing her.

"Breathe, my Star. Slowly, we're safe, remember that," I whispered into her hair, not knowing how long that truth would last.

"Ghost..." She lifted her face. Her eyes were very red, as was the tip of her nose, and seeing her that way, with so much anguish and despair coloring those perfect eyes, sent a sharp pain up my throat. "I'd rather die than go back there," she finally said, more tears streaming from the corners of her eyes, and I found myself cupping her face with both hands, drying them one by one.

"You will never step foot in that place again," I promised, caressing her face with the back of my hand. "Never again, do you hear me?" She did, but she didn't seem to believe it, which was very understandable. "I won't allow it."

"What if there is no other option?"

"They'll have to kill me to get to you, and I promise you, my little tire-slasher, that is something almost impossible," I lied; she didn't need absolute truth at that moment, but a little hope to fight back.

Star flinched at my response, and I felt happy, even relieved, when she nestled better in my arms, not pulling away.

I spent the next hour there, cradling her in my lap. Her slender, slightly elongated fingers were still tangled in my shirt, and gradually, her breathing returned to normal. The tremors faded, and she broke the silence, still keeping her face buried in my chest.

"He liked to hit me," she murmured in a muffled, distant voice, and my whole body stiffened at the comment.

"You don't have to talk about it if you don't want to," I assured her, my lips still in her hair, as if that simple touch could keep my sanity amidst all that madness.

"I don't think I've ever felt as much fear as I do today, even in my other life, the one I'm supposed to remember," she continued. "When I saw him, it was like returning to the place where he trapped me." She held her breath, as if thrown back into hell. "You remember the whip, right? It had a metal tip."

"Yes, I remember." I swallowed hard, recalling the exact moment I found her in the dungeon being beaten with that thing.

I wished with all my might to make Walker swallow it after tearing his skin off with it; that bastard was lucky she was watching us. Star was the only one who could make me stop.

I took a deep breath, trying to expel the violent urge to tear him apart as the scene replayed in my mind. I needed to stay in control and pulled her a little closer, desperate to keep her near me while I listened intently to every detail of her account.

"At first, I felt lost. I didn't remember anything, didn't know those faces. I was so afraid." She sobbed, and the sound, filled with pain, pierced through my ears, tearing me apart irreparably. "When he visited me for the first time, he tried to pretend to be someone he wasn't. He said he was protecting me and that I would be safe there, that he would soon get me out. For a moment, I really believed him, but it didn't take two minutes before he told me under what circumstances I could leave. First, I had to..." She gasped loudly. "I had to..."

"I know." I pressed my mouth close to her ear and whispered, trembling with rage at that son of a bitch for trying to force her, but I kept a cold seriousness and allowed her to continue.

"That's when I refused and took the first beating." She shuddered. I caressed her back, as if the movement could somehow keep her mind here with me. "After the first, the others were no surprise. That's when I discovered his fetish wasn't to rape me; he wanted to dominate me. He wanted me to give in willingly and would torture me relentlessly until he reached his goal, and after the second beating, I had already made a decision."

"And what was it?"

"I wasn't going to give in to him, not even if it cost my life," she revealed with conviction and continued to recount her days in that place.

She spoke of how they left her starving until she lost her strength, the beatings that followed, the humiliation, the fear, the cold, the incessant despair... she told it all. Every terrible detail, and when she finished, I was shaking from head to toe.

"That monster wanted to break me," she said with difficulty. "He wanted me to crumble, but I couldn't." A sob echoed in the night. Painful, broken, from a woman who had been taken beyond the unbearable. "I couldn't give in, I couldn't give him what he wanted."

"You couldn't, because you're a warrior." I kissed the top of her head, then placed a chaste kiss on her forehead and lowered my gaze to hers, without thinking, without reasoning; in that moment, I only knew how to feel... the pain, the panic, the hate, the anguish, and the courage. My God, the courage of that woman was exceptional, and all I wanted was to kiss her... as uncertain as that night was, a sinful desire yet irresistible.

"You were so strong." I pressed my lips to her forehead again. She murmured something unintelligible and sighed at the caress. I trailed my lips down to her temple before I could think better of it.

What the hell, I shouldn't be doing this... but kissing her skin was so delightful that I couldn't resist placing another kiss on her cheek. She closed her swollen eyes and gently tipped her head back. The movement exposed part of her neck, and I traced my fingers along it, mapping her face with the tips of my fingers.

Her slightly uneven breathing brushed against my face gracefully as her chest rose and fell, and I could swear it wasn't out of fear. It was something else, perhaps the same feeling that was igniting my chest at that moment.

She parted her lips slightly, and my eyes were fixated, glazed over by that full mouth so close to mine. What flavor would her mouth have?

I could bet it would be like kissing the goddess of love herself, Aphrodite. I traced her jawline, sliding my fingers over the face that was now taking on a rosy hue, delicate and enticing. How I wanted to kiss her right then and there, my God...

I breathed slowly, realizing what I was about to do, forcing myself to seek a shred of sanity to stop myself from taking her right then. My hands searched for hers, and her slender fingers released my shirt to intertwine with mine, and no touch had ever felt so good.

I brought her hand to my mouth, desperate to kiss any part of her, tracing a path between her fingers with my lips, then lifted her hand until it touched my face. Star looked at me through the darkness of the night and laid her palm against my jaw, gliding it along my stubble.

"Thank you for saving me in so many ways." She exhaled, heavy-hearted. "Thank you for being my guardian angel, Zion."

Hearing my name in that sweet, melodic voice excited me to the extreme. It was the first time she had called me that, and I couldn't help but feel a damn erection imagining her moaning my name.

"There's no need to thank me, my Star." I embraced her and tried to calm myself. "You're making me change my perception of Italy. I can't hate this place like I did before now that I've found something so valuable. Or rather, someone..." She raised her eyes, which held a hint of shyness, and a brief smile threatened to lift the corners of her lips.

"Can you tell me what Italy took from you now?" she whispered. A gust of cold wind cut through the night, flooding the car with icy air through the broken glass.

"One moment, I'll get the blankets. The story is long, and the night is too. We need to stay warm."

I stretched to reach the blankets we had left in the car when we left the hideout and spread both over us, settling into the back seat with my little one in my arms.

God help me, I didn't know how to let her go! I didn't know how to pull away from her, and as much as I should, I didn't want to.

Star

NEVER HAD A PLACE FELT as safe as in Ghost's arms. I didn't know a touch could feel this good. Until now, all I had experienced was fear, terror, and despair, until he appeared with all his bandages and two light feet, all his weapons, and an unreal willingness to save a stranger's life. So, when he pulled the blankets, I nestled against him and took a deep breath, feeling calm invade my heart.

He settled in the back seat, half-sitting, half-lying, and touched my hand to bring me closer to him. I couldn't help but notice the gun he kept resting in the door frame, alert to everything happening around us, but still, I tried to relax.

Ghost pulled me close, and I nestled against his rigid chest. I buried my face in the curve of his neck and inhaled the masculine scent of his skin. It smelled like home, safety, and care.

I sniffled, trying to erase the traces of the convulsive crying that had taken me moments before, and embraced him. He ran his hands up my back in a caress so delightful it almost made me moan.

I blinked and opened my eyes when I realized those caresses were making my body tingle, and a warm heat slowly rose from my chest, through my neck, until it reached my cheeks, which burned. The absolute silence inside the car certainly made the rapid beating of my heart audible, and I wanted to break that stillness before he could actually hear my heart racing from the sudden and undeniably delicious closeness.

"Are you going to tell me what Italy took from you or not?" I felt my face heat up.

"I think I lost faith in people and even in love," she confessed with a low laugh. "It's a little embarrassing to say this, but the truth is one of my biggest dreams was to have my own family. About seven kids running on the lawn, four noisy dogs, loud and crowded dinners..."

"What's embarrassing about that? It's a beautiful dream."

"The embarrassment is in the part where I chose the wrong person to dream with." He exhaled, caressing my arms with his fingertips. "I met a woman in Chicago, an Italian who was studying in my city, and we started dating. Soon, she graduated and got a job here in Italy. Before I knew it, I was visiting this country once a week just to see her. I learned the language flawlessly, as well as the customs, and even considered renting a house to be with her from time to time." I listened to every bit of the story, a latent and intense warmth filling my heart. I didn't know why, but I grew increasingly irritated with the tale. "Then I decided she would be... the mother of all my children, the woman I wanted to spend every day of my life with, whether it was long or not. I decided to buy a ring and surprise her. I came to Italy without telling her, and in the end, I was the one who got surprised. I found out I wasn't the only one she called her boyfriend. There was also a very handsome Italian, that bastard."

"Oh, what a damn, characterless wretch!" I propped myself up on my elbows to face him, and even though we were surrounded by complete darkness, I could see the smile he had on his face, which didn't quell my fury.

"In Brazil, they have a curious saying about this. They say, 'A human being without horns is a defenseless animal,' and I even agree, you know." I bit my lips to hold back a laugh; I was still furious, but the saying didn't help maintain all that anger. "Not with the animal part, I completely disagree with that. I wish we were as pure as animals. Our race is more like something hysterical, evil, and often irrational; some of us should even be sentenced to extinction; maybe a meteor or two would solve the problem. But about the feeling that betrayal can make you stronger, I agree with that. I ended up shutting myself off from new relationships, and everything that was once a dream faded into forgetfulness." He shrugged, and I wondered how much that man must have suffered because of that wretch.

"I ended up using my horns as a defense and pushed away any woman who showed interest in something more serious." He continued, and once again, I struggled to suppress a laugh. "I know you want to laugh."

"I don't want to." I tried with all my might to hold back the laughter, but he poked my arm, and I gave in, burying my face in his chest and laughing until my eyes watered. "You don't make it easy with this horns thing." I wiped my eyes, still giggling.

"I prefer to see you smiling, even if it's based on my disastrous past." He embraced me, satisfied, and returned to the story. "Betrayal, in my understanding, is the lowest form of hurting someone who loves you. Betraying a person who has put all their best into you is an act of cruelty and lack of character. In our family, we value trust above all; loyalty is in our blood. I can't handle anything different from that. For this reason, I developed an absurd hatred for everything involving Italy, from the language to the menu in American restaurants; I ended up exiling the country from my travels until fate decided to show me there would be better reasons to come here."

"How can you say that? You prefer to run away from armed, completely insane criminals, protecting a stranger who doesn't even know her own name, and risking your life rather than dealing with a betrayal?" I shot back, pausing to catch my breath.

"I'd prefer this a thousand times over." There was a soft sensuality in his baritone voice that warmed my heart even more. "I meant it when I said I'd do it again, little one."

"She's a complete idiot, but you're not exactly thinking straight either." He laughed. "It's a shame that woman didn't see who was by her side."

"I wasn't good enough for her," he commented absently.

"I can't believe you aren't good enough for anyone on the face of the earth," I confessed and almost died of embarrassment right after. "Well..." I coughed, trying to change the subject. "I wanted to remember my dreams so I could tell you, but as you know, I'm just an empty sack of potatoes. I feel like I wanted something more than anything, but I don't remember what it was."

"I'm sure your memories will return soon," he said in that unique way that made people believe even in fairy tales.

"And what if they don't come back?"

"Then you'll create new dreams," he whispered into my hair.

A small shiver ran through my body, descending down my neck, passing between my breasts pressed against his hard, muscular chest, until it pulsed between my legs in a way that startled me.

"A-and I..." I tried to keep my thoughts straight, but it was hard when his warm breath touched my skin, scrambling my mind. "I think one of my biggest dreams now is to find out if anyone is missing me, you know? I'm desperate to know if I have a family waiting for me. People who care about me..."

"They are definitely searching for you across the seven seas." I felt the smile forming on his lips, and for some reason, I found myself smiling too.

I tried to look at him in the darkness, but when I lifted my face, I didn't expect him to be so dangerously close.

His eyes locked onto mine, the atmosphere around us became heavy and warm, and for a moment, the world stopped. There was nothing but the whispers of our breaths mingling. He raised his hand until it fit against my face, caressing me. My skin tingled with his teasing touch, and I closed my eyes, overwhelmed.

What was happening? I wanted him to touch me with the same intensity I feared. I wanted to put an end to that uncontrolled desire; I needed to calm down, but how? Zion's hands were like fire, and they burned me more and more.

"Star..." He breathed my new name, making me shudder, and then, as if he were about to cast my soul into hell for good, his fingers traced my lips, observing them calmly.

My stomach was dancing, rising and falling uncontrollably, and anxiety washed over me. I held my breath and gasped in surprise, realizing I might faint if he didn't kiss me.

But he didn't kiss me. For some reason, in one moment his fingers were touching my lips, and the next he pulled me back to his chest, as if fleeing from me.

"Today was long; it's better to rest." His hoarse voice broke the silence of the night, and I had to stifle a moan. "Two chases in less than 24 hours is more than any trained person would endure." He tried to lighten the heavy atmosphere that had settled over us, but his labored breathing told me he was as shaken as I was.

"Y-yes. We need to rest. We don't know if tomorrow we'll face another shooting."

"I'm almost becoming an expert on the subject."

"After a chase in the middle of a storm and a well-executed escape from the second floor of a motel, I'd say you're more than an expert."

"Oh, Vin Diesel, who's the badass now?" he joked, and I noticed the tension in his voice significantly decreasing.

"Who's Vin Diesel?"

"He's an actor famous for his action movies. The kind of guy you know the movie is good just because he's in it."

"Looks like we have a fan." I laughed, snuggling closer to him.

"It would be my pleasure to introduce you to his movies," he said emphatically. "I'll start thinking about which order we'll start with."

That felt good. Thinking about what we would do after all this made it seem real. It was as if we were living a nightmare and would reach its end at any moment; I just needed to be strong enough, brave enough, even if I had to face Scott face to face.

"What are you thinking?" he asked, running his fingers through my hair, sending a shiver down my back.

"Maybe I won't be able to sleep tonight with everything we'll face tomorrow. I can't stop thinking," I confessed, curling up a bit more.

"What if you listened to some music? You said it calms you."

"But there's no sound in the car," I countered.

"Well, there's no sound specifically, and I admit I'm about to do an embarrassing and humiliating performance, but I can sing if that helps you sleep."

"Are you serious?" I almost shouted, propping myself up on one elbow.

A sudden euphoria filled every pore of my being. I loved the only chorus I remembered, but it would be amazing to hear anything else. Especially coming from him.

"I would be honored to hear something." I lay back on his lap again. "Anything."

He stroked my face and ran his fingers down my back until he embraced me against him. I sighed, eager to hear his voice.

"I truly hope not to cause any trauma regarding music in your life; I can't guarantee anything memorable, at least not in a good way." I laughed, intertwining my fingers with his.

"I know it will be amazing," I asserted confidently, and then he cradled me in his lap and began to sing. His free hand caressed me in every corner, and when I heard his voice for the first time, I was certain that God, in his infinite goodness, had chosen an angel from heaven to rescue me.

Nothing... absolutely nothing could be more beautiful than Zion's deep, hoarse, and intense voice. Each note was filled with tenderness, hidden beneath layers of rich, vibrant sound. And the music... oh my, it sank deep into my heart.

I thought all my hope was gone
Until you arrived
You showed this broken body
That this life is worth living
Gave me everything a person could ask for
Made my world so perfect
So I pray every single night
That this love is worth the risk
If I can't face the night
Don't forget me
Keep me in your memory
Let me be your favorite angel
Keep moving forward
Remember
That life always gets better

A solitary tear rolled down my face as I listened to every word he sang. There was something painful and romantic in the sound of his voice, something deeply sad yet hopeful; there was *him*, and I couldn't be more grateful.

"Are you crying, sweetheart?" That word touched my heart and pushed me to the edge. I was astonished by the strong feeling that enveloped me, and all I could do was bring his hand to my mouth and place a chaste kiss there.

"I am."

"Was it that bad?" I couldn't help but smile.

"On the contrary, it was perfect."

CHAPTER FIFTEEN

Ghost

I thought I had faced difficult situations for a lifetime, but sleeping next to Star that night proved me wrong.

Ah, hell... how hot it was!

I spent the night alert to every sound and movement echoing through the cold night in the woods, but no amount of worry could make me forget the presence of the young woman sleeping in my arms, lost in a deep sleep.

I had been so close to kissing her the night before that I could still feel the ghost of her lips near mine, as poised as her nose and as captivating as her eyes... damn, I could only imagine them in the darkness, while her breath brushed against my face irregularly, and I could swear she was aroused.

I even entertained the thought that she might want to kiss me too, but the idea seemed so absurd that I tried to forget it for the rest of the night, which didn't mean I succeeded. The proof of that was the sun was about to rise, and I still felt that frantic desire coursing through my veins, leaving me painfully hard.

"Hmm..." she moaned, sleepily shifting in my arms.

"Couldn't have picked a better time to moan," I huffed, irritated by my own lack of self-control.

"What?" she blinked.

"Are you awake?" My voice came out strangled.

"I believe so, unless I'm dreaming." She stifled a graceful yawn, covering her mouth with her hand. "Am I dreaming?" Her expression grew serious. I chuckled at the sight of her delicate face creased with worry. She was really afraid this was a dream.

"No, Star, you're awake. I'd say just in time, sit up and enjoy the ride." I pulled away from her as quickly as I could and jumped like a rabbit escaping a hunter to the front seat.

"Are you okay?" she asked, sticking her head into the gap between the two front seats. Her disheveled hair was going in all directions, giving her a graceful and slightly messy appearance.

"Everything's perfectly fine," I lied. "If you don't count that we're in the middle of a woods, probably trespassing on someone's land, with one of the windows broken on a day that ominously seems to attract more rain. Oh, and we still have to cross part of the city, and we haven't even considered the bullets lodged in the metal and..."

"Ghost, you seem on the verge of a psychotic breakdown." She pressed her lips with her teeth, holding back a smile and looked at me with those large golden eyes, beautiful like the shimmering waters of an ocean bathed in sunset. The slight pressure of her teeth on her flesh made my heart throb painfully.

"Maybe I'm just babbling too much." I started the car and fixed my eyes on the woods. I needed to focus on anything, anything at all, to stop thinking about her.

"Are you sure you're okay?" she asked as she hopped from the back seat to the passenger side just as we left the woods and returned to the highway. "You seem a bit..." About to explode with excitement and desire? Burning more than hell itself? Crazy with the urge to lay her back in the rear seat and lose myself in her? The damn girl I was supposed to protect? "Sick?" She seemed uncertain about the diagnosis.

I groaned low and frustrated and gripped the steering wheel tightly. What the hell was I thinking? How could I even entertain that idea? She was injured and, worse, trusted me as her protector. I couldn't break that bond, but neither my body nor my heart agreed with me. Even my brain, which should be the most rational, had completely lost it. Traitors, all of them.

"I'm fine." I tried to smile. "Just focused on our next route."

"What's the plan?"

"Look..." I pointed to the GPS, where a blue line marked the route we were going to take. "We'll follow the highway to this point, then we'll travel a short distance and reach the coast, where a boat will be waiting for us with Don Matteo's men."

"My God, so our salvation is right here?" She touched the GPS screen, her voice rising two octaves in pure excitement.

"That's right, my Star." Before I realized it, I had spoken without even allowing myself the luxury of considering she might not have heard me, as her cheeks took on that delightful color I was learning to love. A rosy hue that highlighted her big eyes.

I cleared my throat before I could speak.

"We're close. Too close, so we'll be more careful now and we won't stop for anything." I accelerated down the highway.

Every kilometer less on the GPS was one kilometer closer to Star's safety, and a certain anxiety took hold of me every time I thought about it.

"Ghost?"

"Yes..."

"Can I keep this knife?" I glanced at her, just now realizing she was holding my pocket knife and was about to open my mouth to deny her request when she interrupted me. "I know you're going to say it's dangerous and that I might end up slicing off your ear at some point, or one of my own hands."

"My ear? How in God's name could you do that?"

"But..." she cut me off, ignoring my shock. "Since I found myself in that captivity, I've never felt capable of fighting back. Even when I'm with you, I end up being an easy and unprotected target. But that moment back at the motel, while I was using all my energy to slash those tires, was the first time I felt different. It was as if I could finally be more than a victim. I knew that with it, I could defend myself somehow."

I pursed my lips for a moment, contemplating her words.

"And what if you end up getting hurt?" The chances of that happening were extremely high.

"I promise to use it wisely and only in an extreme situation."

"Still, it's very dangerous, Star." I fixed my eyes on the road, a tightness in my chest as I was assaulted by all the possibilities of that knife cutting her in some way. "I couldn't forgive myself if something happened to you."

"Look, I know we're being optimistic thinking we'll get to our departure point safely, but we both know the odds are split. And if we're surrounded, me getting hurt with this knife would be the least of our problems," she said seriously, staring at the multi-tool knife that had several other accessories besides the very sharp blade. "I don't want to just thrash around while they try to kill us."

"That's a well-crafted argument," I retorted, exasperated. She was right, I had to admit, but I didn't want to. "Maybe you should be a lawyer." She laughed, a pleasant and natural sound that landed directly in my chest.

"So is that a yes?" she asked, euphoric.

"It's a 'Be careful,'" I replied firmly. "Seriously, Star. Only use it if it's an extreme situation."

She nodded, and I spent the next few kilometers trying to remember everything I knew about knife wounds and how to save people who had been injured by such objects.

Star

I WAS LIKE A JUNKIE, watching the GPS signal every inch we traveled. Each distance gained meant so much to me. It was my freedom, and it was so close I could hardly believe it.

It wasn't hard to smile at that moment, and I realized this when I caught Ghost watching me with a quick, charming glance.

"What's up?" I felt my cheeks flush and a persistent warmth coursing through my chest.

"You're smiling... again," he added with visible joy. "I like seeing you smile." The comment automatically made the corners of my lips lift into another involuntary smile. "Are you really that happy to be holding that old knife?" He took on a playful expression.

"It's not just that. Of course I'm happy to carry this knife, but I feel radiant with every meter we cover toward the boat. Soon, all of this will just be a nightmare." Now it was Ghost's turn to smile, though the shine of his grin flickered for a mere moment.

"Not much left." He suddenly narrowed his eyes and slowed the vehicle.

"What—" Before I could finish the sentence, my eyes found the reason Ghost was almost stopping the car. There was a small commotion at the highway exit, where a turn would take us to the coast. "What's happening?"

"Looks like a parade."

The cloudy sky and strong wind didn't scare off the massive crowd gathering from one side of the highway to the other, blocking both those wanting to continue their journey on the road and those intending to travel along the coast. On the contrary, they seemed determined to hold their signs and even lift them up high.

Ghost parked the car at the roadside.

"We're going to have to get out here," he announced seriously, pulling the gun from his waist and checking the magazine.

"What?" I widened my eyes, fear creeping through my pores. "How are we going to get past without being noticed? And... what if one of them is in there?" I pointed to the people using everything to voice their protest. Some wore pieces of cloth with something written on their heads, others opted for painted and expressive faces, while most were holding signs and shouting fiercely. "We have to consider that if we can't get through..."

"They might have been stopped too," he completed. "We'll only know if we try." Ghost exhaled forcefully. "The parade seems quite substantial. That'll help us. We can blend into the crowd and pass unnoticed. It's a protest to draw the attention of the government and politicians to the problems Calabria has been facing and..."

His voice started to turn into a whisper the moment he mentioned the possibility of us entering the crowd. It terrified me. A wave of chills ran through my body at the mere thought, but we were so close to our destination, just a few meters away, to be exact; we just needed to get through the throng of furious people to reach it.

"Star? Star..." I only realized he was calling me when he touched my shoulder. "It's going to be okay, we'll make it," he assured, as if reading my thoughts, and flashed a wide, bright smile, the kind that could light up a cloudy day. I tried to cling to that reassurance as I got out of the car.

Ghost checked the weapons he had with him while his quick eyes scanned the chaotic scene. Somehow, everything in front of me seemed to be moving. The sound of shouts and honking horns ignited the crowd, which was too stirred up and even violent.

"Are you ready?" He approached, and I took a moment to realize my feet were glued to the ground. Ghost looked at me calmly, reached for the hood of my sweatshirt, and pulled it over my head. "This is the moment we've been waiting for; we'll make it, just believe." He adjusted the vest I was still wearing.

"Uh-huh," I agreed, trembling like a twig in a storm.

Ghost framed my face with his hands, and the touch was so deliciously tender and protective that I had to resist the urge to close my eyes.

"Have I ever lied to you?" he breathed, his voice brushing against my ears and cascading down my chest to settle in my heart. "We're both going to reach that boat safely, or I won't call myself Ghost."

"Maybe it's a good time to remind you that's not your real name." I smiled awkwardly, and he laughed, throwing his head back, animated.

"It's like it is." He caressed my jaw with his strong fingers and touched my back. "I need you to go ahead; I'll be right behind you. And remember, if I tell you to stop, you stop. No hesitating, understood?"

"Yes!"

My heart was pounding in my ears as we crossed the space that separated us from the monstrous crowd. I tried to keep the air flowing into my lungs as we approached them, but it was hard to control. I gripped the knife in my pocket, making sure it was still there.

"Stay alert; if you sense any suspicious movement, let me know immediately," he whispered behind me, and I shivered from head to toe, widening my eyes a bit more in fear of missing something. My hands were trembling—no, to be honest, every inch of my body was shaking. "Stay calm." I sucked in a deep breath when I felt Ghost's fingers intertwine with mine. "Remember, we're getting closer with every step we take."

I reflected on that phrase for a moment and realized how right he was. I had spent the entire trip staring at the GPS like a psychopath; I needed to muster courage now that we were just meters away from the end of this ordeal. I straightened my posture and faced the crowd, determined to get through it no matter what.

We reached the tumult that separated us from the coast. Ghost suddenly placed his arm over my shoulder and pulled me closer to him, anxiously.

"What is it?" I nearly shouted.

"Don't look, but there's an armed man to our right." I swallowed hard, reminding my legs that if they failed me now, we would be lost for good.

"I-is he one of them?" I tried to make myself heard over the unsettling sound of shouted words in Italian.

"Probably. Let's go." He pressed his hand into my back, urging me to walk faster when a tall, broad man with numerous tattoos trailing down his wide neck appeared right in front of us as if he had sprung from a hole in the ground. A strange, strangled scream escaped my lips as I recognized him.

"Sergei!" Ghost growled behind me.

"Good to see you again." The man smiled, his nasally and strange voice echoing through the crowd.

My God, it was the guard who always accompanied Scott to the hideout. That bastard had been present every time his boss went there. The last time I saw him, Ghost was dragging him by the feet.

"Did you really think you could escape us?" He didn't even look at me; his full attention was on Ghost, who stood firm at my back.

"Well, my dear, you don't plan to open fire in front of so many witnesses, do you?" My bodyguard tried to buy some time.

"There's nothing and no one to stop me from tearing your skin off after you betrayed us like that, you hellish silent bastard."

The man reached for the gun at his waist, still focused on Ghost, and that's when I realized. He was blinded by rage, so blind that he didn't even notice me. I slipped my hand into my pocket and pulled out the knife with my fingers.

"I won't even need to call for backup. The boss will be so pleased..." He drew his weapon, but before he could aim at Ghost, I pulled the knife, gripped the handle tightly with both hands, and plunged it into the idiot's abdomen with all my strength.

He howled, and I released the knife.

"Shit!" Ghost's eyes widened, and he shoved me aside as Sergei, even with the stab wound, lunged at me.

"You bitch!" he roared, trying to draw his weapon, but my strike bought Ghost enough time to respond with a rapid sequence of punches and precise elbows that disarmed the big guy and sent him staggering through the crowd, now with viscous liquid streaming down his belly where I had struck him. "Run! Go, go, go!" He surrounded me with his arms and pushed me into the crowd. A hysterical scream echoed through the place, rising above the protesters. Then another, and another. "Looks like they found the bleeding man." "Shit," he cursed again as another man appeared in front of us.

I held my breath, but Ghost remained unfazed. In fact, he didn't seem to think before reacting. This appeared to be one of his specialties.

His strikes were too precise and so fast I could barely keep up. In just a few moves, he disarmed the opponent and finished with a high knee that brought him down. He was definitely skilled in some martial art, and I prayed that would be enough to get us out of there.

A tall man shouted and pointed in our direction. I glanced over and, like the others, he had a gigantic tattoo on his neck.

He yelled a few words in Italian and then began to shoot, not caring about the people in the way.

The sound of the parade fireworks mixed with the gunfire, and people seemed oblivious.

"Shit!" Ghost pushed me aside and shot at a man who was very close to us, hitting one of his knees.

Only then did part of the crowd seem to realize they were in the middle of a shootout, and a wild panic ensued. Ghost was trying to retaliate, shooting whenever he had a clear shot. He seemed determined not to hit any innocent bystanders.

"Keep going, Star!" he ordered, shoving me into the crowd until we were hit by a huge wave of people and Ghost's hand, which had been holding me steady and safe, simply vanished.

People rushed past me like horses, about to trample me. I spun in place and stumbled to a distant corner.

"My God..." I whispered, trying to force air into my lungs. All I could see were unfamiliar faces, all coming toward me, pressing in, suffocating me. "Ghost!" I called softly, straining to find my voice. My head began to spin. "Zion!" Dizzier, weaker... the air no longer filled my lungs, and tears started to wet my face.

Where should I go? I couldn't think with all those people pressing in, I couldn't even find my direction. I placed my hand on my chest; the feeling of death began to engulf me, and I wished I could lie down right there.

"STAR!" The familiar voice echoed through the crowd. I blinked, trying to find him, but all I could see were blurs until I felt his hand grab mine and pull me into his arms.

"Zion!" I gasped, burying my face in that embrace I had come to love. I clung to him, desperate and trembling. He wrapped his arms around my waist and placed a chaste kiss on my forehead.

"I'm here, my Star." I shivered, adoring those words like never before, realizing Zion was everything I had, everything I needed, and everything I wanted, and that certainty scared me. "I'm here," he said between gasps. "Come on, we need to get to the coast, now!" He guided me through the chaos, following the direction the people were running until we could pass through.

I nearly fainted from joy when the hill gave way to a slope surrounded by a gigantic sea, where far ahead, a small but seemingly fast boat was waiting for us. That sight restored my legs' strength, and I started to run, forcing myself not to stop even when I heard gunfire behind us.

"GHOST!" The sinister voice that haunted my nightmares echoed in an animalistic grunt, and in that instant, I knew he had found us.

"Don't stop!" my protector ordered, staying close to me while firing back, shooting continuously to keep them at bay.

I heard the sound of the boat's engine roar as they realized we were close. One of the men approached the shore and shouted something as he saw the chaos lurking behind us.

I kept running. I was so close. We were going to make it. *We had* to make it!

"*Come on, come on, come on!*" a man shouted from the bow.

I ran until my lungs burned. My body begged for rest, on the verge of giving in, but I forced myself to keep going. I couldn't stop, even if I collapsed the moment I set foot on that boat.

One step... just one leap, and there was my freedom.

"*Jump now!*" A man shouted, gesturing for me to leap. Ghost positioned his hand on my back and pushed me hard toward the boat.

I jumped over the space where the blue, shimmering sea water glistened and landed flat on the wooden floor of the boat, the impact immediately jarring my jaw.

I sprang up, turning to Ghost, who had stopped in front of the boat to fire back at the incoming shots. Panic struck me as I realized I had only made it this far safely because he had stayed behind. My eyes widened at this realization, and I began to scream.

"ZION! JUMP! ZION!" I yelled with all my strength, only breathing again when I saw him running back toward me.

The men on board began shooting, providing cover as he leaped across the distance between the dock and the boat, which was now even greater than the leap I had made.

My heart stopped for a moment as I counted each of his quick steps toward us. He jumped and landed on the deck of the boat with a thud, but stood up just as quickly, joining the men who were firing at the shore without pause.

"BASTARD! DAMNED BASTARD!" Scott roared from the edge of the hangar, incapacitated to do anything but shoot blindly, and for a moment I felt an overwhelming pleasure seeing him there, savoring the bitter taste of defeat. Until he raised his gun and aimed it at me.

I saw his bloodthirsty gaze locked on mine, heard the shots from his weapon, and even closed my eyes, bracing for impact, but the only thing I felt was a tight embrace as Ghost pulled me into his arms. We both fell to the boat's deck with a strange and forceful impact, while the engine roared to pull us quickly out of the line of fire.

"Oh my God, my God, it's over! It's really over, Ghost..." I smiled, even as his body pressed me against the hard floor. I was so euphoric that it took me a moment to feel something wet on my fingertips. I raised them and my heart stopped as I noticed it was...

"Blood?" I thought I had said. Ghost rolled over me with a pained groan, and I looked from my hands to his contorted face. "IT'S BLOOD!" The men on the boat began speaking all at once, and pure terror took hold of me as I realized what was happening. "He's been shot, he's been shot!" I repeated, shouting. I could barely think of what to do, only scream and scream.

I threw myself to my knees beside him. His jacket was soaked, and his face began to turn pale, devoid of color. I stifled a scream of panic. He jumped... my God, he jumped in front of the bullets meant for me.

"A-are you okay?" he said with difficulty, lifting his right hand to touch my face with trembling fingers, but soon closed his eyes with a grimace of pain that left me desolate.

"Why?" I cried, clutching his hand. "Why did you do that? You made me wear this damn vest everywhere just to jump in front of that lunatic?" Someone touched my shoulder, and I sucked in air forcefully. Ghost held the man's wrist with impressive speed and growled:

"*Non toccarla, non...*" he gasped, struggling to keep the man's wrist and uttered a few more words between brief breaths.

"What?" I questioned, confused, not understanding the damn language.

"We won't touch her, don't worry, I'll inform everyone." A man crouched down beside Ghost, who still held onto him, and I thanked God he spoke my language fluently enough that I thought he was American too. "You need to step back, miss."

"No!" I shook my head and pulled Ghost's hand away from the man's wrist, clutching it between my own hands.

Ghost looked at me, his eyes seemed dull and distant, and then a small smile crept onto the corner of his lips. Suddenly, his fingers tangled in the hair at the nape of my neck, and he pulled me toward his lips.

His mouth touched mine deeply, in a warm and quick kiss, full of meaning, and then he pulled away.

"I'm sorry," he groaned as more men approached with what looked like an emergency kit. "I couldn't help but kiss you, m-my Star." And he closed his eyes.

"Zion... no. No!" I could barely see him. My vision was blurred by the tears streaming down my face, but one thing was clear and desperate to me: the amount of blood spreading across the boat's floor.

"He's going to pass out!" the supposed American shouted at me and said something equally urgent in Italian.

I watched the men surround Ghost as if I were watching the most terrifying horror movie on earth.

There was no pain, no hurt that could compare to what I felt in that moment. It was like swallowing a mouthful of sharp blades. My hero, my guardian angel, was right there, bleeding before my eyes, and there was nothing I could do to save him, just as he had saved me so many times before.

It was then that I discovered what it felt like to descend a few steps into hell, and my only certainty was that I wouldn't be able to escape from there, not without him.

CHAPTER SIXTEEN

Star

Thud!
　　Thud!
Thud!

The sound echoed insistently, reverberating in my skin, soul, and heart. The world spun as the minutes dragged on, slow and torturous.

I watched everything as if my mind had detached from my body, now drifting through a horror movie. From our arrival on Sicilian soil to the moment they lifted Ghost's bloodied body onto an improvised board.

A frantic rush began, and more heavily armed men joined the mission to try to save his life as we set foot on solid ground, which did nothing to calm the painful despair that prevented me from breathing. Everything passed before my eyes as a blur, and I didn't even know where I found the strength to keep holding his hand, which was growing colder, and run alongside him.

"Mamma mia!" a woman exclaimed when we finally arrived at one of the largest houses I had ever seen. More nonsensical words echoed behind me, some more hysterical than others.

I couldn't break the gaze that kept my eyes glued to Zion's weary, sweaty face, as if he would die if I distracted myself for even a moment. I only realized I had entered the mansion when we stopped in a small room, where a huge hospital bed lay next to several machines, trays with sharp and terrifying instruments, and a wall of white cabinets.

A woman with black hair and a pale appearance hurriedly donned a lab coat and began barking orders in every direction. They placed Ghost on the stretcher, and a man in similar attire approached, his white hair not diminishing the vibrant energy radiating from his broad frame; I could have sworn he was no older than fifty.

I found myself watching the two of them as they examined Ghost closely, anxiously trying to discover anything they could. I held my breath when the doctor frowned and glanced at the man, and suddenly her eyes fell on me.

"*Signorina?*" Someone touched my arm. I screamed, panicking and cowering between the bed and the gap of the cabinet beside me, refusing to let go of Ghost's hand.

All eyes in the room turned toward me as if they were just now realizing my existence. A young, very blonde girl opened her lips and withdrew the hand that had touched me, looking at me with her blue eyes in a mix of pity and doubt. I trembled, feeling fleeting despair take over every cell in my body.

"The last thing he said was that we shouldn't touch her." The American entered the room and turned to the woman. "She only understands this language." He looked at me, and I nodded, shaking my head repeatedly.

The blonde scrutinized me from head to toe and took a step toward me, which made me squeeze Zion's hand a little tighter.

"Do you understand what I'm saying?" she asked in impeccable English. If it weren't for her accent tinging each word, I could have sworn she was American.

"Y-yes," I whispered, and she raised her hand, bringing absolute silence to the room.

"Listen, I'd like to ask everyone who speaks English to communicate in it when this young lady is present. She is our guest and will be treated as such," she said, giving a nod in my direction.

"And you can't touch her. She gets a bit strange," the American emphasized.

"You heard them, right? Spread the word." A man entered the room, his broad shoulders accentuated by a long-sleeved white shirt and a striking U collar.

"Yes, Don Matteo!" A chorus of eager voices echoed through the room as everyone agreed with the man. "Can you take care of her, *amore mio*? I'll talk to the doctor and see how he's doing." He touched the blonde's hand, which was still watching me cautiously, then briefly glanced at me, giving a short wave before focusing his attention back on Ghost. "By a thousand hells..." he cursed. "I swore he would make it back in one piece."

"Should we expect a visit from Snake?" the woman inquired.

"I'll talk to the doctor to know what the situation is before informing him of anything." Snake was Ghost's brother, and if Don feared he would show up suddenly, it was because he knew Zion was in life-threatening danger. "If anything happens to him, I fear Italy won't have a peaceful day."

"H-he's going to survive, right?" I whispered.

"Let's let the doctor examine him, and soon we'll know his real condition. My name is Valentina. I'm sorry, but you need to let go of his hand and come with me."

"No!" I refused as she approached. "I can't." I looked at our intertwined hands, and a loud sob rose in my throat. I remembered the first time he offered his hand as a safe harbor, the firm touch, the caring attentiveness, and all the concern he had, never crossing my boundaries. That was our bond, our union. If I let go of him, if he died... my God, everything would stop being real. My heart couldn't take it. "He is my reality; I can't leave him."

"I understand you, truly. I've been in your place more times than I can count, but I learned that if I wanted to see my stubborn husband again, I needed to let those who could save him act in my stead. Do you understand?" She opened her eyes wider, her turquoise blue pupils penetrating deep into my mind. I released Ghost's hand. "That's it. Don't worry, he'll be in good hands." I slowly stepped back and watched as they turned him over onto his stomach, a sharp pain pulsing in my chest. I was about to leave when they ripped his shirt open, exposing Ghost's bare, bloodied back.

A number of surprised gasps filled the room, and both Valentina and I froze at the sight of Ghost's naked, bloody back.

I widened my eyes, unable to breathe. Not even the blood could hide or camouflage the large web of thick, deep scars on his skin. They had no beginning or end, covering everything and any corner of his back like the roots of a tree. His pale skin, stained with red, also highlighted a hole in the flesh where the bullet had entered.

"Dios mio!" someone said, astonished.

"At least one good piece of news." Don Matteo, who was also staring at the scene with slightly wider eyes, crossed his arms and looked at me. "If he survived whatever did this to his back, a gunshot will be nothing."

I left the room shortly after. Valentina expelled all the curious onlookers, leaving only the Don and the doctors.

I huddled on the floor by the door, burying my fingers in my hair. Thick tears streamed down my face and fell onto the bulletproof vest that Ghost had forced me to wear.

"This is so unfair," I sobbed, releasing the cry that had been trapped in my throat. Valentina sat down beside me, sympathetic, and I felt bad for making the lady of the house sit on the floor, but I didn't feel capable of anything other than crying.

"Poor thing, you must have suffered so much," she said in a sweet, delicate voice, and before I realized it, I was pouring out all the despair in my chest through sobs and gasps.

"H-he gave me this stupid thing to protect me." I pointed at the vest, feeling it burn against my skin, then ripped it off in a fit of rage and threw it to the opposite corner of where we were. "And in the end, he decided to be my own bulletproof vest. What a stupid man, idiot!" I cursed, crying even louder. "He's already suffered so much, and yet he has the best heart in the world. Did you know he didn't even know me?"

"Yes, I heard, dear. We learned all about the horrible situation you went through from Snake." The gentleness and care in her words comforted me, like a caress without touch.

"He pulled me out of there without a single fear of getting hurt along the way. Who risks their own life for a stranger?" I looked at her, who, behind the curtain of tears, had become a yellow blur. "If only he had chosen to wear the vest," I lamented. "But no, not for a second did Zion think of himself. He always worried about me, and now..." I brought my hand to my face, sniffling between gasps.

"Get two chairs," she said to someone, and we stayed there until two young women in blue dress uniforms approached with two chairs. Valentina stood and pointed to one of them. "How about we wait together and a little more comfortably while he's treated? After everything you said, I don't think this man is going anywhere without you; he cares too much for that, right?" I lifted my eyes and saw that the two girls were watching me with anxious expressions. "These are Giorgia and Sonia." The first had brown hair and was as delicate as Valentina, while the second had dark blonde hair that fell just below her shoulders and smiled warmly when mentioned. "They will be at your disposal."

"You can ask us for anything," Giorgia affirmed. "What should we call you?" I noticed all three women turned to me, expectantly.

"My name is Star."

"What a beautiful name," Valentina praised in a sentimental whisper.

I held back the absurd urge to throw myself on the floor and cry until I passed out, remembering that he had given me that name, forcing myself to lift my face to them.

"Thank you for all your help," I said and stood up somewhat sluggishly, sat in the chair, and questioned Valentina when Giorgia and Sonia left: "Shouldn't we be in a hospital? I apologize if the question sounds rude; don't get me wrong, but I fear there might be some complication."

"Don't worry; I understand your fear. As I said, I've felt it a few times." She clasped her hands in front of her and settled more comfortably in the chair. "In fact, we've been to the hospital a few times, but after a very suspicious incident that took my father-in-law's life, we had to resort to safer methods. Considering our own problems and that the Marino family is cowardly influential, our chances are all in this place." I nodded as I grasped the situation. "But don't worry. Inside are Doctor Alberto and Nurse Manuela, and there's no one in Sicilian lands with more knowledge than them, especially when it comes to gunshot victims."

I sat in front of that door for long minutes, which soon turned into hours. I was tense, and every part of my body ached in a different way, and I even wondered how anyone could keep breathing after knowing for certain that their heart had shattered into countless pieces. I didn't know, but somehow I was still there, alive.

The door to the makeshift infirmary opened after what felt like an eternity. Doctor Alberto walked through with the Don, and I noticed the doctor was without his lab coat, revealing a crumpled blue dress shirt. I jumped up and placed my hand on my chest when I saw the worried expression on the doctor's face.

"How is he?" I blurted out, anxious, before either of them had a chance to speak.

"He lost a lot of blood; he needed a transfusion to survive the surgery, which, overall, went well. I was worried that the main artery might have been damaged, but we got lucky. The pressure hasn't dropped yet, and we have to worry about a possible blood infection, but before anything else, he needs to regain consciousness."

"I need to see him!" I tried to pass the doctor, who stood in front of me with arms outstretched, blocking my way.

"No way!" he declared, sternly. "We had the hardest time cleaning everything. You can't go in there like this." I looked at my hands, covered in blood, and whimpered at the realization that he was right. "Take a shower first, and then you can stay by his side, but I must warn you there's no estimate for when he'll wake up."

"Can she at least take a peek, doctor? Without entering the examination room?" Valentina asked, and I opened my eyes wider with that brief hope.

"If you ensure she won't take a single step toward the patient, then it's fine."

"I promise!" I interjected before Valentina could respond for me, and I saw the doctor relent, stepping aside from the door for a moment.

My eyes watered as soon as I saw him. Zion looked a bit smaller lying on that large bed, as white as his pale face. Half of his chest was exposed, and a large bandage was fixed to his shoulder, where he had been shot, with several wires connected to him.

I held my breath, not understanding when he had become a vital part of my heart. When did imagining life without him become so devastating and painful? Seeing him there, unconscious with his eyes closed, sent me into a panic. There was the possibility that he might not wake up, and that certainty suddenly drained the strength from my legs. I staggered until I leaned against the first wall I found.

"Doctor, examine her too," the Don requested, but I shook my head in refusal.

"No need; I'm fine. Just a little..."

"Overwhelmed?" I intended to say that I was about to faint from despair, but that would work too.

"Yes, that's it."

"If you insist..." The Don turned to the gray-haired man, his gaze so lofty and assured that he resembled a hawk in flight. "Stay close, doctor; I think we're going to need you. I'll take care of some matters; if there's any change in his condition, I want to be informed immediately." He spoke with a firm, intense voice that perfectly matched his imperious features.

Don Matteo seemed used to giving orders and being obeyed, but when his eyes fell on his wife, something in his expression shifted, and something like affection and love filled his hard eyes. He placed a quick kiss on her lips and hurried down the hallway.

"How about you follow me? You need to clean up to be by his side." Valentina gestured toward Ghost and I forced myself to follow her steps, even though my heart had remained right there, stuck at the door of that infirmary.

✱

VALENTINA GUIDED ME through the mansion, illuminated by many points of light, with elegant walls made of a mix of wood and stone—a combination I would have appreciated observing if I could focus on anything other than keeping my legs moving. We passed through a hall that faced a grand staircase and ascended to a room on the second floor, where Giorgia and Sonia awaited us at the entrance with inviting smiles.

"We've prepared the bath," Sonia informed as we passed through the doorframe.

I entered a very large and dazzlingly bright room. The retro furniture was impeccably arranged, reflecting the weak light of a cloudy day filled with gray, heavy clouds through the glass window that opened onto a small balcony.

"Come, the water is warm; can we help you undress?" Giorgia inquired, opening a side door that led to a bathroom as large as the bedroom, featuring a shower stall on the right with glass walls surrounding it, and a small bathtub on the left, filled with foam and thick steam rising from it.

"She doesn't like to be touched," Sonia reminded.

"I got startled earlier, and I'm sorry for screaming." I turned to Valentina, who by then was also inside the bathroom. "Ghost is teaching me to accept touch better without fear, and I definitely prefer it to be a woman touching me besides him. I just need to know it's happening so I can be prepared," I said in a low voice.

"So is it okay if we help you? I guarantee you'll be safe with us; here, women are protected," Valentina sought to confirm.

"And anyone who thinks otherwise will have their head ripped off by Don Matteo," Sonia added with genuine pride.

"I would appreciate the help. I don't feel capable of lifting a single arm." My lips trembled, and I needed all the strength I had left not to crumble right there.

"Dios Mio, don't be like this; your strength will be renewed after a warm bath," Sonia interrupted, worried, as she gathered towels and various other items.

They then united with a single purpose: to remove my clothes. I raised my arms robotically to help them, and one by one, my clothes were taken off and abandoned in a corner of the bathroom. When they finished, I found myself naked in front of three strangers, who looked a bit shocked.

"Oh my God." Valentina's large blue eyes scanned my body. "What have they done to you, dear?" Both Sonia and Giorgia looked at me with sad, pained expressions.

I knew what they were seeing. The still-purplish bruises, the numerous scars on my legs and arms; they saw the outline of my torment.

"It hardly hurts anymore," I lied, trying to calm them down. Pity, compassion, and a trace of dark anger crossed Valentina's delicate face as she ran her hand through her wavy short hair before responding.

"It's not hurting, or have you just gotten used to the pain? Those are two different things." She guided me to the shower, where she washed my hands and arms, removing almost all the blood before leading me to the bathtub. "Sonia, please get some painkillers."

"Yes, ma'am." The woman hurried out.

"Shitty bastards. *Figlio di puttana!*" I heard Valentina curse behind me just before I stepped into the bathtub.

Giorgia supported one of my arms and helped me into the warm water of the bathtub, which didn't bring me any relief. All I could think about was Zion, unconscious downstairs, and the terrible, unacceptable possibility of losing him. Still, I leaned back in the tub with the water covering my breasts, determined to get clean quickly, and Valentina sat on the edge, beginning to wash my hair.

"You must have noticed that most people living here speak your language," she started to converse amidst my inscrutable silence.

"Yes, I noticed." I tried to focus on that conversation. "Is it some sort of tradition?"

"Almost that. In fact, Matteo's work requires us to be versatile in several languages. English is the main one, a bit of Spanish too, but I admit that the latter I don't master," she explained, sliding her fingers through my hair as she lathered it with shampoo. "Practically everyone here speaks clear English. Some are even American; you'll manage to communicate easily."

Giorgia was on the other side of the tub, scrubbing a sponge with soap that perfumed the entire space with the scent of roses. Soon, she began to scrub me too, washing away all the remaining dirt.

I didn't mind them washing my hair and every part of my battered skin. I didn't care about the sting it caused. I let them help me, allowed them to come close, and they continued, murmuring condescending words now and then, claiming that I would be safe and that they would take care of me.

"All done," Valentina concluded the minute Sonia walked through the door with a pack of pills in one hand and a glass of water in the other. I nodded, trying to keep my thoughts there, in that bathroom. "How do you feel, dear? Are you okay?" I took a deep breath and found three pairs of eyes watching me with concern.

Was I okay?

Did I ever remember being even close to okay? Maybe in that car, after having such a strong panic attack that I could swear I would die, but I didn't die because he was there, willing to save me once again, even from my own thoughts. I didn't die because he was singing to me. And his voice, my God, his voice was so delightful, so strong and powerful. I could live in that sound. I would give anything to hear him sing again, but what if that moment never repeated? Would I still be okay?

Valentina touched my shoulder, and that was all it took for me to completely break down. I started to cry and curled up inside the bathtub. There was so much pain that I didn't know where it had started, nor if it would ever end. Hands, arms, and voices tried to reach me, but everything became a big blur, and I let out what had been stuck in my throat. The pain of what I endured in the dungeon, the despair of uncertain nights, the cold, the hunger, and all the hope I felt when I met that man... who was now dying because of me.

"That's it, let the pain out." Valentina patted my back, and I sobbed even louder, my throat burning, my heart racing like lightning, desperate, fighting to endure the pain. I cried so much that without wanting to, I made Sonia and Giorgia cry along with me.

It took me some time to regain control of my emotions and be able to get out of the bathtub. Once again, I received help to put on a long, floral dress that Valentina had lent me. Giorgia helped me comb my hair, but I refused to dry it. I couldn't waste any more time; Ghost was waiting for me.

"Can I go back?" I turned to Valentina.

"Of course, I'll go with you. Sonia, serve her a strong coffee in the infirmary, and Giorgia, ask someone to bring one of those comfortable reclining chairs over there." And then her blue eyes fell on me. "You need to keep in mind what the doctor said, dear. It could take hours, days, or even weeks for him to wake up."

"It doesn't matter. I want to be there when he wakes up."

✸

I WILL NEVER FORGET the strange, corrosive, and terrifying sensation that filled me when I entered the infirmary a short time later. Sonia had left a tray with juices and warm, filled brioches on a small table, and a large chair right next to the bed where Ghost lay. Manuela informed me of his room and asked me to call her at the slightest sign of change, and soon everyone left me alone with him.

There was no way I could eat, just as I wouldn't find comfort sitting there; nothing seemed capable of keeping me sane in front of the image of the strong man, broad-shouldered, with skin as pale as ivory, unconscious before me.

His muscular chest rose and fell with difficulty, and the only sound breaking the silence was that of a monitor tracking his heartbeat at a steady rhythm.

I forced myself to control the trembling in my legs and approached him. I touched his hand with mine and felt a tear roll down my face upon sensing how cold it was. I leaned in and rested my forehead against his, desperate to touch him everywhere. I ran my hands through his dark hair and traced my fingers down his angular face, outlining his thick eyebrows, nose, cheekbones, and then his mouth. I remembered the kiss he had stolen just before he collapsed. I had never imagined that such a quick touch could trigger so many conflicting feelings.

I wanted to ask why he had done that. Did he feel something strange like I did, as if butterflies danced right in the middle of my stomach every time we touched? Because I certainly felt it.

Warm shivers ran up my neck every time he looked at me with those deep, bright brown eyes, like leaves in autumn. I would remember that color for the rest of my life, but I was desperate to see it again.

"Open your eyes, Zion," I whispered, intertwining our hands. "Let me see them one more time."

✴

THE FIRST NIGHT WAS the worst of all. Not that the following ones would be any less frightening, but the first 24 hours tortured every part of my being through the pain that Ghost felt.

At some point during the night, I rested my head on the edge of the bed and continued holding his hand with both of mine until a low, painful sound made me jerk my head up.

"Zion!" I stood up, leaning toward him. He was breathing irregularly, and small moans escaped his lips constantly.

I called for Madalena, and even after he was medicated, he continued to moan. Beads of sweat appeared on his forehead, and creases began to spread there as he groaned.

"Isn't there another medication?" I questioned, frantic as I saw him mumble strange and disconnected things.

"Unfortunately not; we're at the maximum dosage. He needs to fight off the infection."

It didn't take long for the fever to rise, along with the moans; words began to take shape. He whimpered, sometimes asking for help, begging for whoever was there to stop. At times, his voice became lower, like a frightened child, and I could only imagine that he was trapped in a delirium that took him back to his past.

I began to cry, feeling useless in the face of his suffering as he gasped for air.

"Zion, this isn't real!" I repeated hours later, placing a cool cloth soaked in cold water that Madalena had brought to try to reduce the fever, but nothing seemed to work. "I'm real, remember? We both are." I soaked the cloth again, and I had no more tears left to cry.

We spent the night trying to bring down the fever, and the second day was even worse. Doctor Alberto stayed by our side, trying to control

Ghost's temperature, which would sometimes drop, only to rise stronger again. When night fell once more, I found myself alone again.

I couldn't close my eyes, much less eat. I had swallowed almost a liter of juice that Sonia had brought me against my will, so I wouldn't end up hospitalized alongside Ghost, but aside from that, nothing could pass my throat. I prayed that this night would be different from the last, but my prayers didn't seem to reach the heavens. It wasn't long before the fever spiked again, and with it, the delirium returned.

It felt like every part of my body was being ripped apart as I heard him moaning, pleading, begging, and then he changed. His forehead became lined with creases, and he began to thrash about just as Manuela entered the infirmary to administer a dose of medication.

"Any improvement?"

"No," I replied, weary, watching her inject the medication into the IV bag connected to him.

"The fever is high again. I'll prepare cold compresses, and Star..." she called to me from the door. "Have faith, girl. I've seen worse cases end with a happy ending. Don't you think you should rest for when he wakes up?"

"I can't." I looked at him, who was starting to moan again. "I can't and don't want to leave here."

"You should." I heard the woman's voice fading away, and I leaned in as he began to say something.

"Father!" he whimpered, repeating the word over and over, each time with more intensity, more desperation. His voice rose in my anxious chest and seemed to infiltrate deep into my soul.

I wished I could free him from all pain and suffering like never before, but my pleas went unheard; nothing could be heard but Zion's cries of pain.

Doctor Alberto appeared early in the morning, even before the sun rose, and adjusted the medications as much as he could but assured us we had reached the limit; if they increased the dosages, he could die.

We spent another day there, the third in the midst of hell. I couldn't eat more than a piece of fruit, much less sleep; it was inconceivable. And what if something happened to him while I slept? I couldn't take that risk and had to argue with Valentina to make her understand this, and despite my hostess being determined to make me sleep, something in my gaze made her realize that staying by his side was more important to me than anything else.

When night fell, something different happened. Ghost, who had been delirious and mumbling nonsense, began to repeat the same phrase over and over. Both Manuela and I moved closer to try to understand what he was saying. The hope that he was waking up embraced me completely.

"No... touch..." he said, and we both moved closer. "No. Touch," he repeated.

"No touch?" Manuela looked at me, confused.

"No. Touch. Her." He moaned loudly and gritted his teeth, thrashing about without stopping. "No. Touch. Her. Don't touch her."

A painful knot formed in my throat as I realized he was talking about me, my eyes burned, but there wasn't a single drop to shed.

"You fool," I sobbed. "How can you think of me when you can't even think of yourself?"

Manuela sighed and left soon after, leaving us alone for a moment. She would probably return with more cold compresses.

I stood up and felt dizzy. My vision darkened, and I staggered until I leaned against the bed where he lay. I waited to recover so I could hold his hand with one of mine and touch his forehead with the other.

I wanted him to hear my voice, to know he wasn't alone.

"This can't be the end of our story. You need to give me a decent damn kiss," I ranted. "Something precious, so I can hold it in this empty memory." I knew he had already given me too many precious memories and moments, but I couldn't even think of losing him, and just the thought terrified me and made everything we had seem so little compared to all we could still have. "I hope you can hear me, angel. You're not alone; I would never abandon you, are you listening? You're everything I have." I tried not to cry and keep my voice steady.

I caressed his hair and leaned in until my lips were close to his ear, and I began to sing the only part I knew that always calmed me when I was in the dungeon.

I started softly, rhythmically, pouring all my heart into it. My voice carried a bit of all the torment I felt, but it emitted notes of affection, attachment, and another feeling I couldn't identify, yet I was aware it was strong. It was him who made my heart race when I thought of Zion, and I let that feeling guide my voice, asking the heavens that Ghost could hear it.

Gradually, he began to calm down and stopped thrashing and mumbling nonsensical things. That brought me such joy that I felt my eyes well up again, and I returned to humming the same part dozens of times.

"You have a spectacular voice!" Valentina entered the infirmary accompanied by Manuela. Her frozen expression almost made me laugh. "Seriously, I've never heard such a pleasant sound, and it seems he hasn't either."

"The fever has subsided a bit," the nurse chimed in happily, and Valentina moved closer to me.

"You should rest, Star. You haven't slept or eaten properly for three days. Soon I'll have to arrange a place beside him for you."

"I must admit I'm feeling exhausted, but how could I close my eyes without touching his hand?" She took a deep breath and shook her head in disagreement.

"I have to admit, what you two have is something unique," she said, resigned.

"You have no idea of the things he's done for me. I sometimes wonder if he's in possession of all his mental faculties. Only a madman would face so much for a stranger."

"Maybe you two met in another life, and you're not so strange to his heart after all," she said dreamily, and I pondered that for a moment.

"I miss hearing his voice. Seeing his eyes, feeling the warmth of his hand in mine. I even miss the scares he gives me," I smiled at the thought of his unique personality. "He makes no noise when he walks; it's amazing." I turned to Valentina, who had suddenly become a blur.

A tremor passed through my body, my hands tingled, I lost the strength in my legs, and the floor began to spin out of control.

"Star!" That was the last thing I heard before I lost consciousness.

CHAPTER SEVENTEEN

Ghost

Two Days Later

Ah, how I hated being shot! In fact, the only time I was shot was while protecting one of my VIPs, and the bullet grazed me, which didn't cause anything close to the feeling of being hit by a speeding bus.

I opened my eyes, feeling dizzy, and a sting pierced my body, concentrating on my damn shoulder. I groaned softly. It hurt like hell, and it didn't help at all the burning sensation trapped in my throat.

"Sir?" someone called at my side. A bright light burned my eyes, forcing me to close them again. "Doctor, he's awake!" a woman exclaimed energetically.

I blinked a few times, trying to adjust to the brightness, and slowly the two blurs in front of me gained faces and contours.

"Welcome back!" The man, an elderly gentleman with white hair but a youthful demeanor that reminded me of my father, approached with a stethoscope. "I'm Alberto, the doctor responsible for you, and that one over there with the miracle-witness look is Manuela, my nursing partner. How are you feeling?" he asked, already placing that cold thing against my chest, which I just noticed was bare.

How was I feeling?

I stared at the white coat he wore for a moment while he poked me insistently and tried to remember what had happened. The last thing I remembered after being shot was kissing…

"Star." I gasped sharply and sat up abruptly. A movement that, by the way, caused a sharp pain to hit me. "Damn!" I groaned, placing my hand over the bandage.

"What are you doing, man? Are you crazy?" Alberto touched my shoulders and tried to force me back down, but my mind was racing with just one question, and I couldn't even breathe properly before knowing the answer.

"Where is she? Where's Star?" I asked anxiously, looking around desperately for any sign of her.

"You need to calm down, sir..." Manuela widened her bright eyes at me and raised her hands, clearly unsure of what to do with them in the face of my distress. "Star is sleeping; she's fine."

"I wouldn't say fine," the doctor retorted, averting his eyes when Manuela glared at him.

"What do you mean by that? What happened to her?" Just the thought that something had happened destabilized me. My heart began to race, pounding loudly in my ears.

"Nothing serious. The poor thing refused to leave your side. She's been here, sitting in that chair..." She pointed with her eyes, and only then did I notice there really was a recliner beside the hospital bed. "For three days and three nights. Without sleeping properly and practically without eating." I swallowed hard, a deep sadness washing over me at hearing that. "She only left the infirmary because she couldn't take it anymore on the third day and fainted from exhaustion. She's been sleeping since then; it's been almost two days now," she sighed heavily. "It's a shame she didn't see you wake up; she was so anxious..."

"Is she really okay? Can you guarantee that?" The anxiety in my voice was palpable, and something in my expression made Manuela look at me with what I could only describe as affection.

"It seems you both care a lot for each other." She opened a calm smile. "Yes, she's really okay. I've been monitoring her, and soon she'll be awakened to eat. I think now that you've woken up, she'll finally have some appetite."

"Get this stuff off me; I need to see her." I reached out my arm where a catheter was connected toward the doctor.

"At least you're asking. The men of Don Matteo usually rip everything off before we have a chance to blink."

"I wouldn't consider myself capable of such a feat. I hate these annoying little things; they're sharp—imagine pulling this out voluntarily?" I grimaced at the thought. Needles caused me tremendous agony, and as I looked away to avoid seeing that thing being removed, like a child would, a question occurred to me. "How many days was I out?"

"Five in total. Three of them were terribly feverish," Manuela replied.

"Oh, how disgusting. I need a shower before I see her!" The woman laughed.

"You need to manage to stay on your feet before anything else," the doctor scolded. "We have a sterilized and spacious bathroom right here, with supports to help you maintain your balance. Go take a shower; it'll be easier to help you if you feel weak. The Don has left clothes ready for when you woke up." He pointed to a pile of clothes under a counter in the corner of the infirmary. "And avoid getting the bandage wet, okay?"

I took a shower shortly after getting the lay of the land and how I ended up there. Manuela summarized why we couldn't end up in a hospital.

Don Matteo's father was murdered less than a year ago inside the city's main hospital in a very suspicious poisoning that nearly went unnoticed under the diagnosis of a common heart attack, if it weren't for Matteo's cunning and his contacts, who soon discovered the real cause of death.

Since the whole of Sicily was under the power of the famiglia Vitale, just like the hospital, it could only have been an act of betrayal. Someone from within, perhaps an acquaintance. Since then, Don Matteo took measures, and until they found the suspects, he created a makeshift clinic and brought a trusted team to that place, as his men frequently required medical assistance with alarming regularity.

According to the nurse, it was also difficult to get Star away from my side when we arrived. My little one had been waiting outside, like a guard dog, she said. And nothing in this world would make me happier and even calmer than putting my eyes on her.

I was desperate, to tell the truth. A strange, painful tightness settled in my chest, and all I could imagine was how scared she must have been in front of all that blood, but in the end, Doctor Alberto was right; it didn't take long before a slight dizziness made me stagger out of the shower.

I faced my reflection in the bathroom mirror and was startled by the pale tone of my skin. I had deep dark circles under my eyes, a rough beard that begged to be shaved, and a huge bandage on my shoulder.

"Great," I whispered. "Another scar."

It took me longer than I expected to dry off and get dressed, and when I exited the bathroom, I was surprised to see a man waiting for me.

"Dios mio, he's on his feet!" The man approached, greeting me with a warm handshake. He was large, with impeccable posture and a well-defined beard on his sharp face. His experienced eyes exuded unmistakable nuances of power.

"Don Matteo, I presume." He nodded in confirmation.

"Come, sit down. I don't think you usually have this sickly color." He pointed to the gurney and soon settled into the chair beside it. "It's not good to tempt fate."

"You might be right," I commented, hating myself for the sudden fatigue spreading through my body as I sat in front of him. "I don't even know where to begin to thank you, Don Matteo. For the reinforcements, for saving my life, or for taking care of my Star."

"No need to thank me; I'm just glad to have witnessed this miracle. You suffered from a high fever." He ran a hand through his dark hair. "I carried your name to God in my thoughts... I guess He considered my request. I didn't even want to think about what Snake would do if this story had a different ending."

"Does he know what happened?"

"Not yet. I avoided his calls and waited for you to wake up so you could handle it yourself." He handed me a cellphone. "Call when you can. They're worried, and I advise you not to delay if you don't want the entire Holder family to descend on Sicily."

"I'll do that." I turned the phone over in my hands, knowing that before contacting my brothers, I needed to have a very important conversation with the Don.

"And how are you feeling?" he inquired, genuinely interested.

"Like a fruit that just met the blender, but I'll be fine. Thank you." I pressed my lips together. "I imagine Star must have told you everything that happened."

"If by everything, you mean a great nothing... then yes, she did." He laughed. "All I know was relayed through Snake, and I'd like to understand the whole story."

"To start with, I almost killed Don Gava's son, and if I have any regret, it's that I couldn't do it," I began recounting the entire story.

I spoke about how I met Walker, about his work in the United States and how it facilitated things for Don Gava to camouflage the kidnapping network he operated in Latin America.

Matteo listened in complete silence, his eyes not even moving. He was absorbing every word.

"In the end, I discovered that Star doesn't remember anything before the captivity. I don't know if it was trauma that triggered the memory loss or if she shut down due to the kidnapping and imprisonment situation." I clenched my teeth, unable to suppress the hatred that coursed through my veins every time I remembered the moment I found her. "But the fact is she doesn't remember anything and doesn't like to be touched."

"Valentina noticed that right away," he informed with a tone of sorrow in his voice. "Ghost, as you might imagine, our business here isn't legal. We have the entire population of the city in our hands and the police under the other. The *famiglia* Vitale is old, one of the most respected Italian mafias due to our influence and the number of allies. We also produce the best wine in the state, and it's through that, well, you know. — I nodded, imagining he was talking about money laundering. — We take pride in the empire we've built and manage, and like the other *famiglias* throughout the state, we protect our population and provide a dignified and honorable quality of life for our own. We work with respect, loyalty, and justice. And obviously, our families always come first. However, the *famiglia* Marino challenges every one of our ideals and beliefs. They terrorize the population and engage in human trafficking, which we abhor. We don't believe that human beings are something to be traded.

"I imagine this is one of the reasons my brother holds you in such high regard." I straightened my posture.

"Yes, it was one of the first things he discovered about me when we met. Apparently, we both abhor the same practice. And what Don Gava operates in that place is... disgusting," he continued seriously. "But the bastard has created an impenetrable fortress. Just as we control the police here, he controls them there, just as he controls the population. But here in Sicily, people follow us out of respect and admiration. They know we're here to protect them, while Gava controls everyone through fear." He rubbed his eyes, as if he were replaying a movie that ended in an irreparably horrible way. "Several *famiglias* have tried to dethrone him, but have not succeeded, and to make matters worse, he receives shipments via the sea, through some underground entrance. I regret to inform you that we are tied up regarding him for any retaliation. We have no access to that place, but I sincerely hope for the day I can put a bullet in that bastard Gava's head myself. It would be good to expand business to Calabria."

"Maybe I can provide that opportunity." I crossed my arms.

"How? We don't know what exists there. We'd be lost if the rumors that there are still ancient tunnels in that region were true. Without knowing exactly where to go, we'd fail before anything."

"What if you had a map of that place's layout?" I observed with some excitement as Don's pupils widened and turned into two intense black dots. He stood up, his body language understanding faster than his brain what I was about to offer.

"You got a map of the place?" he asked almost in a whisper, as if someone could hear us at any moment.

"Yes, I have a map." I leaned toward him and tapped my finger on my temple. "It's all right here. Every damn left and right."

"You're serious?"

"An irrefutable truth. I've been there myself and saw the exit to the sea."

He began to pace back and forth in the room, leaving me dizzy.

"Dios mio! This could change everything."

"I'd like to join you. We can leave tomorrow and bring that place down. I can try to get bombs and everything you need, and..."

"Ghost..." he interrupted me, moving closer. "I know the reasons you think you need to be there. I, more than anyone, truly understand what you're feeling." He placed his hand on my shoulder and thought for a moment. "But there's too much at stake for you to get involved. Even though you're an excellent shot and, according to your brother, deadly silent, you're not in a condition for such an adventure. And from what you told me, after almost killing Gava's son, they must have reinforced all the entrances; it'll be a job that requires months of patience. We have to wait a while to strike."

I reflected on those words for a moment and squinted, exasperated when I realized he was right.

"This isn't your job either. You're trained to protect; leave the rest to us. There's honor in taking down a rival *famiglia* Don, and I've long awaited the pleasure of that honor." His voice sounded cold and controlled. "If you give me the map, I'll meet with my *consiglieri* and the underboss, and together we'll devise a plan. I swear on my name that I will do everything in my power to make Don Gava and his son pay for all they've done, but you really need to get on a plane and disappear from here."

"You're right. That fortress likely has double the men protecting it now, and I wouldn't be much use injured, anyway." I took a deep breath, trying to control the feeling of indignation. "But you have to promise me you'll call as soon as you manage to infiltrate that place. We can't allow him to remain unpunished."

"And we won't. Now, rest and recover. Come see me later to talk about that map." He leaned in and shook my hand. "You have no idea of the perspective you've brought to my entire family. It seems I'll be indebted to the Holder family."

"That's already enough for everything you've done for us. Including the clothes." I pointed to the beige shorts I was wearing, made of a comfortable fabric, and the white V-neck shirt that left part of my bandage exposed.

"I hope you recover quickly to try our wine. It's our flagship product," he shared, animated. "The winery was initially just a means to camouflage our business on the coast, but as everything the Vitale family touches tends to prosper, my great-grandfather managed to produce an exceptional quality of wine that's distributed in many places. But we don't expand beyond what's necessary; as you can imagine, we're not looking for unwanted attention."

"A refreshing drink would do me good right now."

"You want to die, don't you?" Manuela appeared in the doorway with a scathing look on her face, and both Don Matteo and I burst out laughing.

"Don't worry, Manuela, the only risk I plan to take now is finding Star," I said, getting up.

"I'll ask Sonia to accompany you. See you soon, Ghost." Don Matteo left right after, and from the agitated expression on his face, he would likely be up all night.

I CALLED MY BROTHERS as soon as the Don left the room, and I had to pull the phone away from my ear when a very furious version of Snake answered.

"Were you going to break your damn hand sending a message? Every time I tried to contact you, I got the same information: that you'd call me as soon as you could. The only thing I don't understand so far is why you chose to leave your family going crazy in American soil." I let him curse for a long ten minutes before I decided to speak.

"I apologize, brother. I've been slacking in our communication, I admit, but I have a good excuse this time." I could only hear his heavy breathing on the other side of the line. "I got shot."

"WHAT? How the hell did that happen? Are you okay? Ghost, don't lie to me. I'll rip your balls off if you're hiding a word from me, and..."

"Don't act like a Neanderthal, brother; it wasn't that serious," I lied to avoid worrying him and couldn't help but smile at the thirty different curses he let loose. I missed him deeply. "Seriously, don't worry. It was a bullet in my shoulder that knocked me out for a few days, but I'm fine."

"Are you sure about that? Did you receive all necessary treatments? How are you feeling? Does it hurt a lot? Are you eating?" he fired off without pausing for breath.

"Don't worry so much; I'm in perfect condition. Don Matteo is taking care of everything, and I'll be home soon." He grumbled, still unsatisfied. "How are things over there? And our father?"

"I can assure you everything is in perfect disorder right now."

"Disorder?"

"I have some shocking news." I pressed my lips together, a mix of curiosity and concern.

"Spill it, man. Or do you want to be responsible for worsening my health? I'm going to die of curiosity." He exhaled impatiently, but pressed on.

"With the help of the CIA and FBI, we managed to locate the girls who were to be transported to Calabria on an unregistered ship over the weekend." I gasped and nearly choked on that information. "Because of you, the entire country is in a frenzy. They were found in a warehouse belonging to one of Scott's various mansions. A sweep was done in every property, even the lab. They found two more girls there; one of them was in the warehouse belonging to the lab, unfortunately already lifeless." I swallowed hard.

"That bastard, cowardly son of a bitch!" I clenched my jaw and balled my hand into a fist with such force that the knuckles turned white.

Another woman had been a victim of that monster, and just the thought that he could have ended Star's life sank me into a dark and painfully unbearable pit.

"He managed to destroy many innocent lives," Snake said sadly. "But thanks to you, all this farce he created—the biotech company and everything else—absolutely everything came crashing down. That's why the country is chaotic. Several of the survivors recognized his face, and more... some photos of him with some of those girls were found in his house. He's now being hunted by Interpol, and all the fans he had have turned against him. He won't be able to return to the country."

"I'm glad to hear that." In truth, nothing would make me happier than knowing he was dead, but being unmasked was already the beginning of a long road. "I'm going to prepare for us to return. I need you to get a new passport for me, since mine was left at that bastard's mansion along with my bag. We'll also need documents for Star..."

"Star? So she's regained her memory?"

"Unfortunately not, but the girl needed a name, right?"

"So..." He paused for a moment, probably connecting the dots. "You gave her a name?"

"Yes. Basically, 'Star' was made for her."

"What's going on, brother?" That question carried the weight of ten more.

"I'm taking care of her, just like our father took care of us one day. Star is my responsibility, that's all," I lied shamelessly. And I could swear that if Snake were in front of me, he would have thrown the first thing he saw in my direction. I was never a good liar.

"If that's what you say... then I need a photo of her and also a last name to arrange a fake document. What should I put?"

"Put Holder. Star Holder." My tongue burned as much as my heart.

"You shameless bastard," he huffed on the other end. "Send me a photo of her face. I can have them sent in two days, and give me your word that you'll return to the United States the moment you receive those documents."

"You have my word, brother. Talk to you later."

"Ghost," he called once more. "Be proud. You saved those women's lives, including Star's. They'll return home safely."

AFTER THE LONG CONVERSATION with my lovely brother of supposedly questionable morals, and all the inquiries he made, I felt infinitely more tired. It was as if I were about to explode from exhaustion. I should probably find a room and lie down, but I knew it would be impossible to rest before seeing Star. After laying eyes on her, I would likely slip into a deep coma, but I was determined to wait a little longer.

"Sonia will arrive any moment to take you to Miss Star," Manuela informed me, handing me some pill packets and a sheet of paper. "Take them as prescribed. Don't delay for a single minute, do you hear me?" I nodded, smiling at her authoritative and worried tone, which reminded me of a mother—at least I imagined it would, since I'd never had a mother to know for sure.

Soon, a young blonde woman with an upright posture walked through the door wearing a blue dress with straight cuts as a uniform, and I soon realized this must be Sonia.

"Good morning, miss! You must be Sonia," I said in Italian, standing up.

"That's me," she smiled shyly, clasping her hands in front of her uniform. "And you don't need to use that language, sir. Miss Valentina instructed everyone to speak in English while you're here, since Miss Star doesn't speak Italian."

I still hadn't met the Don's wife, at least not consciously, but I already felt great admiration for the woman and was grateful for her care for Star.

"That's fine," I agreed and followed her out.

The entire Don Matteo mansion seemed like a well-preserved piece of Victorian art. The stone and wood walls depicted a long and resilient history, as did the retro furniture, old yet impeccably maintained. The doors had rounded, bulging frames, and everything sparkled, illuminated by large crystal chandeliers that adorned each room. It was comfortable and luxurious, like a cinematic house.

"Tell me, Sonia..." I questioned when we reached the hall and paused in front of a grand staircase. She turned to me, attentive. "Is it true that Star is okay? I feel like everyone is downplaying the situation to keep me calm. I don't like that; I prefer to deal with the truth. Facts are usually less frightening." I didn't know why I had said that, but when I realized it, I was already voicing the anxiety that had been nagging at my chest since the Don's visit. I feared they were hiding something from me for some reason.

"It's true, sir," she replied, her radiance soothing the desperation in my chest as I saw her smile. "Miss Star fainted from exhaustion, poor thing. We woke her briefly to help her eat, and she did, even though she was almost unconscious, then she went back to sleep. She seems more rejuvenated now than when she arrived, and we're happy she managed to rest a bit, though fainting isn't ideal; in the end, it turned out fine. Don't worry," she said quickly, with refreshing excitement. "I'll take you to her room."

"That would be extraordinary."

"She'll be thrilled to see you awake."

We climbed the stairs, which drained a good portion of the energy I had left, and I was extremely happy when we finally stopped walking.

"It's right here, sir." She smiled brightly and pointed to a wooden door.

"Thank you." I was about to turn to knock when Sonia called me again.

"Sir, sorry to say this, but I feel relieved that you woke up, and I hope you continue to care for Miss Star." She twisted the fabric of her dress nervously. "She was... quite hurt. It's comforting to know she has you by her side. Only a woman can understand the loneliness of being one of us in a world that doesn't see us and only hurts us." Her dark green eyes widened as if she understood very well what she was talking about.

"No woman should go through any of that, and thank you for the care you've given her," I said sincerely, watching her smile and dismiss the thanks with a wave of her hand. "And don't worry; taking care of her is my greatest pleasure."

"In that case, feel free. I'll be back soon; I'll bring your things and a strong coffee. I'm sure Miss Star's appetite will be renewed in a few minutes." She almost skipped out, smiling, without giving me time to thank her again.

I looked at the door and took a deep breath, uncertain why I was feeling anxious. I had spent the last few days next to Star; why the hell would I be nervous to see her now, after longing for that moment so much?

I placed my hand on my chest, worried about the frantic pounding of my heart.

"Come on, are you a man or a mouse?"

A mouse! A silent, cowardly little mouse, that's what. I closed my eyes and opened them again, realizing my fingers were trembling.

Whatever that sudden electric jolt was, it worsened a thousand times when I knocked on the door and a melodious, soft voice answered me.

"You can come in..." she said. I didn't remember when I had said the same, but at some point, I allowed Star to enter my heart, and it was thinking of that that I took the risk and opened the door, desperate to see her.

Star

I WOKE UP FEELING CONFUSED. The room was dark, except for a bright beam of light escaping from the balcony through a gap in the long white curtain that flowed down like cascading waves to touch the floor. I forced my arms to move and ended up sitting up.

How did I get here?

The question echoed in my subconscious, and a certain fear took hold of me. I rifled through my memories looking for something, but all I found were strange scenes, incoherent words, faceless people. I had felt this way before, when I woke up in that dungeon, and I shrank back as I realized how lost I felt again.

Even though this place was completely different and I was now safe, none of the comfort and soft, warm blankets could take away the feeling in my chest that something was out of place.

I clutched the sheets between my fingers, wishing with all my heart that Ghost was there so I could intertwine my fingers with his. I closed my eyes when a wild longing to hear his firm yet gentle voice overcame me, and I realized I didn't know what I would do when the time came for us to part. And I couldn't fool myself.

"That moment is going to come one way or another, isn't it?" I said softly to myself, and the sadness in my voice frightened me.

The realization made me wake up completely. I couldn't allow myself to think about the future when the present was still so uncertain. Before anything else, he needed to wake up, and I wanted to be by his side when that happened.

I got up, forcing each step that felt slower than usual. I chose one of the pieces of clothing Valentina had lent me with such generosity and selected a long white dress with long, frilly sleeves. It had a subtle but well-defined neckline. The very lightweight and extremely expensive-looking fabric was very comfortable, and I made a mental note to thank her a few more times for such kindness.

I took a quick shower to fully wake up and got dressed. Valentina had also left some hygiene items in the bathroom, including a deliciously scented perfume, slightly sweet.

I had no real reason to go around smelling like a perfume that seemed as exclusive as the fine clothes she had lent me, but for some reason, thinking of Ghost and the moment he would wake up made me want to wear it. What if he liked it? At least I had liked it; in fact, I loved that perfume with all my heart.

I sprayed a little of the liquid on my neck and turned to the mirror. The image reflected back was less haggard than the one I had known in hiding; I had grown accustomed to the fact that the woman in the mirror was me, as if my reflection were a piece of the enormous puzzle that existed in my mind.

The bruises on my face had almost completely disappeared over the last few days, but some still stood out on my legs; however, even those had stopped hurting.

I ran my hands through my hair, ready to head down to meet Ghost when the clear memory of talking to Valentina struck me. We were talking about Zion when I... fainted? Was that how I ended up here?

I returned to the room, thoughtful, and flung open the curtains before leaving, allowing the wind to enter the space. I was impressed when I noticed, for the first time, the lush landscape outside the mansion.

From the second floor, I could see the entire expanse of the property and a bit beyond. In the distance, after a small hill and much of the coastline, a large number of little houses clustered together, tightly packed side by side. Some were as white as Manuela's lab coat, others were colored like a rainbow, harmonizing with the turquoise-blue sea that washed the coast.

On the opposite side, there was a massive plantation. The olive-green leaves stretched as far as the eye could see, and I could see many people working among them. I leaned against the balcony, trying to absorb as much of the view as possible before heading down.

Knock Knock Knock.

Someone knocked on the door, and I could have sworn it was Sonia or Giorgia, probably checking to see if I was still alive.

"Come in!" I said over my shoulder and returned to observing the landscape, which was so lush that it brought a sense of peace to my troubled heart.

The door behind me opened, and I was surprised when I didn't hear the quick, familiar footsteps of the two women entering the room. I turned to the visitors to greet them, but all I could do was open my mouth and widen my eyes, with the sound of a pathetically choked "Hello" stuck in my throat the moment I realized it wasn't Sonia, nor Giorgia.

Holy God, it was *him*!

I leaned my hand against the balcony railing, unable to maintain my own balance. My eyes moved faster than my mind could comprehend, and I began to scour every inch of the man. From his impeccably styled hair back, to the clean-shaven face that revealed his composed and perfect expression, finally stopping at his eyes.

I stared at him from top to bottom, unable to believe he was really there. I didn't even blink, fearing he might disappear at any moment.

"My Star," he called softly and somewhat choked, his eyes glued to mine. An immense joy flooded my chest and made my eyes burn.

My God, he was really there. He woke up!

I took a step toward him, captivated by his eyes as if I were hypnotized, and there was nothing in the world I wanted more than to touch him and confirm that this was real, that he had indeed survived.

"Zion..." A tear rolled stubbornly down my face, and in a rush, I ran, desperate to calm my heart in the rhythm of his.

I didn't know how much I needed to touch him, how much I needed to feel his warm skin against mine, until I entered his embrace like a hurricane and pressed my lips against his.

All I needed was to kiss him; everything else could wait.

CHAPTER EIGHTEEN

Ghost

"Come in!" she said.

And I stepped inside...

I crossed the threshold of the door and took a moment to realize I was holding my breath. The rapid, frantic beats made my heart leap in my chest, and I was sure I would collapse right there the instant I set foot in that room. Nothing had prepared me for the image that awaited me inside.

A woman stood on the balcony. She gazed out at the landscape, seemingly unaware of my presence, but a brief second later, she looked over her shoulder and found me, as still as a statue in the middle of the room, completely frozen in the face of such beauty. Star faced me. Her long hair fell like a veil over her shoulders, cascading around her round breasts, accentuated by the white dress that masterfully outlined each of her curves. Curves I hadn't even known existed.

Her exotic eyes were wide, and the sunlight made them appear even larger, oscillating between gold and warm copper with subtle hints of cinnamon. Her full, plump lips were rosy, just like her cheeks, lightly tinted with a charming ochre hue. It was the vision of an angel.

Holy God, did I die in that operating room? No, God would have spared me all of Snake's curses.

I gasped, unable to move. The sight of Star in those loose black clothes was already extraordinary and impossible to ignore, but now she was dazzling, and my heart, which had been faltering for days, succumbed completely.

"My Star!" I whispered, weak in front of her, excited to my bones with just a distant glimpse.

Damn it, I hadn't even touched her and was already crazy with desire. How would I control myself? It was getting harder by the minute.

"Zion..." her voice came low and trembling as she took a hesitant step toward me, then began to run.

Her dark hair flew in all directions, framing her delicate, fine face. Star was a beauty, a magical being, like those that inhabit the forests in fairy tales.

She crossed the room in a few strides, and I opened my arms to receive her, eager. Her body collided with mine, almost knocking us off balance, and then, to my complete shock, she stood on her tiptoes and kissed me, as suddenly as I had when I was shot.

Her lips touched mine with urgency, and her breath danced on my face like a caress. I inhaled, dazed, and was flooded by her scent. Vanilla, almonds, and honey. A perfect, delicate combination, as sweet as Star.

I couldn't resist!

I wrapped one arm around her waist and pulled her against me, ignoring the sharp pain in my shoulder. Everything I wanted, everything I needed was right there in my arms. I opened her mouth with my tongue, invading it in a kiss that shattered my very foundations. It was quick, urgent, as if we both wanted to prove it was real, my God, that it had to be... *it could only be.*

I slid my hand to the back of her neck, wanting to keep her even closer. Star let out a soft moan and mimicked the gesture, sliding her fingers through my hair, and everything around us faded away.

It was as if nothing existed beyond us and the frantic beats of our hearts, the curve of her round breasts against my chest, rising and falling, the brush of her skin on mine, the trembling sigh she let escape. Nothing was more important than that kiss and all the thousands of sensations that exploded before my eyes.

"And then she said... Oh!" Sonia's voice echoed behind us like a damn kick from fate.

Star startled and jumped in place, as always. I almost smiled at seeing that reaction so familiar to me, but even that couldn't quell the fury and complete loss of control in our breaths. Perhaps that interruption wasn't so damned after all. I hadn't felt so out of control in years, as if I were kissing someone for the first time.

"I'm sorry, Miss Star!" Another woman, a young one with dark hair and slightly shorter than Sonia, exclaimed, startled. "What an inconvenient moment."

She held a loaded breakfast tray, while the other clung to a black square suitcase. Both were as red as a bell pepper.

"N-no... it's..." Star stammered behind me, her trembling hands gripping the edge of my shirt, and I felt an absurd need to touch her, as if I could protect her from any exposure, so I turned to the two of them.

"I don't know you, miss." I pointed to the stranger, trying to change the subject.

"I'm Giorgia, sir, it's a pleasure." The young woman blushed and looked away.

"The pleasure is mine, Giorgia." I turned to Sonia and pointed to the juice. "I assume this is breakfast." I tried to smile, but feared Matteo's khaki shorts were revealing more than I'd like about the immense pleasure still coursing through my veins.

"That's right!" she replied brightly, glancing between Star and me. "We brought your things in that suitcase, where Don Matteo organized your... personal items." She raised her perfectly shaped eyebrows, and I could only assume that all the weapons I had brought with me were inside. "This coffee was recommended by Manuela to help you recover. Are you alright?" She suddenly scrunched her nose as Giorgia set the tray on a small square table in the corner of the room.

Star appeared before me like a mirage, staring at me with those huge, beautiful eyes as soon as she noticed the worried tone in Sonia's question. Her cheeks were marked with a graceful crimson hue, and I couldn't contain my own movements. I lifted my hand and caressed her face with the back of my fingers. She frowned.

"Zion, you're pale!" Star said, worried, joining her hand with mine and holding it against her face.

"What?" I tried to keep the smile, but I felt dizzy and stumbled across the room until I sat on the bed.

I felt a strange tingling rising up my arms, concentrating at the point of pain where I had been shot. I closed my eyes for a moment, and when I opened them again, the three women were almost on top of me, all very attentive to my every movement.

What a humiliation!

"I think I still need to rest," I whispered, a sharp pain in my head forcing me to close my eyes again, and soon I felt Star's delicate fingers searching for mine.

"What are you feeling?"

"I'll let Manuela know he doesn't feel well; she was going to come check on him anyway."

"There's no need to worry." I tried to maintain my calm. "I believe a little rest will make me as good as new."

"Sir, Don arranged some clothes for you, and we've already brought them to your room. They're in the closet next to Miss Star's," someone whispered.

"Your room? You mean this will also be my room?" I inquired, opening my eyes slightly.

"Well... Miss Star told me you two would be together," Sonia stammered.

"You said that?" I looked at Star, who suddenly turned as red as a bell pepper.

"Isn't that what we've been doing since we met? I don't know if I can sleep away from you," she whispered the last part just for me to hear, and I was overwhelmed by a wave of affection that made me even dizzier.

"If that's what you want, then here is where I'll stay." I closed her hand between mine, sleep beginning to lull my thoughts, making them increasingly blurry.

"No sleeping yet." She pulled away from me and reached for the breakfast tray. "You need to eat something first."

"And you too," I retorted. "You don't need to take care of me, Star; you need to rest as well."

"Don't ask me for something I can't do, Zion." She lifted her face, determined.

"They're so cute... Ouch!" Giorgia hissed, receiving an elbow from Sonia. I had almost forgotten they were still there.

"Rest, sir. Manuela will be here soon to see you." Sonia warned and dragged Giorgia out of the room, closing the door behind them. I reached for Star's hand at that moment. Touching her somehow renewed my energy, as if she were my own sun.

"I heard you fainted because of me." She was already lifting a piece of apple, about to shove it into my mouth, whether I wanted it or not. "I can't express how devastating it is for me... to know I caused you even more suffering. I wish I could have prevented it."

"Don't worry about that; I have a stockpile of energy saved up," I joked, which didn't alleviate the pain I felt at all. "You took care of me, now let me do the same, okay?" I opened my mouth to protest, and she took the opportunity to shove the apple in. "Eat a bit before you keep listing the reasons I shouldn't be by your side. But know it's pointless; I wouldn't do it any other way."

Those words flooded my heart with exultant happiness. I had always been busy taking care of others, and there had never been anyone who needed to take care of me, except for my father. It was an extraordinary feeling to know that she cared that much.

I lay down on the bed after we both finished half the breakfast; I was much more tired than I wanted to admit. My eyes could barely stay open, and it drove me crazy. I wanted to keep looking at Star and observe every little piece of her. Everything I had seen, everything I hadn't yet noticed, but exhaustion won out. I leaned back against the soft sheets. Star sat beside me, but I couldn't keep my eyes open for long.

"Are you really okay, little one? You didn't get hurt while I was resting, did you?" I whispered, holding her hand between mine.

"'Resting' is a peculiar word to describe what happened these past few days, don't you think?" I felt her smile through her voice and smiled back. "But yes, I'm fine. Everyone here is very caring."

"It's good to know I won't have to kill anyone." She laughed, and that delicious sound entered my ears like a sacred chant.

I savored the memory of her laughter, and soon after, we fell into a deep and very comfortable silence, and if I stayed quiet, I would surely end up falling asleep, but there was something I wanted to say before that.

"We need to talk about what happened here..." I brought her hand to my mouth and placed a slow kiss on her soft skin, not knowing if she was listening or not. I couldn't simply pretend that kiss hadn't happened. Maybe I'd even dream of it as soon as I fell asleep.

"We have time," she interrupted, with that sweet, worried voice. "Now you need to rest, please, sleep a little. You need to get better soon."

That last sentence sounded like a prayer, a request so soft I almost didn't hear it, but there was so much concern in those words that a burning discomfort rose in my throat.

She was still afraid of losing me. The only person close to her, the only one she trusted.

"Don't worry, little one." I used all the remaining strength I had to pull her into a hug, taking her into my arms. Her small, delicate body soon fit against mine. "I'm not going anywhere, not without you." I touched her face, lowered my eyes to her luscious mouth, and let out a sigh, heavy with longing.

"What is it?" she asked, worried.

"If you only knew what your mouth does to mine..." I was entranced by those soft, well-defined contours.

"Can you show me?" she asked, innocent, and I almost groaned in desperation, unable to control myself.

I leaned in and placed another gentle kiss on those thick, delicious lips. She opened for me, and I slowly penetrated with my tongue, savoring every flavor and nuance of her reactions, which ranged from desire to surprise, from restlessness to tension. She seemed to crave that contact as much as I did, and I cursed the extreme fatigue that forced me to stop that kiss.

I lay down beside her and slept, or fainted, with her scent tattooed in my mind.

CHAPTER NINETEEN

Star

Ghost spent the entire day drowsy and only woke up when the meals were served in the room. Seeing him so downcast was agonizing, but I was so grateful he had woken up, grateful he was there beside me, that I could only feel gratitude and an intense heat rising up my legs every time I thought of the kisses we shared.

We need to talk about what happened here...

The phrase echoed in my subconscious. Just the memory made me shudder, and what scared me most was how much I wanted to repeat it. The feel of his strong mouth against mine, his tongue parting my lips, our breaths meeting in a delicious ebb and flow.

I hadn't known kissing could be so intense, overwhelming, feverish. As if he could take my soul and make me crumble, as if our world were reduced to that precious touch of his lips on mine.

I felt warm all over and had no idea where I would hide my face when he wanted to talk about it. I couldn't lie and say it was no big deal when my whole body screamed the opposite.

I tried not to think about what came next. I needed to enjoy the now, beside Zion. He was sleeping once again, with a calm expression and looking healthier. I soon realized that staying there, watching his broad chest rise and fall with each breath had become my favorite activity, but my eyes began to grow heavier as the minutes passed. Now that I knew he was okay, it was harder to maintain the energy that had kept me awake for so many hours.

I ended up falling asleep, and when I woke up later, the rascal with the light feet was no longer by my side, but there was a note on his pillow.

"Little one, I went to meet with the Don, I'll be back soon. I asked for dinner to be served in the room."

I ran my fingers over the word *Zion,* which was highlighted in cursive in the corner of the paper.

"He wasn't supposed to be wandering around," I grumbled, pushing the covers aside with my feet.

Why the hell was he so stubborn? The only thing he needed to do was the one thing he seemed incapable of fulfilling: stay still, resting.

My heart leaped into my throat when I heard the doorknob to the bathroom turn, and I almost choked when Ghost appeared before me with a towel wrapped around his waist and another in his hands, using one to rub his hair, as wet as his bare chest.

I noticed he held a small package of gauze in his free hand, and my eyes fixated on the bandage on his shoulder. It looked small against the size of his torso and the muscular folds leading down his abdomen, which, even from a distance, appeared rigid. A longing washed over my fingertips, and I imagined what it would be like to touch them. I swallowed hard, a pathetic attempt to control that urge, and returned my gaze to his eyes, which were, by the way, wide open.

"You woke up!" He quickly lowered the towel drying his hair to his chest, covering part of the visible scars in that area.

There weren't many; most were on his back, but he seemed bothered by any of them being exposed. I bit my lips as my thoughts wandered back to a few days ago when I had seen those marks.

Ah, if only he knew... if he only had an inkling of how much I admired him for them. I crossed my arms, exasperated, and when I realized it, I was already staring at his chest again.

"I was changing the bandage," he explained when my eyes fixed on the gauze package in his hands. "I figured you would sleep for a few more hours," he said somewhat confused, pointing at the piece of paper I still held between my fingers. "I'll just grab this and..." He awkwardly slipped across the room and grabbed a pile of clothes from a chair in the corner, abandoning the gauze shortly after. "Give me a minute." He held the clothes in his hand and walked backward into the bathroom to avoid me seeing them.

My shoulders slumped forward as soon as he closed the door, and I let out a breath, realizing I had been holding my breath until then.

I bit my lips, feeling bad for having seen what he was trying so hard to hide. Ghost had been unconscious when they tore his shirt in front of me; there was no way he could know I was right there by his side, but I had already seen.

I had already *felt* those scars. There was no way to stand before them and not feel in my skin what each of those marks represented. How much he *suffered*.

I stayed there lost in thought until the bathroom door opened, and he appeared before me once again, now wearing a plain black tank top and matching pants that contrasted with his ivory-white skin. His hair was tousled on his forehead, and he looked like he had stepped out of a dream. Gorgeous. God help me, but for a moment I thought about jumping on him.

"Are you sure you can be out there walking around?" I forced myself to say something, and he smiled, going to the window and pulling the curtains aside, revealing a bright, starry sky. It was already night, so...

"After almost hibernating all day, I'm refreshed." He approached and touched my nose with his fingertips.

"If you collapse out there, I swear I'll rip one of your legs off," I threatened, narrowing my eyes at him.

I wanted to seem intimidating to lessen the fear I felt that something might actually happen to him. The thought crushed my heart, but all I managed to get from him was a laugh and a kiss on the top of my head.

"Given this threat, I have no choice but to come back in one piece." He caressed my face with his hand and lifted my chin, making me meet those lively, intense brown eyes. "Don't worry, little one. Before you know it, I'll be back. I won't strain myself; it's just a brief meeting on this same floor. Wait for me for dinner."

I tried to cling to the hope that he was feeling more capable when he walked out the door. I couldn't tie him to the bed anyway, even if I wanted to, and I took advantage of his absence to take a long shower.

I even thought about trying to fill the bathtub, but I had no idea how to do that, and washing my hair in the shower was much easier, so I decided on the option that wouldn't risk flooding the room.

I wrapped my hair in a towel when I finished my shower and put on a red top adorned with tiny flowers, which hit just above my navel, leaving my shoulders exposed, and a flared white skirt. The outfit matched my skin tone, and I was pleased to see the reflection in the mirror. I spritzed on some perfume that Valentina had lent me, and when I stepped out of the bathroom, Giorgia and Sonia were distractedly setting up a table on the balcony.

"Good evening, Miss Star," Giorgia greeted. "Mr. Ghost asked us to set up dinner here. Are we interrupting?"

"Not at all, please don't mind my presence; you can continue. I'll just comb my hair in the meantime." I grabbed the brush from the bathroom and sat in a chair positioned in front of an oval mirror, starting to detangle my hair down to the ends.

"Don't you prefer to dry it? There's a hairdryer in the bathroom." Sonia approached with a furrow between her brows, and I felt my face flush at the memory of Ghost behind me, sliding his fingers through my hair with a delirious attention while drying it. I swallowed hard, realizing how precious that gesture was. How he always made an effort to take care of me.

"I don't know how to use a hairdryer," I admitted. "So I'll just comb it."

"Nonsense, I'll dry it for you." I opened my mouth, about to refuse; I didn't like to burden them more than they already had because of my presence, but she had already dashed into the bathroom and soon returned with the black hairdryer in her hands and another wider brush. "I'll be careful drying it."

"Thank you." I smiled at her as she looked at me contentedly through our reflections in the mirror.

Sonia turned on the device and began drying my hair with smooth, slow, and continuous movements, and we barely heard the soft knock that echoed through the room moments before Ghost opened the door and walked through it.

"Mr. Ghost," Sonia and Giorgia greeted him, and I watched as that tall, slender man with an elegant posture approached and stopped beside Sonia.

"May I?" he asked, extending his hand for the hairdryer. "I have some experience with this." Sonia handed it over as if it had suddenly caught fire in her hands and joined Giorgia, who was watching the whole scene from the corner of the room with her mouth agape, dragging her friend out while murmuring something about serving dinner soon.

I gasped as he ran his fingers through my hair, and our eyes met in the reflection. Something crackled in the depths of his eyes, sensual, burning, and even a bit daring. Something that made my stomach flutter.

"You came back quickly." He combed my hair calmly, and his attention behind me left me a bit dizzy.

"I feared I might lose a limb if I took too long." He opened a painfully perfect smile and turned on the hairdryer.

I spent the next few minutes admiring the man who was drying my hair with such care and excessive affection. The touch felt so good that I had to fight to keep my eyes open.

"You're getting better at the art of drying hair. This is the second time you've done it, but you seem very experienced. Are you sure you've never dried hair before?" I questioned, noticing how skilled he was, holding the hairdryer with one hand while the other kept the brush gliding through my hair at a steady rhythm.

"You were my first guinea pig. I think I was born with a gift," he admitted with a smile, and a strange relief filled my chest.

"How do you manage not to pull out half my hair in the process?"

"I'm afraid of hurting you in any way. So it's easy to handle any object near you; there's not much secret to it." He tried to sound simple.

My hair gained volume and shape as he dried it until there was no moisture left. Zion turned off the hairdryer when he saw that my hair was completely dry, set it aside, and placed his hands on the arms of my chair, surrounding me on both sides. He leaned forward until his face was side by side with mine; our eyes met in the reflection, and he leaned in until his mouth was close to my ear.

"What do you think?" His husky voice danced on my skin, sending a shiver down my spine.

"I-it's perfect." I blinked slowly.

Zion slid his firm fingers along my exposed collarbone, brushing the strands of hair away, and lowered his lips to place a tender, lingering kiss at the base of my neck.

"You're perfect," he whispered, and my stomach twisted, as if a thousand damned butterflies had started a rebellion.

His eyes were once again locked onto mine, and not even Sonia and Giorgia passing by as they set up dinner could tear him away.

The women were quick and quiet; when I realized it, they had already left the room once more.

"Can I take a picture of you?" he suddenly asked.

"A picture?"

"Yes, for some documents I need to prepare for you." I nodded, and he pulled out his phone. I was unsure what I should do, so I just stared at the camera, feeling a bit awkward. "Done, it looks perfect." He smiled and glanced at the photo. "Shall we?" He nodded toward a two-person table carefully set up on the balcony and extended his hand to help me stand.

The help was welcome since my legs suddenly felt like jelly. I fitted my hand into his, as we used to, and he didn't let go, even when I stood up, guiding me to the balcony. I sat down next to him and, for the first time, admired the scenery of that place at night.

The sea lapped gently at the shore, creating a soothing sound that echoed through the night. The starry sky was filled with bright points reflecting on the waves and fading into the vastness of the horizon.

A pure gratitude filled my chest. Ghost had survived, and I had become a free woman. That night was precious and meant a lot to me. For the first time, I could sleep without many worries.

He picked up a glass pitcher with a narrow spout, filled with a purplish liquid.

"What is this?"

"I wish it were wine, since Don Matteo's vineyard is quite renowned, but given my bad luck, I won't be able to drink for the next few days, so they didn't even risk it and just sent us grape juice." He assumed a dramatic and disappointed expression and poured me a glass. I took the pitcher from his hand before he could serve himself.

"Let me do this," I wanted to return the gesture and poured the drink into his glass. A strange sensation hit me, and I narrowed my eyes, bewildered.

"What's wrong?" He leaned in my direction, concerned, and took the pitcher from my hands.

"I don't know." I was still fixated on his glass, lost in thought. "I felt something strange when I poured the juice. It felt very familiar."

"It could be," he added. "Maybe you remembered something?"

"I don't think that's it. Nothing came to mind." I shook my head. "What's on the table?" I pointed at the cluttered items, changing the subject. He blinked, still watching me carefully. "I'm serious, I'm fine."

"If you feel something like that again, I want you to tell me." I nodded in agreement.

Ghost leaned over to reach the lid of one of the stacked silver trays on the table, and I gasped as the delicious, homey aroma spread through the air.

We were treated to Spaghetti Bolognese that made my stomach rumble loudly as I watched Ghost serve an astronomically large plate. He must have been really hungry, and how could I blame him? I felt a crater forming in the pit of my own stomach.

"Spaghetti is a typical dish in Italy; it's definitely the tastiest thing you'll try." He set the plate in front of me, and I raised my eyebrows in confusion.

"I thought this would be your dish. Do you think I inherited the world's hunger?" I laughed.

"I know you hardly ate properly since we got here," he said seriously, staring at a spot where the sauce had dripped onto the table. "Your face looks thinner than before." He looked back at me, concern etched in his voice. "I can't allow this to happen again, so please eat."

"You know..." I stuck the fork into the spaghetti and twirled the pasta into a little ball. "It's not a big deal. It's not like I can't go a few hours without eating; it wouldn't be the first time."

I don't know why I said that; it was obvious I was talking about the countless days I had been forced to go hungry, and I even thought I could joke about the situation, but the moment the words left my mouth, Zion's expression darkened, sending chills down my spine.

"You shouldn't have to suffer any of this," he exclaimed suddenly. His hands gripped the table as if he couldn't control them. He was shaking.

"I'm sorry; I didn't think about what I was saying." I dropped the fork, suddenly anxious at the emptiness in his expression.

"No..." He closed his eyes and pressed them with his fingers for a moment, and when he opened them again, something seemed to have changed. That severe, dangerous look had vanished. He released the table and held my hand between his. "I'm sorry," he whispered and lowered his head.

I waited calmly for him to speak again, and when he did, it sent a painful wave through my heart as I noticed the hurt in his voice.

"I thought I wouldn't make it. There, on the boat. When I saw that bastard aiming at you, I was so afraid I wouldn't be able to protect you. Just imagine what he could do, what you would have to suffer again..." He exhaled, heavily. "For me to completely lose control. I'm so sorry."

"You jumped in front of that maniac for me. You took a bullet that was meant for me, and..."

"That's not enough, Star." He lifted his eyes. "I want to make sure you're safe. I want to find your family and see you smile without fear. I want you to be more than just protected. I wholeheartedly wish for you to be happy, so no. I can't accept, or even imagine you going hungry again, feeling cold, or... for God's sake, having someone touch you again." He started shaking again and clenched his jaw.

Anger and concern mixed in his piercing gaze, and he breathed quickly for several long seconds until he turned to the glass of juice and drank it all at once, without releasing my hand.

"I've never wanted this to be fucking whiskey so much," he cursed. "It's painful to imagine the hell you went through while I was unconscious. It's absurd that you spent sleepless nights, uncomfortable in that ridiculous chair instead of being warm in a soft bed after everything."

"I just want to shake you. You don't understand, do you?" I clenched my fists and tried to control myself to not break down right then and there.

What was happening to me? After so long being strong and holding back my emotions, I was acting like a leaky boat, spilling water everywhere. My throat burned with the effort it took to hold back my tears.

"I saw you get shot. You fainted in my arms. I ran by your side all the way here, and your body was so... limp and cold." I sniffled softly and averted my gaze from his. "I had to wait outside while you were operated on. The Don's wife tried to convince me otherwise; she wanted me to rest, but I couldn't." I lifted my eyes to him, who was watching me intently. "It was there that I realized that not even the best food in the world had flavor. A hot shower wasn't relaxing; the bed wasn't comfortable. There was nothing here for me, not while you were between life and death. By your side, that was my place. The place I chose. I couldn't leave there, no way." The memory of seeing him bloodied flooded me forcefully, and a loud sob rose in my throat, and all the strength I had to not cry crumbled completely. "Don't blame yourself for what happened. It was my choice, and I don't regret it for a second, and..."

Zion suddenly shoved the table aside, making everything on it shake, and pulled me onto his lap, holding me tightly. I buried my face in the curve of his neck. He stroked my hair and murmured a few low words, asking me to calm down in a rough, firm tone that warmed my skin. I breathed slowly, and the relief of his touch filled me, and only then did I realize that it was there, in Ghost's arms, that I found my peace. In his protection, in his silent care.

"You fainted, sweetheart. Fainted from exhaustion because of me. How can I bear this pain?" He sighed into my hair, and I turned my face to look into his eyes.

"If I can sit here with you tonight, enjoying this wonderful dinner, it's because you chose to save a stranger. And I will accept everything that happened afterward as a gift. Look, we're both here, alive and well." My eyes fell to the small white part of the bandage peeking out from under his shirt. "Not so well, are we?" I laughed through my tears, pulling a smile from the man who was now watching me with deep, attentive eyes.

Ah, those eyes... they seemed like windows to his soul. So transparent, vibrant, and definitely made me burn from head to toe.

He trailed his fingers up my neck. There was a palpable sensuality in the air. An intimate, forbidden dance, and I couldn't wait any longer; I pressed my lips against his, eager to feel his mouth on mine, and he welcomed me with a rough groan.

His hands gripped my waist and pulled me closer, and in a moment, I was there before him, crying, but when his tongue met mine, all my thoughts vanished, leaving only that wet, deep touch with a taste of grape. His body grew rigid against me, and I knew what that meant. A tingling joy and anxiety surged in my stomach.

Could it be that a man like him, imposing and terribly handsome, was as shaken as I was? I couldn't imagine a reality where a woman who didn't even remember her own name could seem interesting to someone like Ghost, but when he broke the kiss, panting, and wrapped me in a tight embrace, I began to believe.

"We'd better stop, sweetheart, or..." He looked around as if searching for the words to finish his sentence. He was looking for an excuse. "...dinner will get cold." His trembling voice made me smile, and I returned to my place, my face burning, just like the rest of my body.

✷

WE FINISHED DINNER, and Ghost didn't touch me again, but the sensation that burned my skin told me otherwise, as if his mouth were still on mine.

I raised my eyes and stared at my reflection in the mirror after putting on one of the nightgowns Valentina had lent me, the one that covered my body the most, which didn't mean much since it was like a very short, thin-strapped dress made of soft, cool dark blue fabric that left my breasts very pronounced.

I stepped out of the bathroom, somewhat hunched over, unsure if the piece looked at least nice since I had never worn anything like it. Ghost, who was distracted fiddling with his phone, lifted his gaze from the screen to find me standing in the corner of the room, illuminated only by the lamp beside him.

He swept his eyes over my body as I walked toward him, and a crease appeared between his thick eyebrows. His blunt expression bordered on nervousness and left me confused. I climbed onto the bed, ignoring the persistent fluttering of my heart, and had barely settled down when he suddenly slapped his phone on the bedside table and quickly turned off the lamp.

"Are you okay?" I asked in the dark.

"Everything's great." His voice came out strained. "Goodnight, little one." He leaned in and placed a quick kiss on the top of my forehead and lay down on his back, as the bandage would prevent him from turning away from me.

"Goodnight," I whispered back, and I swear I tried to sleep, but the memory of the kiss we had shared kept me awake.

I couldn't shake the image of Zion shoving the table aside and pulling me into his arms with delicious possession, as if our bodies were meant to touch.

I tossed and turned in bed, but Ghost's breathing thudded loudly in my ears, pressing down on me, and I sank into a wave of growing desire. I didn't know what I wanted; maybe he couldn't tell me either, but the heat rising up my legs made the center of my body pulse, and I couldn't stay silent for long.

"Are you still awake?"

"Unfortunately..." he complained, and I ended up laughing at his sudden bad mood. "What's wrong? Can't you sleep?" He turned to face me again.

"You know..." I started, unsure how to begin. My face burned with embarrassment, but what could I do if everything else was on fire? "I wanted to ask you something."

"Just say it, sweetheart." His voice turned tender and affectionate, and there it was, that nickname that stirred my emotions deeply. "Ask for anything. I'll give you what you want."

"Can you kiss me like you did at dinner?"

"No, have a good night!" He grabbed my shoulders and spun me on the bed until I was facing away from him.

"Hey!" I laughed in a mix of embarrassment and amusement. "What happened to '*Ask for anything*'? I rolled back to face him again.

"That's restricted to everything I can control."

"What do you mean by that?" I raised my eyebrows, confused. He pressed his face close to mine, so close that his uneven breath brushed my lips.

"Kissing you away from this bed is one thing, but if I touch you here, I don't know if I'll be able to stop, sweetheart."

"What if that's exactly what I want? For you to touch me and not stop?"

"You don't know what you're asking." He trailed his thumb down the side of my face, and I closed my eyes.

"Kiss me," I whispered, and he groaned, pressing his face against mine.

He kissed the tip of my nose and rested his forehead against mine, battling an internal struggle, but slowly his heavy body moved closer until he was on top of me, pinning me to the bed beneath him.

"Zion... kiss me, touch me."

"I can't resist your mouth, even if I wanted to, sweetheart." He brushed his lips against mine in a subtle caress and placed a chaste kiss right on the corner before pressing his mouth to mine, pulling me into a passionate kiss.

I ran my hand through his smooth hair at the back of his neck as his tongue parted my lips, demanding entrance, urgent. A low groan echoed from his mouth as he slid his hand around my waist, fitting his body against mine.

I felt dizzy, light, and warm as our tongues danced between kisses, bites, and exciting sounds. I lifted my hips almost instinctively as that kiss spread unbearable heat across my skin, and I found his hard, large erection pressing against my belly.

"Sweetheart, do you understand why kissing you is so dangerous?" He pulled away from the kiss and whispered the words, leaving me desperate for more, staring at my face in the dark.

His strong, skilled fingers trailed down my neck, following a hot path, continuing down and down until they found the curve of my breasts, and in a slow, torturous manner, he wrapped his fingers around one of my nipples, pinching it gently. A jolt of pleasure shot through my body, and I whimpered anxiously, lost in that new sensation.

He kissed my cheek and nibbled at my jaw. His agile hands closed around my breast, which now ached, yearning for more.

"Allow me to touch you, sweetheart. Let me..."

"Yes, yes, I allow it!" I gasped, and he devoured my mouth right after. His kiss invaded me, thirsty and strong.

I closed my eyes and arched my body, unable to contain the moan that escaped my lips when he returned to torture my sensitive nipples with his fingers, rubbing and pinching. He ran his fingers along the straps of my nightgown and slid it down my arm, leaving my breasts completely exposed. The night breeze brushed against my hardened nipples, and I bit my lips, feeling Zion's mouth slide down my neck, leaving kisses and bites all the way to the valley between my breasts.

"You're beautiful, sweetheart." He traced his tongue down the valley and nibbled at the flesh, sending all my cells into a frenzied ecstasy.

"Ahhhhhhh!" I threw my head back and tangled my fingers in the sheets as I felt his tongue play with one of my nipples.

The wet touch was devastating and sent shivers through every part of my body. Zion became my abyss, and I was falling, melting in that obsession, holding onto him to keep from collapsing completely while he suckled me between gasps.

I held the hem of his shirt and began to pull it up, desperate to feel his skin and trace those muscles beneath my fingers, but I noticed the brief moment when his body stiffened at the mention of being shirtless near me.

"I want to feel your skin too." My breath was ragged.

"What if I don't like touching it? It could be scary," he whispered, concerned, but he didn't stop caressing me, which scrambled my thoughts.

"There's nothing about you that can scare me, Zion." His insecurity only made him more human and more lovable. "You're different." I pulled the shirt over his head, tossing it aside and placing my hands flat on his back. "I want to touch you with the same desperation that I wish for you to touch me."

I slid my hands down his back; he kept his body tense, but I didn't give up. I traced my fingers over the scars, caressing the dense, wavy folds that made the surface of his skin uneven. I followed the lines along his sides until I reached the welts on his waist. That was his pain, and I wanted to touch it, as if the tips of my fingers could show him how beautiful they were, how valuable he was.

"You are so much more than these marks." He looked at me in the dark, silent, and I continued to trace his skin, feeling my own burn to the bones.

"Oh, my little one," he relented and let out a moan. He buried his head in the curve of my neck and began to kiss me there. "How do I not devour you right here?" And he took my mouth with hunger and a passion that made me gasp.

His slightly rough fingers traveled up my leg, gliding past my knee until they reached my sensitive thigh, and the center of my body began to throb. Continuous shivers climbed up my abdomen, my belly, my neck, until they reached the point where our mouths met. I opened my legs, and a desperate moan escaped my throat as he brushed his fingertips over my panties.

Oh my, he was going to touch me there... I sucked in air, startled by the throbbing ache that almost screamed for him. His mouth continued to explore every corner, uncovering me while he played with fingers that were separated from my intimacy only by a thin piece of fabric.

"Zion..." I moaned against his mouth.

The heat rose in my cheeks and spread across my skin, and when I realized it, I was grinding against his hand, as if every part of my body depended on that touch.

"Tell me, sweetheart, tell me what you want... what you desire, my angel?"

He rubbed his thumb over a spot that, even beneath the fabric, made me squeeze my legs together, and I found myself wanting to beg for something, not even knowing what.

"This heat," I breathed, disoriented. "I want more."

He slid his hand down my legs and spread it across my backside, squeezing the flesh in a delicious way. I noticed his hand was trembling, perhaps with the effort he was making to control himself.

"You are delicious, sweetheart. Your scent, your voice, your mouth, everything and every little piece of you drives me crazy, especially your eyes." He pulled my panties down slowly. "I want to dive into them as much as I want to dive inside you. It's hell to see you and not touch you." I closed my eyes, trembling.

"Touch me! Please, touch me." I jumped in place when his experienced fingers reached my intimacy, and he began to open me.

"Damn..." he growled, and I moaned, arching my back on the bed as I felt his fingers glide up and down my slit. I felt the moisture soaking everything, but the desire pounded so strongly in every throbbing point of my body that I couldn't feel shame and clung to him even more.

His mouth traveled down my neck; he captured one of my nipples between his lips, making me scream, and slid a finger inside me without ceasing to caress the sensitive spot that was about to drive me insane. I began to breathe heavily. I wanted him to possess me.

"Oh, Zion!" I moaned loudly, gasping.

"Did I hurt you?" He stopped moving, and I almost cried out of desperation.

"Don't stop!" I cursed, and he smiled before kissing me, torturing my breasts with one hand while the other slowly penetrated my core.

I wrapped my legs around his waist, opening myself more for him as he began to kiss me hungrily, frantically. The pressure of his erection between my legs made me even more excited, and I reached down, caressing him through the fabric.

The size beneath his pants was thick, long, and pulsing as if it wanted to break free. A mix of anxiety and curiosity washed over me, and I tried to unbutton his pants, but my perfect angel penetrated me with another finger, soaking everything around, and moved that moisture up to place it on the very sensitive spot that sent desperate shivers through my entire body.

I closed my eyes, barely able to breathe. The feeling that time around me had stopped merged with the strong electric impulse that coursed through my skin, and nothing else mattered.

Not where we were, nor the uncertainties of where we would go. Suddenly, the irrational fear that had been creeping in the shadows of my mind gave way to the sounds of our breaths, to Zion's low moans whispering hot words that left me delirious with desire, and the frantic beats of my heart, pounding in my ears, in the breasts he was sucking, biting, and pinching, until he descended to the center of my body, marking it with his fingers. Now nothing else mattered but what was happening between us.

"Ahhhhhhh, Zion!" A violent tremor hit me, and I was thrown into a completely unknown, burning, and uncontrollable place.

I dug my nails into Zion's back and bit my lips, throwing my head back, completely out of control. I had never felt so free as in that moment, trembling with pleasure in his arms.

"What a delicious sound." Zion kissed my mouth and nibbled my lower lip. "It makes me want to hear it all day long." He pulled his fingers out of me and lay down beside me, pulling me to his chest and kissed me slowly again.

I gasped in his mouth, still trembling. My limbs felt loose and pleasantly heavy. I brought my hand to his member, which seemed even thicker, eager to touch it in the same way, and I shamelessly slipped my hand inside the shorts he was wearing.

"Star..." he groaned, hoarse, as I reached the length of his member and opened my eyes at the revealing touch. It was even bigger than I imagined, cold, long, thick, and full of pulsating veins that made me swallow hard, imagining it inside me.

The insane desire I felt minutes earlier surged back, and I was about to pull his shorts down when he grabbed my hand.

"No, sweetheart. If we start this, I know I'll only finish inside you, and I don't think it should happen like that." The combination of words he used made my brain dizzy with excitement. I could only remember the part where he said "Inside you."

"Why do you say that? Isn't it what you want?" I wanted to shout.

"For God's sake, I would kill for this moment." He laughed into my hair. "In my case, this is proof that I'm crazy for you, my angel." He took my hand and placed it over his hard member, groaning softly as I caressed him, even over the fabric.

"So..."

"You've been through so much, little one. I need to take care of your health and make sure this wouldn't hurt you at all, you understand? It's not that I don't want to, my love; I just can't be irresponsible to that extent. Your safety is my priority."

"What if we don't have a tomorrow? We almost didn't have today, and you know that, you know how small our chances are. You're being too rational, aren't you?"

"Not when it comes to saving someone's life, especially yours. I would do anything, anything at all, to protect you."

"If that's the case, you're not giving me another choice... I'm dying, save me!" I dramatized, placing my hand on my forehead theatrically, which made him burst into a fit of laughter. "This isn't a joke; are you really going to let me die of desire?" My face burned with the spontaneous statement, and he laughed even more. He was enjoying himself, the ordinary.

"This is all the fault of whoever had the insane idea to give you that nightgown." He grabbed a piece of fabric between his fingers as if it were the most absurd thing he had ever seen.

"Didn't you like it?" I bit my lips.

"I liked it so much that I'll be forced to take a cold shower in hopes of forgetting it, at least for now." He touched my face and gave me a slow, affectionate kiss. "I'll be back soon." He kissed my forehead and got up, leaving a large emptiness in the bed beside me and a feeling of loneliness in my heart.

I watched his silhouette disappear into the dark room, lost at the entrance of the bathroom, as quiet as always. He was too proper, my Ghost... A just but silent man, quick and lethal.

And I was hopelessly in love with him.

Zion didn't take long to return, and I could only sleep after snuggling into his arms.

CHAPTER TWENTY

Ghost

The early morning arrived with a fleeting warmth. Star hugged me tightly, her legs draped over me, relaxed.

I never imagined I could show such self-control as I had in the past few hours. Choosing not to have sex with Star was the hardest decision I'd ever made, and I wasn't sure how long I could maintain it. Her warm, small, delicate body seemed to be calling for mine.

I caressed her back and pulled her closer. I buried my nose in her hair and inhaled the sweet scent of her strands that brought me so much peace. I traced my fingers down her face, gently touching every little corner until I reached her lips, which formed a cute pout, astonished by the simple fact that she existed, by the great luck of having found her.

I leaned in and kissed her forehead, savoring that closeness. Until a strange sound near the door caught my attention. I looked at the dark wood, suspicious, and another creak echoed through the wooden floor.

Someone was there!

A cold dread rose in my chest, and I turned to the small table beside the bed, where I had left one of my weapons. I fumbled in the dark but found nothing. My heart began to race, and before I could even think, the door crashed down with a terrifying thud.

"Fuck!" I cursed, and Star woke up screaming, terrified. I jumped out of bed, pulling her with me, but I wasn't quick enough. We were surrounded by hooded men in the blink of an eye, and they charged at us.

I began to fight, hitting, punching, kicking, trying to keep Star safe at all costs, but the more I fought back, the more of them appeared before me until I received a blow to the back of my neck that knocked the wind out of me. I fell like a stone, three of them pinning me against the cold floor.

"Zion!" she cried out in pain, and the air suddenly stopped entering my lungs.

"GET YOUR HANDS OFF HER, YOU FUCKERS!" I thrashed in panic; all my efforts were in vain, they barely moved.

"I want him to see," Scott's voice echoed through the room, and a wretched dread froze my limbs.

No, my God, please don't let him touch her.

"Star!" I howled as I saw her being thrown to the floor, struggling against him. "Let her go, you piece of shit. I'll kill you! I WILL KILL YOU!"

"Isn't he your savior?" He pressed her face against the ground, then tangled his fingers in her long hair and began dragging her away. "That bastard is nothing but a dog that needs to be tamed, just like you."

"ZION! Help me, Zion!" she screamed my name, begging me to save her.

My throat closed up, despair radiated through my veins. I knew what he was going to do; I knew that if they took her away, I would never see her again. I fought with everything I had to free myself, but the more I struggled, the less I could move. My eyes burned as her voice called out to me without stopping.

"Star..." I groaned, weak but refusing to stop fighting.

Zion!

Zion!

"Zion, WAKE UP!"

I sat up in bed, gasping for air, barely able to breathe. All the noise faded away, and I fell into the comforting silence of the room we were in. Star looked at me, frightened, her delicate hands holding my shoulders. The light from the lamp glimmered in her wide, golden eyes.

"It was just a dream, Zion. Just that." My chest rose and fell in a frenzy. I couldn't control the tremor in my hands, which quickly spread through my body. I was desperate beyond measure.

I wrapped my arms around Star's waist and pulled her into my lap. Nothing, absolutely nothing but her could calm me. I was burning with hatred, anger, panic, everything.

"My God..." I whispered, burying my face in the curve of her neck.

Soon, her delicate hands moved down my back, soothing me, and she began to whisper tender words in my ear, cradling me as if I were a child in need of comfort, and God knew how true that was.

My eyes burned, and I cursed myself for the sudden urge to cry, which caused a painful knot in my throat.

"What did you dream about?" she asked, not breaking the tight embrace. I had to swallow hard a good three times to force my voice out.

"That they had come to take you back," I admitted in a hoarse whisper, pulling her a little closer. "And I... couldn't stop them. I was powerless to do anything but watch you go." Just remembering that damn nightmare made my hands shake even more.

"It was just a nightmare; it's not real." She caressed my hair, and the tenderness made me sigh. "I'm not going anywhere, not without you," Star repeated the words I had told her once, and those words were like balm to my soul.

I looked at her face, softly illuminated by the lamp light. Her big eyes sparkled, pupils wide and attentive. Her tousled hair fell around her shoulders, making her even more beautiful. I touched her strands and pressed our foreheads together, savoring her rhythmic breathing that had become as important to me as if it touched my skin and traveled down to my heart, pumping it.

A frenzy took over my body when I saw her curvy lips slightly parted. I pressed my mouth against hers, trying to control the urge to devour her, and I groaned hoarsely as her tongue cautiously slipped between my lips. It was enough to awaken the gigantic fire I had tried to hold back at all costs.

I buried my fingers in her nape and wrapped my other hand around her waist. Star wrapped her legs around my waist, pressing our bodies together. I pulsed, painfully hard from that closeness, and began kissing her with an intensity that quickly turned into an inferno.

I lowered my hands, desperate to touch every inch of her soft skin. I was crazy, maddened by the enticing scent of Star that invaded my senses and took everything from me.

I shouldn't... the thought crossed my mind as I cupped her round butt and pulled her against my erection. I shouldn't... I sucked her tongue, lifting her nightgown piece by piece until she was exposed on my lap. I shouldn't... I pulled our mouths apart; Star's face was glowing with her delicate cheeks flushed red and her lips slightly parted in anticipation. She looked like a cherub in my arms. I looked down at her. Her full, round breasts begged for attention, and I couldn't resist. I knew I shouldn't, but when my fingers closed around one of her rosy, swollen nipples, she moaned and threw her head back, and that sound—damn, that low, shy, uncontrolled moan—shook me to my core.

I held the base of her back and traveled my mouth down her neck, kissing every part until I closed my lips around the nipple. Star rubbed against my erection, almost making me lose control right there. I sucked on one nipple, pinching the other.

She slid her fingers and grabbed the hem of the shirt she had put back on, pulling it. I was hit again by that strange feeling of exposure, and a certain fear that she would pull away because of the marks on my back hit me, causing my body to stiffen for a moment.

"Don't be afraid," she whispered, and I took off the shirt, hesitant. Star had already touched them, but what if she saw? What if she got scared? I looked at her, who was watching me with her warm, half-open eyes of desire. "I love them," her surrendered voice threw me into the purest fire of hell, and a shiver coursed through every inch of my body as she traced her nails down my back, caressing the horrible marks that were there. "So please, love me too."

"Little one..." I dove into her mouth, desperate, emotional, and completely lost in the sounds and small moans that escaped her.

The sudden pleasure blinded me, as if I had suddenly entered a fog in the middle of the sea; I didn't know how to return to solid ground, didn't know how to stop.

I couldn't entertain the idea of her getting up from my lap. I held the edge of her panties and tore the fabric with a tug that made Star gasp in surprise.

"I want to feel you, sweetheart." I slipped my hand between her legs, a growl rising in my throat as I plunged my fingers into her flesh. My little one was warm and wet, ready for me.

I played with my fingers, opening her up on my lap. Star began to grind against my hand in a maddening way. My hands trembled with the effort it took not to enter her right there.

"Zion..." She arched her body as I penetrated a finger into her very tight opening.

I could only imagine myself inside her and slid another finger in while keeping my thumb caressing the spot that made her shudder.

I bit her mouth, her jaw, and buried my face in the valley between her perfect breasts, sucking and pinching. Star began to breathe uncontrollably, and her hand traveled down my chest. I gasped when she reached the base of my belly and pulled down my shorts until my rigid erection tumbled onto her stomach, dangerously close to her entrance. She wrapped her delicate hands around the length of my cock. A jolt of electricity coursed through my body, and I shivered at her innocent, curious touch.

I tried to remember that she had lost her memory, tried to force myself to run away, maybe jump into the cold sea, but the only thing I could do while she moved her hand up and down my cock was grunt some words that didn't even make sense while plunging my fingers inside her.

Star moved her hips and squeezed the base of my erection with her fingers. My whole body trembled. I withdrew my fingers from her, and she moaned in disapproval and returned to kissing me. I devoted my attention to the swollen spot I was dying to kiss, and she began to emit louder, throatier, slower sounds, mewing like a kitten, and I sucked in every one of those sounds with my mouth.

She teased the head of my cock, playing with the moisture at the tip, bringing it to her drenched entrance. It was like being on the edge of a cliff; she was pushing me, and I would gladly fall.

"No, my angel, this isn't how it's supposed to happen." I closed my eyes, panting, trailing my fingers over her body.

The heat of her opening brushed against the tip of my cock, and I had to muster all my self-control not to push into her, but instead, I pulled back, still teasing her with my touch.

I was dizzy with desire. Fuck, she was delicious. From the sounds she made to that warm, innocent gaze, her skin soft like velvet and as tempting as the devil himself. Her long hair tangled with my skin, and that became the most arousing sight I'd ever laid eyes on—seeing her naked in front of me, her body pressed to mine... shit, I wasn't going to resist. I didn't want to.

"Show me how it's supposed to happen, then," she asked. "Let me feel you, Zion."

"And what if it's not right? What if there's someone else?" The thought threw me into pure rage, and I swallowed hard, dreading that possibility so much I started to feel unhinged, off-balance.

"There isn't. I feel it."

"How can you be so sure?" I was begging, unconsciously, for some reassurance that what she said was true.

"Ahhhhhhhh..." she moaned into my mouth, her body writhing as pleasure flooded through her. I kept caressing her, now more slowly, savoring that sweet, lost expression on her face. She tried to find the words but stumbled over them as my fingers moved in and out of her hot, tight entrance.

"What were you saying?"

"You're having fun, aren't you?" she laughed, almost closing her eyes, trembling as her excitement grew stronger. She was on the brink of coming, and God, I was one lucky bastard to witness it. "I-I feel things..."

"Oh, sweetheart, you make me feel a lot of things too." I laughed, kissing her jaw.

"N-no..." She dropped her head onto my shoulder, grinding against my fingers, her breathing ragged. "I feel, Zion. Deep in my heart, that there was no one who loved me." Her words sent a sharp pain through my chest. "Believe me, there's no one. There can't be, my heart only burns for one person." A painful lump in my throat made it hard to breathe, as if my airway had closed.

"For who? Who does your heart burn for?" I intensified the rhythm, rubbing my thumb over her clit and thrusting deeper, playing with my fingers inside her. She tilted her head back and clung to me. "For who?" I repeated, pushing her to the edge, and that's when I heard a sound that instantly became my favorite.

"For you, it burns for you... ahhhhhhhhhhh!" She came, soaking my hand, her small body trembling under the control of my fingers. I kissed her mouth, rolling her onto the bed, fully aware that I had lost the battle.

She would be mine tonight.

Star

EVERYTHING WAS SPINNING, my eyes were heavy, but my whole body felt alive, burning. Zion came over me with a look that made me shiver, his weight deliciously pressing me down as I reached out and found the base of his erection.

I touched his cool skin, unable to close my fingers around him completely—he was too thick. I couldn't believe it would fit, but oh my... just the thought made me want to scream with desire.

His mouth sought mine with fervor and passion, his fingers roaming every inch of my skin, teasing and arousing me. It didn't take more than half a second before I could barely control my breathing. I squirmed as he settled between my legs and teased me again in that skilled, possessive, and delicious way.

I opened my eyes and realized once more that this wasn't the Zion I knew. Ghost had many faces, and I was loving this one, where he wanted to devour me.

Every part of his body pressed me into the mattress, which sank beneath us, making the bed creak. The weight of his erection against my belly barely let me breathe, and just when I thought I couldn't melt any further, Zion's mouth moved down my skin, trailing over my breasts that he was still caressing, then down my stomach, kissing all the way down until he reached my navel and spread my legs. I gasped, startled.

"W-what are you doing?" I trembled as he gripped my ass with both hands, preventing me from escaping his merciless mouth.

"I want to taste you, dive my tongue here..." he touched that sensitive spot that drove me wild and slid his fingers down to my entrance. "... and here. I'm going to lick you until you come in my mouth, sweetheart." I grabbed the sheets, feeling my core clench with desire at his words.

I never imagined hearing something like that from a man so composed, but I never thought I'd love him even more for it.

"Oh, my God!" I grabbed his hair, holding back a small jump as his tongue touched me, opening me slowly. The wet caress traveled up and down with torturous slowness.

He sucked, bit, and I arched my back into the mattress as his tongue plunged deep inside me, moving in and out again and again.

"Zion, oh, fuck. Fuck..." He laughed against my opening, and I did the same, unable to say anything else—nothing could describe more accurately what this man could do with his mouth. It wasn't long before another violent wave of pleasure washed over me, leaving me weak and open for him.

I grabbed his shoulders and pulled him up, shocked by the sudden storm that took over me, like the world would fall apart in front of my eyes if he didn't enter me immediately.

He surrounded my body with his, supporting himself on his elbows as he positioned the hard length of him at my entrance. His thick head began to stretch me, slowly, both of us trembling.

Zion started to tease that spot again that made me lose all sense of reason. The heat of our bodies made it hard to breathe. He kissed me, groaning and growling into my mouth as he pushed in. I was tense with anticipation and desire, but suddenly, he stopped inside me, not moving an inch.

I opened my eyes and found an expression of shock frozen on his face, a deep crease forming between his brows.

"Sweetheart..."

"What is it?" I blinked, dazed and confused, his head pulsing at my entrance. The sensation of his flesh against mine was dizzying, making it impossible to think clearly.

"What if no one came before me? What if you're a virgin, fuck..." He took a deep breath. "You're so tight," he growled, his eyes reflecting the flickering light from the lamp, burning with an indecent heat. I ran my nails down the rigid lines of his chest.

"If I'm still a virgin, I want you to be the first." I wrapped my legs around his waist, trapping him there as I saw doubt flicker in his eyes.

His face filled with a strange, warm emotion that made my throat burn when he kissed me again, this time with a radiant, tender devotion. There was concern, desire, and something else hidden behind that touch.

"How can I resist you? How could I?" He moaned against my skin, moving forward, the hard flesh opening me more. "I don't want to hurt you, I'll never want to hurt you..."

And then I felt it, a sharp pain rising through my belly. I dug my nails into his back, and he stopped moving.

"Shh, relax, it'll pass." He pushed a little more, and the burning subsided as he stroked and teased me. "My angel, my sweet angel, you were a virgin." His voice was low, trembling with excitement.

He captured one of my nipples with his lips and sucked it as his cock slid in deeper, the sensation of becoming one with him overwhelming me as he opened me up, whispering romantic words and promises I'd always dreamed of.

Despite the slight burn, nothing had ever felt as perfect as our sweaty bodies pressed together.

"Mine..." He began to move, thrusting slowly, branding my body with his and my mind with his voice. "My star..." He gripped my waist, and I spread my legs wider.

The tremors returned, crawling over my skin as he entered and withdrew, only to plunge deeper, harder.

"Open your eyes, mi amor. Open them and let me see them. I'm in love with them. I'm in love with every inch of you." I blinked, shy to meet his gaze like this, but I did as he asked.

The scorching pleasure I found in his iris made me feel like the most desired woman in the world. His eyes swept over mine as he opened me and entered deep. He increased the rhythm and the caresses without breaking that eye contact until I couldn't take it anymore.

"You... be mine. Just... be mine." I gasped.

I didn't know why I said that, maybe it was my heart, desperate for that moment to never end, and a wave of emotions crossed Zion's striking eyes. His silhouette moved over me, casting indecent reflections on the walls of that room, the bed creaked as our moans met in the rhythm of his body claiming mine. His skin against mine.

I dragged my nails down his back. I traced the scars that marked him and etched them into my mind, into my heart. I touched every curve, every suggestion, every trace... while he made me more and more his.

I screamed loudly when pleasure swept through my body again, sealing that uncontrollable desire. Now everything felt different and more intense with him inside me. I involuntarily squeezed the thick member with my intimacy, and he grabbed a handful of hair at the back of my neck, pulling with moderate force, which made me emit loud, shameful sounds.

Zion buried his head in my neck and thrust deep once more, and a strong moan rumbled from his chest. He hugged me tightly, panting with pleasure.

"I'm yours, *mi amor*, since the moment I saw you for the first time," he whispered between gasps into my hair, and I held back the urge to cry with the sudden happiness that filled my heart.

Nothing could be more perfect than that.

Zion kissed me again, his erratic breathing tickling my face. I ended up laughing, and he joined me.

"Does it hurt?" he asked, still inside me. My eyes were heavy, and my face burned, but I couldn't stop admiring the sight of that strong man between my legs.

"It hurt a little at first, but then..." I bit my lips, about to burst with embarrassment.

"Then?" he insisted, catching my lips with his in a quick, gentle kiss.

"Then all I felt was a crazy desire to never let you go. It was... so strange," I admitted, and he pushed the still very hard member through the length of my intimacy, pulling out of me shortly after. The sensation of emptiness crept into my chest, but he quickly pulled me into his arms, on the opposite side of his bandage. His hair and chest were sweaty, just like mine.

"You drive me crazy, my heart." He kissed and nibbled my ear, and I shivered with a chill. "My perfect angel." I sighed.

"Maybe I'll never remember my past, but I don't want to forget what happened here. Ever." He traced a line with his finger from my cheek to my jaw.

"Remember, *mi* amor. Remember how much I desire you, how much your heart enchants me, your eyes fascinate me. Never forget this, okay?" I turned in his arms to face him, and he took my hand to his chest, where his heart beat as fast as mine. "Only you can make it race like that. In different ways. From the fear of losing you to the desire to be inside you. Don't forget, my heart."

"I won't," I promised, my eyes stinging.

I didn't know this strange and powerful feeling that crept into my chest and made me want to spend my life next to this man, so I hugged him, as if I could keep him between my arms and protect him even from myself and the dangers that surrounded me.

We stayed embraced for a while, just listening to our breaths meet, then he asked me to wait for him in bed while he went to the bathroom. I rolled over the sheets and noticed how wet they were and bit my lips at the sight of a small red mark of blood.

It had been so delicious that I hardly felt any pain, and knowing he had been my first made me weak, especially recalling the uncontrolled sounds he let out as he took my virginity. He seemed as absorbed as I was, in a synchronicity I could barely explain.

The sound of the tub filling took over the room, and soon he returned, completely at ease with his own nudity, at least with the front part. He had removed the bandage, leaving the stitches visible. I could still sense his hesitation about me seeing his back, and that bothered me.

Didn't he realize how perfect he was?

"Come, I've prepared a bath." I squealed as he wrapped his arms around my leg and lifted me into the air, planting a quick kiss on my mouth.

Zion carried me into the bathroom, where the delicious scent of perfumed soap rose through the hot steam of the bathwater. He stepped in with me in his arms among the forming bubbles, and I moaned with pleasure as I felt the warm water against my skin.

He sat behind me and began to caress my body with his fingertips. I curled up shyly when he opened my legs with his hands, sliding them there intimately.

"Relax, my heart, and let me take care of you." I did as he asked and let my body melt into his, enjoying the warmth that spread with every bold touch. How good it felt to have those rough hands against my skin, his breath in my ear, fluctuating as we fit together. "My beautiful..." He kissed the curve of my neck and ran his fingers down the sides of my back, which reminded me of something I wanted to tell him.

"Zion..."

"I love when you call me by my name," he confessed, quietly.

"Your name is important to me."

"What do you mean by that?"

"Ghost is the silent man, the one with scars and a traumatic past, but I don't think that's all you are. There's also Zion, a man with a huge heart, completely in love with his family, who loves music and plays piano, which I must admit, seems pretty fancy." I laughed. "They might seem like the same person, but I see a big difference."

"I didn't know you saw me that way," he said, moved, and I turned in his arms until our eyes met.

"Can I ask you something?"

"Yes, my love." He raised a wet hand and caressed my face.

"Why don't you want me to see your back?" The question caught him off guard, and I noticed that familiar trace of insecurity flash in his eyes.

"There's nothing interesting to see there." He lowered his eyes to our intertwined hands.

"Is that what you believe?"

"Could it be different? They're hideous scars, you wouldn't be the first to be scared by them." A pang in my stomach made me hold my breath as I remembered he had been my first, but I hadn't been his.

I didn't like remembering that, imagining another woman touching him was quite irritating, but worse than that, was imagining someone belittling him because of those scars that, to me, made him unique.

The first I could easily let go, but the second would definitely make me want to rip someone's hair out.

"I've seen them," I confessed, quietly. His usually strong and impenetrable face took on a vulnerable, anxious expression.

"When?"

"As soon as we arrived, and they had to tear your shirt."

"I'm sorry, I tried to keep you from seeing." He didn't look back at me, and I had to hold his face with both hands to make him meet my gaze.

"There's nothing to apologize for." A warmth spread through my chest, and I hugged him, wrapping my arms around his neck. "Do you have any idea how much I love them?"

"How could I?" he retorted defensively.

"How *couldn't* I? They represent your strength, your story? I admire them as much as I admire you. They can't be anything but beautiful if they're part of you." He pulled away from my embrace and took my face in his hands, searching for any sign that I was lying. "Let me see them up close, please."

"And if..."

"Just allow me." I stood up, ignoring his hand that tried to hold me back, and sat behind him, wrapping my legs around his waist.

His posture stiffened; he was nervous, and I understood that. I felt that every time someone got too close, but if there was one thing we were good at, it was getting close to each other.

I touched his scarred skin with both hands, tracing a path through the map of scars on his back. I caressed each one, from the fine ones to the rougher and deeper ones, falling more in love with him. I leaned in, and he flinched in surprise when he felt my lips tracing one of the marks.

"What are you doing?"

"Kissing every part of you." He took a deep breath, two, no, three times, and his strong hands rested on my legs.

We stayed there, motionless for a long time, as I kissed each of his scars, noticing his breathing grow increasingly erratic and euphoric.

"There's no way anyone could say you're less than perfect, my Ghost."

He turned between my legs, pressing me into the bathtub, his body against mine, face to face. His mouth sought mine with a growing mix of emotions.

"Thank you," he gasped, letting a thread of emotion escape.

I looked into his eyes and began to drown in the autumn leaf brown, which reminded me of a sunny autumn day, glowing like a warm fireplace, and there I found all the scars I couldn't touch with my hands, so I decided to touch them with my lips.

I dove into his lips, certain that I had no idea what my past was like, but eager to discover any future I might have, any that included Zion.

My scars hurt less when they were completed by his.

CHAPTER TWENTY-ONE

Star

It was strange not to remember anything. As if I were an empty vessel, without purpose, without dreams. But part of that feeling, which made me feel like a limited woman, changed last night.

Everything changed when he touched me with a desire I had until then imagined was impossible.

I stretched out on the soft bed, surprised to feel so... alive. I had experienced a night without dreams, without thoughts, without anything other than the comfort of being in Zion's warm, protective arms.

I turned over in the sheets, searching for his warm body, and opened my eyes when I saw that I was alone again.

A smile lifted the corners of my lips when I saw the little note he had left on the pillow. I reached for the paper that said a hopeful "Be right back" and let myself fall back onto the mattress.

I ran my hands up my neck and closed my eyes, recalling the intense kisses we shared for what seemed like hours in that bathtub. His hands exploring my body, his breath flowing over my skin—everything, absolutely everything, was still etched in my memory. Creating new memories that I would carry for a lifetime.

We had slept wrapped in each other, and to my surprise, he didn't insist on putting his shirt back on after I asked him not to. I wanted to feel his skin on my fingertips while we slept. That was as real as our union itself. He accepted, which meant he trusted me, just as I trusted him.

I sat up in bed among the covers, lifted my head, and took a deep breath, filling my lungs with oxygen and allowing the wave of relaxation to spread through my loose limbs.

A strange sensation pulsed between my legs after what we had done. As if something was different there, and I knew it was true. My face burned with the memory of him kissing me there, how he filled me until I felt ecstasy, satisfied. I was lost in daydreams when a loud, shrill sound mixed with a terrified scream almost made my heart stop.

I brought my hand to my mouth as I saw the door burst open with a bang, and my eyes widened when Ghost walked through it, Sonia trailing behind him. Both covered in red foam and a dark liquid.

"I'm so sorry, Mr. Ghost!" The woman was frantic, trying to clean him with a piece of white cloth, the only thing that was clean between the two of them.

"No, I'm the one who apologizes." He looked in my direction. His serious face was covered in icing, and there was a strawberry stuck in his hair. I bit my lips in a futile attempt to stifle my laughter, but that scene was more than I could bear. "Don't you dare..." He raised his index finger in a mock threat, which only made it even funnier.

"I can't." I threw my head back and laughed loudly.

"I really am sorry, sir. I was bringing breakfast and didn't hear you coming." Sonia placed the tray she was holding in front of her body; her uniform, once blue, was splattered with various colors. It seemed she had also been hit by the flying food.

Several pieces of what I imagined once were cups were scattered across the hallway floor, along with small utensils. The accident had been quite the mess.

"Don't worry, Sonia. I think I really need to learn to watch where I'm going." The woman still blamed herself for a moment, but ultimately decided to go change clothes.

I couldn't stop laughing, not even when he closed the door behind him.

"How lovely, you laughing at someone else's misfortune. Want to try some strawberry cream?" He ran over to the bed, and I jumped off, weak from laughing as I dodged his dirty hands.

I headed toward the balcony, but he caught up to me first. His strong hands gripped my shoulders and spun me around until my back met the wall. He brought his dirty face close to mine, and my smile faded as his mouth brushed against mine. The smell of strawberries became deliciously enticing.

"Should I teach you not to laugh at me?" He lifted my chin with his fingers until our eyes met, and I pressed my lips together at the sight of the strawberry caught in his hair.

"I don't think you're capable of that," I laughed uncontrollably.

"Damn, so you've figured it out?"

"Figured out what?" I reached for the lost strawberry, but he held my wrist halfway.

"That I can't resist you." He kissed the inside of my wrist and pressed his mouth against mine immediately after, invading me with his warm, tasty tongue. "Wait for me in bed. I'll take a quick shower." He suddenly stepped back, leaving me dizzy. "Giorgia should bring another tray; we'll go down after breakfast, okay?" I nodded, and he guided me by the hand to the bed before disappearing into the bathroom.

I stayed there, in a mix of anticipation and anxiety. Not knowing what he planned to do next, after all, everything had changed the night before.

I heard a soft knock on the door. I got up and opened it, coming face to face with Giorgia and another huge tray of breakfast.

"Good morning, Miss Star." The young woman smiled radiantly. I noticed two other women I hadn't seen before cleaning up the glass shards in the hallway. "I brought the coffee; can I set it on the balcony table?"

"Yes, of course." I walked with her and smiled as I opened the curtains, seeing the sunlight bathing the coast and coloring every bit of the vibrant, lively scene before our eyes.

"Miss, I brought orange juice and cappuccino, and if you prefer, strawberry cream with fresh strawberries—" I held back a laugh at the memory of the fruit stuck in Ghost's hair as if he had suddenly become a human strawberry plant—"pistachio brioche..." She pointed to some stuffed rolls that looked very appetizing. "...and we also have Iris and Cassatelle, which, by the way, are my favorites."

"Cassatelle what?"

"No, miss." She laughed, bringing her hand to her lips. "Cassatelle," she corrected me affectionately. "They are sweet fried pastries filled with ricotta." She pointed to some crescent-shaped pastries. "And the Iris are also filled with sweet ricotta and bits of chocolate." She pointed to something that looked more like a sugar-coated bread.

"Thank you; everything looks delicious."

"If you need anything, just call me." I thanked her again, and she left shortly after.

I sat in one of the chairs, enjoying the gentle breeze against my face, distracted by the waves breaking near the shore.

"Looks tasty," Ghost whispered close to my ear.

"FUCK!" I shrieked like a crazed crow from the huge scare he gave me.

He caught my arms before I stumbled into the breakfast and knocked everything over again. My eyes were about to pop out of their sockets, and the bastard smiled as if he hadn't almost given me a heart attack.

"Should I hang a bell around my neck?"

"I'll hang that shit around your..." I started to curse, still trembling, but that silent rascal silenced me with a slow, rhythmic kiss.

I gasped, sucking in air between the small spaces where his lips separated from mine. That was a wicked trick, I was sure. After all, with one kiss, he managed to make me forget the scare and the anger I felt. In fact, I was being overtaken by a much more powerful feeling.

"I'll let that slide for reasons of..." He raised his eyebrows, waiting for me to finish the sentence. I shrugged. "Your kisses make up for the risk of imminent heart attack I run being near you." He laughed and sat next to me, pushing his chair back and pulling me onto his lap.

His rough fingers brushed a strand of my hair that had fallen over my shoulder, pushing it aside. I gasped when he traced his fingers over the sensitive skin at the base of my neck and placed a kiss right there.

"How many scares do I have to give you to earn more than one kiss?" I closed my eyes as his warm, moist lips glided over my skin. He bit the curve of my neck, trailing down through the small opening of my collarbone to the tip of my bare shoulder.

"Do you really think you need to scare me?" I could barely control the tremor in my voice.

Ghost was a wizard, I was sure, and his spells were spread across every part of his body, from the tips of his fingers to his firm yet soft mouth, the incisive tongue, the exciting voice that could turn me inside out.

"How are you feeling, my love?" He took my face in his hands.

"Very well." I was honest and turned to the coffee, serving myself some strawberry cream that looked very tempting.

"You wouldn't lie to me, would you?" He watched me as I tasted the cream, still seated in his lap.

"Never. Mmm, it's delicious." I took some cream with the tip of the spoon and brought it to Zion's mouth, which he shook his head in agreement.

"It's sweet just right." His voice was heavier as he slid his fingers up my thighs, playing with the short, light hairs on my leg along the way. The sensation was so pleasurable that I shivered and let some strawberry cream fall, landing just above my breasts, sliding down the valley between them, staining everything, including my nightgown.

"Oh, damn!" I complained, about to get up, but Zion held my wrist and stopped me.

I looked at his face, which scrutinized the path the cream had taken with a different kind of glow. I inhaled, surprised to see him lean down until his lips touched my sternum, pressing against the skin above my breasts for a long time before trailing down the valley, licking the path the cream had left.

"Zion..." I gasped. The strap of my nightgown slipped between his fingers as he lifted his eyes to mine, lustful with desire, leaving me half-naked. "What if someone sees us?" He moved his hand up my belly and held my leg, guiding me until I was sitting with my legs open on his lap, facing him. He supported my lower back with his hand and leaned me slightly back.

"No one can see us from here, sweetheart." Zion reached for the bowl of strawberry cream, and I watched in shock as he dipped his finger into it to grab some cream.

"Oh my." I bit my lip when he placed the cream on one of my nipples. The cool touch made me wish I could clamp my legs together, but he kept me there, open and unable to close them.

"I want to taste this cream another way." He did the same with the other nipple, set the bowl aside, and brought his lips to my skin. His tongue touched me, and I dug my nails into his thighs.

Zion wasn't willing to let me breathe. His mouth played with me, licking, biting, and blowing on the flesh around the swollen nipple that begged for his attention. In fact, my entire body was screaming for his.

He reached for the cream with the tip of his tongue and began to swirl it around the mound of white cream. The seconds dragged as the anticipation of his touch there grew. My God, I was about to beg him to suck me there already.

"My sweet Star, delicious..." He took my nipple into his mouth and sucked hard.

A trembling, uncontrolled moan escaped my throat. The center of my body throbbed, wet. I felt frantic, desperate for more. I thought nothing could surpass the touches from the night before, but the sight of Zion sucking that frosting off my nipples drove me wild.

I started lifting his shirt, my trembling fingers fumbling along the way, and he ended up helping me before pressing his lips back against my breasts, torturing me to the limit. I could feel his hard, throbbing erection beneath me, which only made me more aroused. I began grinding against his lap. He slid his hands down my stomach and slipped his fingers between my legs, growling as he reached my intimacy.

"Oh... oh..." I moaned, throwing my head back, breathing heavily.

His fingers parted me with slow, sinful strokes, moving up and down the slick length. He rubbed the pulsing spot that drove me crazy and slid two fingers into my slit. I pulled his face to mine and kissed him desperately.

My face and neck burned, my breasts rubbed against Ghost's chest, grazing the hair there, and just when I thought I'd lose my mind completely, the pleasure ripped through my body in a strong orgasm.

"Zion!" I bit his lip in a rush of pleasure.

"I love the sounds you make when you cum, little one," he whispered against my lips, his fingers still inside me.

Zion was tearing me apart. Every time he touched me, he took a piece of me with him.

I grabbed the bowl of cream and slid between his legs until I was kneeling in front of him. I wanted to do the same to him.

"Can I?" I asked, and unzipped the dark shorts he was wearing.

"Fuck, you're gonna kill me," he moaned, confused, and I slipped my hand inside his shorts until I touched the heavy erection. I pulled down the fabric along with his underwear and knelt there.

Did I know what I was doing? No. But I firmly believed that as long as I didn't end up biting him, everything would be fine in the end. At least that's what I hoped.

I touched the base of his shaft and saw a small drop glisten against the sunlight at the tip of his thick glans. I leaned in and caught it with my tongue.

"Holy fuck," he gasped, gripping the arms of the chair. Watching him experience pleasure made the center of my body ache with desire.

I ran my fingers along the length, enjoying the way the veins rippled beneath my touch, down to the base and back up again. I dipped my finger into the cream and spread it all over the head, sliding down a bit. I leaned in and closed my lips around the glans. Zion growled and tangled his fingers in my hair.

I started sucking the cream, moving my tongue up and down the shaft, and decided to take him into my mouth. I sucked the head of his member and gradually took more into my mouth, caressing him with my tongue as I went.

I sucked as deep as I could and began working my way back to the tip. The guttural sounds he made were intoxicating. His fingers in my hair guided a rhythm that grew more intense, more intimate, but suddenly, he pulled me away.

"Come here, little one." Zion grabbed my waist and pulled me into his lap, spreading my legs, and once again, I heard the fabric of my panties being torn apart without mercy.

"Another pair!" I complained, laughing.

"I can't wait for you to take them off." He plunged into my mouth, his hands dancing over my body until they reached my breasts. He pinched one of my nipples and pressed his thick glans against the warm entrance of my body.

"Ah!" I moaned into his mouth.

"I won't be able to be so gentle, mi amor. I want to fuck you," he confessed, and an overwhelming frenzy shot through me. He entered me all at once, deep and hard. I screamed into his mouth and closed my eyes as he brushed my swollen clit. "Fuck, you feel so good!" he growled against my skin, pulling me down onto his shaft that stretched me to the limit.

I began moving in his lap, panting and making incoherent sounds, moving back and forth, and every time he thrust deeply, he hit something that made me lose my mind. His hands spread my ass, and his fingers dug in, maintaining a fast, strong rhythm. I leaned back, dizzy with desire, and a curious thought struck me. What would it be like to watch him inside me?

I looked down where our bodies met and swallowed hard at the indecent, delicious sight of his cock, wet from my own lubrication, disappearing inside me with each thrust, while Zion caressed and pinched me.

I blinked slowly, feeling a wave of pleasure rise over my skin, and I exploded. The violent tremor threw me off balance. I collapsed forward, moaning loudly in his arms. He quickly pulled away and slipped out of me. His rigid erection rested against my belly, and he groaned in a low, guttural sound, squeezing me tightly as the warmth of his release spilled across my stomach. I panted, completely spent.

I remained still, unable to move. My erratic breathing mingled with his. Zion kissed my cheek, my nose, and even my eyebrow. I laughed and snuggled closer to him as he stroked my back until I regained control over my limbs.

"Sorry about this," he said after a long time and leaned over to reach a pack of tissues on the table, starting to clean up the mess between us.

"I can do it myself." I reached for his hand, burning with embarrassment, but he pulled it away.

"Let me take care of you, sweetheart." He lifted the straps of my nightgown back into place and planted a quick kiss on my mouth, returning to clean us up with care and efficiency.

I closed my eyes, ready to die of shyness.

"Yesterday, even though it was your first time, we took a risk of an unexpected pregnancy," he explained, finishing the cleanup. "Pulling out before the end, which I should point out is as hard as forcing myself to stop, reduced that risk, but it's still not ideal. I asked for some condoms to be brought for us from now on, and I hoped I could control myself until they arrived, but with that delicious mouth of yours, it was impossible to resist." He gave me a peck on the lips.

"You..." I widened my eyes in shock. "You asked someone to buy condoms for us?" I choked on my own saliva and coughed. "Ghost, what will they think?"

"Sweetheart, they think we've already been doing this since before we got here." He played with a strand of my hair. "But don't worry, no one will know, and the person I sent is extremely discreet. Everyone in the mafia is." He tried to reassure me. "You should get back to your seat, or I'll end up eating something other than that Cassatelle."

We finished breakfast between light laughs as he told me why Sonia had spilled the coffee tray on him. As usual, the man with light feet had appeared unnoticed, resulting in that strawberry catastrophe.

A light knock on the door interrupted our conversation.

"I'll see who it is, finish your breakfast." He caressed my face and got up. I glanced through the balcony and saw him speaking with someone who handed him two packages. Ghost closed the door, left one of the packages under the lamp, and returned with the other in hand, a smile tugging at his lips.

"What is it?" I sipped my orange juice.

"I brought you a gift." He sat down in front of me and handed me a white rectangular box wrapped with a very cute pink ribbon.

"A gift?" I pulled the ribbon so fast I ended up tying a double knot, and Ghost had to come to my rescue.

He untangled the knot and handed the box back to me.

"There you go, open it." The feeling of receiving anything from him was thrilling.

"You didn't have to get me anything, you know that," I said as I opened the edges of the box, gasping when I saw the contents inside. "It's a phone!" I gaped in surprise, taking everything out of the box. There was a charger, earbuds, and the heavy black device itself. "Ghost, this must have cost a fortune!" I looked at him, catching his side smile as he watched me.

"Don't worry about it, sweetheart." I bit my lip and leaped into his lap.

"Thank you!" I wrapped my arms around his neck in a tight hug. I rested my head on his chest and began fiddling with the phone, with his help. We spent some time there, nestled together as we set up the device. "There, now we just need a photo for the screen."

"Want me to take one of you?"

"Can you take one of us?"

"Of course, come here." He pulled me closer into his arms, opening the front camera and aiming it at us. And then he smiled, and I got distracted by how beautiful we looked together on the screen, forgetting that I should smile too. "There," he said, satisfied, analyzing our photo between his fingers. "You're beautiful, from every possible angle." He planted a chaste kiss on my mouth, cupping my face with his hands. "I put an app on this phone that gives you access to an endless number of songs." He reached for the earbuds. Then, carefully, he plugged them into my ears. "I added that song you love to the favorites list."

"You found it? Can I listen to it?" My eyes widened as I understood what he was saying.

"You can listen to it whenever and as many times as you want." Ghost opened a green app filled with black waves and clicked on a song titled "Flashlight" by a singer named Jessie J.

I jumped up awkwardly as soon as the beats hit my ears.

"Oh my God..." I whispered, pressing the headphones tighter against my ears, as if I could somehow fuse with them.

I knew that sound, oh, how I knew it. As the music played, pieces of a painful puzzle began to fill in my mind.

My body started to shake, I could barely breathe, everything became blurry, and I closed my eyes, locked in an internal battle between wanting to hear it or throwing that sound far away from me.

My mind was spinning, and the feeling of being lost began to drown me. As if my life, my past, and my future were right there, dancing on the tips of my fingers.

"Calm down, sweetheart, shh!" I struggled against Ghost's arms around my waist, but he persisted, turning me so my back was against him, pressing his lips to the base of my ear, making me hear him even with the headphones on. "You can do this, I know you can. I believe in you, my little warrior."

"I'm scared." I sobbed, realizing I was crying. "I remember her, and I'm scared." I squeezed my eyes shut tighter, fighting against the avalanche of uncertainties.

"Face it, *mi* amor. I'm here to bring you back to reality. I won't let those memories devour you." I gasped and intertwined my fingers with his, desperate for the support I knew was real.

My legs were trembling. Every part of the song invaded me, touching a different point. Each phrase, each line, every meticulous choice of melody...

When tomorrow comes, I'll be on my own
Feeling frightened of the things that I don't know

I groaned, an inexplicable pain split my chest in two. Loneliness, sadness, exhaustion, abandonment. All those feelings flooded my heart, and a convulsive sob rose in my throat.

And though the road is long, I look up to the sky
In the dark, I found the lost hope that I won't fly
I sing along

The smell of alcohol, maybe a bar, mixed with chocolate cookies made me feel tender. A baseball bat, cards on the table, full glasses, empty glasses. I tried to grab any of those strands of memories, but they slipped through my mind. I felt miserable, and the more I listened, the more emotions, smells, and little memories forced their way into my chaotic mind.

I sing along

I cried louder, the words reached my mouth as if they were desperate to come out.

I sing along

I sing along

And then, like a volcano erupting, I let them out. I started singing with my voice, my soul, with all my pain and uncertainties.

CHAPTER TWENTY-TWO

Ghost

I had regretted giving her that phone about five hundred times. I had no idea if what I was doing would help or harm her, and when she started crying like that, filled with despair, hurt, and pain, for a moment I considered taking the earbuds out of her ears, but then something happened.

Star began to breathe in short, frantic gasps. I wrapped my arms around her waist and supported her trembling body, and then she opened her mouth and started to sing between strong gasps, like someone fighting to surface.

I held her tighter, her arms began to move, and she ran her fingers through her hair and kept singing, screaming with all her might, and it was the most intense, anguished, and beautiful sound I had ever heard.

Star had no trouble dancing through the low notes of the music, and when it reached its peak, I had the impression that the air around us vibrated with that unusual sound, which carried so much meaning.

I'm trapped in the dark, but you are my lantern
You guide me, guide me through the night

I heard every word, every cry, every plea, and once again I found myself going mad, wishing to take away her pain with my own hands, desperate to be the lantern she so needed to light that path. And the more my little one surrendered to that music, the more she cried, the more she suffered, and I, who had never felt so powerless, could only stay there, wrapping her body in my arms.

She swayed as she cried and sang, feeling the rhythm of the music.

My eyes burned like embers, and I tried everything to stay calm; she needed me there. I was her solid ground, the point of light in that damn darkness.

I held her close to me. Star tilted her head back and unleashed the full power of her voice in one last chorus. The sound swirled through the air and swallowed everything around us, sending a shiver down my spine, and then she stopped, her hands trembling as much as her legs.

I forced myself to find strength, even as I was devastated to see her suffer so much. I wrapped my arms around her legs and lifted her into my lap. Star fit perfectly in the curve of my neck, her face wet with tears.

"It's okay, my heart," I whispered in her hair as I lay down on the bed with her in my arms.

I caressed her face; her cheeks were very red, as were her eyes. I started playing with the strands of her hair and ran my fingers down her back, as if I could touch her pain with my fingertips. She blinked, but her cinnamon-colored irises were lost somewhere I couldn't reach.

"How are you feeling?" I tried to stay quiet and respect that moment, but her silence was driving me crazy.

"I don't know. There are so many feelings." Her hoarse voice went straight to my anxious heart. Star closed her eyes; she was still trembling. "It's like walking in the dark, picking up pieces and fragments that make no sense. I smell things, like a whiskey made from malted barley and another from unmalted barley. I can specifically tell the difference between the two, and I feel like I've discussed the composition of a Bourbon with someone. I remember feeling cold, wanting to eat some stupid chocolate cookie as if my life depended on it," she laughed, bitterly, "and something tells me that it was an important issue for me. I remember loving something that was on TV, but I can't remember what. My head is full of faceless people, meaningless voices, and you know... when I heard the music, I had a strong, strange feeling that scared me."

"What did you feel, my love?" I held her a little tighter.

"That I wasn't happy," she confessed, trembling as she lifted her face. "And what if I don't like what I find when we go back, Ghost? What if there's only sadness?"

"There will always be sadness in our past, my heart. It will always be there, lurking, but we can't let it come close to us. Don't be afraid that your past is unhappy; our future holds many joys, can't you see?" I lifted her face with my finger until her big, golden, confused eyes locked onto mine. "We will leave soon, and I won't allow anything to make you unhappy, do you hear?"

She blinked and kept staring at me, her expressive eyes overflowing with tears as she threw herself into my lap, making me groan from the impact against the bandage and pressed her lips to mine urgently.

"Thank you for never letting go of my hand," she said between gasps and sobs.

"It's you who saves me, my heart." I kissed her again, lost in the lips of my fugitive. The woman who had decisively stolen my heart before she even realized it.

MAYBE SHE WORKED IN a bar. Republic? No, it could be a pub or a late-night restaurant.

I found myself wondering later, heading to meet Don Matteo.

I was surprised when Star, after calming down, wanted to listen to a bit more of the song I saved on the Spotify app. A terrible fear that she might have another breakdown while listening hit me, and I needed to see her listen to the music one more time to be sure everything would be alright. Still, I felt restless and worried enough not to leave her alone, so I asked her to stay with Valentina, who was about to invite her to join while she painted a picture.

Don's wife was an incredible artist. I had seen some paintings of landscapes by her, and I was truly impressed.

"Please keep an eye on her," I asked Valentina, not wanting to go into details. "You need to warn her if anyone is approaching; you know she doesn't react well to any kind of scare, especially involving a stranger.

Also, don't let her near anything sharp, cutting, or made of glass. Oh, my God, and the cliff—especially the cliff; a fall from there is fatal, and if she's as clumsy as my sister-in-law, it's only a matter of time before she falls. You know what? I'm coming with you..."

"Ghost!" Valentina grabbed my shoulders and laughed loudly. "I'm Don's wife, remember? I'm used to dealing with numerous messy children, troublemakers, and God help me, rebels, and none of them came from me. Star will be fine under my care. A little sunshine and art will lift her spirits, and I'll make sure she doesn't get close to anything that could hurt her, okay?"

I felt like a fool when I realized the excessive worry I was placing on Star, but I didn't know how to shake off the piercing fear in my bones. If she got hurt...

A few minutes later, I still didn't know how Valentina had convinced me to accept that, but somehow I found myself entering Don's office, where he was distractedly reviewing a pile of papers. A sweet fragrance filled the room—hazelnuts, vanilla, and... leather, mixed with fresh fruits and tobacco in the background.

"Can you drink yet?" He raised a glass of wine in my direction.

"Absolutely. If I don't swallow something alcoholic right now, I might end up staring at one of Valentina's paintings for the rest of the day."

"Don't worry about the girl. She'll be safer than all of us under Val's protection." He poured me a glass of wine. I couldn't help but notice the glimmer in his eyes when he mentioned his wife. "Sip it slowly and you'll taste all the nuances of the wine."

I raised the glass, savoring the aroma, which had hints of everything but the usual smell of wine. When I brought it to my lips, I almost moaned in pleasure.

The sweet flavor was the first to stand out, but then a mist of layers took over my palate. From ripe fruits to dry tobacco, subtle as my own footsteps, yet somehow it reminded me of my father's beloved cigar, unearthing all the good memories of those times when he would light one up after one of us drove him crazy.

"It's sensational," I said after a while, getting used to that sensation, which ended with a tropical warmth rising up my neck. "No, sensational doesn't even begin to describe it. This wine is extraordinary." Matteo leaned back in his office chair, crossing his arms over his chest with a satisfied smile on his face.

"I was right all along. The wine made here would surely have a line of titles if it were advertised properly."

"Without attention, remember?" He gathered some stacks of papers and spread a detailed map across the table. "We've drawn it as you asked; now I need you to identify each of the entrances."

I looked at the map, which was an identical copy of Don Gava's mansion, with the same walls and cells. I stared at the point representing where Star had been kept, God knows for how long, and clenched my jaw. All the hatred I had been trying to control since we left the hideout came back to suffocate me, as if it were adrift, just waiting for the right moment to surface. The truth was that all my feelings were chaotic.

"Do you think you can point out every inch of this place to me?"

"It would be my pleasure." I sat down in front of him. If I couldn't destroy that place myself, I would give those who could all the cards I had up my sleeve.

I spent a few hours with Don and a draftsman who joined us for the meeting until every detail was resolved.

"Looks like we're done," the specialist announced at the end of the drawing and left with the assurance that he would be able to put everything into a digital format that would greatly facilitate Don's overall view of the place.

"If all goes well, soon the entire *famiglia* Marino and its reign of power will come to an end," he concluded, satisfied, leaning back in his chair behind his desk.

"Keep me updated on everything."

"You will be the first to know for sure." I smiled at the man, who soon turned his attention to his phone, which was ringing insistently.

I raised my hand in a wave of goodbye as soon as he answered the phone, but Don Matteo raised a finger and asked me to wait.

"Seriously?" he laughed. "What good news. So it's become inevitable. Great, prepare everything," he ordered to whoever it was and turned to me as soon as he finished the call.

"Is there something I should be worried about?" I inquired. His strange smile left me confused.

"Maybe you should be worried. There's a delivery coming for you at the beach." I narrowed my eyes, suspicious. The only delivery I was expecting was our documentation, and I doubted it would arrive by the dock. "Let's go together. I want to see this." He stood up, making me even more alert.

I followed Don Matteo until we reached the beach, where a small wooden dock extended into the very clear waters, and I was surprised to find Valentina and Star in front of two painting canvases, distracted.

Star was laughing and having fun, her hands and part of her face covered in paint. Her canvas was filled with misshapen marks and disconnected strokes, but her genuine smile turned that mess into pure art.

"*Amore mio?*" Matteo called as he approached his wife, who, unlike Star, had a clean face and was precisely painting a replica of the sea before her.

"What are you doing here?" Valentina leaned in and kissed her husband.

"We came to receive a delivery," Don Matteo replied to his wife, taking her hand and leading her closer to the beach. I looked at Star, who was trying to put away the brushes as if her life depended on it, and when she turned to me, I noticed a lock of her hair was dyed blue.

"My little Cinderella." I planted a kiss on her lips and laughed at the mix of colors splattered across her face, as if Star had suddenly become a rainbow of rosy cheeks.

"I didn't expect to see you before a bath." She shrugged, shyly, and I wrapped my arms around her waist. "Are you crazy? You're going to get dirty too."

"In that case, how about taking a bath with me later?" I whispered in her ear, my stubble grazing her bare shoulder. She shivered and jumped, laughing.

"It tickles..." she squealed and squirmed as I nuzzled my jaw into that curve once more.

Star pushed me away and started running through the sand towards Valentina. I chased after her and caught up in just a few strides, grabbing her without a hint of shame.

I spun the breathless, smiling Star in my arms and dipped into her mouth for a moment, craving her taste, if only a little.

"You didn't answer me; are you going to take a bath with me or not? I believe that..." I rubbed my cheek and pointed my yellow-stained finger at her, as she bit her lips, enjoying the situation. "This is your fault."

"Maybe I have a little bit of blame, yes..." She opened a tiny space between her fingers and was about to question that amount of guilt when Matteo's voice brought me back to reality.

"They're coming." Star and I turned to see what the man was talking about.

A small boat was approaching the dock. It looked like a delivery boat, suitable for navigating the area.

"What's happening?" Star shrank within my embrace.

"It's just a delivery, probably our documents."

I held my words when the boat stopped at the dock, and a man of medium height in a black suit jumped off, running so fast that all I could see was his shadow coming towards us, shouting at the top of his lungs:

"MERCYYYYYY!"

Wait, I know that silhouette!

"It's just a snake!" Lyon jumped off the boat, chasing Shaw with something strange in his hands. Wolf and Snake followed closely behind.

I widened my eyes, frozen in disbelief.

"Holy shit!"

"Yeah, I know," Don Matteo added. "Your brothers came to get you."

CHAPTER TWENTY-THREE

Star

My goodness, what the hell was that? Reinforcements?
I wiped my hands on a cloth Valentina had left nearby and widened my eyes, watching with some fear as the four men approached.

The smallest of them, apparently the loudest as well, was running anxiously and only stopped when the guy chasing him returned a slimy thing to a man on the boat, and all four came toward us.

Ghost looked paler than usual, staring at the four figures dressed in black as if he were seeing the end of his own life.

"They're your brothers..." I swallowed hard. "They wouldn't hurt you, would they?"

"Depends on how irritated they are." I held my breath upon hearing his answer.

"Considering one of them is nearly foaming at the mouth, how close to death are you?" I asked softly, shuddering as they grew a bit larger as they approached.

They all wore elegant black suits, their neatly styled hair making them look like a bunch of stickers from the same album, but aside from their clothes and movements, there was a huge difference in each one's appearance.

The tallest among them was also the one who scared me the most. The man had broad, muscular arms and a myriad of tattoos that spread all over. Behind his ears, at the base of his neck, along the length of his hands to his fingers, and I believed there was something on his face too. He had clear, treacherous blue eyes—almost dangerous.

I was even more surprised, as if that were possible, when I looked at the man walking to his right and noticed he had differently colored eyes. Something I had never seen before, or at least couldn't remember. One was blue and the other brown, and he had a sour expression that seemed furious.

Beside him was a more relaxed guy with brown hair and a flawless posture like the others, and lastly, the guy who had jumped off running and was now panting as he stared at us.

He broke into a huge, genuine smile when he saw us. He was the shortest of them, but immediately became my favorite with his dark, slicked-back hair.

"You're done for!" the tattooed one growled as he approached.

"Leave the head to me," the guy with the bicolored eyes retorted.

"This is going to be interesting," Don Matteo whispered beside me.

"Is it helpful if I say I can explain?" Ghost pushed me behind him and was immediately hit by a wave of essential curses.

"You irresponsible idiot, do you have any idea what we've been through? It's been days since I've slept!" the biggest one shouted.

"You got shot. A damn shot, Ghost; I asked you for a daily report on your condition, but you ignored me."

"I should hang you upside down on the beach. A little sand in that brain of yours might solve your problem," the tattooed one shot back and didn't stop there.

I learned four new swear words in that moment as the two biggest ones yelled nonstop, speaking quickly and over each other. The big one was pointing his finger and seemed on the verge of a heart attack. Ghost listened in deep silence, which irritated me.

Why wasn't he reacting? Who did they think they were to talk to him like that?

"Everything Zion did was to save me. If anyone's to blame, it's me!" I huffed, raising my nose, terrified but staring the tattooed one in the eyes. I swallowed hard as he narrowed his gaze and took a step toward me.

"So it's you!" he said quietly, slyly, and my dear Jesus, I preferred when he was shouting. That whispered tone made him even scarier.

"Snake..." Ghost spoke for the first time, mimicking the low tone and stepping in front of me again.

"But it's true; the blame is mine. It was for me that you took that shot, so come on." I pointed at the tattooed guy. "You're big, but you're not two. You can curse me all you want; it won't even tickle compared to what we went through to get here. Go ahead and speak, but don't blame him for anything."

"For my holy patience, you have no memory but have courage, don't you, girl?" He looked me up and down.

"I don't like you." I narrowed my eyes at him.

"Get in line," he shot back without breaking eye contact.

"It's a very long line, sir. It's not worth it," the shortest one commented, and everyone around me started to laugh, even Ghost, while I seethed with anger, contemplating kicking that man.

"Miss, I apologize for my older brother." The owner of the bicolored eyes leaned toward me and extended his hand. I looked at it suspiciously.

"She doesn't like to be touched," Ghost whispered, and he quickly withdrew his hand with a barely audible "*I'm sorry*."

"I'm Wolf. The middle brother; this is Lyon..." He pointed at the brown-haired man. "And that's Shaw." I gave a nod to the funny, smiling young man. "And this here is Snake. Please forgive my brother's shark temperament; it's a burden to be the oldest."

"For sure, being responsible for you two steals all my days of life." He lowered his eyes, pressing them with his index and thumb, then opened a slow smile. "Ghost, you're still going to get me committed or arrested," he huffed and turned to me. "I'm sorry."

"I still don't like you."

"Good girl." Ghost laughed, and I pursed my lips in response.

The three then stared at each other. I felt Valentina's hand touch my elbow.

"It's better to leave them alone for a bit," she whispered, and I hesitated, uncertain. I eventually gave in and stepped away with her and her husband, but Don seemed to read the doubt in my eyes.

"There's nothing these three love more than family, so don't worry; Ghost is not in any danger."

"How's your shoulder?" the tattooed one growled, and Ghost said something I couldn't hear. They talked for a few moments, and then Snake—God, what a nickname—swept his eyes over Ghost from head to toe, as if checking if he was okay, and then hugged his brother.

"Just don't touch me with that paint-covered arm," one of them cursed and laughed.

"Is this how it is to have a family?"

"This is how it is when you're a Holder." Don Matteo chuckled. "Well, Snake, I thought you missed us, but you only came to get your little brother?"

"Matteo!" Snake beamed, which made him less intimidating, but I was still watching every move he made.

I left the brothers chatting and went up for a quick shower. Valentina did the same, and then she organized a spectacular and very quick lunch outdoors, near the cliff, providing an incredible view of both the sea and Don Matteo's vineyards, which stretched endlessly on the horizon.

It was the first time I had a meal with those people, and I didn't imagine it could be like this, as if a thousand things were happening at once.

"And he touched that slimy thing and wanted me to grab it too." Shaw was indignant as he recounted how malicious Lyon had been to grab the boat owner's pet snake just to scare him. "I'm almost certain that living with Lyon will make my entrance into heaven easier." A wave of laughter echoed around the table.

"No one scares more than this man here." Don Matteo pointed at Ghost. "I almost shot him during the time he stayed here... twice. Two times!" He held up two fingers in the air, his incredulous expression was almost funny. "Not to mention he almost cost one of my employees her life." Sonia, who was serving wine to the new visitors, started laughing.

"It was quite a scare. I'm sorry for the strawberry cream shower."

"I owe you an apology, and by the way, the cream was delicious." Ghost, who was sitting next to me, slid his hand down my thighs discreetly and squeezed my skin, making my face burn as I remembered all the places that cream had touched.

"Has he always been like this?" Don Matteo asked.

"He was born in silence, that creature," Wolf replied with a smile, and I noticed the light way they protected their youngest brother's past.

"The blame for our father's gray hairs is entirely his. The old man spent his life being scared." Snake laughed.

"You discover who a person is when they get scared. There are so many different reactions." Zion sipped his wine and continued. "Wolf, for example, always closes his eyes and seems to boil with rage; Snake hits without even knowing what's happening..."

"Miss Jasmin is a frying pan specialist," Shaw added.

"What?" I jumped into the conversation, raising my eyebrows in confusion.

"Jasmin is my girlfriend, and she has a rather aggressive way of reacting to some things," Wolf explained with a smile. "Once, we were at one of my hideouts when Snake and Ghost arrived, but she didn't know them and thought they were after her."

"Ghost, as usual, appeared behind the girl without making a sound," Snake continued. "The crazy girl grabbed a frying pan and whacked that idiot."

"I should remind you that she hit him square in the forehead with that same frying pan?"

"I can't believe it!" I laughed, just like everyone else around. Don Matteo was about to choke.

"And it gets worse. One day, I had the brilliant idea of gathering our closest friends—my brothers, Jasmin, and my father—for dinner at my house. My sister-in-law is a disaster in the kitchen, but she has an unshakeable faith that she'll improve at any moment, and it didn't take long for her to try to help. In the end, Jasmin spilled a bowl full of sugar on the floor and tried to help again."

"Always helping and helping... until she sets something on fire." Snake let out a breath.

"What did she do after she spilled the sugar?" Don Matteo asked, curious, and Ghost continued the story.

"She grabbed the vacuum cleaner..."

"The vacuum!" Wolf, who had been quiet until now, interrupted and started laughing uncontrollably.

"What happened to the vacuum?" I was already laughing and hadn't even heard the whole story.

"Jasmin got startled when I approached her to ask her not to join us since we were in the middle of lunch and that could be cleaned up later."

"Then... she got scared of him," Wolf could hardly speak from laughing so much.

"And she attacked me with the portable vacuum cleaner."

"That thing sucked Ghost's hair right off in one go." Snake shook his head as if still not believing that had really happened.

I burst out laughing, and a wave of raucous laughter surrounded the place.

"It hurt like hell. She ripped out a good amount of hair, that crazy woman." He huffed and then laughed. "Her reactions give me chills."

"You should stomp your feet," Wolf and Snake said in unison, which caused another burst of euphoric laughter.

And the stories continued. Each of them had one to tell, and I had never laughed so much in my life. Watching them became a pleasure.

The three brothers were like pieces of a puzzle. Apart, they were distinct, but together they formed a powerful triad.

One would start to speak, and the other would finish, as if they shared the same thoughts, the same scars, and I could swear the same pains.

So this was a family. I had never wanted to find mine as much as I did in that moment. Did I also have a sister or a brother who knew me as well as they knew each other?

I had no idea, but until I found out, I would keep watching that tightly-knit family.

To me, the Holder brothers had become a reference in family matters. Clearly, those brothers loved each other, even when they hated one another.

Ghost

"WE BROUGHT YOU A SUIT," Snake informed me as soon as lunch ended, leaning against the stone wall that separated us from a deadly drop to the sea.

"Really?" I widened my eyes, surprised.

"I figured you'd need one." He looked at me sideways.

"Thank you." I patted my brother on the shoulder.

"You're thanking him for not killing you?" Wolf sat down to my right.

"No, but I should. What the hell are you guys doing here?" I shook my head, still in disbelief that I was actually with them.

"What do you think we'd do?" Snake shot back, his eyes lost in the vastness of the sea, as blue as his own. "We took our time because I was afraid arriving early would cause an even bigger problem, but I started making arrangements for our trip as soon as you let me know you were here. We just had to sort out the extra documents for you and that little thing over there." He pointed to Star, who was distracted in a conversation with Valentina while the host showed her a color swatch for paint. "How can so much anger fit in such a small person? That girl looks like a miniature pinscher. I thought she was going to jump on my neck."

"Snake!" I warned, trying not to laugh.

"I've never rooted for something so hard." Wolf chuckled.

"'You're big, but you're not two.'" We all burst into laughter as Snake imitated Star in a high, funny voice.

"Snake almost lost his tough guy persona right there." Wolf wiped the corner of his eyes. "I saw the exact moment he made that weird face."

"The one he makes when he's trying not to laugh?"

"That one!" Wolf confirmed.

"No proof, no accusation!" Snake defended himself.

"Who taught you that? Your VIPs?" I mocked.

"Don't make me throw you off this ledge." I laughed. "You said she's afraid of new people, right?" He looked back at Star, and I nodded. "Still, she put that aside to defend you. That made me admire her. She's a brave survivor." That appreciation in his eyes sparked pure pride in my chest. My Star was much stronger than I could imagine.

"You two have more in common than you think." Snake shot me a skeptical look, and I continued. "You both hate new people. You're brave and even a little cheeky. Extremely loyal and root for the Chicago Cubs. I know you're dying to talk about them with her." My brother was fanatical about the team and squirmed uncomfortably.

"Actually, I won't talk about them. She'll have a tough time when she realizes the whole grand story and the amazing games she probably forgot," he said seriously.

"If that's what you say..." I shrugged, disbelieving every word he said.

"Ghost, we need to leave tonight," Wolf interrupted. "We got the documentation, but as you know, it's fake, and we used our father's contacts to get through security in case we have any problems. But that person will only be available in the morning. We'll have to take the boat at dawn."

"And if it wasn't clear enough, for our father to help us, we had to tell him everything." The feeling of a stone rolling in my stomach after hearing Snake's words made me freeze.

"He... fuck, he knows then?"

"Yes, and he's pissed because the exemplary son didn't warn him," Wolf teased.

"I'm going to die." I felt the pressure of my body drop to my feet.

"Only on American soil."

"You guys are terrible." I pressed my eyes with my fingertips. "Is that why you brought Lyon and Shaw? Did my father force you?"

"No, brother. This is our sister-in-law's fault." Snake ran his hand through his hair. "It was either them or Jasmin herself."

"They made a good choice. They know that while we're still here, our safety is limited." The two nodded.

"Our return won't be the best either. Snake has gotten quite famous because of those women's rescues. He and Agent Petrova were surrounded by reporters during the operation. She managed to escape the cameras, but our brother became news in every paper."

"I'm being chased by a bunch of annoying reporters. Scott had a huge name, and the scandal spread all over the country."

"Soon they'll leave you alone to chase another poor soul." I tried to comfort him.

"I'm hoping not to kill any of them before then." Shaw and Lyon approached along with Don.

"I've prepared the library so you can meet with more comfort and privacy. Sonia will take you there," Don Matteo informed, pointing to the young woman who was already waiting for us.

"You can go with her; I'll catch up with you in a few minutes."

My brothers followed Sonia, while Don Matteo and I went after the two women who were animatedly chatting on a wooden bench on the other side of the garden. Matteo called Valentina, and soon the two disappeared inside the mansion.

"What did you think of those two crazies I call brothers?" I settled onto the bench behind her.

"Peculiar." She laughed.

"Is that good?"

"Yes, very good. I'm glad you grew up surrounded by love and protection. Your older brother still gives me chills, but once the urge to strangle him passed, I could see that what you have is very special." I leaned in closer to her and brushed my nose against her shoulder, appreciating the delicate scent of freshly picked flowers that she exuded.

I kissed the curve of her neck, and she turned in my arms.

"We'll leave tonight."

"Oh my God, really?" Her anxious fingers clutched the fabric of my shirt. "W-we're going to the United States?"

"There's no reason to fear, *mi* amor. I'll be with you the whole time, and our safety there is impenetrable." I kissed the tip of her nose and hugged her tightly.

Star nodded and nestled into my arms. I knew that everything new scared her, and I was eager for us to finally get home. There, she would have all the support she needed to face the traumas she endured in that place. I would take care of her with everything I had. That was my only certainty; I would do anything to ensure she was okay.

CHAPTER TWENTY-FOUR

Ghost

I took a quick shower and put on my suit. The soft, black fabric with its sharp cuts brought a nostalgic feeling to my chest. Who would have thought that a well-fitted outfit could rejuvenate a man's soul?

I felt like myself again when I arrived at the library that Don Matteo had set up for me, my brothers, and our friends to converse more peacefully.

I smiled as I approached the place and heard the cheerful, animated voices escaping through the open door. I crossed the threshold and soon found them standing in a circle at the back of the spacious library. Shaw was telling some story, animated and euphoric in that unique way he had. Wolf and Snake listened attentively, laughing from time to time.

"What are you guys talking about?"

"OH MY GOD!" Shaw, who had his back to me, jumped like a rabbit and ran in the opposite direction, and only then did I realize they hadn't seen me come in. "Mr. Ghost, this makes it hard to keep my survival goals." Shaw placed a hand on his chest, barely able to breathe.

"What time did you sneak in that I didn't see?" Snake cursed, clenching his fist, also startled.

"It's always the same, in every country in the world. Ghost is Ghost." Wolf crossed his arms, and Lyon chuckled.

"That damn kid," Snake huffed, indignantly, his hard face taking on a funny expression that sent a wave of laughter throughout the library.

My older brother got furious when I startled him; perhaps because he was the eldest, he tried to maintain an unshakeable demeanor, as if nothing could pull him out of the protective bubble he had created around himself. Meanwhile, Wolf, who was shooting daggers at me with his bicolored eyes, as the middle brother, didn't carry the weight of being the example among us, though that didn't stop him from trying.

My brothers were completely different, from their physicality to their emotions. Snake was the most grounded and least explosive. He was the only one among us who made every decision systematically and precisely; he never did anything without thinking it through first and had total control of his emotions at his fingertips, which, incredibly enough, made him even scarier. Wolf was well-articulated, possessing a mind as precise as the muscles he worked on every day, but he still had issues with self-control and usually said whatever came to mind, often resulting in a fight. But there was one thing those two had in common: their hatred for being scared by their little brother—in this case, me.

I swallowed hard, watching them laugh in a playful way, and a strange pang in my chest hit me. Wolf and Snake had always been by my side since I gained a family. They grew up protecting me even from myself, when they barely knew how to handle their own problems. Those two were my partners in crime, my best friends, my balance and security, and I had no idea how much I needed them, how terrifying it was to face everything without being able to count on the revitalizing and hopeful presence of each of my brothers. I hadn't even realized how desperate I was until I saw them standing before me.

"Why are you looking at me like that?" I crossed the library in a few steps and pulled those two idiots into a tight embrace.

"What's up with this?" Wolf complained, but I ignored him. It took a few seconds, but soon both returned the hug, perhaps not understanding how important that was to me.

"Thank God you're here," I murmured.

"Where else would we be, brother?" Snake clapped my back in an aggressive comfort that almost made me laugh.

"Sometimes you scare me, but right now... what a beautiful thing!" Shaw sniffled behind us and joined the embrace. "Come on, Lyon!"

"No way." Shaw tilted his hand, grabbed Lyon's tie, and dragged him into the hug. "Let me go... damn it!" The man stumbled through the library and landed in the embrace, caught by Shaw's arm. Lyon looked like he was about to faint from the sudden contact. He stared at us with a face as if he had just sucked on a lemon, and a wave of laughter erupted in the library.

"I was coerced!" he complained as soon as we let go.

"You shouldn't see a hug like that and not participate. Human warmth, Lyon. Human warmth." Shaw raised his finger as if he had become the voice of human wisdom.

"What happened to Shaw while I was gone?" I looked at the young man, who straightened up as soon as he noticed he was being watched.

His arms, once very thin, had developed muscles that I could swear hadn't been there before. The kid even looked taller, and his voice, which used to be high-pitched and sometimes annoying, had deepened and strengthened.

"Did you notice?" He flashed an excited smile. "I've been drinking lemon water every morning." He winked at me and turned to Lyon. "See, Lyon? I told you that you should do the same, but you don't listen to me."

I started to laugh.

"I've missed this chaotic environment," I observed.

"As if you haven't faced anything exciting in the last few days, you shameless jerk." Wolf pulled up a chair, and everyone else followed suit. Soon we were gathered around the library table.

"Come on, spill it. I want to know all the details, from the moment you accepted the mission to the instant we crashed here, not knowing if we'd bring you back in pieces." Snake waved his hand in the air and narrowed his eyes. "In detail."

"Except for the sexual details," Wolf interjected urgently, and I narrowed my eyes in his direction with a veiled threat.

"If anyone here has sexual stories that should be deleted, it's you, dear brother; your house isn't safe. I can hardly sit on the couch without imagining some perversion," I retorted.

"If you made noise, it wouldn't surprise us in strenuous situations."

"Strenuous situations? Is that what we're calling them now?" Lyon laughed, and Shaw, who had remained silent, had turned so red that for a moment I feared he might just implode right there.

"Shaw, are you okay?" I asked, concerned.

"In perfect shape, sir, I've told you... lemon is the way. After God, of course."

"He's a virgin," Lyon suddenly blurted out, and silence fell over the room. "Don't look so surprised; just look at him. It's written all over his forehead."

"It's not that I don't want to; I'm just waiting for the right woman," Shaw reinforced his stance, unshaken.

"And you're right, Shaw. There's nothing wrong with waiting for the right person." I tried to comfort him.

"You didn't think that way when you were 15 and brought that girl home and..."

"Brother," I interrupted Wolf before the idiot let anything slip. "Should I remind you of what you did in our father's pool?"

"In the pool?" Snake roared. "I can't believe it; that was a public and sacred place. We swam there, you thoughtless amoeba."

"And you have the right to complain, Snake?" Wolf retorted. "I remember well when our father's silver handcuffs mysteriously disappeared for a long time. If he knew what you did with them..."

"How about you keep your sordid past to yourselves for now?" Lyon slammed his hand on the table, and we all looked at him. "I don't know about you guys, but I'm dying of curiosity. What the hell happened here, Ghost?"

"Alright, let's get back to the main topic." I took a deep breath and started recounting the entire story, from the moment I parked in front of Scott's house, to stumbling upon the dungeon and discovering the whole human trafficking scheme they were running, the car escape, the motel attack, the night in the woods, and finally, the protest, the shooting, the boat, the improvised surgery... "I don't think I forgot anything."

"Holy shit!" Wolf shook his head.

"Holy...," Snake echoed.

"You must be very beloved by God," Shaw added. I looked at Lyon, who was staring into space with his chin resting on his clenched fist.

"Don't look at me. I'm still shocked by all of this. Traveling from one country to another to rescue a prisoner is outside my reality, not to mention the number of women we found in the same situation in our country. It's... surreal."

"Unfortunately, human trafficking is one of the most profitable crimes in the world. A filthy business, run by men and women who cannot be called human." Snake's gaze drifted to a point on the dark table. "I'm sorry you found her in such conditions, brother. I see how attached you've become to her." I nodded, aware that "attached" didn't even begin to cover what I truly felt for Star. "But you know the right thing would be to hand her over to our country's authorities." I suddenly stared at him, clenching my fists by my sides. "But by that murderous look in your eyes, that was never an option. And I understand you, brother." He raised his hands defensively after scanning my face.

"I would do the same if it were my Jas." Wolf blinked a few times and then stood up, agitated. "I can't even imagine that idea. My God, if anyone tried anything..." He gasped, desperation reflecting in every movement.

"She's safe, Mr. Wolf." Little Shaw, who was no longer little, placed a hand on my brother's shoulder in an attempt to calm him. Wolf thanked him with a nod and approached me, resting both hands on my shoulders.

"Brother, remember when I took Jasmin to one of my hideouts and you intercepted me in that..."

"Kitchen of dubious provenance?" He laughed.

"Yes, right there. You lost 100 dollars when you bet with Snake that I wouldn't have the courage to be with one of my VIPs. Was it pretty stupid and childish? Yes, very stupid, but I was more so. I took a while to realize I loved that woman and all the chaos she caused. I see a lot of myself in you."

"Maybe I didn't take as long to realize," I admitted for the first time. "I don't know what I'll do if something happens to her, Wolf. It's as if that woman, whose real name I don't even know, is a part of me. As if with those fine, small fingers, she managed to steal part of my soul. Just the thought of losing her to them again, imagining her suffering, drives me mad." I looked at my brothers, distressed.

Snake stepped forward with a firm stride, and the library fell into a significant silence.

"I know you're scared, Zion." He reached into his pocket and handed me a package. "But if there's anyone capable of doing this, it's you."

"And that's why we're here, to ensure you get back safely," Wolf added. I opened the brown package and found two passports inside.

"And you're mistaken, brother. You, more than any of us, know that girl's name."

"We'll take Star home, then we'll think about the rest, okay?" Wolf patted my arm, and I smiled, nodding, while my eyes scanned the passport bearing the name "*Star Holder*" next to the photo of the young woman with long hair and exotic eyes, smiling sweetly and shyly. My heart raced, and if there was any doubt left, it was now replaced with certainty.

I wanted Star in my life with the same desperation I needed air to breathe. She would be my woman, and whatever her name was, she would carry a Holder name in the end.

AFTER A LONG DISCUSSION about all the possibilities and outbursts my father might have when we arrived with one of his sons shot and carrying a fugitive, which I must admit didn't seem like it would end well, Don Matteo arrived in the library accompanied by his *consiglieri*, Mirko Ferrari. A tall, robust man with countless tattoos starting on his face and descending down his neck, surpassing even Snake's extensive collection.

"Valentina asked me to let you know that our farewell has begun." Don Matteo was beaming. "You look good in a suit, Ghost; you seem less dead." A wave of laughter followed his comment, and I found myself chuckling, happy to be miraculously still breathing after everything. "I feel like I'm watching a free bodyguard showcase." He laughed and guided us out of the library. "It's a shame you're leaving."

"Are you sure you want me around any longer?" Snake teased his friend.

"Of course not; are you crazy? A disaster happens every time one of the Holder brothers sets foot in Italy. You should consider throwing your passports in the trash; it's safer." I laughed and considered the possibility.

The night had already covered the hills in gray clouds, and a gentle breeze wove through the refreshing night air. Points of stars dotted the sky, reflecting the deep blue of the sea, and we followed Don's lead in comfortable silence until we reached the beach.

"Maybe we shouldn't be wearing suits here, ow!" Shaw tripped over a mound of sand and nearly fell.

"Well, where did you think a luau would take place? Of course, it's on the beach."

I looked over my shoulder as my brothers and Don debated about the sand getting into Wolf's sock while Shaw fought to avoid face-planting somewhere, and I noticed that the boat that would take us away was already anchored at the dock. I took a deep breath. Soon that nightmare would end. I was sure I wouldn't be able to sleep until I set foot in the safety of my own home, with Star in my arms.

"There they are." Don Matteo pulled me from my thoughts, and when I lifted my eyes, I saw a few lively figures laughing and chatting animatedly.

Valentina, Sonia, and Giorgia stood around a bonfire. Nearby were two large, firm round poufs holding a candle inside a metal lantern, and a string of lights created a magical and cozy scene, along with some floral arrangements. There was also a table where pitchers of juice and bottles of whiskey and wine were laid out next to a fruit sculpture and cold appetizers like sandwiches, and it was there, near the snack table, that I found her.

Star was distracted, fishing with her fingers for a grape while scanning her options, and I held back a smile as I watched her open a bottle of whiskey.

I approached her as she moved gracefully, radiant in a royal blue dress that reminded me of the Chicago sky on a sunny day. I halted my steps. Watching her was magical, hypnotizing. That girl full of mysteries, with her dark hair cascading like waterfalls down her back, had reached something I never imagined I could feel for someone again.

No, I would be lying if I said I felt for another woman what I felt for Star. Maybe I had loved my ex; I believed that, just as I was sure there were loves and loves. What I had with Beatrice was strong, intense. I suffered for a long time when we separated, but with Star... God, kissing her was like standing at the door of life, a step away from my heart stopping. She could turn me inside out with just one look.

I never slept without a shirt with Beatrice, nor did I ever let her see those marks, and it wasn't easy to hide part of my body in a relationship. But with Star, it was different. She not only saw my scars but kissed each one. The memory still made me burn inside with a mix of shame and passion. The depth of the feelings that embraced me every time I thought of her left me breathless.

"Star," I called, determined not to startle her.

"Zion!" She opened that sweet smile that made her eyes squint. I rushed over, eager to touch her in some way. "Look what I discovered; you take this thing..." She reached for the cocktail shaker, and only then did I realize there was a small table beside her to prepare drinks. "Then you pour in the whiskey, lemon, sugar..." She twirled around me, tossing various other ingredients into the shaker. "And now you just shake it!"

"Are you sure everything in there is edible?" I joked, but I couldn't maintain my own smile as I watched her skillfully handle that thing, making her round, prominent breasts sway from side to side in the dress's low cut. They bounced up and down, hugging the fabric, and at that moment, I felt the growing stiffness between my legs.

"I don't know what this is, but if it has alcohol, I want it." Snake approached.

"Coming right up, a drink whose name I can't remember for the tattooed weirdo."

"You're a sweetheart!" He lifted the corners of his lips and scrunched his nose.

"Give me that, please. You make the potion, and I'll shake it, right?" I grabbed the shaker before the next image of Snake was my woman's breasts swaying.

Holy shit, *my woman!*

The thought made me gasp for air.

"Everything alright there, brother?" I coughed, and Snake gave me a pat on the back.

"All perfect." I resumed shaking the shaker while Star glided across the drink table as if she were at home.

She skillfully grabbed two glasses with one hand and tossed them back and forth, dipped her hand into a small bowl, and sprinkled a fine layer of white powder over one of the preparation boards. Then, almost like a sensual dance, she swirled the glasses, dipping them briefly into a liquid, and then rimmed the edges by dipping the glass into the powder she had set aside.

"Now just pour the drink in here." She ran towards us.

"Don't run with the glasses in your hands, Star."

"She's not 10 years old, Ghost." Snake laughed and took the shaker from my hand, opening it just as Star reached us. "And to be honest, I'm inclined to believe she's an experienced bartender." My brother poured the liquid into the two glasses she held, keeping one for himself and handing me the other.

"Come on, try it!" Star urged us, her eyes shining with anticipation.

I looked at my brother, who raised his glass in my direction. We toasted and downed the drink. I almost groaned in pleasure as the sweet, slightly spicy liquid slid down cold, spreading a pleasurable sensation throughout my body. I could taste the nuances of each ingredient, which, even together, didn't overshadow the intense flavor of the whiskey itself.

"Holy shit, you got the exact measurements right!" Snake blinked, surprised. "That's really hard to do."

"I know!" I agreed, euphoric. She was really good at this, and now we had the first clue about some trace of her past.

"Did you really like it?" She jumped in place, her cheeks flushed with happiness.

"Darling, you're a genius. A true specialist, for sure."

"I can attest to that," Snake chimed in. "It's hard to find someone who knows the right point for a drink without losing the main objective…"

"To maintain the original flavor of the whiskey," she proudly completed.

"Exactly. Anyone who can do that certainly has my respect." She blushed gracefully, and I wanted to throw my brother into the sea.

"Alright, now get out of here." I pushed Snake's shoulder, and he laughed, barely moving that pile of muscles. "I still haven't kissed my favorite bartender."

"I'll look for Wolf; you can exchange saliva at will." Star laughed and then hung on my neck. The scent of whiskey from her lips soon reached my nose.

"It was amazing, angel; I arrived and saw all those things for drinks and felt something strange. I started messing around at the drink table, and when I realized it, the recipes and the correct way to make each detail of the drinks were spinning in my head." She was so euphoric that she didn't even realize what she had called me, but I did.

Angel... A four-letter word that felt like it was the size of the world and warmed my heart.

"You have no idea how happy I am that you remembered, mi amor." I leaned in to touch my lips to hers, wrapping my arms around her waist and pulling her closer. The taste of whiskey spread across my palate, and I had to control myself to not pull her against the painful erection she caused.

Her tongue, usually so shy, eagerly slipped between my lips. Her delicate fingers tangled in my hair at the nape of my neck, and she let out a soft moan that made me even harder.

"How much of this did you drink?" I questioned, brushing my mouth against hers. "One?"

"Actually..." She looked up at the sky, trying to remember, and as she raised her fingers to count, my jaw dropped in disbelief. "It was four or five."

"And you're still standing?" My eyes nearly popped out of their sockets.

"Like a soldier!" She saluted.

"Star, save meeeee!" Valentina came bouncing through the sand with Don Matteo hanging on her arm. It was funny to see a man who was usually extremely dangerous transform into someone else around his wife. That was undoubtedly his best version.

"Valentinaaaa!" my little one sang and spun in my arms, rubbing her backside against me, and I almost bit my tongue trying to suppress any inappropriate sounds.

"Please, show my husband what a real drink is? I beg you; I want one too!" Valentina also had flushed cheeks, and just one look from one to the other told me what had happened there.

"They started the party without us." Don Matteo approached, and we stood together watching the two rush toward the drink table. "My God, is that safe?" Star was pouring the drinks, and Valentina kept cheering for her new friend.

"For God's sake, I hope so."

CHAPTER TWENTY-FIVE

Ghost

That night became one of my favorites.

The gentle breeze, the romantic and friendly atmosphere, Star smiling as she ran along the beach with Valentina in tow, while Sonia and Giorgia tried to keep up with them. Everything was in perfect harmony.

The men gathered near the bonfire. Snake calmly recounted the moment he met Don Matteo in a trap that almost cost the man his life in Chicago.

Apparently, one of Don's allies had deceived him, landing him in the middle of a delivery for an unknown mafia that would surely consider him a threat to be eliminated immediately. If it weren't for Snake, who had immense influence within that mafia, almost as a chief advisor, he would have been a goner. He was working that day and realized that Don Matteo had been misled and intervened for him.

"Snake had to escort me back to Sicily. He trusted me, saw the truth in what I said, and if it weren't for him, the worst could have happened," Don Matteo continued the story, which Lyon and Shaw followed with rapt attention.

"Hey, Wolf." I gave a nod and stepped away from the circle for a brief moment. Wolf followed me.

"Everything okay?" he asked, suspicious.

"Actually, maybe I've had too much to drink, but I'd like to ask you for some advice. After all, you're the only one of us who knows what it's like to live with a woman."

"I think I'm the one who hasn't drunk enough." He laughed and crossed his arms. "When did my little brother grow up so much?"

"I was never that small," I pointed out, shoving my hands into my pockets with a hint of a smile. I saw Wolf searching for Star with his eyes and found her playing with the pebbles on the beach alongside Valentina.

"I can't explain what I feel for her," I confessed. "It's like Star is in my thoughts all the time. I'm terrified just thinking of any possibility where she gets hurt, and I've been struggling to control that impulse you know well." I let out what had been bothering me for days. "My nightmares are now about her. I go crazy with worry; it's something I can't even explain. As if..." I tried to find the right words.

"As if it hurt in your own flesh when she gets hurt." He looked into my eyes. I nodded with a defeated sigh.

"Do you understand that?"

"It's how I feel about Jasmin. I wouldn't think twice before jumping in front of a bullet for her." He touched my injured shoulder carefully. "And looking from here, you don't seem that different from me." He smiled. "I don't think you need advice, brother."

"I'm afraid of making her unhappy somehow."

"Then you're on the right path."

"How can you say that? I'm more lost than your damn keys."

"You heard she stole from me again, didn't you?" Wolf laughed. My sister-in-law was known for her light fingers, and from time to time, she would swipe Wolf's motorcycle keys, a collector's vehicle she was fascinated by.

"Dad told me. He was the one who asked her to take your keys, you know? The old man adores her."

"There's no other way. Jasmin charms everyone." He smiled, smitten. "And when I say you're on the right path, I mean that like you, every day I worry about making her happy. It's become my greatest pleasure and goal. Every day I choose to make her happy, and I'm sure this will be your decision from now on. But don't be fooled; now and then, you'll want to strangle that delicate little neck, but even when she irritates me, Jasmin makes me feel like the happiest man on earth." He turned to me, a gentle sincerity displayed in his bicolored eyes. "Snake may not believe in love and continue this life of a different woman every night, but when his moment comes..."

"And apparently it comes for everyone in the most varied ways." I laughed and added.

"Yes, and only when it happens will he realize there's a huge difference between a life alone and one with the woman you love. Everything changes, for the better. We're lucky, brother."

That's how I felt, like a damn lucky fool for having found my Star amid so many misfortunes.

MY FRIENDS AND BROTHERS exchanged stories near the bonfire, distracted by drinks and laughter when someone brought a guitar to Don.

"Come on, Matteo, it's been ages since I heard that voice. The bastard is good." Snake clapped his friend on the shoulder and pointed to the guitar. Soon Star and the other women joined us around the fire.

My girl was electric, sweaty, and delightful in that flowing dress. Star stumbled over and flopped onto me. We formed a circle, and everyone sat on one of the thousands of cushions scattered around. I nestled Star between my legs and wrapped my arms around her waist. Don Matteo strummed a few notes, tuning the guitar, and began to sing a beautiful song in Italian.

His deep voice resonated through the night. Star followed along with her intense, sparkling eyes, even without understanding a word he was saying, and she cheered loudly, just like the others when Don Matteo finished the song.

"Star, *mia amica*, can you sing a little?" Valentina asked. "I heard you singing to Ghost when he was, well... in the infirmary." She laughed, and I looked at Star. I hadn't known she had sung while I was unconscious. "You have a beautiful voice."

"Would you grace us, miss?" Don Matteo requested, and all eyes turned to Star. I imagined my little one would decline the invitation, but the drinks had made her lively and much more at ease.

"Can you play, Zion?" she asked softly.

"Which song, sweetheart?" I touched her face with the back of my hand.

"That one..." Her big eyes met mine, and I knew what her answer meant; the piercing fear of seeing her cry like the first time I heard that song hit me.

"Are you sure?" I held back the urge to throw her over my shoulder and run away.

"Yes. I spent the day with Valentina, listening to her, and I remembered it's my favorite song." I pondered for a moment, searching her face for any sign of danger, but when I didn't find any, my only option was to accept.

"It would be a pleasure; I just need a moment to find the sheet music for that song." I grabbed my phone and searched online.

"It's all yours." Don Matteo handed me the instrument, and I positioned myself next to Star.

"Are you ready, sweetheart?"

"Yes." She took a deep breath and closed her eyes.

I slid my fingers across the guitar strings and began to play.

Each time I heard Star sing, I was more convinced I would never get used to the surprise of hearing her voice, and now my little one wasn't just surprising me. There was an audience frozen in pure shock as she focused solely on singing.

Her melodious voice danced through the lyrics of *Flashlight*, making it difficult to keep my attention on the sheet music. Star surrendered to the music, soaring and diving in high, intense tones. Her body leaned forward, and she placed her hand on her chest, feeling the lyrics in every sense.

A shiver ran up my spine and spread through my body as she reached the climax of the song, tossing her hair to the side like a goddess. Yes, how I longed to worship her—with my mouth, with my fingers, marking her with all my essence. And when she stopped singing, the only sound audible was the waves crashing against the shore.

"I told you she was incredible." I returned the guitar to Don and wrapped my arms around Star's waist.

"I wouldn't have imagined in two lifetimes that I would meet a voice like that. Star is one in a million." Valentina leaned in and touched her friend's hand.

"To me, she's one of a kind." I kissed the top of her head.

Everyone was so astonished that they still stared at us with wide eyes, even Wolf turned to Snake as if the words were burning in his mouth.

"Singing bartender!" He pointed suddenly.

"That's not fair; an extra chance is a hundred bucks more, and I already chose Bartender." My older brother retorted, and I narrowed my eyes, jumping from one to the other.

"I can't believe you bet on her," I growled at the idiots I called brothers. "I'm going to rip both of your balls off!" I stood up, about to grab Wolf by the hair.

"It's nothing, I swear." He raised his hands, laughing.

"What do you mean, they bet?" Don Matteo asked, curious.

"It's something we sometimes do among us," I explained, squinting. "We try to guess something about one of the brothers without the victim knowing, then we bet between the two involved to see who wins. I've lost count of how many times we've done this, but never with anyone outside of the three of us."

"And with our dad," Snake added, assertively.

"And with our dad!" I gritted my teeth and glared at him. "It wasn't supposed to involve anyone else besides him, remember?"

"Don't you think we're grown up enough to stay quiet about her past curiosity?" Wolf retorted.

"What are you talking about, huh?" Star stood up and faced Snake, who for the first time in ages decided to apologize for something.

"I'm sorry, miss, but we bet a hundred bucks on who would discover something about your past first. We saw some of your skills and decided to bet on what your profession would be, like the children we are." I raised my nose, counting the seconds until Star started to curse him out.

I waited for that moment with all my might, but when she opened her mouth, she almost knocked me back.

"Can I bet too?"

"What?" A chorus of surprised voices echoed through the night.

"Come on," she turned to me with a smirk as if she was about to pull a prank, "I have no idea what I did as much as they do, and if I happen to guess right, I'll be a hundred dollars richer than now."

"I want to bet too!" Valentina jumped in place.

"Well, if that's the case, I want to as well. I bet on the singer!" Don Matteo got excited.

"Great, you've created a lottery, haven't you?" My brothers started laughing along with Star, and I couldn't stop the corners of my lips from betraying me, breaking into a smile against my will.

"I'm thirsty; I'll get something to drink," Star said, and I touched her hand.

"I'll go with you." We turned our backs without anyone paying attention to us. They were so absorbed in the possibilities of Star's past that they wouldn't notice us even if we set that guitar on fire.

"What do you want to drink?" We stopped in front of the drink table.

"Straight whiskey, no ice, please," she requested with alarming certainty.

"Maybe you really do work with this." I poured two shots and watched her down hers in one long gulp, savoring the warm drink.

"The pure flavor is even more invigorating." I tilted my drink back and took the glass from her hands. Our fingers touched, causing a small electric shock that made her let out a delightful squeak of surprise.

"What was that?" She widened her eyes. The tousled hair framed her delicate, stunning face, giving her the appearance of a wild warrior in that blue dress. Star was indecently beautiful.

I brushed the hair from her shoulders and leaned in to plant a kiss on the vein pulsing in her neck. She gasped, surprised.

"The human body allows electric charges to move freely." I traveled my lips along her skin, reaching the curve of her cheekbones. She closed her eyes at the touch. "And thus, it allows the passage of an electric current from one body to another."

"My God, you're such a nerd!" She gasped when I nibbled her jawline.

"You got me; I admit I could extend this explanation and talk about protons and electrons, but to summarize, the human body is a good conductor of electricity, and your body, *mi amor*, is leading me to a cliff."

"I can't let you fall," she whispered, affected, and I moved my lips to her ear, nibbling the tip carefully.

"Then hold me." I tightened my grip on her waist and slid my fingers to graze the side of her beautiful, round breast. She let out a soft moan.

"You make me feel things." I looked into her face and parted my lips in desire, noticing her flushed cheeks.

I turned to our little crowd of friends where Don had returned to singing. Everyone was focused on the private show, and I was sure they wouldn't notice our absence if we disappeared from there.

"Sweetheart, how about a walk on the beach?"

"A walk?" She blinked, confused. Then I took her hand, glanced around to confirm no one was watching, and placed it over the painful erection she had caused me.

"I want to show you a place before we leave, what do you think?"

"Are we going to have sex on the sand?" She almost shouted, and I had to cover her mouth with my hand.

"Shh, speak softly." I laughed and buried my face in her hair. I was loving this tipsy, straightforward version of Star she was showing me.

"But I want to have sex on the sand, come on, come on!" She escaped from my embrace and started pushing me.

"Should I feel violated?"

"Not at all," she laughed. "Let's make love, so please, cooperate!" I laughed and wrapped her in my arms, kissing her mouth slowly.

"Say that again," I requested.

"What?"

"That you want to make love to me. Say it." I needed to hear her say it again; maybe then I could etch that deliciously exciting combination of words deep into my mind.

"Make love to me, Zion. *Always* make love to me," she repeated, and I stayed there for a few more seconds, absorbing her words, her scent, her voice.

I held Star close to my heart, and as I ran with her across the sand, I felt for the first time in my life that I would find a happy ending to the nightmares that had tormented me for so long.

That night, I laid my mermaid on the sand of the beach, with the waves crashing behind us, and dove into her, crazy with desire. The sand dirtied our clothes, our skin, but I didn't care. I was lost in the desperate, surrendered moans she made as I entered her slowly, filling her up, my skin marked by her nails pulling me closer. In her half-open, hungry golden eyes. I was completely lost in her.

My heart began to race, burning with every thrust. I inhaled deeply, quickly, fiercely, as if marking her with my essence, mesmerized by the image of her flushed face, her full, parted lips full of desire.

She whimpered my name, and I stored every part of that dream in my mind and heart. Every thrust, every sigh, every moment she tightened around me in her warm, wet body. We exploded together in intense pleasure, and I settled her in my arms afterward.

Nothing was as perfect as the sight of her sandy skin under the moonlight. I kissed her mouth possessively, unable to control myself, and that's when I realized my heart had already made a choice. It was her. The love I had sworn never to believe in again.

CHAPTER TWENTY-SIX

Star

We said goodbye to Don Matteo and Valentina at the dock in the early hours of the morning, and after thanking them, I hugged the delicate woman with a strange knot in my throat.

"Will I see you again?" I asked, holding back tears, and Valentina squeezed my hands affectionately. Giorgia and Sonia joined us, and I hugged both of them tightly.

"I would love for you to visit when you come to the United States. My home will always be open to you, as will my eternal gratitude." Ghost shook Don's hand firmly.

"It will be a pleasure, and yes, dear, we will see each other again." Valentina gave me one last hug. Her bright eyes shone with emotion.

We boarded the boat, but I spent long minutes watching the figures waving from the beach. Words could not capture all the gratitude I felt for them; I hoped Valentina knew how important she was to me. To ensure she did, I left a small note next to one of her favorite drinks on the table in her room. It was something simple, but it carried all my affection, and I said goodbye to Sicily, sincerely determined never to return.

※

AFTER A FEW HOURS ON the boat, we arrived at an airport that, according to Ghost, was protected by Don Matteo's men, but that didn't stop the five bodyguards from forming a perimeter around me as we walked to the boarding area.

Curious glances fixed on us with each step we took. I had to admit, despite the constant fear I felt that something bad could happen at any moment, it was an exceptional and even hypnotic scene. The way they moved was precise; their steps seemed synchronized, as if each of them were interconnected in a rigid and threatening posture. Like a dance, they seemed to share the same soul.

We passed through the boarding gate, and part of the fear I felt was left behind in the Italian lands that bore no guilt for all my suffering but were marked by my pain.

Still, I was grateful to be returning home, even though I couldn't remember it.

I DOZED OFF ON THE plane after taking a calming pill, and when I woke up, I had a vague impression of dreaming about lying on the sand, underneath Zion.

Even after a shower, small grains of sand could still be found in my hair and on Ghost's impeccable suit. My intimacy was slightly sore, but the sensation was pleasant and reminded me of the exact moment he was filling me up.

Ghost had a naughty, perverted side that I loved more and more. The way he came over me on that sandbank, using my dress as a carpet for the indecent and very hot dance between our bodies, left a mark on me.

It was the first time we used a condom, and it was infinitely more enjoyable to feel him raw, but still, I experienced one of the strongest sensations of my life that night. The fear of being seen made everything more intense, and the memory of his hand on my butt, pulling me against his erection, thrusting deep, swirled in my mind. Our sweaty skins stuck grains of sand like glue, and I didn't want to stop; I couldn't.

My face burned as I realized how much I wanted to feel that sensation again.

We were about to disembark from the plane, a long trip that had almost terrified me, but recalling what we did and how we did it kept my mind distracted.

I ended up dozing off again, resting on Ghost's lap in the cabin reserved just for the Holder family.

"Sweetheart," he called in a soft, gentle voice, kissing my temple. "We've arrived." It took me a moment to realize we had stopped.

"Are we in the United States?" I yawned.

"Yes. We're home." I looked at him, filled with a strange and singular emotion, as if I was about to find an important part of myself. A part I had been searching for for a long time. "Come on, there's nothing to fear." He smiled, his relieved gaze studying me affectionately as he extended his hand.

"We made it." My choked voice revealed all the mixed feelings I was experiencing, and he nodded slowly. I intertwined my fingers with his in that touch that was so important to us.

We disembarked at a small, almost empty airport. Except for a cluster of people dressed in black waiting near the arrival gate.

Ghost guided me with firm steps, staying to my left. Snake walked to my right like a shield of muscles, Wolf followed behind us, and together, the three brothers formed a triangle around me, completed by Lyon and Shaw on the sides. It almost seemed rehearsed, and I started to wonder if this was some kind of bodyguard maneuver.

I noticed Ghost's body posture changed completely as we approached the men in black. He was staring at someone specific in the small crowd.

"Who are they?" I whispered.

"Our ride back," Snake replied.

"My father's clan," Ghost added, his voice very low, which worried me.

I scanned the crowd until I found the man he was staring at. A tall, strong guy with gray hair and a very youthful expression was looking at us with a neutral gaze. There was no expression in his cold gray eyes. He was an elegant and very handsome man, with that feline beauty that makes you never know when he'll strike.

In addition to Zion's father, there were about six other bodyguards standing like statues beside him.

"Father." A deafening silence filled the space.

Ghost stopped in front of him, and I felt his hand lightly squeeze mine. My protector angel was nervous, and I wanted to hug him, trying to comfort him somehow, but when the man stepped toward us, a sovereign tension fell over us.

I could feel it spreading through my sides, my back, through each person present. That man commanded respect without even needing to speak.

"I'm sorry for not saying anything." A painful tightness took my heart as I heard Zion's insecure voice, as if he suddenly wasn't the grown, dangerous man anymore. There, in front of his father, he was just a little boy. "I didn't want to..." The man pulled him into a hug that made Ghost wince. I released his hand and stepped aside.

"I'm grateful you came back alive and whole."

"Maybe this is a good time to remind you that I got shot in the shoulder," Ghost groaned, and his father stepped back slightly, sweeping his gaze over him from head to toe.

"A hug? I'm outraged; I expected at least a world war." Wolf crossed his arms.

"What's it like being the favorite, Ghost?" Snake teased.

"Oh, you two." The man scrutinized his sons one by one. "First, I'm grateful you're still breathing; then, I try to make you stop breathing, and with Ghost, it'll be no different, this irresponsible kid." The man cursed, pointing a finger at Ghost, making the three brothers laugh. Then his clear eyes landed on me, and suddenly I took a step back from him, almost hiding behind Zion.

He ran a hand over his tailored black suit almost unconsciously and took a step toward me. His eyes became slightly gentler, as if he saw something in me that I hadn't even noticed, and he showed the shadow of a smile.

"So, you are Miss Star?" His voice came out softer and kinder, and I nodded my head in confirmation, scared.

"Star, this is my father. Reid Holder." Zion introduced, and the man continued to stare at me.

"It's a p-pleasure, Mr. Reid." I clung to Zion's suit, and soon Reid turned to his son.

"She needs medical attention." His voice was urgent and concerned, and I shrank at the speed with which everything was happening. "We'll take her to a safe place, Star, don't be afraid. Each of these men is here to fulfill two missions: to escort you safely and to prevent me from killing one of my sons."

Another wave of laughter echoed around us, and I felt more relaxed. I nodded in agreement and heard a strange sound right afterward. A persistent *knock knock* seemed to speed toward us. I searched with my eyes to find where the sound was coming from and widened them as I noticed a young woman, very blonde and, my goodness, very beautiful, with large blue eyes and a little red dress matching her lipstick, walking quickly toward us, balancing on a fine, high heel. She looked like a doll out of the box.

"Finally, you guys are back!" she said loudly before even getting close to us.

Wolf passed by me almost running and went to meet the woman, who jumped into his arms as if she hadn't seen him in decades. They kissed, and the exchange of glances between them made it clear all the love they shared.

"Where is she?" I heard the blonde ask, and Wolf gestured in my direction.

Her bright blue eyes swept over the small crowd until they landed on me. Her face took on an expression that varied between pity and compassion, and she crossed the distance between us, dancing on her high heels.

"Jasmin, she doesn't like that..." The blonde reached me in a few strides, pushed Ghost aside with one hand, and pulled me into a hug with the other.

"It's too late now," Snake said softly.

I froze for a brief moment until I felt her thin, delicate arms wrap around me with such affection that I couldn't help but sigh. She seemed to care about me without even knowing me.

"This is Jasmin, my sister-in-law," Ghost introduced while she still held me in her embrace.

"The one with the frying pan?"

"That's the one. But don't believe everything these brothers say about me, okay?" Jasmin laughed and held my shoulders. "Welcome." She examined my face as if touching each of the small traces of bruises still visible on my skin, and I saw what seemed to be anger cross her clear eyes. "Everything will be okay now."

"Thank you," I whispered, grateful and surprised at the same time. She looked at Ghost and released me to point her slender finger at his face.

"If you dare to scare us like that again, I swear to God I'll rip your teeth out," she threatened, serious, making Wolf and Reid laugh.

"I'm also happy to see you in this astral plane."

"Idiot!" She hugged him affectionately. "You better get ready. Someone followed you, father-in-law." She turned to Reid and hugged him. "There's a considerable number of reporters at the airport entrance. All thanks to the new star of Chicago." She narrowed her eyes and glared at Snake.

"I didn't know I was being recorded when we blew that damn hideout," he growled, running his hands through his hair. "Damn, what now? These pests are like ants; they're everywhere. They firmly believe I have relevant information for the media about the case."

"Indeed, you do have relevant information for the media about the case," Shaw interjected, whispering a "sorry" when Snake growled at him.

"Now we only have one option." Reid straightened his body and looked at the six men waiting for him like shadows. "We're going to do what we do best: escort you out of here."

"Stay by my side, okay?" Ghost whispered and took my hand again. I tried to contain the panic that crept up my throat and started walking alongside them.

Reid walked in front alongside Snake, surrounded by the same triangle I had seen a few minutes earlier. The men spread around us and formed a barrier. Each of them wore sunglasses and earpieces through which they communicated. I also noticed the weapons they carried.

I shuddered, having no idea what to expect when I saw a small crowd at the exit.

"We need to get past them to reach the parking lot," Wolf instructed.

"Move quickly and concisely. Remember all the times you've done this for some movie star. Dealing with reporters is never different." Reid quickened his pace, and before I knew it, we were almost running through the courtyard, and not a single person passed us without staring. I noticed a woman pull out her phone and start recording us.

"Don't worry about her; she probably thinks we're escorting some celebrity and wants to capture the moment," Zion whispered in my ear and removed his suit jacket. "Lower your face, sweetheart, or the flashes will burn your eyes." He barely closed his mouth when a shower of bright flashes fell upon us, and a shouting match began.

"How did you find the hideout?"

"Snake, can you give us a statement?"

"Talk to us, please! Where is Scott Walker?"

"More crimes discovered?"

"What is the connection between Holder Security and the case revelation?"

The questions kept coming until a specific one made me freeze.

"Who is she?" someone shouted, and all the cameras' attention turned to me.

My eyes widened in panic. My feet stuck to the ground, and my legs lost the ability to move. Everyone around me stopped in their tracks with me; Ghost threw his blazer over my head and hugged me in the fabric.

"Come on, you can do this. Breathe, sweetheart." A shiver ran through my body, and I tried to force any movement, but there were so many voices, so many people... "Hold my hand; I won't let it go. Trust me."

"Trust us." I was embraced from the other side by a pair of thin arms. Jasmin squeezed me against her. "If any of those vultures come near you, I swear I'll poke their eyes out."

"And then I'm the violent one, right, Dad?" Snake complained, and I ended up laughing between gasps. It was hard to stay serious in the middle of that strange family.

"I've dealt with reporters chasing a scoop before. They are extraterrestrial beings with unlimited energy, but I know how to beat them, and we'll do this together." I bit my lips; I couldn't see anything under Ghost's suit, and I would have to trust them to guide me through the crowd, but if there was something that gave me confidence, it was the pairs of arms trying to keep me protected, and I decided to trust them once more.

I crossed the courtyard with my eyes glued to the asphalt under my feet. I felt a few pushes as we advanced, and the voices grew dangerously louder, but soon began to fade behind us.

I got into the back seat of a car with Ghost still hugging me, and I only removed the blazer from my head when he closed the car door. Snake took the wheel, and Shaw sat next to him.

"Oh my God, how wild they are!" Shaw complained as he settled into the seat. "I thought they were going to devour my precious little body." I laughed and shook my head.

"My little body..." I repeated in a whisper to Ghost, who looked at me with a funny expression.

"He's a character." Zion caressed my face with the back of his hand; his bright eyes were livelier since we landed. He felt safer at home, and just imagining that we were a country away from that dungeon made me infinitely happier. "Are you okay?" He lifted my face.

"Yes. Very much," I was honest, and he planted a warm kiss on my lips when Snake started the car, which was followed by three more black vehicles with the rest of the team.

I looked out the window and found a city completely different from the one we had been in. Full of tall buildings, crowds of people running around, many cars, and large buses scattered across wide streets. A constant noise pollution echoed under the blue sky's brightness, and all that commotion felt very familiar to me.

I was overcome by a strange feeling of finally having returned home.

CHAPTER TWENTY-SEVEN

Ghost

How could I believe that this was real?
How could I understand that part of the nightmare was over?
The thought crossed my mind as we passed through the door of my house.

My house, damn it!

We really had made it back, and it seemed so crazy that I was the one holding Star's hand, trying to accept that this was really happening.

"We've arrived, sweetheart. This is my home." Star twirled in place, observing every corner of the living room with curiosity. From the dark furniture, climbing the walls with recessed lights, to the grand piano, black as the suspended reclining couch nearby.

My siblings, Jasmin, and my father entered, each looking for a comfortable place to sit. Shaw and Lyon had gone to their own homes and would return to Holder the next day, and everything seemed to be okay.

"Star," my father called.

"Yes, it's me, but I'm not me." She stopped in the middle of the room, agitated. "I don't know if you know this, but I don't remember my real name, but I like this one. Zion gave it to me, so..." She paused to catch her breath.

"Alright, Miss Star who isn't Star, can you sit here for a moment?" my father asked, and I guided my little one until she sat on the large leather sofa next to him.

I should admit I was nervous and anxious while waiting for my father to say anything. I knew he would welcome her, but I was desperate to hear what he had to say.

"Listen, girl..." He turned to her with a serious expression, but the warmth I saw in his gaze relieved me. "I can't imagine the horrors you've been through and how terrifying it must be not to remember anything." She blinked, her large eyes widening even more. "When I decided to raise these three, I knew each one also came with a suitcase full of problems. They were stubborn, loud, and fighters, but that wasn't the worst. To me, my suffering revolved around theirs. I knew exactly the scars behind each of their behaviors, and I see the same in you. A young girl who was forced to be stronger and braver." My Star sniffled, trying not to cry at all costs, but her teary eyes betrayed her. "I know you must feel confused and lost, going back and forth from one country to another without knowing who you really are, but don't worry, there is indeed a light at the end of the tunnel, and you will reach it with a little help and care. Look at my children, each one lived through hell, and even though they have flaws that sometimes make me want to kill them, they are incredible. They are my greatest pride, and I know how hard they fought to overcome their past. In your case, the past isn't very distant, but what remains, what you've suffered, you can count on all of us to help you overcome."

"Overcoming." I startled myself with my hoarse and emotional voice. "That's the kind of thing my family specializes in." She smiled and wiped away a discreet tear.

"Thank you, Mr. Reid. I am very grateful. To Zion, for saving me, and to you all, for helping a stranger."

"You don't seem so strange to the Ghost." Jasmin smiled and shrugged, making me smile too.

"We need to decide the next steps. We have to investigate her, try to find out where she came from and if she has any living relatives," my father said. "But I believe before everything, you all need to rest."

"And see a doctor," I added.

"And clothes..." All eyes fell on Jasmin. "Well, I didn't see any suitcase, how do you expect her to survive in this nerdy house full of weird stuff?"

My sister-in-law scanned the hallway wall, where five rare silver miniatures of the Knights of the Round Table were arranged on short, transparent shelves that gave the impression they were floating in the hallway. I had become a collector of rare pieces a few years ago and acquired them on a trip to Great Britain. Another item I loved was my 13th-century Kamakura katana hanging in my room, a sword I had won at an auction thanks to one of Snake's quirky contacts, among other pieces for which I had good reasons to use extra alarms, in addition to insurance.

"She's going to need a world of things. Clothes, shoes, creams, underwear..."

"Jasmin!" I widened my eyes at my loudmouthed sister-in-law, and Star turned as red as a pepper.

"These are facts, Ghost!" She rolled her eyes and hid in Wolf's embrace.

"In any case, there's no way to go out after that reporter attack," Snake pondered, leaning forward, thoughtful. "They took pictures of her, they'll probably notice at some point the bruises that are still visible, they might try to link her to me, and soon they'll get to the warehouse with the victims."

"Victims?" Star opened her lips, her eyes widening even more.

"My dear, you weren't the only one taken by that bastard, as you might imagine. We found a hideout with some other victims." She shrank back, and I saw fear cross her cinnamon-colored eyes. "But they were saved. All of them," I lied, hiding the fact that two of them hadn't survived. "They're already with their families. And you're right, but I need to think of something. Star needs to see a doctor urgently."

"I can ask my doctor to come see her," Jasmin suggested. "I think the lab tests can be done here. She'll feel less uncomfortable."

"Yes, if possible, I prefer that." Star leaned toward my sister-in-law.

"Of course it's possible, dear. And my goodness, how beautiful you are. I still can't get used to it," Jasmin commented randomly, like almost everything she did. My sister-in-law had no filter, and a lovely rosy hue took over my girl's cheeks.

"Then it's decided." I went to the small office next to my living room and grabbed my spare credit card from one of the drawers. "Jasmin, do you think you can handle the shopping?"

"Ohhhhhhhhhhhh!" She jumped on the sofa and snatched the card from my fingers. "It will be a pleasure."

"Buy everything you think is necessary."

"Deal, I'll be back later. I'll call the doctor on the way. She should arrive in a few hours." Jasmin kissed my father and turned to Star. "In the future, we'll go shopping together." And she skipped out of the room. Wolf stood up and placed a hand on my shoulder.

"Good luck with your credit card, brother."

Alena

I SAT IN THE LIVING room while Zion took his family to the gate. My eyes were fixated on that beautiful, shiny piano, but my thoughts had turned to the appointment I would have later that day. I had no idea what it would be like, and the unknown always made me anxious.

Poft, Poft, Poft, Poft

A strange sound caught my attention and pulled me from my reverie. I shoved the fear I felt under the rug and looked over my shoulder to see what it was.

"What are you doing?" I laughed loudly when I saw Ghost lifting his knees as he walked to make noise when his foot touched the ground. He looked like a heron with back problems, and I burst into laughter that made my stomach hurt.

"I'm trying to make noise so I don't scare you. You should thank me for this!" He wrinkled his nose. "Such a lack of appreciation for my effort." He played it up, which didn't help at all. I laughed so hard I started to cry, and even he couldn't resist and laughed too.

"Come with me, funny girl. I want to show you the house." He extended both hands and helped me stand up.

"It's very luxurious," I observed as we entered a hallway where some miniatures were displayed. "I'm scared I'll bump into something ridiculously expensive and break it all."

"Don't worry about that, sweetheart. Accidents happen, although I would prefer if you avoided any that involved the sword in my room. For your own safety." He opened the last door in a hallway that, like the rest of the house, had a variation of light and dark grays, along with white.

"A sword?" I entered the room, which was very clean and spacious, with light plaster walls, a built-in closet that looked more like an extra room, and a double window that allowed sunlight to bathe half the room.

The bed was gigantic, and there was a lamp on each side, on retro wooden stands, which matched the serious furniture.

"My goodness," I whispered, noticing the massive sword hanging on a wooden panel in front of the bed.

"I'm a collector of special pieces, and I must admit I really like each of my acquisitions, like the vase on the pillar near the piano or the painting in my office, but this sword is among my favorite pieces."

"It looks like it must have cost a lot. At least can you stab someone with it?" He laughed.

"If you want to know if it's sharp, the answer is yes. It can hurt."

Zion showed me a microchip that had been carefully and discreetly placed in each piece of his collection so he could track them in case they were stolen.

"I planned this house to be safe. There are cameras at the entrance, the gate has a sensor and alarm, and I also have cameras at all strategic points on the roof that allow me to see around us, and the master bedroom is like a panic room. If you close the door, only you can open it, and the window is bulletproof." He didn't even pause to breathe.

"I don't know if I understood everything, but it looks like we're pretty secure." I laughed and followed him through the house, which was large and spacious, divided into a kitchen, two bedrooms, a dining room with a solid mahogany table and a strange painting that must also be worth a fortune, an office with a library, and another painting as ugly as the first, and the living room, which extended into a small hall where the piano was.

"Now, I want to show you one of my greatest treasures." We stepped outside the house and went down a small hill to the parking lot. "My

BMW Nazca. It definitely outshines the sword, and with it, I can go out." He laughed.

I widened my eyes as I approached the very shiny gray car that looked more like a spaceship. I opened my lips as that strange feeling of having seen something before hit me again, like a Déjà Vu.

The vehicle was imposing, seemed very powerful, and I had the impression that its designer shape gave it a constantly irritated appearance, as if it were glaring at me, pissed off.

It was incredible!

"It must be like the Don Matteo of cars," Ghost laughed.

"Yeah, it really does look like a mobster. I'll take it out to show you some places as soon as I can." He promised, cheerfully.

"I would love that." I looked at the reflection in the car's windows, which were flatter than normal, and I straightened up when someone honked in front of the large steel gate of Zion's house.

"It must be the doctor. Are you ready?"

No, but I would have to be.

CHAPTER TWENTY-EIGHT

Ghost

Dr. Madison arrived within two hours, accompanied by Rose, a nurse carrying a blood collection kit.

Jasmin had explained the entire situation we went through and assured me that the doctor was extremely trustworthy and would not report anything to anyone.

Star seemed a bit standoffish when they approached, but she soon began to feel more comfortable as she answered the endless questions from the doctor, who was visibly concerned about my little one's condition.

I stayed by her side, calming her, until the doctor looked into Star's eyes and asked in a routine tone:

"When was your last menstruation?" Star's face turned very red, and her posture became rigid.

"Maybe two weeks ago. I didn't really know how the days passed where I was." She lowered her gaze.

"That's alright, dear. It's okay." The doctor patted her hand, her expression fluctuating between anger and concern. "Now you are safe. We will take care of you."

"I'll leave you alone. Make yourselves comfortable." Star looked up at me but didn't ask otherwise.

I knew it must be hard for her to remember everything. There was no way she could handle it with dignity during her captivity, and although I wanted to tell her that there was no reason to feel that way, I understood.

I waited in the living room while the examination and tests were done in my office with the door closed, and about an hour later, the doctor emerged from the room and came to me.

"Well... Rose is just finishing up the blood samples, but I must warn you, Ghost." I swallowed hard, nervous and worried. "Her condition seems good. Stable blood pressure, good motor and perceptive responses. But the overall situation could become alarming. She is a kidnapping victim who lost her memory." She placed a hand on her hip and shook her head, as if she couldn't believe what was happening. "We will run tests to see where we stand, but she needs to see a multitude of specialists. Especially a neurologist. We need to investigate why she lost her memory. At the hospital where I work, I have several colleagues who can help her discreetly and safely. I will provide you with the contacts to schedule the appointments."

"Okay, thank you, doctor."

"I'm done." Rose came out of the office with the kit in hand.

"Great, for now, that's all. Let her rest, and I'll call you tomorrow to discuss the results."

I took Madison and Rose to the exit, and when I returned to my office, I caught Star rummaging through the books in my small library with one arm bent, where a bandage had been carefully placed. She wore a red dress that Valentina had given her. After enduring a boat trip and two flights, the fabric was wrinkled and disheveled, and I hoped Jasmin would arrive soon with everything Star needed.

I was tired, exhausted to be honest, from seeing her always needing something. A sharp desire to be able to fulfill all her wishes and needs tightened in my chest.

I entered the office and approached her.

"How was the..." She screamed and swung a slap in my direction. I caught her wrist in mid-air before the slap hit my face.

"What the hell, Zion!" She gasped, startled, and I broke into a slow smile. "What's so funny? It's not funny at all, you almost gave me a heart attack!" I wrapped my body around hers, pressing her against the bookshelf and ran my fingers over her rosy cheeks.

"I wasn't laughing at you; I was just enchanted watching your face turn red." She blinked, confused, and blushed even more as she understood. "Your cheeks turn red when you're scared, when you're embarrassed, and especially when you're excited. It's charming." I pressed a kiss on the sensitive skin of her wrist.

"After that scare, I must definitely be red with anger." She wrinkled her nose, but soon a small smile lifted the corners of her lips.

"Sorry about that."

"I know you didn't mean it."

"I'll try to do better, without waddling like a lame duck." She let out a graceful and charming giggle. I loved seeing her smile.

"Just try not to surprise me when I'm holding anything sharp, okay? That's enough." I nodded in agreement.

"How was the appointment? Did it hurt?" I ran my fingers over her skin until they brushed against the bandage.

"No, it was just a little prick. I liked the doctor; she asked... a lot of questions." She bit her lips. "Some pretty embarrassing ones, but she just wants to help, so I told her everything she wanted to know."

"Good girl." I held her hand. "I'm going to prepare dinner; tomorrow I'll look for a housekeeper, which will help when I'm not here. I think we'll also need a cook."

"Listen, Zion," she called softly, diverting her eyes from mine. "You're doing so much for me. After everything we went through in Italy, you even mobilized your family to help me, gave your card to Jasmin so she could buy me clothes, and took me into your home." She sighed, anxious. "I don't know if I'll ever be able to repay all of this, but I plan to leave your house and stop bothering you as soon as possible, and..."

"Stop," I said, seriously.

"I don't want to be a burden."

"And you never will be." I took her face in my hands. "You have become very precious to me, Star. From the first moment I met you, I felt I was meant to take care of you. I want to protect you, little one," I said softly. "Don't worry about anything, and I would never accept you paying me back. I'm one of the major partners in my father's company, sweetheart. Money is not an issue."

"But..." I kissed the stubborn girl before she could continue.

"I'm your guardian, and you'll have everything you need and everything you want. Just let me be your safe harbor, okay?" I asked, anxious for her to agree.

"Just until I can get myself sorted."

"Yes, until you can get sorted and blah-blah-blah!" I rolled my eyes and hugged her.

"How old are you?" she laughed.

"Five, if that makes you forget this story."

"DOES A PERSON REALLY need all this to survive?" Star asked, her eyes wide after seeing all the boxes and bags that Jasmin had brought with Wolf's help, now piled throughout my living room.

"A woman does." Jasmin winked at her.

"I think I saw a pair of ears over there. Should I be worried?" I turned to Wolf.

"Definitely. She's going to implant the sovereignty of stuffed animals in Star; it's best to stay alert. I've seen Jasmin in action, and soon you'll come home to find a panda in place of Star."

My sister-in-law loved personalized stuffed animal outfits, and I could only imagine how my woman would look stuffed into one of those.

My woman... I loved that combination of words.

We spent the afternoon organizing all of Jasmin's purchases, and by the time night fell, both Star and I were exhausted to the bone.

I took advantage of her shower to sort out a few things.

I called Sicília and informed Don Matteo about our arrival. I also reminded him of my desire to be notified when the invasion of Don Gava's house was over. Even though we were on American soil, safe in my house, which was practically a fortress—second only to my light-fingered brothers and their advanced technology—I was still extremely worried about the fact that Scott was at large.

There was no way that man could set foot in the United States; his entire life had been destroyed, his followers abandoned him, and he had been severely punished in both the real world and the virtual one, becoming one of Interpol's main targets worldwide. But I couldn't feel at ease until I saw him locked behind bars, or in a coffin. Whichever came first.

I ended the call just as Star stepped out of the bathroom.

"Zion," she called. Her low, slow voice revealed the sleep that was creeping over her. I looked over my shoulder and held my breath the moment I laid eyes on her. "Does it look strange?" She yawned and let her hands glide down the black lace ensemble that draped over her curves, making them even more enticing. I swallowed hard, resisting the urge to pounce on her.

"I can't draw a conclusion; could you do a little spin so I can evaluate better?" She laughed, probably aware of my hungry gaze. She slowly turned and revealed her rounded, perky backside, adorned by the dark lace that made her look even more delicious.

"Do you like it?"

"Sweetheart, there's nothing you wear that looks anything less than perfect." I got up and walked over to her, desperate to touch her.

I wrapped my arm around her waist and slid my hand down to her rear, squeezing the flesh and sucking in the soft sound she let escape. Her eyes were warm, desirous, but her tired expression begged for a long night's sleep.

I leaned down and slid my arms under her legs. Star squeaked when I lifted her into my arms.

"What are you doing?" She laughed, and I kissed her.

"Putting you in bed." Star was already light and relaxed as I laid her down on the sheets and pulled the covers over her, tucking her in.

She closed her eyes and held my hand.

"Can you stay until I fall asleep?" she asked without opening her eyes.

"Of course, sweetheart, I'm not going anywhere." I lay down next to her and pulled her close to my chest, stroking her hand, her face, her hair, and she sighed, relaxed. The view of the arc forming a heart on her lips was graceful, and I couldn't resist the urge to touch it with my own lips.

"Your house is beautiful," she whispered and shivered.

"Our house, *mi* amor," I replied, but my little one was already asleep.

CHAPTER TWENTY-NINE

Star

I woke up the next morning feeling like I had experienced the best night of my life. It was as if I had slept in paradise on that high, extremely soft mattress, and to top it off, there was the owner of the muscular arms who had spent the night holding me.

I opened my eyes and stretched. I realized I was alone in the huge room. My still-drowsy body begged me to enjoy a bit more of that comfort, but I forced myself to get up and headed to the bathroom, determined to wake up for real. After washing my face and getting ready, I rummaged through the closet that Ghost had divided in two to make space for my clothes and shoes.

I looked for something to wear for the day and pulled out a pair of straight-cut denim shorts and a white shirt that were among the pieces Jasmin had bought. As if she knew I was thinking of her, a gentle knock on the door was followed by the energetic voice of the blonde echoing through the room:

"Star?" she called.

"Come in!" I replied, and I saw her open the door a crack as if stepping into forbidden territory.

"Can I talk to you for a minute?" I smiled at her and nodded in agreement. I sat on the bed, and she did the same, facing me.

Her big blue eyes looked at me, and she gave a half-smile.

"You must think I'm weird, right? Invading your room so early." She smiled. Is it possible to like someone without even knowing them?

Jasmin had a trustworthy aura, something that made me feel comfortable around her. Her big eyes seemed like a window, and all I saw in them was pure kindness. I really liked her.

"I don't think you're weird. A bit different, maybe, but that's why I liked you."

"Different... I like different." She laughed and looked into my eyes. "Star, I want you to know that you can count on me for anything you need. I'm not sure what you must have gone through, but I believe it was terrible." She glanced at the small visible spots on my face, remnants of bruises that hadn't completely faded yet, and swallowed hard. "I'm sorry that this happened to you. I know there's nothing I can do to erase what happened, but if you want to talk, I'm here for you. I also have my share of moments I'd like to forget; it seems like a prerequisite to be part of this family." I laughed.

"Thank you. It's really nice to have another woman around."

"I know, I'm so happy you're here. Well, it's not easy for me to trust people. Not since I lost my little sister."

"Oh my, I'm so sorry." I put my hand to my mouth.

"Thank you." She shared a brief summary of how she lost her. At a dance, after being attacked by a hitman, and what shocked me was that Jasmin had such intense and cheerful energy, but when she spoke of her younger sister, Magnolia, her eyes took on the weight of grief. From what I understood, we were all in the same boat in some way. "She is a daily absence in my life, but I've learned to love her from here, while she looks after me from there. After all, we have to move forward, and that's why I wanted to come talk to you. Our past is biased; it will always try to pull us back, but the people who love us don't want to see us giving up on happiness, so we need to react. Count on me for that, and my goodness, you're so beautiful." I couldn't help but laugh at the sudden change of topic. "I'm serious, those huge golden eyes, look at that hair..." She ran her hand through my strands.

"Thank you, Jasmin. For everything." She raised her eyes, which sparkled with understanding. Her support filled my heart with strength and affection, and she seemed to know it, as if someone had once done the same for her.

"Yes, right, Doctor!" Ghost burst into the room with a troubled expression, catching our attention. Wolf was close behind, and both Jasmin and I turned to face him as he hung up the phone. "It was Dr. Madison," he said to no one in particular.

"What happened?" I asked.

"The results of your tests are ready." He ran his hands over his face, the weight of concern growing in his eyes as he approached me.

"What did they say?" I opened my eyes wider.

"We need to go to the hospital, sweetheart. There's no way to delay this; your results showed significant changes. The doctor has already diagnosed anemia, but we need to do more complex tests to investigate further." He hugged me tightly as if the end of the world was knocking at our door. I felt scared.

"Is anemia very serious?" Wolf asked.

"Apparently, for Ghost, it's the apocalypse." Jasmin laughed. "Calm down, brother-in-law, I've had anemia before. It can be due to poor nutrition, but it's usually easy to treat. It's nothing that deserves that funeral expression on your face. She'll be fine with the right medication." I felt calmer with Jasmin's words, my newest friend, which didn't stop Ghost from dragging me to the hospital anyway.

✴

I SPENT THE NEXT THREE days at the hospital. I underwent more tests and went through yet another array of consultations. I also entered a strange machine that spun and made a loud noise. Afterward, I spoke with three different doctors, in addition to Dr. Madison, who accompanied me every step of the way.

At first, it was difficult to walk among strangers who occasionally stared at me with speculative expressions. Ghost didn't go unnoticed either. His posture beside me drew a lot of attention. He kept one hand on my waist while the other extended slightly ahead of my body, preventing anyone from getting close enough to touch me. He looked handsome in a dark gray suit. Each of his steps made it clear that he was a powerful man. He was elegant, attractive, and his presence had the strength of an army. I calmed down as I noticed that by his side, I felt safe.

By the end of the third consecutive day of tests, as we were passing through the last doctor, a neurologist with startlingly large eyes, even my soul was exhausted, but Ghost refused to give up on discovering even the origin of my hair strands.

"We'll wait for today's test results, but it seems to be a pre-established and variant condition. She may have received a blow to the head that could have caused a traumatic brain injury, resulting in decreased brain function, which significantly affects memory. Alternatively, the trauma from everything she lived through could have caused the disturbance. It's quite common in cases like hers; the brain shuts down as a protective mechanism, and in some cases, it erases everything."

"Is there any treatment to reverse this condition?" Ghost asked, staying by my side.

"The human mind is an imperfect variable. I've treated patients who lost their memory in similar circumstances and never regained those memories; however, there are cases where it returns without any treatment. It's an uncertain factor; there are no guarantees she will remember anything, but we will do everything possible to minimize long-term effects and keep her stable moving forward."

An uncertain factor... The words echoed in my mind on the way back home. Ghost had all my prescriptions, both for medication and diet. According to Dr. Madison, we had to take certain precautions to prevent the anemia from progressing to an alarming state, but overall, I was doing fine.

"Do you think I'll ever get my memory back?" I asked as I got into his car in the hospital parking lot. Ghost turned to me and held my hands between his.

"Are you afraid you won't?"

"Terrified," I admitted. "I don't want to be stuck with the feeling that something is missing in my life." I pressed my eyes shut with my fingers, which burned with a sudden urge to cry. "What if I never discover who I really am?"

"You may not remember what happened in your past, but your personality, your character, your love, none of them abandoned you. Your values are still there, along with your strength and spirit." He caressed my face. "It's like your voice; you may not remember the songs, but that doesn't stop you from having a beautiful tone. That can't be lost because it's your essence. You may have forgotten part of your story, but not who you are."

I reflected, immersed in those words.

Zion was right; even not knowing who I am, I wanted to fight to survive. I remain true to my values and true to myself.

"You're right," I whispered, resting my head on his shoulder. He wrapped me in a warm, cozy hug. The fresh scent of his skin soon enveloped me, and I raised my lips, searching for his. Zion kissed me and held my face between his hands.

"Sweetheart, now we need to address a slightly more complicated situation. Perhaps the hardest step."

"What?"

"We can't delay a formal conversation with the police any longer, sweetheart. They need to investigate your disappearance, see if there are any reports on the missing persons list, and check for any contact from your family." I swallowed hard. I knew this moment would come, and I tried to prepare for it, but despite wanting it very much, I couldn't shake the sudden fear that gripped me. But Ghost was right; there was no way to delay it any longer.

"Let's resolve this once and for all."

Ghost drove to a police station downtown, and a few minutes later, I found myself sitting in front of three large, unfamiliar men. According to Ghost, the chief at this location was a family friend and a trustworthy man.

"Miss Star, I'm Chief Russel, and I'm here to understand your story." The serious man, with a thick beard that connected to a prominent mustache, wore a large chain around his neck with a shiny badge, just like the gun at his waist.

He began asking questions while the other two officers took notes on every word, and Ghost stayed protectively by my side.

"We'll take your fingerprints and a photo for our missing persons database, alright?" I nodded my head in agreement.

According to him, there might be a missing person report that could help me find my family and discover what happened.

I left there with renewed hope. It was real; perhaps very soon, there would be some information about my past, and just the thought made me extremely happy.

✷

WE GOT HOME LATE AT night. Ghost ordered a pizza, and we ate in comfortable silence, accompanied by a glass of wine that, according to him, couldn't compare to what was produced at Don Matteo's vineyards but was still of exceptional quality.

We were too tired to say anything, but even so, I could hardly tear my eyes away from the man sitting comfortably in front of me.

Zion was wearing a loose white linen shirt that gave him a casual yet elegant look, along with black shorts.

I shifted uneasily in my chair, unable to believe I was really wearing one of the strange panties Jasmin had bought for me.

Earlier, when I came out of the bathroom, I searched for a light dress to spend the rest of the night in and rummaged through some of my new clothes, pulling out a short, cute pink dress with little sleeves that draped off my shoulders—very comfortable.

When I opened the underwear drawer, I came face-to-face with a strange and unusual piece. It was a black lace thong, but unlike what I was used to calling underwear, this one had a huge slit right in the middle, leaving my entire vagina exposed. I actually wondered if I'd wear it, and I could barely believe I was sitting in front of him, wearing the damn thing and feeling a cold, unexpected breeze hitting right between my legs.

"Everything okay, sweetheart?" Zion's concerned voice snapped me back to reality.

"Yes!" I almost shouted.

"What were you thinking about?" My panties. Or rather, the lack of them, because there was no way in the world those two straps could be considered panties. "The day was really intense, wasn't it?" He touched my hand over the table.

"You're right."

In a way, he was right. I couldn't shake off the hectic day and the questions that kept surfacing in my mind.

Would anyone show up looking for me? The hope was suffocating, but I didn't want to get my hopes up.

"I found a great therapist who offers online sessions. What do you think about starting that way? This way, you won't have to go out often for now, only when you feel safe." Zion brought the glass of wine to his lips, and all I could focus on was how his lips touched the crystal, slow and precise, reminding me of when he'd done something similar to very intimate parts of my body.

"Y-yes, it would be amazing to have therapy at home." I tried to keep my thoughts together.

"Are you sure you're really okay?" He raised his eyebrows, and a shadow of a smile crept onto his lips.

"It's just... I was thinking, could you play the piano for me?" I improvised. "I'd love to watch you play."

"It would be my pleasure." I smiled at his response, and when we finished eating, Ghost stood up and came over to me. "Come with me." He held my hand.

My heart started pounding harder, as if that simple touch was capable of sending signals all through my body, making my skin burn.

He led me to the suspended divan, and I lay down, resting my head on a high pillow that left me almost sitting.

Ghost walked with elegance and confidence to the piano and sat down. I noticed how captivating he looked in that position. Everything seemed to fit—the contrast of his light shirt against the dark piano, and the equally sophisticated aura between Zion and the grand piano. He gave me a sideways smile, indecently beautiful, removed the piano's key cover, and began to play.

The light notes started to echo through the air, as if each one danced to its own melody. I held my breath, feeling the intensity of the sound. It was like a caress, a hug. A declaration of love. It was everything. Delicate and profound, as beautiful as the man who let his fingers glide over the piano keys with such grace and agility.

His skill was remarkable, and he controlled the sound with the tips of his fingers, moving along with the melody. I propped myself up on my elbow, captivated by the sexy vision in front of me. His hands moved quickly, the muscles in his arms flexing, revealing veins I wanted to kiss.

The delicate melody was like a whisper to my heart, and the warmth it spread through my body left me aroused. I slowly opened my legs. My core burned, and I wanted him to see. To see how wet I was, how crazy with desire he made me.

He turned to me, still lost in the music, but when his eyes fell on my open legs, a hungry and surprised expression crossed his face, and he missed a note. The mistake jolted me back to reality, and my body burned with both desire and shame. I pressed my legs together and parted my lips. His eyes were still on me, hungry, wearing that dark, delicious expression.

I was addicted to that image of lust and excitement.

He stopped playing, swiveled on the bench, leaned forward, and rested his elbows on his legs. His narrowed eyes scanned me from head to toe.

"Open your legs, sweetheart," he commanded, and I shuddered at the low but extremely authoritative tone. "Now," he repeated when I didn't move, and I swallowed hard.

I slowly opened my legs, never taking my eyes off him, and my entire face started to burn, the heat sliding down my neck, chest, and into my abdomen, which pulsed with need.

"Take off the dress." His possessive gaze pushed me to the edge of insanity.

"Take it off?" I gasped and trembled with desire.

"You teased me, little one. Now take off the dress and open your legs for me." The absolute and sexy tone left no room for doubt, and I could hardly believe my heart was racing, desperate to obey.

I did as he commanded, sliding the fabric down my body until it fell to the floor. I opened my legs, leaving myself completely exposed.

His eyes traveled down my open body, his parted lips seemed to touch me with the sheer lust burning in his gaze. I started trembling as I watched him rise from the piano bench and remove his shirt. His sculpted muscles matched the excited, hungry look on his face. Zion unbuckled his belt and unzipped his pants, revealing the hard tip of his member beneath his white briefs, which showed a small wet spot from his arousal.

"How can you be so delicious?" He came over me, his heavy body pressed me against the suspended sofa, making it move. He rubbed his hard erection against the rigid, wet, and pulsating point in the center of my body.

I moaned and arched my back as his firm fingers traveled down my belly, marking my skin on the way to opening my legs and placing his hand over all my intimacy.

"Oh my god!" I hissed, anxious, and started to squirm when he placed his mouth over one of my nipples, hard with desire. His fingers invaded me completely, thrusting deep. I opened my legs wider, agonized. "Zion... damn!" I gasped, and he continued to thrust with his fingers, his lips leaving my swollen breasts and starting to travel down my belly.

"What a delight, my gorgeous." He blew softly against my swollen clitoris and sucked it hard. His fingers filled me deep and fast. The sound of our breaths intensified, mixing with moans and curses.

Zion took everything from me, with his mouth, with his fingers, with his deep voice whispered against my wet intimacy. He drove me crazy. And just when I was about to explode, he lifted me in his arms and placed me on my knees on the piano bench, with my back to him.

"Put your hands here and lean. That's it, I want you open for me." His hands spread my thigh, opening me to the limit. I lay over the piano and moaned at the feel of the cold wood against my stiff nipples.

He continued to tease me, now opening me more with his fingers, thrusting, torturing until I felt my vagina drip and throb. I was desperate, pushing my butt up. His mouth traveled down my back, marking me with small bites until he reached the base of my back. I tensed when he grabbed one of my buttocks and opened it.

"Shh, relax, little one. Trust me," he asked, and I stayed there, caught in a mix of anticipation and nervousness.

I held back a scream as I felt his tongue slide over my butt's opening, and I shrank back in panic, but excited to the limit. He held both sides of my butt firmly, and I closed my eyes as his tongue entered there, in that spot that had been untouched until then.

The pleasure was so absurd that I exploded in an orgasm while he thrust into me with one hand and pinched my clitoris with the other, shamelessly plunging his tongue into my butt. It was indecent, shocking, and terribly delicious.

"Zion." I gasped, shaken.

He was igniting every part of my skin. His tongue left my butt, and he thrust his fingers deeper inside me, until he returned with them coated in my own pleasure, and slowly he pressed the tip of his finger against my butt and placed the head of his member at the entrance of my vagina, which pulsed as if my body wanted to pull him in.

"You drive me crazy, hungry," he whispered in my ear, slipping one hand into my hair, at my neck.

He sucked my neck and thrust forcefully inside me. I screamed as I felt him stretch me completely. He released my hair, and his hands danced over my bare breasts, rising and falling, and he began to torture me in every corner, in every space of my body.

The sounds coming from my mouth were shameful, desperate, and very loud. I lifted my butt higher, trembling with desire. He went deep again and again; the heat of his finger penetrating behind began to become an extreme point of pleasure, and I couldn't take it anymore.

"Oh, angel..." I shuddered, delirious.

"Come for me, love." He sucked my neck, pressed his mouth to my ear, and ordered: "Come, my Star."

I dug my fingers into the sides of the piano, holding on as best I could, and closed my eyes as a strong, overwhelming sensation made me scream, as if ecstasy danced in every corner of my body, exploding me into particles that spread from the tips of Zion's fingers. He moved his hand up my neck and squeezed, growling and thrusting hard.

It was delicious, intense, wicked, and it made me burn.

"Damn!" he roared and pulled out of me. His member fell hard on my back, and the frantic pulse spread warm liquid all over my butt. Until that moment, I had never experienced a more delightful sensation.

Ghost kissed my neck and caressed my breasts, pulling me into his lap without caring about the mess between us. I still felt trembling and unable to say a word.

"My Star, small and delicious..." he gasped into my mouth. I looked into his eyes that revealed a warm passion, so intense it made me swallow hard.

My racing heart beat wildly against my chest. Zion made me feel so much in such a short time that I was dizzy.

"I want you to be my wife, officially."

"What do you mean?" I blinked, moved to see the wave of feelings tightening his eyes.

"I'm in love with you, little one, and I want you in my life, even when you find your family or regain your memory. I want to be able to hug you every day, to make love to you every night. To sleep smelling you and to wake up in your embrace. I want you to be my girlfriend. Do you accept, sweetheart?" He looked at me for a moment, a certain insecurity taking over his brown eyes, and my chest warmed in a different, intense, desperate way.

"Yes, I accept," I replied, hopelessly in love with my guardian angel. And he kissed me again with urgency, as if the distance between our lips were unbearable, and I knew it was.

✸

"PLEASE, LET ME OUT!"

A very small, thin, and weary little girl was curled up in a dark corner of a low and terrifying attic. She trembled, whether from fear or cold, I couldn't tell, but an overwhelming desire to go to her and hug her took hold of me. I tried to reach her, but I couldn't move as everything passed before my eyes like a film.

"I warned you, you little brat. I don't want to see you in my way. I can't stand your face; you're lucky to have a place to stay, and yet you still challenge me." — An annoying voice sounded from outside the door.

"I was just playing."

"Shut up, you pest, and don't pretend you don't know what you did. What did I say about playing in the house?"

"That I could only play in the attic, but I'm scared here." — The girl looked back at the room behind her, and that's when I saw her golden eyes, very red from crying. A rare, cinnamon tone, exactly like mine. *"Please, let me out!"*

The door burst open, and the shadow of a woman passed through it. I couldn't see her face; no matter how hard I tried, she was just a strange figure, like a blur, but a searing pain pierced my chest as I watched her grab the girl by her little arms and throw her onto a strange bed with dark blankets.

"Daddy! Daddyyyyyy!" — the girl screamed, terrified, as the woman took off her slipper and began to hit her hard.

"Shut up, you little bitch! Shut up!"

Stop!

I tried to scream, suffocated by the horrific scene.

Stop, please, she's just a child!

But she didn't stop, and the girl lost her voice from crying so much.

I thrashed with all my strength, wanting to grab that bitch by the hair. I was blinded by hate and rage, and suddenly I was taken by the terrible sensation of falling into an endless hole until everything disappeared. The filthy bed, the dark attic, and that demon in woman form gave way to Zion's calm and safe room.

"My God!" I sat up in bed with a jolt and gasped for air as if I were drowning. Pain and despair threatened to tear my heart in two. I felt deeply the pain of that child. I began to cry uncontrollably, desperate.

"Star?" Zion sat next to me, alarmed. "What happened, my love?"

"A nightmare." I cried loudly, without shame. I didn't know how to express the pain I was feeling.

"Calm down, it's over, it was just a bad dream." He tried to soothe me, which only made me cry more because I knew it hadn't been a dream.

"It wasn't a dream." I sobbed, feeling like yet another piece of the puzzle that was my life had been thrown into my lap.

"How?" I told him about the nightmare and how real it felt, as if I were right there, in the body of that little girl. I could barely speak through my tears, but somehow he understood.

"It was me, I'm sure. I saw that girl's eyes." A dark fog passed over his face, and his brown eyes widened a little more. "I think I had a memory, and it was so horrible, Zion. I still feel that girl's suffering; she was so alone." I cried for all the sounds of pain and hurt that little girl left etched in my subconscious. I felt so much anger for her. "Do you believe me?"

"Of course, sweetheart." He held me a little tighter in his arms; the veins in his muscles were bulging. "A dream like that can have many meanings." He held my face in his hands and wiped the tears that still streamed down my cheeks, and I curled up there in the safety of his arms, unable to stop crying as the memory repeated in my mind. I wanted to see the face of that evil woman, but she was just a blur. A swirl of hatred and malice that made me feel anger and fear at the same time.

Zion caressed me, and I cried until I felt emotionally exhausted and finally fell into a deep sleep, this time, without dreams.

CHAPTER THIRTY

Ghost

I barely managed to sleep after last night. Star cried for long minutes until she finally fell asleep from exhaustion, and that hurt deep in my heart. She firmly believed that the nightmare was a memory, and just the thought of her having suffered something in her childhood made me sick with rage.

I lifted my eyes to her, who was staring at breakfast with a tired expression. Her big eyes were marked by dark circles, and I needed to touch her hand with mine to feel calmer. I no longer knew if I wanted her to discover everything about her past, not if it brought her so much pain.

"Sweetheart," I called, but before I could finish the sentence, my phone started ringing, and the name of the delegate flashed on the screen.

"Is it the delegate?" she peeked.

"Yes. Good morning, Russel," I answered with a strange feeling.

"Ghost, we have news." I opened my eyes wider and stood up from the table.

"What happened?" I tried to keep my tone calm, but Star straightened her posture immediately and looked at me with a worried expression. I started to wonder if there was any way to hide something from the women.

"We investigated the records of missing persons and looked for something related to her. Star, as they call her, has no record in the fingerprint database, nor any police record, and we also found no formal missing person report, but I discovered something very interesting." I brought the phone closer to my ear. "Less than a month ago, a man named Walt Jenkins went to the police with a photo of a girl he claimed had disappeared. The police contacted the family of the supposed victim, but the father and stepmother said the young woman had run away on her own, so the report was filed away. However, as a rule, everything that happens in the central office is recorded, and that's how we found a connection between the photo we took of Star yesterday and the photo that Mr. Walt brought to us. They are the same person, Ghost. Star's real name is Alena Farrel."

"Fuck," I whispered in shock, unsure whether to feel happy or worried.

"I tried to contact Walt, who apparently has no blood relation to the young woman; he might be a friend, a godfather, something like that, but the number he provided goes straight to voicemail. I sent an officer to his house, but it was empty." I exhaled and brought my hand to my mouth, attentive to everything the delegate was saying. "However, we had more luck with our database and found her family. Father, brother, and stepmother. They lived on St. Vincent alley, behind a bar that also belonged to the family, but they moved recently to another place across town, and it seems they sold the other properties. One of the officers tried to contact the family by phone, and now they are aware of Alena's return to the United States and her memory loss. I'll send you the address where they are living now; we can go there immediately."

"Yes, we will," I said almost automatically, trying to absorb all that information. Star looked at me anxiously.

"Great, but I must warn you. They insist that she ran away, that she left on her own. I don't think they are expecting her return. The stepmother seemed uncomfortable with a possible visit; be prepared for the worst-case scenario in situations like this."

"What would that be?"

"One in which the family doesn't want to welcome her back."

"If they don't want contact, that's fine. She doesn't need them anyway." I hung up, irritated but very aware of the pain that rejection could cause Star.

"What did he say?" Star nearly jumped on me as soon as I hung up the phone.

"I think you should sit down, love."

WE GOT INTO THE CAR a few minutes later, on our way to the address the delegate provided. Star was terribly silent, her eyes lost on the dashboard, which made me worried.

I knew it was a lot to take in; I felt dizzy myself. The name Alena kept spinning in my mind, as if challenging me to believe it was real. A strange feeling overtook me.

I was desperate to find anything about my wife's past since the moment we landed in the United States, but now a certain apprehension gripped me as a trio of strangers was about to call my Star by another name. However, that wasn't even the worst part. I feared those people would make her suffer in some way, and I wouldn't hold back from choking anyone who hurt her.

I turned a corner, already close to the address. Star maintained an uncomfortable silence, and I could barely think, unsure of what was going through her mind. Was she scared? Anxious?

No, that was me—I was sure of it.

"It's there." I stopped the car a little way from the house, which was small and located on an empty street. The delegate was already waiting there, leaning against his vehicle next to another officer right in front of the house.

Star squinted and scanned the house from top to bottom. I took her hand, and she turned to me, her big eyes brimming with tears and overflowing with an almost palpable uncertainty. I hugged her, trying to calm her down.

"There's nothing to fear, sweetheart," I whispered in her hair. "We don't know who these people really are, so I don't want you to get your hopes up, but I promise you'll be safe during the meeting."

"Can you stay by my side?" she asked in a faint voice.

"Where else would I be?" I lifted her face and planted a warm kiss on her lips. "Shall we?" She took a deep breath and got out of the car.

A new knot formed in my throat with each step I took toward that house. I hadn't imagined I would feel this way when the big moment of reuniting Star with her family arrived, as if I were plummeting into a hole, terrified of how she would react to what was coming.

We walked a few meters until we stopped next to the delegate.

"Are you ready?" he asked, as the officer beside him ascended the steps leading to the front door and positioned himself next to it.

"Yes, I am." Star didn't hesitate, and the officer knocked on the door.

A woman opened it moments later. She was elegant and beautiful, looking no older than fifty. The officer said something to her, and she stepped outside, her dark eyes like her hair scanning the entrance until they landed on Star.

Her eyes widened, and she brought her hand to her mouth, surprised for a brief moment. Soon, surprise gave way to something different, even dark. Something that worried me. A tall young man stood beside her. He had long arms and deep eyes like the woman's. In fact, they resembled each other quite a bit. So, he was the brother.

"She really came back, mom," the young man tried to whisper, but shock made his voice louder.

"Alena," the woman spat the name as if it made her nauseous. I went on high alert, already regretting having allowed her to come here. There was something strange about those two; I could feel it even before they opened their mouths. Generally, my instincts never failed.

"Do you recognize this woman, Alena?" the delegate asked. She was shocked by the mention of the name and shook her head negatively.

"Call her Star, Russel; she doesn't remember that name."

"So you really lost your memory?" The stepmother approached the three steps leading to the entrance of her house. Her expression seemed tense.

My girl was paralyzed. Her hand gripped mine tightly. All her expression displayed one thing while she faced those two: purest fear.

I began to dread the outcome of that meeting.

Star

I DIDN'T RECOGNIZE anything at all. Neither the house nor the two strangely intimidating people standing before me. I stared at the young man who scrutinized me from head to toe, a pulse of disappointment thrumming in my neck. I thought I might be able to remember something, but all I felt when looking at them was fear.

"This is Norah Turner and her son, Calebe. They are your stepmother and half-brother. You don't remember them, do you?" The delegate stepped closer to me, and I jumped, startled. Immediately, Ghost's arm wrapped around my waist in a protective hug.

"Why did you bring her here?" the woman interrupted before I could respond. "I thought I made it clear that we didn't want to see her face." There was a lot of anger in that woman's voice, and a strange pain shot through my chest.

"Ma'am, I imagine you don't have a friendly relationship, but I thought maybe the young woman's father would want to see her. She survived a kidnapping, went through a lot, and will need her family." Norah glanced over her shoulder at one of the windows of the house, and I noticed the shadow of a man watching us from one of them.

I swallowed hard, already knowing who it was. It was my father. A shiver ran down my back, and I realized I didn't know if I wanted to see him, something that seemed very mutual, but the overwhelming desire to discover anything about my past filled me with a courage that bordered on madness.

"Ma'am," I said for the first time, and I trembled from head to toe as she turned her attention to me. There was something in her gaze; Norah seemed to hate me, while a flicker of fear appeared on her face every time she looked at me. "Can you tell me what happened? They said I ran away, but as you can see, I don't remember anything. Can you help me? There must be something about me—photos, clothes, anything."

"As if you deserve any help," she spat, and Ghost growled beside me. I felt the muscles in his body tense up behind me. He was on high alert.

"Ms. Turner, please cooperate. Can't you at least hand over the young woman's belongings?" Delegate Russel intervened.

"Not even if I wanted to." She turned to me and descended the steps toward me, her son trailing behind, furious.

"Don't come any closer." Ghost stepped in front of me with impressive speed.

"And who do you think you are to stop me?"

"I'm her boyfriend and her bodyguard, so keep your distance if you don't want me to intervene." His voice was dangerously cold.

"I'll answer her question, and I want you all out of my house, understood, officer?" she said over her shoulder. "You left because you wanted to. You had a home, clothes, and food, plus a job, but you were always a rebellious troublemaker. Disobedient, irresponsible. You only brought distress to our family and heartache to your father." I shrank back from the fury of her words, trying to imagine living that way. It made no sense. That woman said one thing, but my heart disagreed.

"Besides being a stupid brat," the young man beside her added.

"You don't want to get into this conversation, you piece of shit," Ghost shouted, taking a step toward him, and he hid behind his mother.

"You might not want to see your girlfriend's reality, kid." She wrinkled her nose at Ghost. "But she just ran away, abandoned her family and her father. Thanks to you, we had to move. Because of you, we sold the bar and the family house. It's obvious that your father doesn't want to see you; you only brought pain and suffering to someone who raised you with everything good and right." She pointed to the window. "I don't know why the officer brought you here, but go back where you came from. You turned 21 a week after you ran away; you're an adult now, not our responsibility anymore, and there's nothing here for you. I threw all your things away after you left. There's nothing left." I tried to hold on to the information she was giving, but a sharp pain in my chest threatened to blind me.

Had I really abandoned my family?

"Why? Why did I run away? And my mom? Where is she?" Calebe, the weird guy who might be my half-brother, broke into a sinister smile.

"She's dead."

"Dead?" Shock hit me for a moment, but there was something familiar about that feeling of grief, as if I had already gone through it.

"Yes, that idiot died, and it was my mother who had to take care of you, girl." Calebe narrowed his eyes and looked at me darkly, as if he had held those words for a long time, and a sudden rage surged up my neck as I heard him speak about my mother that way. I didn't remember her, but I was sure she was an incredible woman—I could feel it.

"I guess I didn't miss much by forgetting you," I shot back. My hands trembled with the urge to throw something at his head, and I didn't know where all that fury mixed with fear was coming from.

"This is you for real. Spoiled, sassy, and annoying. You always caused trouble for my mother to deal with. We were lucky when you ran away." His dark gaze seemed unshakeable and full of hatred. He raised a finger at me. "Look at what you did to my family, see the tiny house we live in now, all because of you. Go away and don't come back, you wretched brat," he shouted, and I flinched at the shock of his loud voice.

Ghost grabbed his fist in the air and twisted his arm in a quick, sharp motion, making it crack.

"You'd better watch your words if you don't want me to rip your arm off." Ghost flashed a side smile, a dark expression I knew all too well taking over his face, and Norah began to make a scene.

"Let go of my son, you lunatic. Officer," she pleaded for help.

"Ghost," the delegate called, and he released Calebe the moment.

I began to feel dizzy, short of breath. Emotions churned in my stomach, and the sensation that the world was upside down hit me hard.

"Damn it, Ghost, what are you doing?" the delegate cursed.

"This idiot needs to learn some manners," Ghost retorted.

"What the hell, mom, he twisted my wrist!"

"You left because you wanted to, but it was the best thing that ever happened to us." Norah hugged her son and shot me a fierce look. "Don't come near us again. Come on, son." They turned their backs on me.

"Norah, you, your son, and your husband are invited to give a formal statement," the delegate announced, and she glared at him in disgust. "I want to know the last time you saw this young woman, and you better have time because the list of questions is huge. This girl was kidnapped, and we will find out how it happened. If you don't cooperate, you'll be treated as suspects." He handed her a card, which she received with a disgruntled huff. "I'll be waiting for you at the station. Have a good afternoon."

Zion exchanged a few brief words with the delegate, who instructed him on how to issue a second copy of my true identity, and we left there as quickly as possible. I only realized how tense I was when I sat in the car seat and started to tremble.

"I'm sorry it turned out this way, sweetheart." He stroked my hand, and I noticed how cold his palm was. "I wish I could have avoided all this shit."

"It couldn't have been different. I needed to meet my family, after all. I just didn't expect to feel this way."

"How?"

"Like I'm about to break into a million pieces," I confessed. "I thought when I found my family, I'd feel happy, whole, but I'm confused and scared. I didn't recognize anything, except the anger they feel toward me." I sighed, exasperated. "What if I really am like they said? What if I ran away out of pure rebellion and ended up getting kidnapped? Could I really cause so much suffering to my own father?"

"Star, I have a different perception of people, you know that." He kept his focus on the road and continued. "While the police work with 'innocent until proven guilty,' a bodyguard's motto is the opposite. They're all guilty, end of story. I prefer to be suspicious and keep my VIP safe than leave it to chance, and over the years, I've started to identify certain telltale signs people give off without realizing it, and I didn't believe a word those two said. I know your essence, and I never doubted it for a second."

I clung to that comment to try to feel a bit better. I was still nauseous, sad, and downcast, but I needed to react. Maybe they really were lying, and if that were the case, it would be best to distance myself, even though my heart beat with desperation, crazy to see my father. To know what he was like, but the man hadn't even bothered to look at me through the window. Maybe it was better this way. I would have to start over somehow, and it seemed it would be far from my family. If I could still call them that.

✸

"HE'S A TOTAL IDIOT. Where does that jerk live? Let's go over there and slash his tires." Jasmin jumped off the sofa as Zion finished telling what had happened to his sister-in-law, who was with Wolf, Snake, and Shaw.

I still felt down and probably wouldn't be able to sleep, but Jasmin's refreshing presence helped calm me.

"What a ridiculous situation, Miss Star." Shaw was perplexed. "I'm sorry your reunion with your family ended this way."

"They're still trying to contact the man who made the first report, a guy named Walt; maybe he has more information than that snake did," Zion huffed and took a swig of whiskey.

"We have a crisis right here, and no one seems willing to talk about it." Wolf stood up, worried, gaining everyone's attention. "How are we going to refer to you from now on? Star or Alena?"

"I prefer to be called Star. I don't remember that other name, so..." I shrugged.

"Alright, Star." Snake approached. "Listen, you've been through a lot to get here. You need to choose which fight you want to take on next. Pick one you can win. Family doesn't always mean perfection. Just look at the three of us. We were abandoned by those who share our blood and found a real family outside of that bond. Those idiots might share your last name, but they don't mean a thing. They're not your family."

"But we're here," Jasmin added.

"Your name already carries my last name." Zion placed a long kiss on my hand, and a simple touch had never felt so intimate. My eyes burned. "You know my family can also be yours if you want it to be."

"Thank you, everyone. Even you, weirdo." I looked at Snake, who gave an almost imperceptible side smile. "I guess it was a shock, but I'll be okay."

"How about we watch a movie together? It'll help distract you," Jasmin suggested cheerfully.

"That would be perfect. What movie?"

"The Twilight Saga!" she almost shouted.

"No!" Ghost and the brothers shot up in unison. The only one who seemed to love the idea was Shaw, who was doing a quirky, silent dance in the corner of the room.

"For God's sake, Jasmin, again?" Wolf looked indignant.

"Is the movie bad?" I asked, amused by the exaggeration.

"They're terrible, and she made each of us watch them," Ghost crossed his arms.

"Each one of us!" Snake echoed. "She attacked us when we were separated."

"Which means she's probably seen the saga a thousand times herself." Wolf ran a hand through his hair.

"And I'd watch it a thousand more; they're perfect, and I'm sure you've seen them once, Star, but forgot. If there's any advantage to losing your memory, it's being able to watch the entire Twilight saga again as if it were the first time, believe me," she exclaimed and stood up. "I'll go grab the movies; they're in the car."

"Who wants to get drunk in the next room while the three of them marathon this crap?" Wolf suggested.

"I definitely do." Ghost wrapped one arm around my waist and gave me a quick kiss. His loving eyes hid a deep concern. He had been attentive to every one of my steps since we arrived, and I hugged him, overwhelmed with gratitude for everything he was doing for me.

"I wonder if Miss Star will root for one of them. I've always liked Bella and Edward more, but Lyon said he preferred Jacob," Shaw commented as he sat next to Jasmin on the sofa.

"Lyon told you that?" Snake looked at the young man, incredulous.

"He growled less when I asked about Jacob."

"That's what I figured." And he disappeared down the hallway behind Wolf. Ghost kissed me and shouted as he was about to follow his brothers:

"I hope you don't return a starry-eyed girl enamored with that stupid vampire, got it?" He pointed at Jasmin, who stuck out her tongue in response.

"Just hit play before I die of curiosity." I sat between Jasmin and Shaw, pushing all the confusing feelings that occasionally threatened to overwhelm me under the rug.

I didn't know if I had really run away or if I was the horrible person those two described, but I had one certainty. The Holder family welcomed me, and the person I had become was different from the one Norah and Calebe knew. I had lost everything I had and started my life from scratch, but at least I wasn't alone.

CHAPTER THIRTY-ONE

Ghost

Two Weeks Later

A sunny morning bathed the porch of my house, and sunlight streamed through the window, spreading across the leather sofa where Star lay, distracted, researching on my notebook.

I received her identification a few days after the meeting with the delegate, and little by little my girl was starting to get used to her new life and the presence of new people.

I approached her as she was once again engrossed in research about a business administration course; she seemed to really enjoy the topic and all its systematics, which was fascinating. According to the therapist, from now on, Star would start anew, but gradually her tastes and preferences would emerge.

"Little one," I called as I got closer.

"AHHHHHHHHHH!" she screamed, losing her balance. The notebook went one way, her phone the other, and Star fell off the sofa with a thud.

Fuck!

"Star!" She stood up, furious, and glared at me with her fists clenched at her sides. A part of her hair fell across her face, making her look even more intimidating. I had to bite my lips to avoid laughing. "I'm so sorry, my dear, I didn't mean to scare you. Did you hurt yourself?" I tried to step closer, but she raised a finger threateningly in my direction.

"Don't you dare," she cursed, her face red with anger, and the scene was so cute that I couldn't help but smile.

"Sweetheart..." I took a step toward her.

"No sweethearts, I almost lost mine because of you." She placed her hand over her chest.

"Could you forgive me? I can't handle that angry look on your face." I feigned drama, and she opened a half-pouty smile. "But it was so funny. Ouch!" I laughed when I received a light slap on my arm and held her wrist, pulling her into my arms.

"You absolute silent idiot," she complained, and I kissed her.

Star touched my face, and her expression turned slightly more serious.

"Zion, can you take me somewhere today?"

"Sure, where do you want to go?"

"To the old house that belonged to my family. The one near the bar." I raised my eyebrows, confused.

"Why did you decide to go there all of a sudden?"

We had barely talked about her family in the past two weeks. She didn't show many feelings about it, other than a moderate coldness. She hadn't cried or asked many questions. Sometimes it seemed as if it hadn't even happened, but I felt in my heart that it was painful for her to touch on the subject, and I tried to avoid it as much as I could, but I was starting to get worried.

Star had lost weight; her eyes were sunken, and although the medical exams were normal, her heart seemed to be suffering, and I was just standing there, unable to do anything to ease her pain. Occasionally, it made me want to strangle someone, just imagining that she might return as hurt as she had been when we went to see her family.

"I want to see all the parts of my story to try to discover something that makes sense." She pursed her lips, uncertain. "I've been mentally going over everything those people said for days, but nothing fits, as if my mind is saying one thing and my feelings the opposite. I don't remember them, or the house they lived in, but maybe I'll recall something when I return to where I lived. They say there's a bar there, right? We know I must have worked in one, given my current age..."

"That would have been against the rules."

"Exactly." She jumped, excited. "What bar would allow a minor to work there? According to the research I've been doing..."

"None."

"Or one that belongs to your family and feels safe breaking the rules," she said quickly. "I'm sure I worked there."

"What other types of research have you been doing?" I glanced at the notebook, unsure, and she quickly stepped into my line of sight.

"Nothing important. So, are we going?"

"You're right; you might remember something when you see the place, but I want you to promise me that from now on, you'll tell me what you're thinking and researching about this case. I'm worried, little one." I cupped her face with my hands.

Star was trying to show calmness, but I knew every one of her body signs. When she was scared, she slightly raised her eyebrows, furrowed her forehead, and her lips parted briefly. Her eyes would expand and become round whenever she was very happy, but they would narrow to almost a line, warmer and more engaged when she got excited, her pupils dilating and her breath becoming shallow and panting.

In recent days, it had become common to see Star tapping her feet in a steady rhythm whenever she wasn't speaking, or with her eyes lost on a point in the newspaper or magazine she liked to read. She often stared off into space with her eyebrows raised, distant from the real world and trapped in her own thoughts, and knowing everything I did about that woman, I could tell she was tense and worried.

"You know you can tell me all your worries, right? All your fears and uncertainties. You can tell me everything you want, okay?"

She looked deep into my eyes and then hugged me. Her small, delicate body fit against mine like pieces of a puzzle that were meant to find each other. I wanted to protect her from all pain, but it was too late for that. Now, all I could do was tend to each of her wounds, and I feared that many of them were yet to come.

I DROVE TO STAR'S FATHER'S old house, north of Chicago. It was a two-story place at the back of an alley that led to the bar, right in front of it. The entrance was simple, but the house looked cozy and empty, though Star didn't look at it for more than two minutes. Her attention was focused on the battered iron door to our left, where the bar's entrance was.

I had visited the place almost two weeks ago. I was curious to know where she lived. It was a rough neighborhood; all sorts of illegal activities happened right next to that bar, the place where she probably worked.

Star was young, innocent, and a certain anger surged within me at the thought of the kind of things she must have faced there.

"I know this place," she whispered, staring at the grimy walls of the alley. Both the house and the bar had peeling walls and looked abandoned.

"Do you remember being here before?"

"It's not exactly a memory; it's more like a certainty." She gasped. I noticed her eyes were misty and fixed on the bar. She shook her head, and her expression was filled with such deep pain that I had to swallow hard to say something.

"Come here, my love." I embraced her, and she curled up in my arms. She was trembling but kept staring at the bar. "Are you sure you want to stay here? We can come back later, a little at a time." She slid her cold hands between mine, and when she spoke again, her voice was so heavy with sadness that I felt a reflection of her pain touch my own heart, and it was hellish.

"You said I could tell you all my worries."

"Yes," I replied quickly. "Anything."

"I feel like I spent a lot of time here." She looked at me through the tears that were gathering in her beautiful eyes. "But I can't find many good feelings, just... some strange ones that scare me, and in the end..." She gasped for air and sobbed. "... I think they're right about me, because looking at this place I feel like I would do anything to get away from here." Star brought her hand to her mouth, and I watched her being engulfed by sadness right before my eyes. "But I don't know the truth." She began to cry loudly. "I want to remember my life. I want to remember my mother, but I can't. I can't!" I held her tightly against my chest, and my eyes burned with the effort she made to breathe between the pauses of her painful crying.

"That's it, love, let that feeling out. Allow yourself to feel it. You're not alone," I repeated into her hair, continuing to whisper, trembling with anger at what they had done to her and anguish for not being able to take away her pain.

Star cried for a long time until she lost her voice. The sound began to fade until it turned into a whisper, and gradually she stopped trembling. I kissed her forehead, and she took a deep breath, searching for calm to speak.

"Can we go home?"

"Right away," I assured her, starting the car.

"Zion, can we pass by my father's new house on the way?"

"How?"

"I'd like to go there one last time. Maybe now I'll see it with new eyes." I looked at her little red face from crying and wanted to be able to deny that to her, but I couldn't.

I took Star to the street where her family lived and parked the car a reasonable distance away. She stared at the house for a few minutes, her eyes shining with a serious expression.

"Are you okay?"

"Yes. I'm okay. I think in the end, I really did run away."

"If that was the case, I'm sure you had good reasons," I assured her.

"Thank you." She smiled a smile that didn't reach her eyes but maintained a determined expression. I drove home with the feeling that something had changed.

LATER, MY SIBLINGS came to visit us with some drinks and the intention of a lively night, which came at a good time. I wanted Star to have a little more distraction, and nothing beats the lively chaos of my family.

"I brought a little party along." Jasmin pointed to a box of beers in Wolf's arms as she passed through the door and rushed to hug Star, who smiled at her friend.

Jasmin had been a great help during those tumultuous days. My sister-in-law visited my house almost every day and became a great friend to Star.

"You guys arrived right on time," I greeted Snake, who placed his hand on my shoulder, and I turned my attention to the whiskey he was holding.

"I hope you've improved at poker, brother; I don't want last month's massacre to happen again, for your own good. And you, you little thing..." He pointed at Star and tossed something black in her direction. She raised her hand quickly and caught the object.

"What is this?" She squinted, suspicious. The two had a funny love-hate relationship.

"A USB drive. I brought the best moments and historic games of the Chicago Cubs." He pointed to the bracelet she was still wearing.

"I thought you weren't going to mention the baseball team to her," I scoffed, finding it amusing.

"As a fan of this team, it's my duty to remind her of the best times it's had." Snake twisted his lips. "You won't be able to forget this story twice." He pointed to the USB drive.

"What's this, Snake? A sudden outburst of empathy?" Wolf teased. "I bet you want to binge-watch the team's games. Again." He laughed, knowing that Snake was as obsessed with the team's games as Jasmin was with the Twilight saga.

"Every fan deserves to relive their team's best moments. It's almost a global rule; I'll have to watch it with you," Snake retorted.

"Alright, I'll prepare some drinks for us to watch; in the meantime, Jasmin, can you start the game?" She interrupted the discussion and handed the USB drive to the blonde.

I followed Star to the kitchen to help her.

"What do you need, sweetheart?"

"Can you grab the shaker?" She picked up the bottle of whiskey.

"Sure, what else?" I turned to her just as Star opened the bottle.

"Oh my gosh!" She quickly brought her hand to her face and dropped the bottle on the counter as if it suddenly were on fire.

"What happened?" I stopped next to her as she struggled to breathe.

"The smell." Star opened her eyes wider, as if she couldn't believe what she had said. She went back to the bottle and leaned her nose toward it. "Ahhhhhhh!" She covered her nose again. "What whiskey is this? The smell is so strong it churned my stomach." She looked at me, and I noticed her lips were pale against her white face.

I went to the bottle and grimaced when I realized there was nothing different about it.

"Do you think it could be related to your memories?" She became very unsettled whenever she started to remember something. A smell or a familiar sound, like when she heard a snippet of a song at Don Matteo's house, even the missing gaps in her story, like what had happened earlier that day.

"I don't know." She was still pale, which worried me. I grabbed a glass of water and handed it to her.

"Drink a little." She did as I asked, and a few minutes later, away from the whiskey, Star's lips regained their color. I went to her and hugged her.

"Let me handle the drinks, okay? I know I don't have the same gift as you, but I think I can manage here. Go watch the game with Snake before he invades the kitchen."

Star went to the living room and sat next to Snake. I kept an eye on her and noticed she started to relax as she focused on the TV. A certain relief filled me. In the end, everything was okay.

We had an amazing and pleasant night with our family, and Star allowed herself to live in the moment for the first time in two weeks. Perhaps she needed to go through all that pain to be able to move forward.

I had to get used to the idea that I couldn't control everything around her; sometimes Star would get hurt, but as long as I could prevent it, I would. I would protect her from her past so she could rebuild her dreams for the future.

I WALKED INTO THE ROOM after a shower and caught Star sprawled on the bed, staring at the ceiling. She looked like a mirage, her long hair spread across the white sheets, her round breasts prominently outlined by the pink lace baby doll top, and it left me hard. My woman was incredibly sexy.

She caught me watching and gave a mischievous little smile. Her eyes traveled down my shoulder, where the scar from my stitches still marked my skin, down to my bare chest, and finally landing on the underwear I was wearing. I bit my lips at the sight of her blush. My little one was innocent, barely able to control her own desire, and that drove me wild, exciting me to my bones.

"Something on your mind, sweetheart?" I lay down next to her on the bed and played with a strand of her hair, inclining my nose toward the delicate, addictive scent in her hair.

"I was here wondering what my mother would be like." She traced her finger across my chest. "If I look like her, if she liked numbers and music like I do. I don't know." She shrugged, as if it were nothing important.

"How do you feel about that? Do you think you were alike?"

"Yeah, I don't know why, but I feel like I have a lot of her in me." I ran my hands along the lace of her baby doll, trying to ignore the hard erection throbbing between my legs. "I wish I could remember, but I need to start understanding that it might not happen, and according to the therapist, that's okay. I want to live in the now. After what happened today, I realized I'm getting a second chance. One in a million, and I want to make the most of it." Her small body curled up against mine.

"Your mother must be proud of the daughter she has, wherever she is." She lifted her face until her emotional eyes met mine. Her heart began to beat strongly against my chest, and she leaned toward me.

I kissed her lips and ran my hands down the soft curves of her body, sliding my hands under the sheet, reaching her butt and realizing...

"Damn, you're not wearing panties?" She laughed and bit her lower lip. I slid my hands over her exposed skin.

"I thought I wouldn't need them for long," she confessed softly. "Since the day we first did it, I can't stop thinking about the sensations you make me feel." She closed her eyes and shuddered when I pinched one of her hard nipples under the fabric of her nightgown.

"What do I make you feel, my love? Tell me," I commanded, twisting the nipple between my fingers. She moaned and whimpered.

"Everything." She gasped. "You make me feel everything. Oh, Zion!" I closed my teeth around the fabric and squeezed the nipple with too much force. She dug her fingers into my hair and arched her body, opening up to me.

I continued the teasing, biting, sucking, and licking the fabric while rubbing my erection against her wet entrance. She let out delirious sounds that drove me crazy, and I couldn't hold back; I needed to taste her, her excitement on the tip of my tongue.

I rose over her, pinning her small body against the mattress. I grabbed the nightgown she was wearing and pulled it up. Star let out an excited, happy squeal. A smile that turned into a long moan when I buried my mouth between her legs and bit the lips of her already slick vulva.

Damn, what a delight.

Every time I touched her, it felt like soaring to heaven and falling into the heat of hell. My body begged for hers every damn second of the day. Star became my downfall, and I succumbed to her beauty, the sweet and addictive scent, the warm gaze of desire. I was more than aware that she had me in her hands.

I stopped sucking her when I felt she was about to climax, which made her moan, unsatisfied and trembling.

"Today I'm going to tease you, sweetheart." I kissed her mouth and made her taste herself. I got rid of my underwear and rubbed the head against her soaked pussy. I pushed a little and watched her eyes nearly close with the sensation of my cock slowly entering her, her thick lips parted, and she gasped, pulling me in deeper.

Damn, who was going to torture whom?

I fought the urge to penetrate her fully and pulled out, collecting her dissatisfied moans with my mouth. I entered again, just enough to drive her crazy, and with one hand, I massaged her clit while with the other I opened her ass and began to caress that spot that made her even more sensitive.

"Zion! Zion..." She clung to me, digging her nails into my back.

I couldn't stand hearing that surrendered voice and plunged deep into her the moment an orgasm took over her. I felt her walls squeezing me, and I thrust hard and fast. I reached for the drawer of the desk and grabbed a condom clumsily. I needed to put it on quickly. I pulled out of her, put the condom on, but when I lay on top of her and filled her, Star was looking at me with a different gaze.

"What's wrong, sweetheart?" I stayed still inside her.

"Remember what we saw on TV at that motel?" Her sweet face flushed gracefully, and I moved slowly, watching her close her eyes.

"Yes, my love. I remember." I nibbled on her soft skin, and she let out a quiet moan, losing her train of thought for a moment.

"They were having sex in a different way." I stopped kissing her, trying to remember exactly what it was about. "He was, well... doing that... oh my god, how do I say this?" she stammered, nervous, and only then did I realize what she was talking about.

"You mean they were having anal sex?" I whispered softly, pushing deeper inside. Her thick legs closed tightly around my waist, and I swallowed hard, unable to believe what was coming next.

"Yes." She buried her face in the curve of my neck, embarrassed, and I continued to thrust slowly, going deep until I felt her pulsating strongly.

"You don't need to be embarrassed, sweetheart. What you saw is just one of the many things a couple can do if both want to; there's no reason to feel ashamed about wanting to know anything like that." She lifted her face and suddenly stared at me.

Her deep eyes were filled with desire, her mouth slightly open and delicious, letting out air slowly, and then, as if she wanted to throw me deep into hell, she said, still gazing deeply into my eyes:

"Can you do that with me?"

"Fuck, damn."

"My dick hurt from so much arousal. No, I must have heard that wrong."

"What did you say?"

"It's just that..." She diverted her gaze to my mouth. "Every time you touch me there, I feel something very strong and a crazy desire to feel you there, like I saw in that video. Damn it, what am I saying?" She covered her eyes with her hands, but I held them until she looked back at me.

"Is that what you want? For me to possess you here?" I slid my fingers down her ass and pressed against the tight entrance of her anus.

Damn, I never imagined she would be ready for that, but now all I could think about was my dick filling her ass.

"Yes!" She shuddered. I touched her neck and pulled her in for a quick, desperate kiss. Our tongues met. "Is it going to hurt?" she asked worried, but without hesitation. I spread her ass with my fingers, not stopping my thrusts, and caressed her there.

"I'll make sure it doesn't hurt, my love." And I continued to tease her.

I sucked, bit, and licked every corner of her skin. I made her come on my dick once more, then teased her with my mouth again, determined to make that night unforgettable for both of us.

Star

ZION TURNED ME ON THE bed and pulled me to the edge of the mattress. I was wobbly, trembling, and felt my own liquid running down my legs, which made me even more delirious. His lips touched the base of my back with a kiss. His hand spread over my butt and squeezed the flesh until a delicious sting spread there. Then he opened me more and slid his wet tongue over my butt. I moaned, shaken, and arched against him.

Ghost tortured me with his tongue and fingers until he took all my sanity. He began to lick me and reached the little hole at the center of my butt.

I gasped loudly when he penetrated me with his tongue and began to swirl it there, pushing it in more. I grabbed the sheet with the strong sensation that rose through my skin. It was too indecent and delicious, oh my!

He penetrated a finger and spread a cold liquid that made me gasp. I could hardly describe what I was feeling; it was a mixture of libidinous pleasure with the desire to be possessed by him. Strange sounds began to rise from my throat and I began to beg without even knowing why. He inserted another finger, and I writhed with the invasion. Everything was more intense there, as if he were able to fill me without even entering me, and I already felt about to climax once again, while I sweated and panted.

"Stay still..." he ordered and twirled his fingers inside me. "I want you to lie on your side." He pulled me into his arms and fit himself behind me, thrusting the two fingers into my butt and opening me more.

"Zion..." He inserted another finger and bit my back. I leaned back and whimpered when he pinched my throbbing clitoris. I pulled in air sharply, succumbing to that wicked and extraordinary sensation.

"Relax, love, don't tense up. Just open up for me."

"Y-yes... oh, yes!" I began to rock against the three fingers, and an intense pleasure rose in waves through my legs, belly, and chest.

I heard the wrapper of another condom being opened. Zion poured more oil on his fingers in my butt and spread it around there, going in and out. He grabbed the flesh of my buttock and pulled it toward him.

"I'm going to f*** your ass, baby." He placed the head of his penis at my very tight entrance, and I tensed my body impulsively.

He caressed me until I relaxed and pulled my leg over his waist, fitting himself there. Then he began to push slowly, opening me. I felt my anus pulsate from the invasion; the thick flesh of his erection opened me forcefully, while he caressed me all over, barely giving me time to think from so much desire.

"Ah!" I gasped when he entered a little more. The pain was both intense and pleasurable. The sensation of being possessed by him was delicious. "Don't stop..." I moaned and pushed my butt back more.

"So hot!"

Zion plunged two fingers into my wet and warm vagina and moved up to the swollen clitoris. That back and forth made me dizzy, trembling. I wanted more, and that's what he gave me. I trembled and whimpered against the mattress. Zion opened me to the limit, and I screamed loudly when he buried himself deep, to the hilt.

"Fuck, Star, what a delicious ass, love," he growled breathlessly against my back.

Zion began to whisper indecent words right into my ear, while he stayed still inside me, waiting for me to get used to it. It was strange but delicious and very intimate too. I could feel him deep inside me.

"You unbalance me, Star." He inserted his fingers at the base of my neck, pulled my hair, and pressed his lips to my neck. "You have all my reason at your fingertips, sweetheart. Without you, I'd go crazy." He began to thrust, sliding through the previously untouched channel, possessing it ever more strongly. I closed my eyes, being possessed by the purest lust.

"You... ah, oh, Zion!" I screamed his name and exploded in a very intense orgasm, trembling from head to toe, and arched my butt even more against his shaft.

He thrust hard and took me to another consecutive wave of pleasure. His pelvis slapped against my butt; the sounds echoing through the night would surely be etched in my memory forever. He came inside me and growled, uncontrolled. There was something different in the sounds he made, as out of himself as I was. We stayed still for a moment, and I moaned softly when he pulled out of me slowly, leaving a strange emptiness.

He settled me in his arms after getting rid of the condom and slid his hands over my legs until reaching my wet vulva. His experienced fingers caressed me there, and I shuddered, imagining that I would not have strength for anything else; however, I began to burn again when he turned me to him, and his teeth closed around my nipple. He began to suck it, marking the skin until he had me restless and excited once again.

"Hearing you moan makes me hungry, baby." He climbed over me, surrounded my body with his, while I whimpered against his fingers. I closed my eyes, and he kissed me, opened another condom, and entered me deeply, all at once.

"Aaaaaah, what a delight, Zion..." I arched, unable to stay still in the face of the strong desire that whipped me. I ran my nails down his back; he thrust deep, and it wasn't long before we fell onto the bed, both exhausted after coming once again.

Every day, I felt on the tip of my tongue a new flavor that Zion presented to me, and that night, I experienced the taste of being completely possessed by him. I realized that I was a little more in love, a little more lost in love with that mysterious man.

CHAPTER THIRTY-TWO

Star

"Star, I'm going to tie you up, I swear!" Jasmin threatened, and I started to laugh. "Stay still, for God's sake." The blonde couldn't hold back and laughed too, holding an eyeliner brush in her hands.

"This thing tickles," I complained, wrinkling my nose. I was doing my best to keep my eyes open while she did my makeup.

"It'll be worth it." She bit her lip and focused.

"Should I intervene? I fear you're torturing my girlfriend." Ghost poked his head through the doorframe.

"Get out of here if you don't want me to throw a palette at you."

"I don't know what that is, but it sounds terrifying. Sorry, buddy, you're on your own." He laughed and left.

"Almost there..." she huffed. "Okay, look at me. Let me see the... damn!" she suddenly shouted.

"What happened?" I opened my eyes wider and leaned toward the bedroom mirror. "Oh my God!" I covered my mouth upon seeing how Jasmin's makeup highlighted the gold in my eyes with a dark cat-eye liner and a light earth-tone shadow.

"Star, you're the most beautiful woman I've ever seen." She smiled, satisfied with the result. "Your golden eyes match that huge dark hair." She tied my hair up in a high ponytail, exposing more of my face. "My best friend is prettier than a magazine model. We were born to be together."

"Jasmin, I loved it." I smiled at my reflection, still enchanted, and turned to hug Jasmin.

"Now change clothes, or we'll be late." I looked at the blonde, who wore a fitted white dress that highlighted her light eyes.

In the last month, Jasmin and I had talked a lot, and I began to shift my focus in research. I was no longer just looking for articles on management; I was researching everything about starting my own business, and the more I thought about it, the more certain I felt about my decision.

I started planning for the future as I progressed in therapy, and I was sure that in a few months, I would be psychologically ready to find a job to save money and start my own business, and Jasmin was willing to help me. Zion wanted to cover all expenses, but I refused. It had to be something I did myself, earned by my own hands.

Although I didn't know what my dreams from the past were, I began to outline plans for the future, and that day there would be a special and exclusive Workshop on entrepreneurship at a renowned venue.

The event was small, with fewer than twenty guests, including famous and Forbes-listed successful entrepreneurs. It would be a unique experience, and Jasmin had gotten a ticket for me to accompany her. It would be the second time I went out with her since returning to the United States, and it was getting easier to walk among people without feeling so claustrophobic.

The first time happened two weeks ago when I went shopping with the blonde at the mall. Zion almost had a fit when I told him I intended to go out for the first time and ended up tagging along with Shaw, who that week was responsible for Jasmin and me every time we stepped outside. It was a memorable event, especially because Zion didn't know where to look when we entered a lingerie store.

This time, he and Wolf were supposed to accompany us, but due to a last-minute meeting at Holder Security, Jasmin, Shaw, and I would go ahead and they would meet us there later, which caused quite a stir, as Ghost was worried about my acceptance of more people, but Shaw assured him that no one would approach us, just like Jasmin. So everything would be fine, and it would be a new step toward normalcy. I had to start somewhere, right?

Still, I woke up feeling nauseous that morning. Pure nerves, I was sure, but I took a deep breath and put on the dress I had set aside for the occasion. I slipped on the heels Jasmin had given me. When I stood up, it felt like I was walking on stilts.

"What a strange feeling." I widened my eyes and stared at the closet mirror. I never felt more like a circus performer than at that moment, wobbling toward the bedroom. "How do you manage to walk in these things?"

"AHHHHHHHHHHHHHHHHHHHH!" Jasmin screamed, almost making me trip as soon as her blue eyes landed on me. She stared at the dress, which was a pale pink, elegant, with a shiny fabric and a sheer section at the bust that made my breasts look more prominent. I could swear they looked bigger than before. "You look amazing. Beautiful, stunning. My God, I can't stop looking at you."

"What happened..." Ghost and Wolf skidded through the door after Jasmin's shrill scream, her eyes fixed and shining on me. "Damn." I held my breath as I felt Zion's gaze on me before even looking at him. I had never worn makeup before, and perhaps the lost and excited look on his face was a sign that he liked what he saw. "Wolf, do we really have to go to this meeting?"

"Wipe that drool, brother." The man with two-colored eyes laughed and walked over to Jasmin. "Let's wait for them in the living room," he said, taking the blonde by the hand.

"My friend is beautiful, isn't she? Did you see those eyes? I did her makeup," she told Ghost before leaving, making me smile shyly. Jasmin was a great friend.

"She's right," Zion said quietly, and the weight of his words reached me before his hand calmly touched my waist. He looked exceptionally handsome in one of his completely black suits that highlighted the tone of his skin. His dark hair was perfectly styled, and he exuded a natural charm, both alluring and dangerous. A deadly combination. "You stole my thoughts; I think I even forgot my own name." He brushed a finger along my face. "I can't stop looking at you."

"Thank you." My face flushed. "Today is an important day." I shrugged, as if justifying my pathetic attempt to keep my balance in those scary heels.

"Everything will be fine. There, you'll have the chance to talk to important names in the industry. Investors, entrepreneurs. And I want you to think about my offer afterward." Zion had made an offer he dubbed a "partnership." He would start a business for me. Period. He didn't intend to make a profit afterward, and I didn't want to accept. It was important for me to earn that with my own hands, and if I ever accepted his help, it would be as a businesswoman. He would get all the investment back, with interest. But for that, I needed to understand how that world worked, which is why today's workshop was so important.

"Maybe I'll make a counteroffer after today," I warned, and he stepped closer to me, wrapping me with his body without actually touching me. His citrus scent, mixed with the aftershave I loved so much, filled my nostrils.

"I'm looking forward to negotiating with you." He pressed my body against his, and I noticed how hard and excited he was. "I'm not going to risk kissing you right now because I'm sure I wouldn't be able to stop," he warned. "And if you show up with a hair out of place, my sister-in-law will kill me, but I want you wearing those same heels tonight; I have plans for them." A shiver ran up my neck at his veiled threat.

"I'm excited for that moment, sir." I smiled at him as he offered me his arm.

"How are you feeling today?" he whispered just before we reached Wolf and Jasmin.

I started having nightmares again after the last time I visited the home of those I should call family. I never went back there or saw them anywhere; it was better that way, but that little girl crying in the corner of a dark room seemed to haunt me since then, and just remembering her made me tense.

"I know you always say you're fine, sweetheart, but I'm watching you. You keep eating like a bird; maybe it's time to visit Dr. Madison to retake your iron tests. What do you think?"

"We'll do that," I assured, not knowing if that would help.

"Take care of them, Shaw. We'll meet you there soon," Ghost warned as we were leaving.

"Don't worry, sir. The mighty Shaw is on the case." The young man gave a thumbs-up, and both Jasmin and I started laughing at his enthusiasm.

"That guy is something else." I heard Wolf laugh as Shaw started the car.

SHAW USUALLY HAD AN upbeat and funny demeanor. The young man, who always saw the bright side of life, frequently had a chat with God in his unwavering faith, and I had the impression that he was harmless—until I saw him in action.

As soon as we got out of the car, his posture changed completely, and it became clearer as we entered the very fancy event. His usually calm expression turned serious and focused. The rigid stance made him appear a bit taller in his tailored black suit. For the first time, I saw Shaw, the usually small and funny Shaw, become intimidating. He walked behind us, guiding us through the small crowd, alert to every new approach.

"Wow, it's beautiful," I commented as we passed through the entrance and stepped into what looked like a silver spaceship, adorned with decorations and monuments of various shapes. There was a stage, equally ornate, and soft, comfortable chairs everywhere. In a slightly more distant area, a crystal-clear fountain flowed continuously, creating shimmering waves against the silver decor.

"They really went all out this year," Jasmin commented. "Hello!" She waved at some suited men who raised their drinks in her direction as a greeting.

Jasmin was famous among the businesspeople. I discovered this a few minutes later when I found myself surrounded by them, intercepting her as if their lives depended on it. I was enchanted, to say the least, by how effortlessly she handled all that attention and the countless questions, constantly steering the conversation back to me, through which I learned more about investments and starting a business in the current economic landscape.

The subject fascinated me, and I spent hours talking with successful entrepreneurs during the lectures. My mind was opening up to a new world, and I couldn't have been happier.

Ghost worried about my future. Whenever I saw him with that distant look in his eyes, I knew what he was thinking. He feared that someday Scott's shadow would come back to haunt us, and that fear occasionally stole my sleep, but I wouldn't allow that bastard to take that from me. Living well and happily was the greatest revenge I could give him, and I wouldn't let Scott take that from me.

"There are areas of the city that are begging for something different, an innovation based on creativity. Something that makes people feel like they're not in the middle of Chicago, like they're at home," a chic, jovial man commented in our current conversation circle. Jasmin was distracted, talking to another businessman, and didn't notice the fascinating comment from the man.

"Like a portal to another place. Traveling without leaving home," I added, excited by an idea that had sprouted in my mind.

"Exactly, what's your name again, miss?" He leaned toward me, his light eyes scanning me from head to toe. "Unfortunately, I haven't had the pleasure of being introduced to you; I'm Max, CEO of Comfort Technology." He flashed a toothy smile, and his voice dropped to a lower tone.

"My name is Star," I replied, shy under the strange gaze he was giving me.

"That's a beautiful name, and it suits you well. I fear you shine so brightly that I can't pay attention to anything else. Shall we take a walk? Perhaps I can show you one of my most famous projects." He winked suggestively, making it clear what kind of project he wanted to show me, and raised his hand toward my arm. I froze at the mention of that stranger's touch, but before his hand could reach me, Shaw was quicker and grabbed the man's wrist almost reflexively.

"Keep your hands off the lady, please."

"Who do you think you're talking to, you idiot?" he spat, irritated by Shaw's intrusion, who remained unfazed by the man's aggressive tone.

"Someone about to take a dive into that fountain right there. It's better you obey; I won't warn you again." He released the man's wrist with a jerk that made him stumble.

I stared at the bodyguard, shocked. The stance Shaw took was unlike anything I had ever seen; his narrowed eyes were dangerously dark and alert. His hand resting on his gun left no doubt that he was ready to draw.

"You just lost a great opportunity, Star, since you can't even control your bodyguard." I opened my mouth, about to curse him out, infuriated to the bone, but Jasmin was quicker.

"What opportunity are you referring to, Max?" She emerged behind him. Her blue eyes were darker with anger.

"Miss Cahill, you should choose your companions more wisely. This lady and her bodyguard have just disrespected me. You know I'm not a name to be disregarded in this market."

"Who are you trying to fool, Max? You might be important to your partners, but you know I know you well. You're not fooling me; you think more with your lower head than your upper one." He opened his mouth, pretending to be shocked. "Her eyes are on her face, not on her breasts, you know?" She didn't even pause to breathe, and each word seemed to slice through the man's throat. "You've been disrespecting my friend since we arrived and have the gall to blame my guest and our bodyguard? You can't even control yourself at a professional event?"

"How dare you say something like that; you're tarnishing my reputation."

"A reputation based on your dick doesn't count." The businessmen around us seemed to be enjoying the scene.

"I love when Miss Cahill takes someone by the neck," a male voice commented from behind us.

"I won't stay here listening to this nonsense!" He turned his back and stormed off.

I turned to Jasmin to thank her, as well as Shaw, who defended me without hesitation, but my head spun and I staggered, dizzy.

"Are you okay?" Jasmin stepped closer.

In that moment, a strong and sudden wave of nausea hit me. I widened my eyes in panic and stumbled to the nearest trash can in the corner of the hall. I made it just in time to drop to my knees in front of it and let everything out.

Jasmin held my hair without a second thought and tried to calm me while I could barely breathe.

"That idiot made you nervous. I should have shoved a shoe down his throat," she cursed, not letting go of my hair.

"Is she okay?"

"Poor thing!"

"What happened... oh, wow!"

Voices crowded around us. I held the handkerchief Shaw had given me and lifted my face. They were all there, surrounding me. People kept arriving. I took a breath, dizzy, my hands began to tingle.

"Jasmin, can we go home?" I whispered, still on the floor. I wasn't feeling well.

"Of course, sweetheart, come on."

She helped me to my feet, but everything went dark as soon as I stood up. A strange sensation rushed down to the tips of my fingers, as if suddenly the world had turned upside down. I was swallowed by darkness.

"Star!"

"Mercyyyyyyyy!"

That was the last thing I heard before I blacked out completely.

CHAPTER THIRTY-THREE

Star

I woke up with a strange taste in my mouth and took a moment to realize that Shaw was carrying me down a very bright corridor. Jasmin's frantic voice echoed behind me as she explained what had happened to someone.

"Put her on the stretcher. She's regaining consciousness."

"I'm fine," I whispered, but no one seemed to hear.

"Oh my God!" Shaw was pushing the stretcher, desperate.

"I'm fine!" I raised my voice and squeezed Jasmin's hand.

"SHE'S AWAKE!" the blonde shouted and received a hush from the nurse. "Sorry. Star, how are you feeling?"

"Like I'm in a car with no brakes, Shaw. Can you go a bit slower?" I pressed my hand to my head. "But seriously, I'm okay."

"We're taking her to one of the recovery rooms right now. Dr. Madison is already on her way to see you. She's your doctor, right?" a nurse asked.

I nodded in agreement. Shaw pushed the stretcher along the path the nurse had taken, and I ended up sitting on one of the hospital beds.

"I've already notified Ghost. He's on his way with Wolf." Jasmin smiled fiercely and stood by my side.

"He's going to freak out," I predicted, aware of how protective he was, and I buried my face in my hands.

"At least we have a little time before that happens." She held my hand and took a deep breath. "I was really worried, Star. You fainted and turned as white as a ghost."

"I'm sorry for worrying you."

"It's all that idiot Max's fault. I swear I'm going to throw a heel at him the next time I see him, that shameless jerk." She barely paused for breath, and I smiled at her, realizing she was becoming much more than just a great friend.

"What do we have here? Star!" Dr. Madison entered the room and interrupted our conversation. "For a moment, I was confused by the name on the chart; I'm used to calling you Star, Alena still feels strange to me."

"Don't worry, doctor, it feels strange to me too." I smiled. "I'd like to say I'm happy to see you, but as you can see..." I shrugged.

"You don't look too well; I'm going to check your blood pressure. Tell me what happened." I briefly summarized the recent events while the doctor examined me closely. "Your blood pressure is very low. You may have fainted due to your nervous state. Aside from that and the nausea, have you had any other strange symptoms in the last few days?"

"Not that I can remember. I've had no appetite for the past few weeks, but I think I was just anxious after finding out who I really am. You know how it is—knowing and not knowing at the same time."

"Alright." She began taking notes on a clipboard. "When was the last time you menstruated?" I pressed my lips together, trying to remember.

"About 15 days ago, give or take."

"Was the flow normal?"

"Actually... this time it was very light; it only lasted three days." The doctor glanced at me for a brief moment before looking back down at her clipboard.

"Stress is one of the conditions that can affect the menstrual cycle, but we'll redo some tests to be sure. When you came here for the first time, I ordered a BETA HCG test; I'll repeat it to draw a conclusion."

"That's the test we do when we want to find out if we're pregnant, right?" Jasmin's eyes widened.

"PREGNANT?" I shouted, straightening up in the bed.

"Calm down, it's just a hypothesis. If we rule that out quickly, we can find the real problem."

"But she menstruated, doctor. Isn't that a clear sign that she's not pregnant?" Jasmin seemed absorbed by the hypothesis, just like I was.

"Not exactly; some pregnant women do menstruate in the first months of pregnancy, it can be a normal occurrence, but we have to analyze on a case-by-case basis."

"Oh my God, I can't believe even menstruation can deceive us. What a total mindfuck!"

"Jasmin!" I laughed nervously.

The doctor gathered the blood collection team, and a few minutes later, they left the room with blood samples, while Jasmin and I stared blankly into space.

So many emotions flooded my heart that I could hardly concentrate on them. I felt lost, caught in a hurricane. The heels I had fought so hard to balance on lay in the corner of the room, staring back at me with a question that terrified me.

Pregnant?

My chest rose and fell along with my unsteady breath. What if it were true? How would I take care of a child, my God, I barely knew how to take care of myself.

I was breathless with fear.

"Hey, Star..." Jasmin quietly approached and placed her hand on my shoulder. Only then did I realize I was rocking back and forth. "Don't worry, whatever the result is, you're not alone." Her big blue eyes were brimming with affection. My lips trembled as I pulled her into a tight embrace, desperate for any comfort.

"Excuse me." Dr. Madison returned some time later and pushed the door closed behind her. Her composed expression gave away no hint of the results, but she carried them attached to the chart in her clipboard.

"What was the result, doctor?" I asked in a shaky voice, and she got straight to the point.

"Positive, Star. You're approximately 7 weeks pregnant."

"A-are you sure? Are you really sure about this, doctor?" I brought both hands to my mouth, unable to process it.

"Absolutely. All the symptoms pointed to a suspicion. I also noticed that your blood tests showed another change related to anemia. You're apathetic and dehydrated. We'll start the appropriate treatment, and you'll be referred to an obstetrician..."

I stopped listening and stared at the blue hospital sheet. My lips parted, and my breathing began to alter.

Pregnant?

Oh my God, I'm pregnant!

I couldn't believe it.

"Star?" Jasmin called, feeling my hand in hers. I realized I had pulled half the covers from the bed and was clutching them between my fingers.

"I'll leave you two alone and come back when Zion arrives."

I almost fainted at the mention of his name.

"Everything will be fine." Jasmin was controlling herself from freaking out along with me, and her spaced-out breathing was a clear sign that it was just as hard for her to believe the result as it was for me. "It has to be okay." I turned to her in panic, on the verge of collapsing, a painful knot forming in my throat.

"How can it be okay, Jasmin?" I sobbed, tears I had held back began to stream down my face. "I'm pregnant. Oh God, what am I going to do?" I started to hyperventilate, in a panic. "What will Zion think? W-what if he gets mad at me?" Jasmin laughed.

"Mad? My God, I'm shaking." The blonde ran her fingers through her perfectly styled hair. "Star, don't you see how he looks at you? It's as if you're the only woman in the world. My brother-in-law would kill for you; it's written all over his face how much he loves you. He'll freak out, in a good way. Oh my God, I need to sit down." She went to the nearby chair.

I paused to think about her words and brought my trembling hand to my belly. 7 weeks. That was about two months, right?

There was an innocent life growing inside me. I pressed my hand harder against my abdomen, and a sob rose in my throat. It was my child. My little child, and I didn't know what to do. Could there be a greater despair than this?

"I don't even recognize my own name," I said, my eyes fixated on a point on the bed. "How could a woman like me, with no past, nothing, and now pregnant, be anything other than a problem?" My shoulders trembled, and Jasmin climbed onto the bed, embracing me with her thin, comforting arms. "I'm scared, Jas," I confessed. "He won't like this. Who would? How am I going to raise a child if I don't even know how I was raised?" I succumbed to the fear in my chest and cried uncontrollably, overwhelmed by pure panic.

Ghost

THE SOUND OF MY HEART pounding in my ears began the moment Jasmin called to inform me that Star had fainted at the event. A cloud of possibilities settled in my mind, and none of them were even remotely pleasant.

"Ghost, I'm sure everything is fine. Nervousness causes this, brother," Snake tried to calm me as I sped toward the hospital. My older brother had joined us at the meeting and decided to come along to see how Star was doing, and I was certain my father would show up soon too.

"Don't make us admit you too. Look how pale you are," Wolf poked me from the back seat.

"I heard that idiot from Comfort Technology made her nervous. I'm going to rip his throat out if anything happens to her." I gripped the steering wheel, barely able to breathe.

"First, try not to kill us in traffic and drive carefully. Just because we're heading to the hospital doesn't mean we have to end up in a bed there, right?" Snake pointed out, and I did as he asked.

We arrived at the hospital many long minutes later, and I jumped out of the car without even properly parking it. I started running down the hallways as if my life depended on it, stopping when I spotted Shaw sitting near a door at the end of the corridor. His eyes were distant, arms crossed. He was tense, and before I realized it, I was already running toward him. The sound of my hurried footsteps caught his attention.

"It's the first time I hear you walk on the ground, Mr. Ghost!" Shaw broke into a cheerful smile.

"Where is she?" I skidded to a stop near him, barely paying attention to what the young man was saying.

"Right here." He pointed to the door beside him, and I passed by it, opening it with an anxious bang.

"Oh shit, Ghost!" Jasmin jumped when she saw me burst in like a hurricane. "You're scary when you're silent, but it's infinitely worse when you make noise. What the hell, do you want us to have a heart attack?" My sister-in-law was lying in the hospital bed next to a tearful Star, her cheeks as red as the tip of her nose.

Time stopped for a moment, and Star cried even more as I approached her.

"What happened, sweetheart? Why are you crying?" I hugged her, anxious.

"I'll leave you two to talk. And you..." Jasmin jumped off the bed, pointed at me, and narrowed her eyes. "I think you'd better be careful what you say to her, got it?" My sister-in-law made a sign with two fingers toward her eyes, then pointed them at me as a clear indication that she was "keeping an eye on me" before leaving the room.

"Should I be worried?" I asked anxiously as I sat on the bed in front of Star. I wrapped my arms around her back and pulled her into a hug. "What is it, little one? What happened? I heard Max intercepted you right before you passed out. Did that idiot say something?" She sobbed in such a painful way that it broke my heart.

"Zion, I'm so sorry." She gasped and cried, devastated. "I'm so sorry." She repeated it, and I started to feel more apprehensive, the nervousness making me hold her tighter against my chest.

"What happened, love?" I pulled her back, concerned, and held her by the shoulders to look into her eyes.

"I fainted at the event after I vomited," she explained between gasps. The tears kept rolling down, and I framed her face with my hands. "W-when I got here, the doctor did some tests."

"And what did she find that left you so distressed, my heart?" She raised her tear-filled eyes, which shone behind the tears in a sumptuous, intense amber tone, full of emotion, and I could see the fear etched there. My world stopped when she spoke again.

"I'm pregnant, Zion." She brought her hand to her mouth. "Pregnant." I smiled, somewhat confused.

"What do you mean?" Star's lips trembled again, and she tilted her head forward, crying heavily. My mind started to spin.

"I said I'm pregnant."

I opened my mouth a few times, then closed it again.

Holy shit! I wanted to scream, but the only thing I could do was stare at her. The news infiltrated deeper into my subconscious until it became real. Like a lightning bolt, strong and absolute.

"Pregnant?" My voice came out low, and Star trembled.

"Yes. I think it happened the first time we were together." The exotic eyes of my little one filled with tears once again, and I embraced her, kissing each drop that rolled down her face.

Oh my God, the news caught me off guard. I was expecting anything, absolutely anything, but not a pregnancy. A strange and powerful feeling swept through my chest. Anxiety, fear, joy, surprise—everything, absolutely everything—and I didn't even know what to say. I could barely believe this was really happening.

"I'm so sorry, Zion."

"Why, my love? Why would you say that? Oh God, please, don't cry." I pulled her small body close to me.

"I know you weren't expecting this news. I can't even take care of myself without making you worry. How will I be able to take care of a baby?" She cried, and I wished with all my might to show her the strange and wildly desperate beats of my heart at that moment.

Pure euphoria coursed through my veins.

My woman was pregnant.

Pregnant!

"Yes, I wasn't expecting this." I buried my face in her hair, my hands started to shake. "I didn't expect this gift so soon." I laughed, unable to maintain my composure. "Shit, I'm going to be a dad!" I kissed her worried little face. "This is the best news I could receive, the best, sweetheart."

"Are you serious? Or are you just trying to make me feel better?" She gave an uncertain smile, and part of the pressure weighing on my chest eased. I held her face in my hands.

"I've never been more sincere in my life. It was my fault, love. I knew we were taking a risk, even being the first time. And now..." I opened a smile as wide as the world, so happy I could barely think. "Oh my God,

I'm going to be a dad," I repeated. My voice trembled with emotion, and I buried my face in her neck. "Oh, my love, thank you." I took her mouth with mine, kissing her anxiously, trying to confirm that this was real.

My heart was pounding in my chest, and I spread my hand over her still flat belly and smiled, looking at her.

"We're going to have a baby." She brought her hand to her face, insecure, fearful.

"We are!" she whispered.

I kissed her again until her anxious breathing calmed down.

"I'm going to call the doctor. I have so many questions, and I want her to guide us. I'll make sure you and our child get the best medical care." *Our child...* damn, I was about to burst with joy, and I couldn't help but embrace her again. "I'll be back in a moment. I'll ask Jasmin to stay here until I find the doctor."

"Don't you think you should breathe first? You're speaking so fast I can barely understand you." She sniffled, her little nose red, and I leaned in. I gave her a playful nibble and a kiss on the tip of her nose, making her laugh.

"I'll be right back." I stumbled out the door and bumped into Snake, Lyon, Shaw, my dad, and the small army of bodyguards that followed him everywhere. In one corner of the hallway, I saw Wolf hugging Jasmin.

Everyone, except my sister-in-law, who was grinning at me with a cheeky smile, wore worried expressions, and my dad was the first to speak.

"I came as soon as I could. What happened to Star?" He frowned, bracing himself for any kind of news.

A swell of pride and deep love filled my chest as I noticed once again my dad was there, ready to face any problem alongside one of his children. Reid Holder was my greatest role model, and I realized I wanted to be like him; I wanted to care for my child just as my father had cared for me.

"Is it serious, brother?" Snake got up and came toward me as soon as our eyes met.

My eyes burned and were probably red from trying so hard not to fall apart right there, but when I began to speak, in the safety of my family, I couldn't resist.

"She's pregnant. The first Holder baby is on the way!" I shouted, euphoric, and I watched my brothers' faces shift from worry to surprise until they understood the news and began to cheer.

"A GRANDSON!" My dad jumped up, excited, and ran to me, wrapping me in a tight hug. "Finally!"

"I was the first to know. Auntie already loves you!" I heard Jasmin's voice echo as she bounced around, and even Shaw and Lyon joined in the raucous celebration, which ended with a lecture from Dr. Madison about keeping quiet in a hospital area.

I returned to the room with the doctor a few minutes later while my family was still celebrating outside, absorbing the news. I embraced Star, feeling as if I were touching happiness itself with my fingertips.

That woman, who couldn't remember her own name, who punched me every time I surprised her, who moaned with surrender when we made love, that strong, energetic woman with an angelic voice was pregnant with my child.

I was the luckiest bastard on the face of the earth.

CHAPTER THIRTY-FOUR

Star

My thoughts swirled in confusion as I tried to process everything happening around me. When I left home earlier, I had intended to gather information and learn a bit more about a world of entrepreneurship I didn't know, and I never imagined I would end up sitting on a hospital bed with my eyes burning from crying.

I raised a hand to my head, where a painful throb emerged. Loud voices echoed down the corridor, and I held onto the sheets until I saw Dr. Madison walk through the door, followed closely by Ghost.

"So there are no doubts, doctor?" he asked with a gigantic smile on his striking face. He was genuinely happy, and seeing him excited about the news that would change our lives eased my anxiety a little.

"It's a very accurate result, Mr. Holder." Madison laughed.

"And how is she? How are they?" Ghost stepped closer and took my hands in his. His words tumbled over each other.

"Star will be referred to an obstetric gynecologist. I've already recommended Dr. Audra in the file; she's one of the best doctors I've ever worked with."

"Doctor..." I interrupted her, too worried to remain silent.

"Yes?"

"Can my memory loss harm the baby?" I squeezed Zion's hand, anxious.

"No, not at all. You will be monitored at all times to prevent or diagnose any issues early on, but there are no warning signs related to your memory loss. Don't worry about that, okay?"

"Doctor, I want to ensure the best medical support in the country. I want her to have access to absolutely everything, no matter what."

"Alright." Madison smiled. "I'll schedule the first ultrasound and appointments with the obstetrician right now. I'll keep a close eye on the team."

"Is that all? What if she throws up again or faints?"

"Bring her in immediately. Fainting is more concerning than nausea during pregnancy, as it's a common symptom, but we also need to be cautious about that. She can't get dehydrated. So, drink plenty of fluids, young lady. We'll see you soon." The doctor left through the door.

I blinked, anxious and confused. Zion sat in front of me, his serious face filled with an emotion that made my own chest ache.

My God, this was really happening. I curled up, fear making me apprehensive and emotional.

I sobbed, a river of feelings threatening to drown me, and I found myself unable to control my tears, as if all the water in the world now resided in my eyes. He traced a finger down my face, wiping away the tears that had formed there.

"My love." His voice came low, and he gave a sideways smile, affected. "I will take care of you and this little part of us that is growing right here." His hand rested on my smooth belly, and a part of me wanted to dwell in that touch. He caressed my stomach with devotion. "I thought I knew what happiness was, but nothing I've experienced compares to the news that a child is on the way." His trembling voice shook me. "I'm happy, my love. You make me very happy."

I started crying again when I saw Zion's eyes glistening with tears. He leaned in and took me in his arms, his mouth brushing against mine, a multitude of feelings dancing between us. He kissed me hungrily, fiercely, and his hand remained protectively at the base of my belly.

"What are we going to do now?"

"We're going to start our family." He held my hand between his and brought it to his lips.

A knock at the door caught our attention, and soon Jasmin's blonde head popped into the wooden frame.

"Have you accepted the news yet?" I couldn't help but smile. "Great, come in." She swung the door wide, and one by one, all the members of the Holder family entered, including Zion's father, who carried himself with that impeccable, elegant posture of someone who held power at his fingertips.

"Star, what wonderful news." He embraced me.

"Do you really think so?" I smiled, relieved.

"Of course."

"And who would think otherwise?" Jasmin scoffed as if the thought was absurdly unacceptable.

"Our whole family is thrilled about the news. You and Zion have just given me another reason to live for the next fifty years, aside from keeping my children alive." Snake and Wolf grumbled something to each other and crossed their arms in identical fashion.

"Pregnant women need attention and care, and I can visit you every day if you want." Jasmin raised her delicate nose, sure of her decision. This filled me with gratitude and affection for that woman.

"Was that supposed to be comforting?" Zion complained, and a wave of laughter echoed through the room.

"You should feel grateful; I'm a valuable friend."

"I would feel that way if your presence didn't threaten the perfect alignment of my teeth. I never know what you're capable of if I scare you."

"I regret to inform you, brother, but I don't think any kind of scare would do Star and the baby any good," Wolf chimed in as he approached me, extending his hand in my direction. "Congratulations, Star. I can't wait to meet my nephew."

"Or niece." Jasmin jumped beside him.

"Your brother is right, son."

"Is the glorious moment finally here when Ghost will need to wear a bell around his neck? I don't know any other way we can protect this child." Snake looked at me sideways and pursed his lips. "And congratulations, little one. I know you'll be a good mother," Snake whispered so low and fast that I almost didn't understand.

"You get weirder when you try to be nice," I retorted, and he laughed.

✵

I ADMIRED, FEELING all giddy, that family committee that had gathered at Zion's house. Mr. Holder, to my surprise, took off his suit jacket and poured whiskey for his sons and daughter-in-law. Then he fetched a glass of juice from the fridge and handed it to me, proposing a toast. His gray eyes were deep and experienced, and he scanned each face present in the dim room before continuing.

"I'm not a man given to romance," he began. "I never married in my entire life, nor did I wish to get involved with anyone beyond work, but I found love through my children. It's strange to be responsible for another life that isn't your own, but that's the meaning of having children. We hand over our hearts to a small being that needs our protection," he continued with a serious expression. "You no longer worry about your schedules, your commitments, your own nights' sleep. The only thing that matters is that your children sleep well, that they are safe and happy." His eyes drifted to a point on the wall, and he paused for a brief moment. "There was a time when I didn't believe in love between a man and a woman. I thought the feeling was trivial, selfish. I didn't believe in it, just as I didn't believe a person could suffer for something that didn't exist. At least not until I saw my children growing up. Until I saw them suffer from their first heartbreak." He looked directly at Zion. "That's when I realized it didn't matter if it existed for me. It existed for my children, and all I ever wanted was for them to find that love. To be happy beside whoever they chose, even if it broke one rule or another." He fixed his gaze on Wolf, who smiled emotionally and hugged Jasmin. "The child that is coming will be your world, Zion, just as you three will always be a vital part of mine." I blinked, trying to wipe away the stubborn tears that continued to fall down my face.

Zion swallowed hard, continuing to look at his father, visibly moved. Snake barely moved from the corner of the room, and I had the impression that Wolf wasn't even breathing.

"Your father is a stubborn old man, who made many mistakes raising you alone and without any experience, but who cares? I'd do it all over again, and if there's anything I can do to help with my grandchild's upbringing, please count on me."

Zion bolted across the room and hugged his father tightly, almost knocking the whiskey out of Reid's hand.

"How beautiful!" Shaw wiped his eyes.

"Shut up." Lyon elbowed him, almost making me laugh.

"You guys are impossible. My makeup is going to smear all over..." Jasmin looked at the ceiling, blinking to chase away the tears.

"I love you, Dad," Zion whispered. "Thank you for this."

"Damn, we're going to have a baby in the family." Wolf laughed, and Snake punched Zion's arm.

I wished more than anything for my mother to be by my side, even though I didn't remember her. I wanted to tell her about the emotion that was splitting my heart in two. To ask if she was scared when she found out she was pregnant with me, and if it took her a while to accept the idea. I was terrified when I found out, but not a day had passed, and I was already in love with that little piece of us growing in my belly.

I took a deep breath; she wasn't physically there, but I felt that wherever she was, my mother was watching over us.

I smiled and turned to the Holders. That joy and unconditional support filled my chest with an intense, liberating feeling. It mixed all the emotion I felt with the hope of never being alone again.

"So this is it," I thought aloud.

"This is what?" Zion approached.

"Being part of a family." He smiled and gave me a tight hug, full of meaning.

✶

IT WAS FUNNY HOW EVERYTHING with the Holder family turned into a big event. I never imagined that the next morning, they would all be at the hospital again, eager to accompany us during the ultrasound. Even the doctor didn't expect so many spectators and, I must admit, she was thrilled with the charming way they embraced the news of my pregnancy.

"I think this is the first time I've done an ultrasound with so many eyes on me," Dr. Audra, a cheerful obstetrician with long dark hair, joked. "Do you all know this is the first ultrasound? You won't be able to see anything beyond a little dark spot."

"That little spot belongs to this family, doctor. So we want to see it," Snake said seriously, crossing his arms.

"We're very involved," Reid added, perching beside Jasmin, right by the large monitor in the middle of the room.

"Move over!" Wolf shoved Snake.

"I got here first," the biggest and oldest brother growled, refusing to budge.

"You don't even like kids, why do you want to see it up close?" Wolf retorted, narrowing his two-colored eyes in dissatisfaction.

"The baby will be my niece, it's my duty to like her, now shut the hell up."

"It's better if everyone stays quiet, because if I get kicked out of this room because of your noise, I'm going to kill you!" Jasmin exploded, and I couldn't hold it in; I started to laugh.

"My God, you're so loud. Can we get started?" The doctor smiled, and Zion stood by my side, shielding my exposed belly from any wandering eyes.

"I'll start the ultrasound, but I'll need all of you to leave afterward so I can continue the exam, okay?" A wave of agreement echoed through the room.

"Even the father? There's nothing about Star that I don't already know!" Ghost complained, outraged.

"Zion!" I burned with embarrassment.

"Dad stays," the doctor conceded, exasperated, and spread cold gel over my belly. Then she placed a round-tipped device on my skin and slid it up and down. I shivered at the ticklish sensation spreading across my skin. "Here it is..." The doctor pointed to the screen, but I didn't see anything. "Do you see that little dot right there in the middle? The size of a blueberry."

"It's the prettiest blueberry ever." Jasmin waved her hands, excited.

"Looks like you, brother. We can barely see it," Snake teased, and Wolf laughed loudly.

The doctor quickly ushered them all out and proceeded with the consultation.

"Now we'll perform a transvaginal ultrasound to listen to the baby's heartbeat, and I believe you'll want to record it to show your family at home."

"Alright, doctor." Ghost straightened up with a jerk, and all I could think about was that word: transvaginal.

"Doctor, are you saying the ultrasound will be..."

"Inside your vagina. I'm going to insert this imaging device here." She pulled out a long, thin instrument. Ghost swallowed hard at the sight of it.

"You don't need to be scared, sweetheart," he said quietly, his hand cold. I pursed my lips, not understanding why he was worried.

"I'm not scared, just curious. Look how thin this thing is. You're much thicker than this and it fits."

"Woman, for God's sake!" he grunted, hoarse. His ivory-colored face turned vivid red.

The doctor laughed.

"Can we start?" she asked, a few minutes after preparing everything for the exam.

"Yes, I'm ready."

At least I thought I was. But when the doctor began the exam and a very rapid little sound echoed through the office, a strange, desperate, and unique feeling swept through my chest. That was the most beautiful sound I had ever heard. It was my baby's heartbeat.

"Should it be this fast?" Zion stammered, emotional, as he focused on the thumping on the monitor.

"Yes, it's perfectly normal."

He brought my hand to his lips. His serious face, framed by a well-groomed beard that made him even more handsome, didn't hide his watery eyes. He leaned in and kissed me, trembling, just like I was.

"I love you, Star," he declared, and the doctor stepped back for a moment. I opened my eyes wider; even though Zion made it clear at every moment how much he loved me, he had never said those words before, and my heart raced so hard I feared it would explode. "I love you so much, sweetheart. I love every part of you and this part of us. Our child." He placed his hand on my belly, which was beginning to form a tiny bump. I bit my lips and spent the rest of the exam emotional and tearful.

"And finally, something that couples often ask me about is having sex during pregnancy." Ghost's face lost some color, and he coughed. "As long as Star feels comfortable, there are no contraindications."

"We won't risk hurting the baby?" I asked, anxious.

"Intimacy won't harm the baby. He's protected inside the womb; you don't need to worry." I smiled, my cheeks burning just thinking about what we could do. "I'll see you all soon. You have my contact information; you can reach out whenever you have any questions."

✳

WE GATHERED WITH THE whole family later, in front of Zion's TV that took up half a wall.

He held my waist possessively as he watched the ultrasound recording once again.

"I'll never get tired of this sound," he remarked, and Reid turned to him.

"I want a copy. Arrange for one first thing tomorrow." My father-in-law maintained a stance with rigid shoulders and straight legs, like an off-duty cop, but his gray eyes overflowed with emotion.

Snake watched from the corner of the room, a glass of whiskey and ice in hand. His usually serious expression remained unchanged, but the way he focused on each part of the sound told me he cared too, just like

Wolf, who wore a silly grin on his face, with an emotional Jasmin by his side.

Our family wasn't traditional, but I could guarantee it had the most love to give.

✸

THE HOLDER FAMILY LEFT after a few hours, and I took a shower, but before going to bed, I went to the kitchen to take my daily medications, which included an iron supplement, and I smiled when I found Zion at the stove making hot chocolate. One of my favorite drinks.

"I was going to bring your meds with the chocolate; you didn't need to come." He quickly pecked me and returned his attention to the stove.

"I would have had to come anyway; I wanted to take a look at the newspaper." I swallowed the medication and pulled out some newspapers that were on the marble countertop dividing the kitchen.

I flipped through the newspaper until I found the job section. I didn't feel comfortable depending on Zion for everything, and since I discovered I was pregnant, I became even more worried. I needed to help in some way and should start while I still had the strength for it, not to mention the plans to start my own business that would have to be postponed for at least nine months.

I kept turning the pages and began to wonder if I could handle working as a bartender; it was certainly something I could do. My only hindrance would be the possibility of some man approaching me. Just the thought sent shivers down my spine.

"What's on those pages that made you go pale like that?"

"N-nothing," I stammered, trying to shake off those thoughts. "Actually, there are some bars hiring bartenders, and I considered the idea of applying for one of those positions."

"Wait." He put his hands on his hips, turned off the heat, and looked at me in a funny way. "You're looking for a job?" His voice came out strangled.

"Am I? I am!" I hesitated, confused by the angry expression he was giving me. "Why are you looking at me like I scratched your car?"

"Right now, I want to understand why you're thinking about looking for a job in a bar." He stepped closer.

"I already said I don't want to be a burden to you. So I'll do something, anything."

"Honey, you're not a burden, and this child is our son. It will be a pleasure and an honor to take care of both of you." He kissed my forehead. "I know I can't force you to stay idle at home, but I ask that you consider the option at least during the pregnancy. I would also feel more relieved after hearing news about Scott's whereabouts before letting you go out without a bodyguard." His gaze reflected fear and insecurity. The need he had to protect us was palpable.

"You're right; I'll wait for a while, but sooner or later I'll have to start over in some way."

"And I'll support you, without a doubt, especially if there are no crazies on your tail." I laughed, and he slid his hand over my belly, his smile turning warm and filled with feelings.

"We need to start preparing for the baby's arrival. The months fly by; I'll call an interior designer this week so we can start decorating the room." He sighed and looked into my eyes, his hand still resting on my belly.

"All of this feels a bit surreal, but I'm already dying to know if it's a boy or a girl." He curled his lips and suddenly burst out laughing. "What's up?" I smiled, confused.

"I still can't believe you had the guts to say that to the doctor." He pressed me against the countertop.

"What are you talking about?" I feigned ignorance and watched him bite his lip. He took my hand and guided it down his abdomen until it landed on a hard erection, pulsating against his pants.

"You know what I'm talking about." He slipped both hands under the floral dress I was wearing and raised them to cup my butt. His fingers squeezed my skin, and I resisted the urge to close my eyes.

"Zion!" I squeaked when he lifted me and set me down on the cold countertop.

"I want you to repeat what you said in the office." His face took on that commanding, intense, and perverted expression that seemed ready to devour me. His fingers tangled with my panties and he pulled them down my legs. "Now, Star." He covered my vagina with his hand, and I felt the center of my body jump with desire from the sudden touch.

"I said, ah!" I couldn't hold back a moan. "If, oh my..." I bit my lip; the invasion of two fingers into my intimacy mixed with the overwhelming sensation of his lips closing around a nipple over the very thin fabric of the dress. "If you keep doing this, I won't be able to... speak," I stammered, and he opened my legs wider.

"I think I didn't hear you. What did you say?" He removed my dress and left me naked on the countertop, then leaned his lips close to a hard nipple and blew on it. I tried to close my legs in excitement, but he stopped me.

"I said you're rough. Too rough; I feel you opening me up, filling me."

"And do you like this? Do you like that I'm opening you up?"

"I love it." I shuddered at the slow, lascivious smile that spread across his face.

His mouth devoured my free breast in one go, sucking it mercilessly, his fingers slipping inside me, penetrating in a constant rhythm, and a shiver ran up my chest. He sucked my neck, bit my mouth, and continued to roll his thumb over that pulsing spot that drove me crazy. I trembled, desperate. I was about to explode. I heard the sound of his zipper opening and felt the broad tip of his member at my entrance.

"Zion..." I arched my body between his arms as he slid inside me slowly.

He plunged his tongue into my mouth, and I opened up more, taking him fully until I felt him deep. He stopped moving and stayed there, just filling me. I clutched at his dress shirt, crumpling the light fabric that highlighted his eyes. My ragged breath met his, and his eyes sparkled in a different way.

Zion slid his fingers over my face, caressing my cheekbones, and swallowed hard, his face taking on an emotional expression.

"What's wrong, angel?" I whispered, unable to formulate a more complex sentence. I was a bit dizzy with his member buried and pulsating between the walls of my vagina.

"Thank you, sweetheart." He pressed our foreheads together and began to move. "Thank you for this." Zion spread one hand over my belly while keeping the other torturing my clitoris.

The emotion surrounding us went beyond intimate contact. A phantom entered my heart strongly and quickly, as if we were destined to belong to each other. Again, the feeling of having seen that look somewhere before washed over me.

My angel... I thought, opening my lips, overwhelmed by the sensation of his skin against mine, of his member sliding inside me.

Yes, he was an angel. Protective and kind, who also knew how to be dangerous and unpredictable. He had refined manners like someone from the elite, yet was irritatingly silent like a thief. That man touched me in a unique way. He made love to my body and my soul, savoring each of my feelings. Zion did much more than save me from a terrible end; he showed me what it was to love and be loved.

"Star," he growled, out of control, shoving his hand at the base of my neck, pulling my hair roughly until I bent over.

"Ahhhhhhh!" I moaned loudly.

My whole body shuddered, and I bit my lips, lost in a powerful orgasm. Ghost buried his face in my neck and bit my skin. A rough, deep sound escaped his mouth, and I felt his member swell as he spilled inside me.

He kissed me for long minutes. I was still in ecstasy and a bit limp in his arms when he spoke again.

"I can't wait to see you more pregnant." His thumb brushed my belly.

"What would 'more pregnant' mean?" I laughed.

"I want to see that round belly, your swollen breasts." He kissed the flesh of my breasts one by one. "I want to be there when the baby kicks for the first time. To go find strange things for you to eat in the middle of the night, I don't know. Pregnant stuff. I want to be part of every step, no matter how small."

I kissed him, unable to love him more than in that moment.

CHAPTER THIRTY-FIVE

Ghost

The first few weeks after discovering the pregnancy were very difficult. Almost every night I took her to the bathroom to vomit. She cried, and it broke my heart in two. We tried various options for the nausea, but nothing seemed to help. Her appetite had decreased even more, and she struggled to eat anything besides instant noodles. She was addicted to junk food, and I was sure that if Star had to choose between a pack of chocolate cookies and me, she would definitely pick the pack.

I took some time off to care for her and still remembered the nights I spent awake, just praying to God that she could sleep. I couldn't stand seeing the dark circles under her pale eyes or watching her cry every time she vomited. At one point, I had to take her to the hospital. Gradually, she started to improve, but it took almost a month for my prayers to be answered.

Today marked five days since she last felt sick. Her appetite returned, and she was already eating without difficulty. It was a great victory, and to top it off, I had managed to hire two employees with excellent references.

Deloris and Bertha were recommended by Ruth, the housekeeper who worked for Jasmin's family. Bertha was Ruth's cousin, and like her, she was a serious, focused, and straightforward housekeeper. Her very short hair highlighted her attentive and helpful gaze. She was a bit intimidating at times, but she seemed like a soldier ready to fight a war to keep everything organized—very helpful and loyal.

Deloris, on the other hand, the new employee responsible for the kitchen and part of the house, had a completely different personality. The slender woman with brown hair had round, friendly eyes. She was more sensitive and loved to chat. Star took to her immediately, and I felt more at ease when I returned to work.

In a few months, we would have a baby in the family, and I was eager for that moment. Every day, I felt an insane desire to see her little face, and aside from all the anxiety, everything was fine. Perfect, until that afternoon when I received a call from Don Matteo that changed my perception.

"What did Matteo say?" Wolf asked, holding the phone with a call from Snake on speaker.

I had parked my car in the garage and decided to tell my brothers what was bothering me. I had been keeping that information secret all day and couldn't take it anymore.

"Finally, Don Matteo reacted and attacked Gava, but the outcome wasn't what we expected. Not entirely."

"What happened?"

"They took Don Gava's house," I said quietly.

"Wonderful," Snake cheered. "The human trafficking scheme is over."

"Don Gava, his advisor, and the underboss are dead, but Scott hasn't been found in the country," I revealed.

"What? How is that possible?" Wolf cursed.

"Impossible. Where would he be if not in Italy?" Snake ran his hand through his hair. "He's being searched for everywhere; that bastard would only find refuge in Calabria."

"I don't know, brother, but I'm very worried that he might have returned to the United States. You know how sick he is; he's probably a psychopath."

"If that's the case, he will definitely try to get close to her again," Snake said.

"I don't want to tell her for now, so keep this information to yourselves. It won't help to worry her at the moment."

"Okay, I'll reach out to my contacts and see if anyone has heard anything about that bastard on American soil." Snake hung up.

Wolf and I got out of the car and walked toward the house, enveloped in a tense silence.

"He won't get close to her," Wolf tried to comfort me.

"I really hope not, brother—or I'll have to kill him," I wanted to add.

I would do anything to protect my wife and the child she was carrying.

I tried to push those thoughts aside for now and smiled as I passed my sister-in-law Jasmin's car, parked in front of the house entrance.

Star was adapting well and already had some ease in getting along with others. The constant visits from Jasmin and the joy my sister-in-law brought were of tremendous help, and as I climbed the steps to the entrance of the house, I tried to remember to thank her for all her attention to my little one when a strange sound echoed through the door.

I hurried my steps, horrified by the horrifying noise, and found Shaw and Lyon standing outside on the porch, near the living room. My eyes widened when I realized that Shaw was wearing a pair of bunny ears and swaying his body from side to side, to what was supposed to be music, but sounded more like a fatal collision of instruments and voices.

"What a horrifying sound is that?"

"Mr. Ghost!" Shaw said, pulling the headband off in one swift motion. His wide eyes almost made me laugh.

"I told you someone would see that nonsense on your head," Lyon grumbled, the sound of a furious wild animal providing a background soundtrack. "We're being tortured!" Lyon covered his ears and glared at me.

"Miss Star and Jasmin decided to have fun with karaoke."

"Star has a fantastic voice, but Jasmin..." Lyon ran a hand over his face.

"It sounds like she swallowed a little bird, and the poor thing is there, gasping for breath," Shaw added.

I walked through the living room and was stunned to see a tone-deaf panda singing next to a little kitty complete with ears, tail, and everything.

I couldn't help but smile when I saw her. Star became more beautiful every day, and her light seemed to fill the room as she cheerfully sang beside Jasmin. Her little belly was already starting to round out, and it was hard not to touch it all the time.

There was no more perfect sight than my pregnant wife.

"Ghost, you arrived just in time! This one's for you..." Jasmin pointed her finger at me, but I grabbed the remote and turned off the sound before she could blow out my eardrums. "Hey, you party pooper!"

"Hands up, panda of the apocalypse. Hand over the kitty and nobody gets hurt." I aimed the remote at Jasmin, who burst out laughing.

"Just take her already!" She pushed Star in my direction.

I opened my arms to receive her and placed a quick kiss on her lips, eager to see her up close. She looked so adorable in the plush costume that I had to squeeze her against my chest.

"You're going to suffocate me like this," she laughed. "I missed you." I smiled, enchanted by that delicate pout on her lips.

"Did you have lunch, princess?" I hugged her, inhaling a bit of her sweet scent.

"Actually, it was a snack," she replied quickly.

"Miss Star hardly ate, sir!" Bertha, our new housekeeper, appeared by my side as if she had sprung from the ground. I placed a hand over my heart, trying to mask my surprise. I wasn't going to give my brothers that satisfaction.

"I had a sandwich, Bertha! That counts."

"In the morning."

"It was a really big sandwich." Star tried to trick me and started to laugh. Even she couldn't keep a straight face.

"Can you ask Deloris to make a hearty snack for this stubborn one, Bertha?" I requested.

"For this stubborn one here too, please!" Jasmin jumped beside Bertha and raised her finger. "Who am I kidding? I'm extremely easy; I'll eat whatever's in front of me."

I laughed and pushed the two human girls dressed as stuffed animals toward the dining room.

WE ENJOYED JASMIN AND Wolf's company, turning the snack into a small family gathering, complete with drinks, of course.

"Jasmin!" Star raised her voice as my sister-in-law handed her a square white box. I approached Star as she hurriedly opened the gift and pulled out a tiny all-white outfit.

"It's a coming-home outfit," Jasmin perched beside Star on the couch.

"Is that an ear?" I squinted and picked up the little hat that was part of the set. I cracked a half-smile seeing the bunny ears on the outfit, and I could only imagine how adorable our baby would look in it.

"Of course it's an ear; it's a personalized outfit," Jasmin said, lifting her nose. The two had changed out of their costumes, making it possible for me to have a serious conversation with my sister-in-law. It was quite complicated to talk to a stuffed panda.

"Are you going to turn the baby into a bunny from an early age?" I asked, and she stuck out her tongue.

"I loved it. It's going to be the cutest thing in the world." Star sniffled. My little one had been sentimental lately.

"Thank you, Jasmin; it's the perfect gift," I said, still fixated on the tiny outfit.

"The ultrasound day is coming up, right?" Wolf asked, pretending to be casual.

"It's scheduled for this week. We're going to try to find out the baby's sex," I replied.

"Who do you think will win?" Jasmin let slip and then covered her mouth immediately.

"Win what?" I narrowed my eyes at Wolf.

"Well, we made bets," my brother revealed, and Star laughed.

"You bet on the baby's sex?"

"Don't tell me you didn't think about it because I know you did," Wolf laughed, and I ended up doing the same.

"And what did you bet?"

"Wolf and Snake think it's a boy; Reid and I disagree and believe it's a girl," Jasmin said.

"Did my dad bet too?" I opened my mouth in shock.

"Yes. Do you think he would sit it out? It's the first grandchild on the way, the baby of the youngest," Wolf sang the last part playfully. "He's going to be involved in everything."

It was strange and even a bit scary to know a child was on the way. A mix of sensations embraced me from the moment I woke up until I went to sleep, the strongest being love. A strange knot formed in my throat as I looked at the outfit. It was real; our baby was real. And I needed to protect them.

I looked from Jasmin to Star. The two were excitedly talking about the baby's room, hardly noticing the latent worry I now shared with my brothers. It was better this way; I didn't want them to carry that alert beyond us.

I blinked and turned my attention back to Star, who was smiling, serene and distracted, and the certainty that filled my heart was that I would destroy half the world to keep that beautiful smile on her face.

She was so happy, dreaming of our baby, making plans and more plans, and just the thought that she could get hurt made me feel sick.

A deep fear washed over me, almost like a bad premonition whispering something in my ears.

CHAPTER THIRTY-SIX

Ghost

I woke up before her that morning. Like almost every day. Watching Star sleep and caressing her round, small belly had become one of my greatest pleasures.

I spread my hand over her and she stretched, letting out a soft moan that reminded me of the delicious indecency we had shared the night before. A sideways smile crept onto my face as I kissed the purple mark at the base of her neck. The memory of having sucked on that piece of skin made me hard.

"Hummmmm!" Star whispered, arching her back against me. I swallowed hard and resisted the urge to possess her, which, by the way, felt like it was burning me from the inside out.

I had a meeting scheduled with my father and my brothers to analyze major investments and discuss three new expansions. The international calls were usually timed, and if I was late, I would halt a department in my country and another abroad.

So, I placed a kiss on her lips and fled from that temptation before I changed my mind.

I took a quick shower and was ready to leave in a matter of minutes, dressed in my usual elegant black suit.

"I'll be back by the end of the afternoon, my love." I kissed Star and whispered in her ear.

"Let's organize the baby's room..." she murmured, still sleepy.

"Yes, we will," I assured her. "Remember to eat and call me if you need anything or if you feel unwell." It was the first time I would leave her alone for so many hours in a row, and I was crazy with worry. She turned in my arms, her plump lips seeking mine in a sleepy kiss.

"I'll be fine," she said confidently.

"Aren't you going to miss me even a little? I'm hurt!" I joked, and she smiled without opening her eyes.

"I can't say I already miss you, or you'll end up staying home." She was right; I was about to move that important meeting to my kitchen table.

I said goodbye to Star and headed straight to Holder Security.

Star

I WOKE UP LATE THAT day. I could still feel Zion's strong touch on my skin from the night we had together. All it took was a distraction for the images of what we did to resurface, and I couldn't help but smile at the reflection of my marked skin in the bathroom mirror.

I placed my hand on my round, protruding belly. The more days passed, the more the certainty that I was living a dream surrounded me, but there was one difference. I had nightmares within that dream I called life.

I stepped out of the bathroom and went to Zion's office in search of a book. I was loving the adventures in the novels Jasmin had gifted me, and when I entered the room, which served as both an office and a small library, I was met with the wall dedicated to Zion's diplomas. Many frames hung side by side, some featuring photos of men in suits whom I could swear must have been important in some way. Zion was well-versed in martial arts, the top of his class in speed and precision, a distinction that occupied the center of all his diplomas, issued by an Israeli training academy. I admired the countless diplomas and honors stretching across the wall.

He was good at everything he did. A-class bodyguard, as some called him. One of the most sought-after and even feared. Anyone who looked at Ghost was sure to face a strong and courageous man, with no idea of the dark past behind that impeccable demeanor.

Then I realized that living was just that. The good moments, those that seem like dreams, sometimes give way to nightmares. It was up to us to know what to do with each phase. The only certainty was that there was no fairy tale with a blessed "happily ever after." At some point, we would encounter a bad dream along the way. Ghost chose to turn his nightmare into protection.

My heart swelled with pride for the man who would be the father of my child.

I smiled, picked one of the books, and placed it on the couch—my favorite reading spot. I would start it as soon as I ate something.

"Breakfast is ready, miss." Bertha appeared behind me, almost as silent as Ghost. It was already late afternoon, and the housekeeper knew that with my altered sleep, I had been eating at the wrong times, something I intended to change as soon as I managed to wake up earlier. Her care for me was evident once again.

Her always hardened face did not hide the gentle and worried gaze with which she always addressed me. Both she and Deloris had been essential in each of my days here.

"Thank you, Bertha." I smiled, happy to have them by my side.

I had a hearty breakfast while looking at my phone. I was almost done when I came across an ad for a store in Chicago. A baby clothing store that sold personalized gifts for moms and dads. I was enchanted when I saw a decorated wooden box with an engraved phrase on the lid: Daddy, inside Mommy beat two hearts that love you.

My eyes burned with a sudden urge to cry. There was also a tiny bootie, a small bodysuit, embroidered as well, a teddy bear, a "promoted to dad" pin, and a bottle of wine, all decorated with ribbons. Apparently, customers could customize the gift as they wished.

I smiled at the screen, imagining Zion's face when he opened the little box, and I stood up, eager to buy it. I saved the store's address and looked out the glass window that overlooked the entrance gate, where there was a small security room where the bodyguard of the week spent most of his time.

Henry, a tall man with broad shoulders but a friendly demeanor, was different from Shaw, who entertained the whole house when he was here, and from Lyon, who was willing to watch the games Snake lent me with me. Henry was more reserved.

I saw the shadow of the man, focused in the little room, which also had cameras, especially by the gate.

I grabbed one of the bags Jasmin had bought. The small model was dark and discreet, and I used it to store two things: the card Zion left with me so I could buy anything I wanted and my ID.

I stared at the document and the version of myself printed there.

Alena Farrel.

That name again... it was annoying, like getting a shot. As if Alena had become the reference for something I wanted desperately but couldn't reach: remembering my past.

I shook my head and turned my attention back to the plan I was executing. I reached for my phone and called Zion. Even though it was a surprise gift, I promised that if I decided to go out, I would let him know, but I bit my lips when it went straight to voicemail. I checked the time. According to the GPS, the place was far from our home; if I didn't leave now, I wouldn't make it in time to buy the gift.

I shrugged and stuffed my phone into my bag. I would try to call him again on the way.

I passed by the mirror, already on my way to convince Henry to go out with me, and stopped when I saw my reflection. I was wearing a long, loose black dress, the same color as my bag, which conveniently disguised the object and my round belly. I pressed the fabric with my hand until I saw it in the reflection and smiled. Since the moment I discovered the life I was carrying in my womb, nothing seemed more important than her. It was as if half of my heart now beat in my belly. I was carrying the most precious thing in my life there.

I was still smiling when I went down to the parking lot.

"Miss!" He stood up and assumed a cordial yet serious posture. "Is something wrong? Do you need anything?" I smiled, trying to calm him.

"Actually, I need you to take me to this address." I pulled out my phone and showed him the store, which made him purse his lips.

"It's almost on the outskirts of town." He raised his eyebrows. "I'll let Ghost know, and we can go."

"I tried to call him, but it went straight to voicemail. Maybe if you try now, you'll reach him, but if he answers, don't tell him which store we're going to; it's a surprise." Henry nodded quickly and made the call, not taking long to confirm what I had found out.

"I'll notify headquarters, miss. They'll track our trip."

"Okay."

"I would prefer if you didn't take too long at the place. We need to return before nightfall; it'll be safer."

"It's not like there's an army waiting for us, right?" I said as I got into his car. "But don't worry; I'll call the store and ask them to speed up the order. That way, we won't have to wait."

"Okay, please fasten your seatbelt."

I did as Henry asked, and we drove for almost an hour to the store's address. I was so eager to get there that I could hardly contain myself and chatted away in Henry's ear the whole way.

"Wow, it really is far," I commented as all the hustle and bustle of the city faded behind us, and we entered a quiet road surrounded by bushes. I swallowed hard as I briefly remembered the roads I traveled with Zion in Italy. A shiver ran through me.

"This address is almost out of town." He glanced briefly at me in the rearview mirror, but his eyes soon fixed on something behind us. I noticed he began to speed up on the one-way street, and a massive tunnel loomed ahead of us.

"You don't need to go that fast, Henry. We have time before night falls." He didn't listen to me. His eyes were suddenly darting from one rearview mirror to the other. Something was wrong.

We entered the dimly lit tunnel, and he accelerated further, grabbing the radio to try and make contact, but all he got was a bunch of static.

"Shit!" he cursed, throwing the radio aside.

"What is it, Henry?" I gasped as I saw him draw his gun.

"We're being followed." He barely closed his mouth when a violent impact hit us on the right side.

"Oh my God!" I screamed, gripping my seatbelt. Another hard hit came, this time on the left.

"Hold on, miss!" he shouted, doing everything he could to keep control of the car. I could barely move, paralyzed by fear and shock. I couldn't believe this was happening.

Another impact. Two cars surrounded us, and when one of them hit us for the third time, the car spun on the road and slammed hard into the tunnel's wall. The sounds of screeching tires mixed with the crash of steel and concrete and shattering glass; it was a nightmare.

The car came to a stop, and the sounds of vehicles braking around us reached my ears. I tried to move; someone was coming. Panic blinded me for a moment, and I took a deep breath; I needed to think quickly.

I blinked, forcing my eyes to focus, and saw Henry, unconscious, his head slumped over the deployed airbag. My head was spinning. I unbuckled my seatbelt, lost in the smoke that began to spread through the car, but before I could move, someone opened the door and a pair of arms grabbed me roughly by the shoulder as soon as my feet hit the ground.

I started to struggle and kick at the air, trying to hit someone. The panic gave me strength, but not enough to stop the stranger, who pressed a damp cloth against my nose. I started to feel weaker. I tried to fight the guy, but all I managed was to push him away weakly. I lifted my eyes, half-dizzy, and he released me onto the ground.

"What do we do now?" a young man said, and I realized I knew him.

"Take her to the attic; he'll come for her in a few hours, and we can start our lives far away from here," another man spoke.

I lifted my eyes, still dazed, and that's when I saw him.

The man was tall, strong, and robust, with golden hair like Caleb's, who was standing next to him, and like mine. His deep eyes stared at me without a hint of feeling, and my heart ached at recognizing him, even without remembering him.

"Father?" It was the only thing I could manage to say before I blacked out, affected by the vague memory that this wasn't the first time I called out to him asking for help.

I sank into darkness. He had abandoned me again.

CHAPTER THIRTY-SEVEN

Ghost

I got into the elevator and pressed the button for the fourteenth floor, where the executive office was located. Two employees entered the elevator on the next floor and congratulated me on my impending fatherhood as soon as I greeted them.

My father had almost placed an announcement in the company's internal newsletter, and everyone already knew I would soon be a dad, which led to a wave of congratulations and advice that seemed never-ending. Usually, one came right after the other, and this time was no different; however, those maternal tips left me in shock.

One of the employees recommended a YouTube channel that provided tips on breastfeeding and added:

"If her breast gets sore, there are lots of great tips there." I froze inside.

"Sore breast? Excuse me, miss, what do you mean by that?"

"It's normal during the first breastfeeding. The breast can get sore; it's very painful and... oh!" Another girl, much younger than the first, lightly elbowed her friend. "Oh, I'm sorry. It's just a tip from an experienced mother."

"Thank you for the suggestion," I said in a panic and stumbled out of the metal box.

"Where did you get the idea that Mr. Holder wants to hear about sore breasts, woman?" I heard the younger one comment before the door closed, and I staggered down the hallway.

Sore breasts? Dr. Audra hadn't mentioned anything about that. A knot tightened in my stomach at the thought of my Star going through that, and I quickly noted the YouTube channel that woman had suggested. Still, I would have a meeting with the doctor later that week. I would do everything in my power to ensure my wife had our child in peace.

"I'm on my way, Emma!" I called out as I approached the receptionist to avoid startling her.

"Mr. Holder!" She stood up, excited. "I want to congratulate you on your fatherhood. I hope everything goes well. If you need home remedies for baby colic, just call me, okay?"

"Thank you, Emma. I think I will need that."

Great, now I had to deal with colic too.

"President Holder is finishing up a meeting and will join you shortly."

"Thank you."

I entered the executive meeting room, and my two brothers were already seated at the large mahogany table, waiting for my father.

I glanced at the watch on my wrist just to confirm that I had arrived earlier than scheduled and sat down next to Wolf, who was sizing me up through a narrow slit in his two-colored eyes.

"What's up?" I laughed.

"Nothing much, just think you've lost weight, brother." He smirked, and Snake chuckled. I raised my eyebrows, not understanding.

"It's clear you haven't slept a full night in days. Seems like what they say about pregnant women is true. She's going to wear you out, brother." They started laughing louder, and only then did I realize what they were talking about.

A few weeks ago, Wolf and Snake had been researching baby stuff. According to them, they would be experienced uncles. That only made me more worried, and while sifting through tips, Wolf found an article about pregnant women that said some women had an increased libido during pregnancy, and it was normal for their sexual appetite to rise significantly.

At the time, I already suspected something like that, but I denied it when my brother asked if the information was true. I didn't like talking about my wife's desires with anyone, so I lied. And he was right; we were having sex frequently enough to exhaust me. But it felt so good, fulfilling, and perfect that I couldn't resist. Yes, I was the luckiest bastard in the world, but I decided to steer the curious away and told a different version.

"Fuck off. I've been having sleepless nights, but it's taking care of my pregnant wife, you idiots," I said seriously, putting on my best poker face. Snake straightened up quickly, and both he and Wolf stared at me seriously.

"Is she feeling unwell again?" Snake asked, his eyes slightly wider and attentive.

"No, she's doing great." I couldn't lie in the face of their worried expressions and ended up laughing.

"Look at you, you bastard," Snake cursed and laughed.

"Don't joke about my sister-in-law's health, you idiot." Wolf slapped my shoulder, but his expression softened, and he was almost back to teasing me when I threatened:

"Brothers, I don't want to hear another word about assumptions involving my sex life, you hear? Otherwise, Dad is going to find out who broke the naked angel statue he loved so much. And let me thank you here, that thing was monstrous and..." I raised a finger when Wolf opened his mouth to speak. "He's also going to find out that the signed crystal figurine of the Chicago Bears he adores *is not* the genuine Chicago Bears figurine he treasures."

"But it's an identical copy; no one will ever find out." Snake nearly stood up, irritated, but kept his voice in a whisper that sounded more like a growl. "How do you know this?"

"How did you manage to make a copy of something like that?" Wolf cut him off. "Dad had that figurine made just so they could autograph it; there's no way to make another one like it, let alone get all the identical autographs."

"Snake knows more than you think." I smirked.

I would obviously never reveal my brothers' secrets, especially Snake's. My dad was a fan of that football team, and if he found out that there was now a counterfeit version of the figurine he had specially commissioned for autographs, he would probably kill him. Snake could be annoying and scary at times, but I loved him, and I was glad to see him breathing.

"Alright, you win; I won't say anything more." Snake raised his hands in surrender just as my father walked into the room and set his eyes on me.

"Have you lost weight, son?" I nearly growled in response, and my brothers burst into laughter.

"Go to hell!"

"HOW IS MY DAUGHTER-in-law? Has the nausea stopped? That girl needs to eat her vegetables; don't forget to check her diet," my father instructed, taking his prominent place at the conference table.

"I read that babies absorb their mother's nutrients while in the womb. We don't want him to be born sick or for Star to end up hospitalized," Snake added, serious, tapping his fingers on the table.

"You really have been researching babies?" I questioned, perplexed. "I thought you gave up in the first week."

"He tried, but I insisted." Wolf lifted his chin, proud of himself.

"Yeah, I know. It's kind of scary. They're small and strange. You have to be very careful, which is why I refuse to hold a baby. They're fragile and breakable," Wolf laughed.

"You don't seem like the same guy who pushed a kid into the pool just because he made fun of your hair." I narrowed my eyes at our older brother.

"Did you really do that, Snake?" My father's gray eyes widened.

"It was a pool party; he was there to swim. I just gave him a little push."

"My God, where did I go wrong?" My father threw his arms up.

"That's not the point. That brat was just a meddling stranger; Star's child will be my nephew. It's different; I'll have responsibilities."

"If I were you, I wouldn't trust him with the baby. You might find it stuck to the ceiling fan." Wolf crossed his arms. "You should leave it with me. I'll be the cool uncle, and Jasmin will definitely be like a second mother."

"You, the cool uncle? Look at me; I'm the cool uncle!" I laughed at Snake's response, and my father chuckled too as they argued for the twentieth time over who held the title of "cool uncle."

"Let's start the meeting," my father began, and I straightened up, paying attention to what he was saying.

"You three, more than anyone, understand that Holder Security is more than just a project to me, right? It's my life." He opened a small projector and displayed the design of a structure featuring three large towers of at least 20 stories.

"However, a man's legacy isn't in the material wealth he leaves behind but in his family, which is the only treasure we should cling to. And when I realized this, I started a new project aimed at expanding our reach across the country and growing our name even further. The Three Powers." I raised my eyebrows at the new information, and my father smiled wider, getting up, restless, and moving toward the images on the screen.

"What happens when a VIP approaches Holder Security these days?"

"In most cases, they're placed on a waiting list," Snake chimed in, and Wolf continued:

"Depending on the level of service, it can take from one to seven days to secure a contract."

"Exactly. We don't operate on an instant booking basis because we don't have the support for the high demand we already have, and this is a scenario I've always wanted to change."

He skipped to the next slide, and an illustration with three circles titled "The Three Powers" appeared on the screen. The company logo was in the center, but there were three other names I had never heard of.

"And there's only one way to expand without losing the Class A standard we work with. Three new branches, three new companies, under the leadership of the most capable men in this company—my three sons. And that's why I created a project where new branches will be established for different audiences." He pointed at the slide as he spoke.

"Holder Loyalty, Holder Sincerity, and Holder Family. Those are the names of the new buildings."

"Dad, do the initials mean what I think they do?" I inquired.

"If you thought I chose each of those words because they match the initials of your codenames, then you're correct. Loyalty for Wolf, Sincerity for Snake, and Family for you. These are the words we were forged from. Our company, our family. Everything around us. It couldn't be different; I want you to be the presidents of each branch." A silence fell over the meeting room. The surprise was palpable in the air. "You will have complete authority over the partners you choose, and all actions and results will be in your hands. You won't have to report to me, but you will need to exercise the same power I do."

"You mean that starting with this project, we'll stop working directly with the VIPs?" Wolf questioned, his quick eyes analyzing every part of the project on the screen.

"Yes. I've been preparing you for a lifetime to one day take my place, but at a certain point, I realized my sons had become better than I ever was. It's time for you to make history." My heart raced as I recognized how significant that decision was. "I want to prepare you to lead your own team of bodyguards. You will determine who your clients will be and be responsible for every life that hires a Holder's protection."

"Be careful, Snake, or you might end up creating a mafia from this project." I laughed and shook my head at Wolf's provocative comment, and Snake muttered a curse.

My father watched us and leaned back in his chair. His wise eyes wandered for a moment.

"With the Three Powers, I want to pave the way for you to fly. I know what you're capable of, and I am very proud of each of you." Snake coughed and disguised his emotion, and I did the same.

"Thank you for the opportunity, Dad. We won't disappoint you."

"I know you won't, son." He gave my hand a confident pat, and we joined one of the partners to discuss all the changes we would face in the coming months.

According to my father's project, within a year, the new branches of Holder would be inaugurated, and we would have a lot of work ahead.

I STOPPED NEXT TO MY brothers in the parking lot after long hours of meetings. My head was buzzing with the new information, but there was something I wanted to ask them, and I decided to do it all at once since we had a lot of work to do and I didn't know when I'd see the two of them together again.

"Listen, I need some advice." I stopped next to my car, and they both approached me. "Even though I truly believe neither of you can help me."

"It's motivating, the faith you have in us, brother." Snake leaned against the car. "What's going on?"

"I want to marry Star," I blurted out.

"Since you want to make this mistake, can't you just go over and say: 'Will you marry me?'" Snake stretched out his arms.

"That's why I wasn't too confident about talking to you."

"Don't listen to Snake; you know he's skeptical when it comes to love."

"I'm not skeptical; I'm realistic."

"Do you think Wolf and I are lying when we say we love our wives?"

"I don't think you're lying; I just don't believe in love like that. It doesn't work for me, but I'm happy if it works for you."

"That's a start. And you, Wolf? No creative ideas?"

"If you consider the five I've already used on Jasmin..."

"Have you asked for her hand?" I gasped, and Snake leaned forward, attentive.

"Yes, FIVE TIMES!"

"Damn, you really suck at this. We need outside help. Urgently!"

"That's not it, you idiot. Jasmin wants to wait until she becomes CEO next year before we officially marry. It's her goal, and I had to accept it for now. I plan to keep asking."

"I don't know what I'd do if Star says no. Just the thought drives me crazy."

"See? That's why I don't like love. It drives sane men mad. And the only thing I allow to take my sanity every now and then is a strong drink, which, by the way, we don't have here," Snake complained, and I grew serious at the memory of the first time I saw Star.

I would never get over that scene. She was so hurt, so scared, and I ended up letting her see part of the monster I keep inside my chest. That was one of my biggest fears—allowing it to come out again, especially around her.

"It's clear she loves you; I'm sure she'll say yes." Snake tried to comfort me.

"Actually, I was thinking about when I met her. Just remembering that scene fills me with rage. I almost killed Scott in front of her, in that place. I don't want that scene to repeat itself because I lose control one day, and we know that can happen." I clenched my jaw, hating the bitter loss of control that anger spread through my body, then felt Snake's heavy hand on my shoulder.

"Listen, brother, your only problem is wanting to fight the anger you feel," he said firmly and decisively. "Anger is just a form of protection. It's the way your body makes you confront something that hurts you."

"Maybe it's easier for you to say since Wolf is explosive, and I go blind with rage, but you're different. I've never met anyone so calm and absolutely terrifying."

"I prefer to plan for a fatal, flawless destruction rather than mess things up and fail. I think before making a decision, and when I do, I'm unyielding. I only achieved this when I stopped fighting all the anger I felt."

"How did you manage that?"

"By accepting it as part of me. I'm always angry." He cracked a sideways smile. "It sharpens my aim, clears my thoughts, and protects me. We're not ordinary people, brother, and for us, there are no ordinary solutions."

Therapy, that's what we all need.

I wanted to say, but I focused on his words and said goodbye to my brothers before getting into the car. They started the engine and drove off. I picked up my phone and only then realized it was off. I frowned when I noticed some missed calls from Star and Henry, the bodyguard responsible for her safety, and I returned the call, but it went straight to voicemail. I tried to call Henry and began to feel nervous when I couldn't reach the guy.

Immediately, I called Bertha, who told me that Star and the bodyguard had left some time ago.

I ended the call with a strange feeling and dialed the central office. All the cars were monitored, and it would be easy to locate any of them, so I provided the license plate to the operator and asked her to contact me immediately once it was tracked, a process that took a few minutes.

I tried calling Star while I waited and felt terrified when once again I was greeted by the robotic voice of voicemail.

Damn, where had she gone?

I accessed Star's cell account, which allowed me to track her phone. It felt invasive, and I was sure there were rules against that sort of thing, but given my wife's situation, having lost her memory, it seemed like a good option to have nearby, and it was much faster, too.

"But... what was she doing there?" I gasped when I saw that the phone signal showed she was stopped in the alley behind her father's old house.

I started the car and sped toward the address, trying to ignore the nagging worry that felt like it was splitting my chest in two.

CHAPTER THIRTY-EIGHT

Star

I woke up lying on a cold wooden floor, half-asleep and dizzy. A bitter, horrible taste left me nauseated, and my head kept spinning. Then I remembered the accident, seeing two familiar faces, the wet cloth on my face...

"My God!" I suddenly sat up and immediately placed my hand on my belly.

The fear that those lunatics might have hurt my baby made my eyes well up, but thank God, everything felt normal; only my body ached.

I looked around and stifled a scream when I realized where I was. It was a low, cold, strange room. It was empty except for some old furniture and a very small bed, already without a mattress. My blood froze. I recognized that place with its moldy walls; it was the attic that terrified me in every nightmare.

I panicked and got up; my bag with my phone was gone. Thick tears rolled down my face as I ran to the wooden door only to find it locked.

"Hey, is anyone there?" I shouted. "Help!" I tried several times, but silence answered me.

I began to tremble.

Why were they doing this? Why?

I felt weak with fear, terrified, to be honest. My legs threatened to give out, and I had to lean against the wooden door to think. The attic had no windows, and the sensation of hands tightening around my neck began to overwhelm me.

There was so much pain and suffering in those walls. So much loneliness; I could feel it deep in my heart, as if I had spent many years there with that little girl who only knew how to cry from sadness.

I slid down the door to sit back on the wooden floor, trying to force my mind to function.

I tilted my head and stared at the floor. I was sure those men in the tunnel were Caleb, my half-brother, and my father. But why? What kind of father does something like that?

Remembering his face, even for a brief moment, left me agitated. His dark eyes looked like a pair of demons lurking to attack, and I realized how much Norah resembled him.

I narrowed my eyes when I saw a wooden object fallen behind the bed and crept over to it. I couldn't afford to just sit there crying; I needed to act.

Maybe that piece of wood could help me escape that place. I pushed the bed aside to reach it, and a baseball bat rolled to my feet. I picked up the object, which had the Chicago Cubs logo stamped on the wood, and my eyes widened with the feeling of having done this at least a thousand times before.

I pressed my hand to my forehead as a sudden pain surged there and realized that part of the wooden floor felt different, right where I had moved the bed, as if it were a false floor.

I crouched down and fiddled with the gap until I freed the wood from the floor. I gasped in surprise when I found a pink box inside. I touched the box, my heart racing in my chest. I recognized that faded pink that adorned all four sides.

I opened the box and was confronted with stacks of hundred-dollar bills inside, along with some photos and colorful papers that looked like letters. I pulled out the printed images.

There was a beautiful woman in one of the photos. Her ivory skin was dotted with freckles. Her large, expressive eyes were a warm, vibrant gold, just like mine. Identical to those of the little girl she held, as if the love of the world could fit within those arms. I placed my hand on my chest, the sharp pain that shot through made me hold my breath. A tear rolled down my face and landed on the picture, which began to shake as I trembled.

I knew that woman; my God, I knew her. I sobbed, reaching for the other photos and pulling out some letters.

I didn't need to open any of them to know what they were about. They were letters to Santa Claus. Ever since Norah and Caleb moved into my house, I hadn't received a single gift. I played with the same dolls for years until they fell apart while Caleb got new, expensive toys.

Norah said I was a bad, messy, and disobedient girl. That children like me didn't deserve gifts from Santa Claus, but I kept writing those letters because I never lost hope, even knowing I couldn't deliver them. Even knowing that no one but my mother cared enough about me to even know they existed.

My head began to spin. I grabbed one of the photos where the woman was holding a baby in her arms, her golden eyes overflowing with love, and saw something written on the back.

"*Alena, Mommy loves you.*"

"Mom." I dropped the box and curled up with the sharp pain I felt in my head. The word kept spinning, everything felt out of place, and I could only think that my mother loved me. Even sick, even weak from the cancer that took her, she always said: Mommy loves you.

With all her strength, with all her heart.

I remembered her, the tight, loving hug, the warm cake in the late afternoons that she often let me help her make. The bedtime stories, the nights and nights we slept together because my father didn't come home. I remembered her eyes, sincere and big like mine. The promise that she would love me from wherever she was and the miracle she always told me about, already preparing me for her departure.

My mother got pregnant by accident; she was already diagnosed with a rare cancer. According to the doctors, she wouldn't survive even a year, but she said I was her miracle, and the truth was that her love for me was so strong that she turned one year into ten.

She left, but she stayed as long as she could. She stayed for me.

I sobbed as I realized that yes, I was loved. My mother loved me.

I howled, and an animalistic scream rose in my throat. I closed my eyes tightly as more and more details of my life resurfaced.

The bar where I worked my whole life, Uncle Walt and his daily visits, Norah, her surgeries, and all the unfounded punishments that turned my days into pure hell. The pinches and hair pulls Caleb inflicted on me, and he... my father. The man responsible for me, who should have protected me, but instead handed me over to Scott to save his own life.

My mother would risk her life to protect me, but my father wanted me to die in his place, without feeling any remorse. That man never loved me.

It was him. I placed my hand on my chest; the pain was so strong that I thought I might faint. It was my father who sold me to the man who tortured me!

I couldn't bear it and leaned over, vomiting everything in my stomach. The photos now scattered in a corner as I could only tremble.

The gaps that tormented me for months began to fill in, and only then did I realize how much Norah, my father, and their son were liars and hypocrites.

I cried out loud, from rage, from hate, from sadness. I cried until my eyes burned and not a single tear was left, taking a few minutes to lift my head once again.

I was strong, dedicated. I never abandoned my job at the bar and became an exceptional bartender practically on my own. I dealt with all kinds of men, from troublemakers to drunks and perverts. I was responsible despite being young, and that money scattered on the floor of my room belonged to my savings to get out of that place.

Cliff, Norah, and Caleb underestimated me. They tried to take everything from me, but I learned to survive when I was just ten years old, and now I was the survivor of a fucking kidnapping, and they would remember my name.

Alena.

That's how my mother called me, and I would make each of them pay for both of us.

I leaned against the bed and forced myself to stand. Thick tears streamed down my face, and I felt like I was floating over a minefield, about to explode at any moment.

Those people only destroyed my life. I never did anything to deserve that; I only gave love and only got hurt in return.

The sudden sadness and confusion gave way to a transcendental rage. I grabbed my pure wood Cubs bat and turned to the door, ignited with hatred.

I needed to get out of there and ask for help.

My anger grew even more when I realized they could hurt my child. Those bastards thought they knew me, but they had no idea what I was capable of doing to protect my baby.

I raised the bat and struck the doorknob with all my strength, and it flew off. If they had any sense, they would know my door was as old as a museum piece; it could come down with a kick.

I exited down the hallway I had known my whole life; my skin burned with rage. I couldn't believe they really did this to me. No matter how much Norah hated me, no matter how worthless her child was, I never thought that together with my father—who, by the way, shared my blood—they would be capable of such a barbarity. They hurt Henry, and just the thought that he might not survive threw me into a sea of fear and rage.

I always gave my best to that fucking family, but all I got in return was hate.

"What the hell do you think you're doing?" Caleb came up the stairs and only noticed my presence when he looked up from his phone. He was already close to my bedroom door.

I was right. The three of them were part of this.

His expression faltered when he realized I wouldn't back down from his threat, but he came at me right after, as if his size would scare me.

Star was sweet and naive, afraid of closeness, but that version of myself was no longer there. In that moment, I was Alena, and I was going to beat that son of a bitch to a pulp.

"You motherfucker, you'll regret showing up in front of me again!" I shouted, crazed with rage, and he widened his eyes.

"You remembered." Caleb was startled, but I didn't give him a moment to think.

I raised the bat and swung my hips hard, mimicking one of my favorite players; however, instead of hitting a ball, I aimed for that bastard's knee. Caleb howled and fell, and I struck the middle of his legs mercilessly.

"AHHHHHHHHHHHHHHHHHHHHHHHHHHHHHH! MOM, MOM, SHE'S GOING TO KILL ME!" he started screaming, and I lifted the bat once more.

"You bastard! Bastard!" He tried to grab my foot, but I jumped just in time and paused when I heard hurried footsteps coming up the stairs.

"CALEB!" Norah shouted as she rushed toward her son. "You savage, you little bitch, look what..." I struck the bat against her shoulder, and she fell near the stairs. I looked around and saw no one. I tried to run down the stairs, but she grabbed my legs, and I fell on top of her.

We rolled on the floor. She tried to pin me beneath her body, but years of dealing with men bigger than me made it easy to toss her aside and spin until I was sitting on top of her with the bat pressing against her neck.

"Why?" I shouted, panting. "Why do you hate me enough to kidnap me, you sicko? I never did anything to you, and you, along with these bastards, ruined my life. Why? ANSWER ME!"

"Because you've always been a thorn in my side, you useless piece of trash. You ruined everything," she spat. "Your father only tolerated your sick mother because of the inheritance that bitch would leave when she died, but you messed it all up when you were born. And as if that weren't enough, because of you, that maniac threatened your father. We just had to hand you over to him, and we would have gone back to our life. The one you stole when you ran away from that man."

"Scott." The memory of his name made me hold my breath, and I jerked up, distancing myself from her to escape down the stairs.

Norah wiped the blood from her mouth and smiled.

"You won't get away, you little bitch. This time, I will never lay eyes on you again." I raised the bat, determined to get out of there at any cost, but froze in place when the edge of a razor touched my neck.

"You haven't changed a bit, Dove." The dark voice slipped into my ears as a man positioned himself behind me.

That voice... it was him. Scott found me.

CHAPTER THIRTY-NINE

Ghost

I focused on Snake's words as I reached the alley leading to Cliff's house, Star's father. I parked before the narrow lane, where a simple two-story house with brick walls and dark windows stood behind a bar.

Cliff's Bar.

I knew something was wrong when I saw a black van with its lights off near the front door of the house. Night had fallen, leaving the alley in complete darkness. What the hell was that van doing there?

I observed the scene for a moment, taking in as much information as I could. I drew my gun and placed my hand on the car door, about to get out, but froze when I saw a man moving in the darkness. He was large, and even speaking softly, I could hear his annoying duck-like voice.

"Sergei," I whispered in panic.

If that bastard was there, Scott was definitely around too. My phone rang. I answered almost in a whisper, listening intently to the information from the young operator at Holder Security, speaking quickly without pauses.

Henry had been found unconscious in a tunnel, completely alone. The bodyguard was fine, but the car had sustained a bilateral impact.

I don't know how I found the strength to ask her to issue an alert, and I immediately called the detective, who told me to stay away from the area and wait for the police to arrive. I hung up, promising I would wait—another lie. I texted my brothers and got out of the car, gun in hand.

I wasn't going to stand by while my wife might be hurt inside that house.

I took a deep breath; rage coursed through my veins and made me tremble. I would kill that bastard if he touched her.

I crossed the street, watching Sergei from behind. By his body language, he was alert and alone, and it didn't take long for him to seek the safety of the van. I went around the vehicle and got very close. I could even hear his heavy, raspy breathing from the front seat.

I tried to remember what Snake had said and focused. Rage was becoming more and more a part of me. Then I acted, quick and precise. I struck the man, who fainted before he even realized what had hit him. I secured his hands to the steering wheel with nylon straps that were part of the work material we carried in the car. I searched the bastard, grabbed his phone, and a loaded gun that I tucked into my waistband. I needed to be precise if I didn't want to endanger Star's life.

I approached the house and realized I couldn't stop; if I didn't keep moving, I would start thinking about the danger my pregnant wife was in—and about my desire to tear that man apart down to his soul. So I kept my attention focused on every step and took control. I would strip away my feelings; I had to rid myself of all that fear of losing her to fight for her. Like I did with my VIPs, paying attention to signals, sounds, facts. Far from emotional blindness.

I stopped next to the door, where one of the windows was broken, and carefully kept to the shadows to avoid being noticed. I tilted my head and surveyed the place. There was movement upstairs. I held my breath when I recognized Scott's voice and analyzed the situation coldly. Until I heard a soft cry that I knew all too well.

Star.

My breath came in gasps, altered. He had her, my God. For a moment, all the self-control I maintained slipped away. I wanted to split him in half and rip off the hands that dared to touch her again.

I quickly glanced at the entrance of the house and found another door, a smaller one, probably used for trash disposal. I had to get in somehow without him seeing me, so I slipped through the tiny entrance and quietly descended into the kitchen.

The sound of voices grew louder, and every cell in my body contracted as I realized Star was in the next room with Scott. I knew

I was ready like never before. My family was there, and I would do anything to save them.

Star

THE SHARP BLADE PRESSED against my neck, and I could already feel a slight sting where it touched. But nothing compared to the despair that consumed me.

Scott pulled me against his filthy body, his voice cold and cruel.

"Drop the bat, now." I did as he commanded and watched the wood roll away.

"You've gotten what you wanted. Take her and let us go now." Norah crawled over to her son, who writhed in pain on the floor.

"You two, lock yourselves in the bedroom until Cliff comes back. And you, Dove..." He inhaled close to my neck. "Our ride is waiting for us. We'll be leaving soon, and then it will just be the two of us again."

The ground disappeared beneath my feet. He stared at me with a twisted smile that he tried to hide with a large black hood.

"Where's my husband? What did you do to him?" Norah threw herself beside her son and hugged him.

"Don't worry, Cliff will soon be free and loaded with cash, but first, he's off to fetch one last delivery for me. Now you both get out of my sight before I regret letting you live." Norah dragged Caleb into the room that once was mine and locked the door.

"And you, come down now and be quiet." I obeyed, terrified of what would happen next. He kept the knife pressed against my skin; any misstep would be fatal.

I felt a jolt as we reached the first floor, and he shoved me against the wall to look into my eyes. The knife lowered to my abdomen. I could barely breathe from panic. If he noticed, if he saw that I was pregnant...

All the crises I had managed to suppress after weeks of therapy, all the fear I overcame to face other men again, every bit of control I had began to slip between my fingers as he tightened his grip on my neck.

"Ah, Dove, what a mess you've made." He grinned a macabre smile that froze my blood. "You killed them all. Destroyed my family." He didn't know the trouble I went through to recover it. He inhaled deeply, taking in the scent from my neck, and I almost vomited from his closeness. "I blackmailed your father, watched you for weeks, and almost lost hope. Can you understand? I risked my life to reclaim my acquisition." He squeezed my arm hard. "And now you will pay for everything you did. When I'm done with you, I'm going to hang your guts in front of that bastard Ghost's house. He'll find out he never should have messed with me." I jerked my body and pushed him, unable to stay still. He lost his balance in surprise, and I dashed toward the door, but he grabbed my hair and slammed me to the living room floor, immediately closing his hand around my neck, forcing me to stand until he was positioned behind me.

A strange burning intensified. He pressed the knife so hard it cut my skin, and a cold trickle ran down between my breasts.

"Still feisty." He smiled.

"You don't need to do this. You can run now; no one will ever find you."

"You think I want to run? You ruined my life. Destroyed everything I spent years building. Do you know how many came before you? How many were trapped in that same dungeon that that bastard Don Matteo destroyed?" He yanked my hair and pulled hard until my neck bent against his chest. I screamed at the sharp pain. "I'm going to make you pay for all the other women I killed there. I will destroy every part of you, Dove," he threatened, his eyes constantly scanning the door. He was waiting for someone, and despite my fear, I tried to think. I knew what that lunatic was capable of, and I needed to escape before he had the chance to hurt me again.

"I didn't want to give in before, but you will have to now." He pulled the knife away for just a moment, enough to grab one of my breasts with that filthy hand.

I trembled, unable to move or react. The beatings he gave me in the dungeon were cruel and terrible; if he did that to me, if he beat me, he could kill my baby. Just the thought paralyzed me.

I cried. I couldn't react. I would allow him to do whatever he wanted with me. I would do anything to keep my child safe.

I closed my eyes, feeling trapped on a thorny beam. He filled me with disgust, fear, and horror. Each of his touches made me nauseous. The air barely reached my lungs, and I couldn't imagine a happy ending to this story. He was about to kill me, and he had nothing to lose, unlike me. I had never wanted to survive as much as I did in that moment.

"Cliff is going to come with my money, and we're leaving. Come on, we are," he started repeating endlessly like a lunatic. "You're mine. You're going to make everything go back to normal. You have to do it, do you hear?" He shook me by the base of my neck, and I whimpered, unable to say anything with his knife pressing against my neck.

I was so scared that it took me a while to notice a figure lurking in the gap between the living room and the kitchen, where a dark corridor concealed him. I tried to control my breathing and stay quiet, but the emotion that washed over me almost made me faint.

It was him.

"Stay quiet, damn it!" Scott shouted and shook me again; his wild eyes were too focused on the door. He seemed to be waiting for someone.

Zion stared at me, a life passing through his serious and concentrated gaze. His posture was different; I had seen him like that in Calabria when we were attacked at the motel, like a cat poised to strike, ready to retaliate.

He raised a finger to his lips and then closed his hand into a fist. I immediately remembered his signals. The closed fist meant I should stay still at all costs, even if he shot in my direction, and I widened my eyes when I noticed he was raising the gun, aiming at us. I did as he instructed. I lifted my hand to Scott's forearm and leaned against it without him realizing, already preparing myself. When Zion fired, I would use the small gap to push the knife away from my neck, and I didn't move an inch after that.

Scott grumbled, agitated by whatever he was waiting for. Ghost tilted his head to the side, positioned the gun, and fired. I shoved Scott's arm just as the man screamed and threw myself to the ground at the same moment. Ghost lunged at him and aimed again, but Scott staggered and crashed into a small shelf where Norah kept a collection of crystal glasses, which came crashing down on both of them.

The furniture shook, and all of them fell at once. I covered my face with my arm, trying to protect myself. The apocalyptic sound of everything shattering around me made me question whether I was living a nightmare.

I summoned all my strength to sit up and saw Ghost on top of Scott. The gun had been lost among the shards of glass, but he didn't stop.

"Son of a bitch! Never, never touch her again, you piece of shit!" Ghost pounded on him violently, punching without stopping in a quick rhythm that seemed terrifically synchronized until the man stopped moving.

Then he released him the moment the police broke down the front door and dropped to his knees in front of me.

"Star, my love, are you okay?" Zion held me by the shoulders, scanning my body for injuries.

"Ghost... what the hell!" Snake stopped beside him with Wolf right behind, both observing the chaotic scene with expressions bordering on shock.

Zion's eyes fell to my neck, where most of the pain concentrated. He looked at the wound from Scott's knife with a dark expression.

"Let me go! You filthy scum, do you know who I am, you trash? THEY HAVE TO PAY!" Scott regained consciousness and began to roar and thrash desperately. "They destroyed everything. EVERYTHING!"

His face was even more deformed, and he writhed in a pool of blood while struggling with two police officers trying to restrain him. Ghost leaned his body to the side, blocking my view so I wouldn't see him again.

"Get him out of here, Snake, or I'll kill him." The older brother didn't hesitate and positioned himself between the two.

The veins at the base of Zion's neck pulsed, his face red from the effort of maintaining control, but even in his anger, even as dirty with blood as I was, I could find in his dilated brown pupils that look full of care and protection. That look I loved so much.

Suddenly everything made sense, that angry and protective expression, that proud face knowing the power he possessed... I knew him. My eyes widened as I remembered.

The man from the football stadium!

The one who drove a BMW over a median to defend a stranger from three harassers. It was him. My guardian angel whom I thought I would never see again.

I cried out loud and threw myself into his warm embrace, surprised that we had met before, shocked by the luck I had in crossing paths with that strong, mysterious man who never grew tired of protecting me. My God, how could I have forgotten him?

"Zion!" I sobbed and buried my head in the curve of his shoulder. "Henry, he..."

"He's fine, don't worry. He wasn't hurt."

"It wasn't h-his fault, I asked him to..."

"Don't worry, sweetheart. I know you were cornered." He kissed my hair and exhaled in bursts, as if he could hardly believe our torment was over. I knew well I didn't believe it. "My God. You were so brave; I'm proud of you." He kissed my forehead, trembling. "Did he hurt you anywhere else? Tell me, love, what did he do?" He stopped speaking and touched my belly; I shuddered, an overwhelming fear of what could have happened crashed down on me. Only then did I realize how close I had come to death with my baby.

"I think I only hurt my neck." I managed to say, shaking from head to toe. He embraced me carefully, our erratic breaths mingling.

"I'm so sorry, so sorry, sweetheart. Now you're safe. It's over, little one."

I clung to his black suit, my fingers weak and trembling. I closed my eyes and breathed slowly.

"They..." I gasped and lifted my face. "Caleb and Norah are on the second floor," I told.

"They're still here?" A strange shadow crossed his gaze, and I confirmed. "Snake, inform the police, her brother and stepmother are on the second floor. Can you help them down?"

"It would be my pleasure." Snake smiled on his dark face, displaying an exotic and intense beauty. He looked more terrifying when he smiled, as if he were planning the end of the world. "Deputy Russel..." he called.

"There's a box..." I whispered, grimacing at the sharp pain the cut caused. Wolf knelt beside me, his eyes glued to the wound on my neck.

"Don't speak, love. The paramedics are on their way," Zion said anxiously.

"I need to. There's a box, the only photos of my mother are there, in the attic. It's all I have left." My eyes welled up.

"I'll get it. I'll bring everything." Wolf placed his hand on my shoulder. "You're incredibly brave; I'm relieved you're okay." He smiled, but his expression changed when we heard things crashing upstairs, and suddenly Caleb came tumbling down the stairs, his face very red.

"He tripped." Snake followed him down, and the police officers who had gone up alongside him brought Norah down handcuffed. "Come on, get up, that was nothing. A fall like that is no worse than kidnapping your own sister, right?"

"You liar, he didn't fall; you hit my son!" Norah screamed.

"It was your son who hit first." The officer on Norah's right interrupted her.

"As if he could take on a man that size." The other officer holding her on the left laughed.

"Save your breath, ma'am; you're going to need it in jail," the deputy warned her.

"No, I didn't do anything. We were coerced; my husband..."

"Your husband was arrested with a large sum of money leaving town. He was fleeing."

"He was going to abandon us?" She opened her eyes in shock, and one of the officers took her away.

Ghost touched my face gently. He was sweaty, dirty, disheveled, his suit completely wrinkled, but how in God's name did he look like a beautiful angel marching off to war?

"Here!" Snake waved to someone, and a few paramedics entered the small house.

"She's pregnant." That was the first thing Zion said to the paramedic, his eyes glazed with worry.

"Ghost, we need to talk about you ignoring a direct order and putting yourself in danger. I told you to wait for the police to arrive."

Deputy Russel approached while the medical team examined me, but he didn't seem angry.

"Deputy, my specialty is protecting people. How could I do anything else with my wife?"

I WAS PLACED ON A STRETCHER, even after insisting that I could walk just fine. Ghost followed by my side, helping the paramedics carry the stretcher to the ambulance, and as we passed through the door of the house, a crowd of police officers, reporters, and some civilians awaited us.

I held Zion's hand and looked into his eyes while one of the paramedics finished a temporary bandage on my neck.

"I remembered, remembered everything," I said as soon as she stepped back.

"How?" I briefly recounted the details of how I had gotten there.

"And when I saw the little box, the memories came rushing back. I thought my head would explode."

"Damn," he cursed, his surprised and disbelieving expression almost made me laugh. "You remember everything?"

"Everything." I sniffled, overwhelmed with emotion. He looked deep into my eyes, as if trying to see something in my soul.

"I'm still the same, if that's what you want to know. I still love you with all my heart." His eyes welled up with tears, and he kissed me quickly, urgently.

I sighed, grateful to have survived. Despite the betrayals of a family that never loved me and the pursuit of a cruel, psychotic killer.

Other women lost their lives in that place, and just imagining what they suffered threw my soul into pure hell. I tried to hold onto the hope that this cycle had ended. Scott would not make any more victims. We had won, and I would be happy—for myself, for my child, and for them.

I tried to feel joy for simply being alive, but all happiness faded quickly when I felt a sharp pain in the base of my belly, and a cold liquid trickled down my legs.

"Zion," I could barely speak.

"Yes, *my* love." He looked at me intently as I lifted the hem of my dress to run my fingers through the liquid.

I raised my hand and felt the world around me lose its color, just like Ghost's pale face as he stared at my bloodstained fingers.

My eyes burned, and I saw fear and panic flash across his.

"I'm bleeding," was all I could say before I broke down in deep sobs.

CHAPTER FORTY

Ghost

I could barely breathe as we passed through the hospital doors. The paramedics pushed the stretcher with Star, who was softly crying, and the sensation spreading through my chest felt like I was being torn in half.

My heart was right there, on that stretcher. Beating fiercely for that woman and the small life growing in her womb. I wished more than anything to take her pain away, to free her from that nightmare once and for all.

"This way, quickly!" I heard Dr. Audra's voice approaching, and she skillfully took charge of the situation next to Star. Her reassuring smile tried to support my girl.

"Doctor," Star sobbed, and the physician took her hand.

"I'm here, we'll take care of you both, okay?" She turned to me, where I stood beside my wife like a statue. "Are you sure you don't need medical attention? You look like you're about to faint, Ghost."

"I'm fine, I just need you to take care of her, doctor. Star is bleeding," I said with immense sorrow. I tried to control my own despair, but it was difficult. All I could think about were the injuries that that bastard had caused her once again. The fear, the physical and psychological torture. The pain.

I clenched my fist. I wanted to kill him, and I had to give everything I had not to end that miserable bastard right then and there. Scott was lucky; both times I encountered him, it was because of her that I held back. I didn't want to become a murderer in my wife's eyes.

"I need you to stay here, Ghost," the doctor requested as we reached the entrance to the examination room.

"No way."

"Not for long, I promise I'll call you in a few minutes. We need to run some tests and... a doctor will come to talk to you."

"Doctor..."

"I don't want to be away from him," Star pleaded, squeezing my hand. That only made me want to storm into that place at any cost.

"It will only be for a few minutes," Audra assured and disappeared with Star behind the double white doors of the hallway.

I leaned my back against the wall, dizzy and weak, and slid down the tiles until I sat on the floor. A nurse approached, and I waved her off; I didn't want help. I was on the brink of an abyss, about to fall. I could barely breathe, but there was nothing and no one to help me.

I heard footsteps running down the hallway. A small army was approaching. My brothers, Shaw, Lyon, and my father, who looked at me with attentive, worried eyes. Seeing them there shook me even more. My heart was about to break. My father came over and placed his hand on my shoulder; his silence spoke for both of us.

"I promised she wouldn't get hurt again." Guilt and despair gnawed at me. "I told her, Dad, that I would protect her. That I would keep our baby safe, but I couldn't."

"You can't blame yourself for what you can't control, son." He sighed. His own security team waited at the end of the corridor. "Star knows, we all know you wouldn't hesitate to swap places with her and protect her. Don't blame yourself," he repeated. "Let's just be grateful for my daughter-in-law being back safe." I swallowed hard; my eyes burned, and my whole body began to tremble.

My father's voice could open an emotional hole in my chest that left me vulnerable and anxious.

"He's right, isn't he, brother?" Snake questioned, concerned. His attentive eyes probed me. "Is she okay?"

"Star started bleeding," I whispered, and I didn't need to look at anyone to feel the heavy aura that settled around us.

Snake sat on the floor beside me, while Wolf did the same and sat on the other side. Both too big for our elbows not to bump into each other.

"Dude, she's strong. She'll pull through, and the baby will too," the oldest said, optimistic.

"It couldn't be any different being your child." Wolf nodded. "He's been a fighter since before he was born." I thought about that, but the feeling that everything was out of my control hit me.

What if he didn't survive? If he couldn't make it, what would I do?

"Shaw," I called hoarsely, and he came closer. His dark eyes were wide and alert; that boy was kindness in its most genuine form. "Can you talk to God? Like you did when Jasmin was hospitalized? He... He heard you. Can you ask for my Star and the baby?" I sobbed, unable to contain the pain that felt like it was splitting me in half.

"Why don't we do it together? God will like to hear your voice." And that's what I did; I closed my eyes, and as Shaw led a quiet prayer for Star, I elevated my thoughts to Him.

"God, I know I haven't been a man of faith throughout my life. I know I've made mistakes, far more than I've made right, but I also know You are a God of mercy, so I beg You, I beg You to take care of Star and my child in her womb. Give my girl just a little more strength. Please, God, watch over them both. Help me, God, to protect my family."

I implore.

When I finished, I noticed everyone around had taken a moment to do as Shaw and I had, and despite feeling grateful that even those without much faith were willing to seek some form of refuge and comfort in God, some help, I couldn't control the panic that suffocated me.

My shoulders shook, especially when my father knelt before me and placed his mature, experienced hands on them.

I thought I might die from crying so much. Seeing that feeling of despair and helplessness was new. For many years my torment had focused solely on me and what I was living through. The pain I felt in my own soul, but ever since I first saw Star in that prison, everything stopped being about me and became about her. And how hard it was, how desperate it felt not to have control over the bad things she might face.

"Everything will be alright, son. You've placed it in God's hands, so let Him help her, okay?"

"Ghost!" Dr. Audra appeared in the doorway and pulled me up with a strong jolt. "Please follow me."

"How is she, doctor?" Snake asked, anxious, and everyone stepped closer to the doctor.

"As I expected, Star is fine."

"And my grandchild?" My father leaned in, his gray eyes wide.

"In perfect condition." I heard a chorus of "*Thank God*" behind me and realized I had said it too, in a worried whisper. "She experienced some bleeding due to the stress she endured, but ultimately it wasn't significant. But that woman needs peace from now on." She looked each of us in the eyes.

"We'll make sure of that," Wolf asserted beside me, confident.

"Absolutely." Snake squared his shoulders, appearing a bit taller.

I followed the doctor and couldn't contain myself when I saw Star's weary face, anxiously staring at me with tear-stained cheeks.

I hugged her desperately, feeling that if I didn't touch her, I would die right there.

"How are you feeling?" I slid my hand down her belly and pressed my palm against the round, firm bump.

"I'm okay." She smiled, leaving me confused. "The doctor said our baby is also in perfect condition and..." She bit her lip. The fear I had seen on her face before entering the exam room had almost completely disappeared.

"And?" I asked, perplexed.

"She said she was able to see the baby's sex." I looked at the doctor with my eyes wide open, almost popping out of my face.

"Are you serious?"

"Yes," the doctor confirmed. "Star was waiting for you so you could find out together. Are you ready?"

"I'm more than ready." I nodded and stood by the stretcher, holding Star's hand between mine, watching as the doctor spread the gel over Star's belly. Soon the image formed on the screen.

"Do you have a preference?"

"No," we said together.

"I just want her to be healthy." I looked at Star, still in disbelief that she was really okay.

"Congratulations, it's a girl," the doctor said simply, and I couldn't contain the huge smile that spread across my face.

"A girl," I whispered, in a mix of shock and joy.

Star broke into a beautiful, sweet smile full of love. I hugged her again, the tears betraying me once more as they lost themselves in my wife's hair.

"Thank you, my love. Thank you for surviving, thank you for making me so happy."

"I want to see her!" A familiar, high-pitched voice shouted from outside the door. "She's my best friend, move aside!" The door burst open as an angry Jasmin stormed in, crying. "Star!"

"Young lady!" The doctor stood up, about to block her way, but I gestured for her to let it be, watching my sister-in-law run to Star and wrap her in a hug.

"I'm so sorry." She cried, and Star began to sob too. "That bastard," she cursed upon seeing the marks on her friend's neck. I saw so much love between the two that I felt grateful.

Extremely happy that two strong women, who carried so much pain, betrayal, and suffering, could love each other that way. As if they were sisters.

I noticed the crowd at the door of the exam room where Snake, Wolf, and my father shared space with Lyon and Shaw. Everyone anxious to see her.

I breathed calmly for the first time in hours, now aware that everything was okay. I turned to my family.

"I think it's a good time to tell you all that I'm going to be the father of a girl!" I announced, proud as hell.

"Holy shit!" Snake shouted with a huge smile, and a commotion erupted in the hospital corridor.

"Shut up or I'll kick you all out!" Dr. Audra called out, jumping to make herself noticed amid the chaos. The scene was so funny that it made us all laugh, and even she couldn't resist and began to laugh too.

I hugged my brothers and friends, grateful to my core, and later, as we were leaving the hospital heading home, I could only think of one thing.

Thank you, God. Thank you so much!

CHAPTER FORTY-ONE

Star

The news of what happened in that house spread throughout the city, and I ended up making headlines in the newspaper. The detective called us, informing us that thanks to the article, they had found the man who tried to report my disappearance, even against my father's wishes.

I could hardly believe it when I heard the name of the responsible person and recognized him. The detective immediately took him to Zion's house, and my eyes widened when I saw the man with ridiculously black hair, visibly thinner than I remembered, standing next to his wife, Ava, who was smiling anxiously as if she couldn't believe what she was seeing.

"Uncle Walt," I said softly, overwhelmed, and started to cry when he embraced me.

"He was hospitalized. He fell ill after Alena went missing; his wife was with him in the hospital, which is why there was no one home for weeks."

"His phone was turned off, and I was so worried about this stubborn man's health that I ended up forgetting him. I'm so sorry, dear. If we had received any call at all..." Ava hugged me affectionately.

"I knew it; I was sure you wouldn't run away without telling me."

My uncle had been the only one to show me care, love, and concern. Both he and his wife held me in high regard. I was so happy to see him that I couldn't stop sobbing.

"The nightmare is over, my love. It's over!" Zion held me in his arms.

✱

WE GATHERED IN ZION'S small office for nearly an hour as Uncle Walt spoke about his suspicions, and the detective updated us on what had happened.

"Alena is like a daughter to me. Her mother was a great friend since childhood. I witnessed every step of her battle against cancer. A battle that lasted ten years. It was a miracle because according to the doctors, she wouldn't survive more than a year, but even medicine couldn't predict the love she would feel for her only daughter," he said, looking down. "Her mother would have killed Cliff if she had any idea what he would be capable of when she left. I saw that girl grow up without being able to interfere in the cruel upbringing she was subjected to."

"What are you talking about?" the detective inquired.

"Cliff never liked Alena; the only one he considered his child was that boy, Caleb. The girl, however, was left to fend for herself. My wife visited her often, bringing her things she needed, but that monster wouldn't allow it to continue. He remarried a woman as detestable as he is and forced the girl to work in the family bar. I tried everything to stop it; I even contacted the police to report it, but that man had ties with important people there, detective." The man nodded and took note of the complaint.

"I would like to know more about this; it could help with the investigation. Cliff was running part of a human trafficking network. He worked for Scott, and from what we've gathered, the bar was just a front. Unfortunately, there may be undercover police involved."

"Even with my reports, they never went there," Uncle Walt added with regret. "I realized the only way to keep caring for her was to stay quiet, and that's what I did. I was seeing her every day, and I was desperate for her to turn twenty-one soon." He leaned toward me. "Alena, you have an inheritance from your mother to receive. One that she inherited from your grandfather when he passed. Your mother made sure to leave around 70% of the amount for you when you turned 21."

"So it's true," I whispered, and all eyes turned to me. "Norah said something about an inheritance."

"Your father was certainly waiting for the right age to steal it from you. Poor girl..." Uncle Walt wiped his eyes; he looked somewhat defeated, more fragile. "Was it you who brought her back?" He turned to Ghost, who nodded in confirmation. A wave of emotions crossed my uncle's dark, deep eyes. "Thank you for that."

We spent more time talking. The detective explained that Scott and Sergei had entered the country illegally and sought out Cliff. According to reports, sick as he was, Scott believed I belonged to him and threatened Cliff and his family to ensure his cooperation with my kidnapping, and there was no resistance after he warned that he would pay well for the service. In the end, they all accepted to participate and would be compensated for it, which disqualified them as victims.

Scott had some money saved, and that was why he didn't send Norah and Caleb away from the house after he had me; he had asked Cliff to gather the money and was waiting for my father to return with his wife and child upstairs as a ransom. He just didn't expect my father to try to escape with the money, caring little for his wife and child.

All those bastards ended up arrested, and I would never lay eyes on any of them again.

"Now you can sleep in peace." The detective also seemed relieved.

✶

I YAWNED AND HUGGED Zion, tangling my feet in the bed sheets, exhausted to the bone after all that nightmare. Sleep made my eyes burn, but I couldn't stop talking, and Zion listened to each of my stories with rapt attention while gently stroking my hair in a calming rhythm.

I told him everything.

How my life had been, my desire to one day open my own business, which I would now realize with my mother's inheritance that had accumulated over more than ten years and turned into a small fortune.

I revealed my wish to have my own family to love and be loved, the affection that Uncle Walt always gave me and how important it was for surviving those horrible people. How I fell in love with the Chicago Cubs and then, intertwining our fingers, I revealed:

"Do you remember a girl you defended in the back at Wrigley Field during the Chicago Cubs' playoff games?" He thought for a moment, releasing our embrace to look into my eyes.

"How do you know about her?" I pulled out the bracelet I still wore from the team.

"I bought this bracelet that day. It was the only money I had left after buying my ticket. I know what happened because I was there. The girl was me."

"What?" He widened his eyes and sat up on the bed.

"I had gone to the stadium to see if I could catch a glimpse of the players arriving on the bus, but I couldn't. Then I climbed the steps; there was a small view of the field. The rest of the story you already know." I shrugged. "You became my hero that night, and I couldn't thank you because I had to get back to the bar. Otherwise, I would be punished. It was that night that Scott kidnapped me, with my father's permission," I repeated what I had told the detective earlier.

"My God, so the mysterious girl was you? Seriously?"

"Yes." I smiled and sniffled, emotional. "You've saved me more times than I can count." He gave me a hug full of love and care.

"I thought about the girl from the stadium every day after that. I didn't know what happened; when I looked for her, you weren't there anymore. Maybe I searched for her with my thoughts, and fate decided to show me where I should go to see her again."

"Thank you for finding me."

"I will always find you, sweetheart. Wherever you are, half of my heart beats in your chest and the other half in your belly." I laughed and nestled into his arms.

He whispered something else, still impressed, but a heavy sleep engulfed me, and I ended up drifting off.

Ghost

AFTER LONG HOURS OF talking with my family and updating them on everything that had happened, I helped Star take the medications the doctor recommended, including a mild tranquilizer to help her in those first days. I thought she would fall asleep as soon as she lay down, but she was so euphoric about regaining her memory that it took her a while to doze off.

I was still enchanted to learn a bit about Alena and how small the world was. So she was the mysterious girl from the stadium. She was my destiny.

I smiled and ran my hands through my hair, leaning against the doorway of the room, watching her sleep under the soft light of the lamp. I couldn't take my eyes off her small body sprawled on the bed. Her dark hair cascaded over the pillows. She was lying on her side, making her little belly more pronounced—the place where our treasure was sheltered, our girl. The bandage on her neck was the only thing capable of stealing the joy from that scene, and I felt nauseated every time I looked at it. Still, the sight was so beautiful and full of life that I took out my phone and snapped a picture. I would cherish that image for the rest of the night.

The next day wouldn't be easy; Star would need to testify and recount what happened. But from the brief conversation I had alone with the detective, her father, stepmother, and brother were colluding with the kidnappings that Scott had perpetrated, and she was one of the victims. Thus, none of them would see the sun again except from behind bars, especially since they would also be charged with murder due to the deaths of the innocents who did not survive in Scott's warehouse.

For the first time since I laid eyes on her, I felt truly relieved. Now my girl was safe and would be surrounded by all the love that filled my heart. And I wasn't the only one; every member of my family, every person around us loved her, and it couldn't be any other way. Star was a being of light.

Star... I had asked her how she would like to be called now that my little one had regained her memory.

"Alena is part of me, my past, and my story. I like who I am with her."

"According to Snake, Alena knows how to wield a baseball bat." She laughed.

"Even if everyone calls me Alena, I would like you to continue calling me Star. That is also my name. It was with it that I discovered what it meant to survive, to be happy, and to be loved. I'm proud of that name too."

The memory of her confident response still made me smile. I walked to the bed, kissed her hair, and covered her up. I closed the curtains, turned off the lamp, and was almost out the door when I spotted the box Wolf had brought from that house at Star's request.

I picked it up, curious, and went to the living room. I began to take each item out, examining the photos scattered inside.

There was a girl in one of them. I didn't even need to think to know it was Star. The golden, intense eyes left no doubt, but what surprised me was the beautiful woman next to her, with eyes identical to hers. Star looked so happy in that picture that I started to smile. I pulled out another image and stared at it in admiration as I looked at a teenage version of Star.

The young girl in the photo had a fuller face, a lively, mischievous smile, dressed in a gray Chicago Cubs sweatshirt and a black cap covering part of her face. I immediately remembered the cap. It was the same one she wore when we met at the stadium. Next to her was her Uncle Walt, also wearing the team's shirt, his fist closed in a gesture of pride.

I traced my thumb over her stunning smile and thought. Would our daughter inherit her eyes? Would she have that sweet, charming smile?

I was dying to see our daughter's little face.

I continued rummaging through the box and found Disney princess stickers, an old notebook, and a bundle of letters tied with a ribbon. I turned one of the papers and saw it was written and addressed in small, shaky letters that looked like a child's handwriting.

To Santa Claus, up in the North Pole

I opened the first letter with a smile and began to read.

Hey, Santa, my name is Alena, remember me? Last year my mommy took my letter to you. Now I'm 10 years old and I'm a good student. My teacher says I have the quickest answers of all and that I just need to improve my handwriting. I'm sorry it's like this, kind of hard to read. Christmas is coming, and I've been good all year. Can you please give me a cookie jar? My aunt always makes them, but she says I'm not good and don't deserve to eat them, but she didn't see how hard I'm trying to be as smart as little Sara from school. You saw it, didn't you, Santa? If possible, I'd also like you to talk to my mom because I miss her a lot since you fly so close to the sky.

I pulled away the old, stained paper with my eyes burning with rage. I was shocked, perplexed.

How in God's name could that wretched woman have denied cookies to a child? A child who had lost her mother?

I stood up, indignant, and started reading the other letters.

Santa, it's been a very difficult year. My favorite doll was killed, Candy, remember her? She was my best friend. But Caleb, Mrs. Norah's son (she doesn't like me to call her aunt), smashed her to pieces. I won't tell you how I found her to not upset you, but it was horrible. She was my only companion, and now I feel more alone than before. I would like to ask for a teddy bear, if you have time to pass by here. Maybe Caleb wouldn't want to tear it apart.

I'm going to die... of rage, I thought as I finished the second letter, where Star was only 11, and I threw the paper into the box, utterly outraged. That little bastard had been tormenting her life since she was young; hell's pest. Knowing he would rot in prison for a long time was far too little compared to everything. I exhaled sharply and grabbed another letter, like a masochist.

Santa, last month we passed by an amusement park; we couldn't go in because dad and I needed to work, but Caleb went there on his last birthday, my friends from school did too. So, I would like to ask for that as a present this year. I promise I've been a really good girl, I even improved my handwriting. Believe me, please.

"What hell! What a damn hell..." Knowing what she suffered in childhood was even more painful now. Because I simply didn't have the power to turn back time and beat the hell out of each of those idiots.

I opened another one. I was already in the shit anyway.

"Santa, are you mad at me?"

I sighed, unable to not feel the emotion in those words. In that letter, Star asked for a "sparkly" dress as she described it, having seen a girl from her class wearing one at a birthday party and falling in love with what she called "a dress of stars."

"What the hell, she just wanted a dress. How could they have neglected her like that?"

It was a stupid question. The bastards had the nerve to sell her to a psychopath. In the end, evil knew no age; there were no exceptions.

In the next letter, she asked for a prince charming.

"If he comes on a white horse, that would be really cool, Santa. If you can send just the horse, I'll accept that too. I love horses."

I laughed nervously and grabbed the last letter from the bundle, thinking that nothing else would surprise me. However, I was wrong.

"Hey, Santa, how are things up there?"

"You know, I turned 15 this year, and I thought long and hard before deciding whether to write this letter or not. For the past few years, you've been like a beacon of hope for me. Someone I knew deep down didn't exist, but you were the only one I could dream about. I wished so much that my letters would be answered, but I always kept them under my bed. I knew they would never be read, but it made me feel good. Thinking that someone might care about me made me happy. But this year I understood that this will never happen; it's just me by myself, right, good old man?"

"Thank you for being part of my monologue these past years. Thank you for being my thread of hope. And to keep our tradition, I'll say goodbye as always, asking for something that won't happen."

"I would like to watch a Chicago Cubs game at Wrigley Field. The stadium is beautiful, and I dream of one day being able to see it. If you can't help me with that, I'll be happy if they at least keep winning."

"Thank you, Santa. This is a goodbye."

Damn, my eyes burned.

There, in those last words, were also the last hopes of a girl who lived through pain and abandonment. Who had simple dreams, dreams she never fulfilled.

I needed to swallow hard a good three times to compose myself. I gathered the letters and picked up my phone.

Snake answered on the second ring, his voice startled.

"What happened? Is it Star?" I laughed; everyone in my family was sensitive.

"Calm down, brother, it's nothing about her. Star is sleeping. Thanks for your concern."

"Then why the hell are you calling me at this hour?" I glanced at the letters in my hands.

"Brother, I know you have direct contact with that guy, W. L. something, one of the Chicago Cubs' coaches."

"Yeah, he's an acquaintance. We haven't talked in a while."

"Doesn't he owe you a favor?"

"Who in this city doesn't owe me something?" He laughed, and I did too.

"Great, I need your help."

I hung up the phone a few minutes later and started plotting a plan. I couldn't erase Star's painful past, but I would do everything to ensure that every piece of her future would be like a dream.

I would make her happy.

CHAPTER FORTY-TWO

Star

The following week was filled with love and care. I was starting to get used to being with Ghost, who stayed close to me like a shadow. It felt like his hand was about to create a tattoo on my belly.

The entire Holder family was rotating shifts, and every day one of them appeared at Zion's house, except for Jasmin, who visited me almost daily and became a highlight of my day. There was no room for sadness or worry around that cheerful and irreverent woman. Even when the police came to hear my testimony, she stood by my side, with Zion on the other, like two bodyguards, and now and then she made me laugh.

The housekeeper Bertha also dedicated herself to making me comfortable, while Deloris prepared my meals with great care and affection. The woman cried every time she saw the marks on my neck, which were already starting to heal.

I rolled in the soft sheets, relaxed, and yawned, ready to get up. The bedroom door opened, and Zion walked in with a small tray in his hands.

"You're already awake," he said softly.

The white tank top showed off his well-toned arms. His brown hair was neatly styled, and his broad shoulders gave him a stunning, beautiful appearance.

"Yes, I woke up a few minutes ago," I yawned. He placed the tray on a stand by the bed. "What's all this?" I opened a huge smile when I saw a pile of fried bacon, my favorite, scrambled eggs, toast, orange juice, and a heap of heart-shaped chocolate cookies.

"It's the start of our day. I want to take you to some places today, so you need to eat well," he warned.

I attacked the chocolate cookies, which were sweet and crunchy.

"Hummmmmmm, delicious!" I ate two more under Zion's watchful eye. "Aren't you going to eat too?"

"I already had breakfast, princess. This is for you; there are more cookies in the kitchen. I asked Deloris to make them regularly."

"I'm in love with cookies like these. Once, I bought a pack at the store, but they weren't good. Actually," I took another bite, "the homemade ones are definitely the best in the world. There's nothing Deloris makes that isn't delicious. I had no idea she knew how to make them." And I certainly didn't have the courage to ask.

After regaining my memory, I understood why I always had difficulty asking someone to do something for me.

I grew up taking care of myself, and allowing someone else to do it felt strange, different from my nature.

I ate another cookie under Zion's watchful gaze. I took a sip of coffee and opened my eyes wider when I remembered something important.

"We still haven't chosen our daughter's name." I placed my hand on my 17-week belly. He smiled and leaned in, giving me a quick kiss on the lips, his hand spreading across the bulge of my belly.

Our baby moved for the first time under his touch. I opened my mouth, feeling a strange and perfect sensation.

"That movement... She moved?" He sat beside me, and in two seconds both his hands were pressed against my belly. Zion couldn't even close his mouth; he was in shock, just like me.

"Yes, she moved when you touched my belly."

My eyes burned as he leaned toward my belly and pressed his mouth close to my skin. Zion had been doing this often; he loved talking to our daughter, and I watched them there, talking about all kinds of subjects, as if she were right there, understanding every word, and I had to give everything I had not to cry. This time, however, I couldn't resist. I cried as I heard him whispering words of affection with eyes shining with love.

"She moved again," he said, a mix of excitement and surprise. I wiped away the tear rolling down my face.

"It's me who is carrying her, but she moves when she hears your voice. How absurd!" I joked, my voice choked, and I saw Ghost staring at my belly with a thoughtful expression. "What is it?"

"This is magical. Soon I'll be holding her in my arms. It's like..."

"She is our heart beating outside the body?"

"Precisely." He leaned in and whispered, "I love you, daughter; I can't wait to hold you." I bit my lips, my own heart beating warm in my chest. "Let's think of a beautiful and meaningful name today." I kissed him, unable to express my feelings in words.

"Right, that way we can invite the godparents."

"Who do you have in mind? Jasmin? I know she's so attached to you that she will probably end up being a second mother to our daughter." He smiled.

"Of course, I thought of her, but I also thought of Wolf and Snake." I shrugged and shoved a piece of juicy bacon in my mouth. "Everything they did for me, for us." I placed my hand on my belly. "It would mean a lot to me."

"Three godparents." He considered the idea for a moment. "I'm sure they'll be ecstatic, especially Snake."

"After saying he'll only accept because she's his niece..."

"And he's obliged to love her."

"But he won't hold her..."

"Because babies are strange and fragile," we completed together, and I started laughing.

"Finish your coffee; our agenda is full today."

"What should I wear?"

"Whatever you want, but choose something light and comfortable. As if we're going to spend the day at the park."

✷

ZION PREPARED HIS BMW, the one that looked more like a spaceship, and we left his house with the roar of the engine shaking the air around us. It was exhilarating and attracted attention wherever we went. I had to admit, he looked even sexier behind that wheel, his strong arms steering as if the car were an extension of his body.

Zion drove across the city and parked in a large private lot, where each car was housed in a protected section. We had barely exited the vehicle when two teenagers approached.

"Look!" one of them exclaimed, punching his friend's arm.

"Holy shit, it's a Nazca!" The boy's strangled voice made me laugh. He jumped in place and snapped a picture from afar, as there was a large barrier separating us.

"Our day has begun. Shall we?" Zion offered me his arm.

✸

I OPENED MY MOUTH WHEN we passed the entrance and was confronted with a gigantic amusement park.

"When you suggested I dress as if we were spending the day at the park, I didn't think you were serious." I wanted to jump for joy at the sight of the colorful lights creating a magical rainbow, but I held back to avoid looking too childish; still, I couldn't hide the huge smile on my face. "Am I really going to be able to go on the rides?"

"On all the ones that allow pregnant women, as many times as you want, my love."

"Even the bumper cars? That sounds so fun." I started jumping with excitement, and he smiled.

"Even there."

"If you don't want to join, or if you think it's too childish, you don't have to come with me, okay?"

"Sweetheart, let me tell you something about men—" he leaned in and whispered, "Rarely does one of us completely cross the line of maturity; of course I want to ride every ride with you."

I bit my lips, unable to believe that happiness could feel so absolute. Ghost, with his light feet and questionable temperament, managed to surprise me every single day we were together, not just with the scares he fought to contain, but with all his love, care, and dedication.

"Then let's go." He pulled me, and I ran alongside him toward one of the most unforgettable afternoons of my life.

Unfortunately, I couldn't go on the bumper cars, but I enjoyed all the other safe rides, like the Ferris wheel. I ate cotton candy and hot dogs, along with countless fried chicken skewers. We spent almost an hour at the stuffed animal machine, where Ghost used all his techniques to try to win one, but in the end, he couldn't. Then we went to the shooting range, and he came out with a bear bigger than me.

"Do you think it will fit in the car?" I questioned, already at the end of the outing.

"If it doesn't fit, we'll tie it to the roof, but this bear is yours. We fought bravely to win it."

"You fought, my hero," I whispered, getting close to the car.

"What did you say?"

"My hero!" I giggled as he tossed the bear carelessly onto the hood of the car and hugged me, kissing me urgently. His touch, his scent, his body against mine... it became so intense that it felt like Zion was a part of me. That man had my heart in the palm of his hand.

"Don't make me commit a public indecency crime." He pressed his waist against me, and I bit my lips, feeling tense. "I want you to call me that when we're in a less public place and not in a park, about to be late for our next appointment." His arm wrapped around my waist possessively.

"What's our next appointment?" He opened the car door, reached behind the seat, and pulled out two caps, handing me one. I parted my lips at the sight of the Chicago Cubs logo.

"To watch a game that starts in half an hour at Wrigley Field."

"Wrigley Field? But that's the official stadium of the..."

"Chicago Cubs?" He pointed to the cap in my hands. "Yes. I used Snake to score two last-minute tickets since they were sold out. We'll see them from the front row."

"You're kidding, right?"

"I would never lie to you, sweetheart."

"WHAT?!" I shouted, unable to pretend it was normal. "I'm going... oh my gosh, are we really going to watch the game in their stadium?"

"I'm scared I'll lose my girlfriend to one of the players, but yes, that's the plan." He laughed, and I jumped into his arms, ecstatic.

"Thank you, Zion! This was one of my biggest dreams. Thank you."

I thought I might faint from excitement during the game, which also had Snake's imposing presence.

"Where there are two tickets, there are three." He shrugged as we met and cheered together for every positive point our team scored.

In the end, to my utter disbelief, the team's coach, W.L. himself, came to us and handed me a jersey signed by all the players. Ghost looked briefly worried, afraid I'd faint right there in front of them.

No surprise could top that moment. At least that's what I thought, but in the end, Ghost was right, and the night still held one last surprise that was infinitely better than watching my favorite team play.

"I WANT TO KNOW EXACTLY what's being shoved into my head," I complained.

"Be quiet, you're safe. I have great taste, and it wasn't easy to do your makeup. What's with the aversion to a little blush, Star?" Jasmin replied, irritated, making me laugh.

Ghost had planned some surprise for the night, a date, he said, but for that, he blindfolded me as soon as Jasmin finished my makeup and asked her to dress me, which I found very strange.

"You look divine!" Deloris commented, excited.

"Careful, miss, you can't twist your ankle in those heels; aren't they too high for her?"

"They were the smallest I could find," Jasmin lamented.

"They're comfortable, Jas. Don't worry, but I really would like to see how I look." I ran my hands through my hair and felt the curls my friend had meticulously crafted.

"Hey, take your little paw away; you'll ruin my perfect curls. Ghostyyyyyy!" she yelled, sounding like a goat. I laughed. "The order is ready, and I think you should be careful taking Star around blindfolded."

"Don't worry, sister-in-law. Here are my most valuable treasures; do you think I wouldn't take care of my two princesses?" I felt his hands slide around my waist.

"Ugh, how gross. Have a good night."

"Thanks, Jas!" I said, but squealed when I felt Ghost lift me up. "What are you doing?"

"Preventing you from tripping over something," he said simply, carrying me to the car and placing me in the seat with the blindfold still over my eyes. His agile hands fastened the seatbelt around me. "All set, sweetheart." His hand slid along my jaw. "You look so beautiful it's hard to let you go."

"I'd like to see something."

"Just wait a little longer; I promise it'll be worth it."

And I waited. A few long minutes later, Ghost helped me out of the car, and we walked slowly. There was background music, something light, romantic, growing louder as we approached.

"Alright, stay here for a moment, my love," he said. I obeyed and felt his body behind mine. He took the blindfold off my eyes, and I blinked until I got used to the low light of the place. We stood before a mirror that was part of the decor.

"Oh my gosh, it's me!" I laughed, incredulous as I faced my reflection in an absurdly beautiful one-shoulder silver dress that accentuated my cleavage with a deep neckline. The soft fabric was covered in tiny lights from start to finish, sparkling like diamonds, and opened in a slit that showed off my legs, enhanced by the heels.

Jasmin's makeup was perfect, flawless. The red lipstick she chose highlighted the vivid color of my eyes. I was so shocked by the gorgeous image before me that I took a moment to notice the stunning man beside me.

Ghost was looking at me through the mirror, attentive to each of my reactions. He looked divine in a crisp white suit. He seemed comfortable with all his beauty, and once again I realized how lucky I was to have found that specimen. Well, actually, it was he who found me, three times in total, and I loved him so much it hurt.

"Thank you, Zion." My lips trembled, and I continued to watch him through the reflection. "I've never felt so beautiful in my entire life."

"You've been looking in the wrong mirror all this time, my love. There isn't a day you're anything less than fascinating." His hand rested on my belly, also adorned with sparkling stones, and I felt like I was living a princess's dream. "Come with me."

He guided me through the place. A very fancy restaurant, high up in the city, where glass walls offered a view of a glowing Chicago below. Several lights hung from the restaurant's ceiling, filling the whole place with them, as if there were a private sky just for us, and that's when I realized there was no one else wandering around except the waiters, who were already approaching.

Ghost asked for two drinks. A neat whiskey for him and a non-alcoholic cocktail for me.

"Why is there no one here?" I smiled as I sat at a table where a candelabrum with candles was positioned, transforming everything into a stunning scene.

"I rented this place for a night with you," he revealed as the drinks arrived and downed his whiskey in one quick gulp.

"Why would you do something so crazy? You know I'm getting used to people; maybe not all, but I can handle most of them."

Regaining my memory had also helped me regain control over my life, and the panic of meeting new people had almost faded away. But the fear of being kidnapped still lurked in my mind. It was easy to manage a conversation in a crowded hall, a busy park, or even a night party, but walking alone on the street, for example, was something I felt incapable of doing. Apparently, some scars would last longer than others.

"No, sweetheart. To be honest, I asked them to close it for a much more selfish reason." He smiled and stood up. "Because I wanted to play for you."

"Play?" He stood up and kissed me without answering the question.

I shook my head, a mix of disbelief and excitement. There was a grand piano, similar to his, positioned a little to the right. The dim lighting had prevented me from seeing it right away.

Zion took his place at the piano. His eyes found mine, and he began a beautiful, slow melody, one I knew well.

It was "Turning Page" by Sleeping At Last.

And there went the makeup Jasmin had done. I started to cry as his baritone voice echoed through the space, filling my senses.

I waited a hundred years
But I would wait another million for you
Nothing prepared me for the privilege it would be to be yours
If I had just felt the warmth in your touch
If I had just seen your smile when you blush
Or how you pout when you're concentrating
I would know what I was living for all this time
For what I've been living
Your love is my turning page
Where only the sweetest words remain
Each kiss is a cursive line
Each touch is a redefined phrase

How could I not love him with all my strength? I thought, trembling, when I saw him stand up as the music ended.

He picked up a pile of papers that had been hidden in the piano and came over to me, elegant, handsome, with the posture of a model at ease on the runway. My red, swollen eyes couldn't stop streaming tears.

"Zion," I called softly, seeing him kneel before me. He held up the letters and handed them to me. I recognized my handwriting on the yellowed paper immediately and my eyes widened as I flipped through them. "My God!" I gasped, incredulous, and stared at him. "You... The chocolate cookies, the park, the game, and even the dress." I covered my mouth and sobbed, unable to control my emotions. "You fulfilled all my wishes, Zion."

"There's one left." He held up another letter. "In this one, you asked for a prince. Or a horse; I didn't quite understand." He smiled sideways, a wave of emotion and warmth crossing his gaze. "If your wish is to have a fairytale prince by your side, I must warn you that I'm far from being one of them, my love. I'm full of flaws, but everything in me, from my values to my faults, absolutely everything, loves every little piece of you. My heart races every time I see you, I feel sick when we're apart, I imagine your smile, your cinnamon-colored eyes, your angelic voice. You've touched me like no one else. There's nothing I wouldn't do to see you happy. And even though I'm not a prince..." He reached into his blazer and pulled out a small velvet box. "I want to fulfill all your dreams and wishes. I want to be your safe harbor, the person you trust most, your lover, your friend, your protector."

He opened the box, revealing a huge, sparkling diamond before my eyes. The edges of the stone were slightly pointed. I realized in shock that the diamond was shaped like a star.

"I want to be your husband, Star. Will you marry me?"

"Yes, yes," I affirmed, euphoric and trembling. He slid the sparkling ring onto my ring finger and placed a kiss there.

"My fiancée!" he whispered against my skin.

"Who needs a prince when you have a guardian angel? I love you, Zion," I kissed him, too happy.

Zion Holder

I could barely take my eyes off her during dinner. Star was beautiful, every little piece of her carried a sweet perfection, one I became addicted to with each deep kiss, each tender touch, and oh my, she had said yes. The word was too small for the magnitude of feelings it caused me. Euphoria, gratitude, and a wave of love that threatened to tear me apart.

I loved that woman with every part of my body, my mind, and my heart. And to finish the day I had prepared for her, I guided my fiancée to the presidential suite I had arranged for our night, on the top floor of the same building.

I opened the door to the room, and Star walked through it, curious.

"Zion," she called with a smile upon seeing the white rose petals scattered around the dimly lit room leading to a very large round bed. Small candles were placed throughout the room, creating points of light everywhere, as if we had our own sky full of stars, and I couldn't help but smile at the sight of Star's emotional eyes taking in every detail.

My little one looked like she had stepped out of a royal movie. The shimmering dress reflected the tiny light spots, and she seemed to float as she walked, until...

"Ouch!" She turned her ankle, and the panic of her falling to the floor almost made me jump on her. I wrapped my arms around her waist and held her close to my chest. "I'm not used to heels."

"How about never wearing one of those again?" I joked, and she laughed at the exaggeration. I spun her delicate body in my arms until she faced away from me.

"Wow!" she whispered, encountering the view.

We were atop a hill that offered an exclusive and special view of the entire city, sparkling like a Christmas tree through the glass wall that took up half the room.

I caressed her bare back and ran my fingers over the small, fine scars she had there. There weren't many; thank God, nothing compared to mine, but I knew how much they still hurt. Even if she didn't tell me, I saw the sadness, anger, and fear that crossed her gaze every time she looked at the marks on her legs. Knowing how hard she fought to carry on every day, to smile and live made me want to kiss them. I leaned in, and she sighed as I brushed my lips against the scar that ran in a thin, disfigured line until it disappeared into her dress.

"Look." She pointed to the sky and rested her head on my shoulder. The starry night made the city lights more intense, as if they were one and the same. The feeling of looking at them was good.

"It's beautiful." I pushed her hair away and placed a kiss on the curve of her neck, leaving a little bite at the end.

"Remember when you said stars gave you hope?"

"You gave me hope," I corrected her and saw her smile form through the reflection in the glass.

"No, my love." Her voice choked, and I hugged her, fitting her back against my chest. "That was everything you gave me. Ever since you helped me in that stadium. You were the only one who truly protected me. The only one who was able to see me. You gave me hope when you saved me from that harassment; that's why I couldn't stop thinking about you. You gave me hope when you pulled me out of that prison, when you brought me into your world. You were my thread of hope even when I had stopped believing, and now..." She held my hands around her round belly. "I know what name I want to give our daughter."

"What is it, sweetheart?" My own voice was trembling.

"Hope. She is the hope of our love." I smiled into her hair and turned her to me until I had her in my arms. Her tear-filled eyes were watching me.

"Hope," I said in a whisper. "It's perfect, sweetheart."

I kissed her mouth with passion, urgency, and even a little anxiety. As if everything I felt for her couldn't fit into a single touch.

I ran my fingers to the opening of her dress and slowly unzipped it, wanting to savor every second, to capture in my heart every sound Star made under my touch, every moan, every spasm of pleasure. I turned her to face the glass wall and slid the fabric down until it was completely off. The thin panties accentuated her very round bottom, just like her breasts, and I fit myself against her back.

"Are you sure no one can see us from here?" She giggled as I nestled against her back.

"No, my love, we're on the top floor. No one can see us here." I took the flesh of her swollen breasts in my hands. Star pressed against my chest, her eyes closing as I began to tease her there. Her reflection in the glass was indecent, delicious.

I kissed the line of her neck and moved up. I captured the lobe of her ear with a gentle bite and pinched her brown nipple, recalling the moans she let slip in my memories.

"I love you, sweetheart." I caressed her belly and moved lower, slipping into her panties to touch the center of her body. I smiled, realizing how wet she was, feeling possessive of her.

Star was a virgin when I met her. No one had ever touched her, and I couldn't suppress the pleasure of knowing I had taken her innocence, that all her first sensations were with me, given freely and intensely. Her pussy was dripping from my touch, her moans were for me. Star chose me when I already belonged to her.

I pressed the swollen flesh and opened her lips between my fingers, teasing her to the limit.

"Zion!" She rubbed against me and whimpered when I pulled my touch away to lift her into my arms.

I walked over the white rose petals with my woman in my arms, aware that all my happiness was there, between my arms.

I laid her on the bed and admired her on the silk sheets, enjoying the sight of her swollen breasts and hard nipples of desire. Her warm, golden gaze shone brightly under the countless flickering candles. I removed my blazer, then unbuttoned each button of my shirt. I took off piece by piece until I was completely naked, never stopping to look at her, ready to prolong our night.

I lay down beside her and tucked her into my arms, playing with her exposed, beautiful breasts.

"You are the reason I still believe in human kindness," I said, biting the flesh of her breast, circling the nipple without touching it. She arched her back seeking pressure, relief, but I didn't give in. "You exude love." I blew on her swollen nipple. "Even after everything you've been through, you remain strong and dreamy."

"Ahhhhhhh!" I closed my lips around the nipple with too much force, alternating between sucking and biting. She grabbed my hair and let out a long, deep moan full of feeling. I slid my hand down her legs and caressed her, hard to the bone. Her delicate, slender fingers closed around my rigid erection, and I couldn't help but let out a muffled groan at the pleasure of that touch, which went up and down in an exciting slowness.

I turned her on her side and pressed my body against hers. I placed one of her legs between mine, forcing her to open up for me, and I caressed her butt. If only she knew the things I intended to do once she had our daughter... but now, there were risks I wasn't willing to take, not in two lifetimes, and I was going to love her safely, but all night long.

I slid a finger inside her, and she rolled her hips, seeking more. I caressed the center of her body, thrusting one finger, then two, slowly, focusing on teasing her to the limit and always stopping when she was about to climax.

She pushed her butt against my erection, and I pressed the thick head at her wet entrance. I stifled a curse as she pulsed, pulling me inside, surrendered, warm. I increased my caresses, penetrating her only a few inches.

"Zion, make love to me. I can't take it, I just can't..." I went deep the moment her body began to tremble and she screamed loudly. Her small body shook in my arms, and I had to breathe deeply to avoid climaxing without even moving. I thrust hard, prolonging her orgasm, which came energetic, impetuous. She grabbed the sheets between her fingers and began to roll, seeking more.

She was so delicious, I thrust deeper, harder until I felt my own limbs tingling with pleasure. I couldn't hold back as that round butt rolled against me, while she let out soft sounds, surrendered.

"I love you, Alena." She turned her face, her cheeks red contrasting with her surprised eyes. It was the first time I called her by her real name. "Every part of you is important to me. Whether it's Star or Alena, I love both."

She broke our contact and climbed onto my lap, facing me. She gripped my erection in her hands with a hungry look and guided it to her entrance. I slid inside her with a hoarse groan, and she began to roll her hips.

Her nails traced down my chest, outlining the scars marked there. I closed my eyes, opening her up for me.

"I love each of your versions. From the bodyguard to the warrior angel. From who you were in the past to who you are in the present... ahhhh." I returned to pinching her swollen clitoris and started thrusting her harder. "I love the father of my daughter, I love my future husband," she said, surrendered, languid, just before falling into another strong orgasm.

I couldn't resist, I rolled her body on the bed until she was underneath me. I opened her legs, controlling my own weight over her and thrust hard, strong, fast. My flesh opened hers, and she gasped, red from head to toe. Her delicious mouth open, lost in the spasms of her own orgasm. The ring on her right hand glimmered against the candlelight, and the sight was so intense and stunning that I exploded.

I buried my face in the curve of her neck, and a type of trembling growl rose in my throat as I spilled inside her.

The night was just beginning, but I knew that when I closed my eyes, exhausted from making love to my woman, two names would resonate in my subconscious, and I would sleep knowing I was the happiest man in the world.

Alena and Hope.

My wife and my daughter.

My Star and my Hope.

EPILOGUE ONE

Star

We got married in a cozy, intimate gathering that was meant to be a peaceful celebration among our family members, but who was I kidding?

I was talking about the Holders. What were the chances of everything going as planned?

I laughed nervously and clung to Uncle Walt's arm, who looked handsome in a black suit adorned with a gray tie. A mild, refreshing late afternoon served as the backdrop for the union of our love, and the excitement coursing through my body made me sway.

My eight-month belly felt heavy, and I could barely see my feet from up here, but I wanted to marry before Hope was born, and I felt more beautiful than ever.

My impeccably white dress resembled that of a princess. The bell-shaped silhouette cascaded down my figure, concentrating an intense shimmer right at the end of the bodice. Jasmin and I had spent weeks searching for the ideal model until we found it, and it was tailored specifically for me. My veil was long and adorned with tiny sparkling stones, beginning at the base of my hair, cascading down my back.

"Let's get started." Two wedding planners approached us, and I held my breath, struggling to stay calm. One of them handed me a bouquet of lilies and orchids in the color of my dress, beautiful like everything else.

I faced the path created by the green grass leading to the aisle where Zion would be waiting for me. There was a red carpet sprinkled with white rose petals, identical to the room where we spent our first night as newlyweds, and my eyes burned at the thought of my future husband at the other end.

We had opted for a simple wedding amid nature, where only our relatives, who were already few, and close friends would be present. In a lush green grove that seemed touched by a fairy godmother, the velvet benches extended like a carpet under very tall trees. The temple where the altar was carefully placed was surrounded by white lilies and orchids of the same color, just like the entire aisle, blending with the countless points of light throughout the place.

It was a dream come true. Marrying a prince, pregnant with a princess. Our Hope, the hope of our love.

"You look amazing, dear," Uncle Walt commented as we began walking toward the altar, and a slow, enveloping wedding march embraced us.

It was hard to control my emotions and the urge to cry, especially when I walked down the aisle and all our guests rose, awestruck.

Shaw, who barely laid eyes on me, started to cry; Lyon and Ray beamed animated smiles; Aunt Ava, Walt's wife, watched us through a curtain of tears that only made me want to cry even more. Jasmin's father was also present, along with Bertha and Deloris, who waved subtly; the latter surrendered to tears as I passed by them, embraced by a wave of immense gratitude.

Those people didn't know me. In another reality, we might never have met, but now they were part of my life, my family. A family that truly loved me, one that fought for me above all.

I sniffled and lifted my face. I almost choked when my eyes landed on the elegant, drop-dead gorgeous man waiting for me at the altar, in a dark gray suit custom-made by one of his father's favorite designers, enhancing Zion's beauty in every possible way. His broad shoulders were straight and erect, his posture always firm and attentive. His brown eyes sparkled; he was emotional, I could feel it. I realized I knew that man beyond anything else. I saw his heart, touched his soul, and gave him mine along the way.

I took another trembling step. Beside him at the altar stood the groomsmen: Jasmin, in a shimmering gray dress; Wolf and Snake, in their usual black suits, but with gray ties highlighting their looks, just like my father-in-law, Reid Holder, who watched me with a loving, even affected, gaze.

I walked among the flowers, hardly able to breathe. Hope was restless. My daughter seemed to feel what was happening there—the union of her parents, and that moved me even more. Zion's eyes gleamed strangely, and he kept gliding them up and down my body, as if wanting to memorize every detail. I knew full well that no amount of pictures could capture the beauty of walking toward him at the altar. And then, my fiancé came to meet me.

"Take care of her," Uncle Walt said, handing my hand to him.

"With my life," Zion's low reply came, but instead of taking my hand, he turned his palm up, and I knew exactly what he was doing.

It was my choice. Once again, Zion was telling me I could trust him to come and go, to protect me, to find my peace.

"This is real!" I raised my hand and interlaced my fingers with his.

I thought I couldn't love him more than I already did. Yet, he lowered his lips to place a kiss on my hand, and his vibrant gaze locked onto mine, as if he could read my mind and dive deep into my thoughts.

"You are the most perfect vision I've ever seen. A work of art. You look beautiful, my love," he said, his voice a heartfelt whisper. His hand rested on my round belly. My lips trembled. "Shall we? I can't wait any longer to make you mine, forever."

He walked slowly beside me. We reached the altar, and Zion helped me up the two steps and planted a kiss on my cheek. Jasmin came to me, took my bouquet of white lilies, and the wedding began.

I should have paid attention to what the priest was saying. The beautiful, sweet words he emphasized with such passion, the commitment, the union of two souls, but I could only focus on Zion's intense eyes, which were fixated on mine.

A wave of feelings hid behind his brown irises, and I understood because I felt the same. It was as if I were being embraced by the world; the joy of that moment left me euphoric, dizzy.

I couldn't contain the tear that rolled down my face. He caught it with his fingers, that simple gesture containing everything we had been through together. He took the microphone to say the vows. He positioned himself in front of me and flashed a lovely side smile.

"There are moments in our lives that we will never forget unless I end up losing my memory along the way. But that's one of your specialties, my love." A wave of laughter rose behind us, and even I started to laugh. "As for me, I'm silent. Many times, I've wished I could be different from who I am. I tried to be someone else to fit in, to bury the past and move on. Until the moment I met you, when I needed more than ever to be exactly as I was. When I had to accept that being silent is part of me, just like the many scars I have on my body, marks of a past I couldn't erase. I thought I would be happy if I became someone else, but when you saw my scars, when you touched them with your hands and your heart, everything changed. I realized how grateful I was to be who I am. If I were different, I wouldn't have found the love of my life." He flashed a smile that didn't reach his eyes, which were, by the way, misty. "Star, you taught me what it means to love someone more than myself and gave me a daughter I can't wait to meet. But more than that, you gave me your trust. Your angelic voice when I come home exhausted and your love when I'm burning up."

"Zion! That shameless boy... didn't I teach you any manners, kid?" my father-in-law scolded us from behind, and I burst out laughing, my face burning with embarrassment.

"Sorry, Dad." He bit his lip. "Today I wanted to make a declaration worthy of what you mean to me, Star. You and Hope are my life, my hope, my happiness. My heart is yours, and I will take care of you, forever."

I loved him so much it hurt deep in my heart, and I completely broke down when he took one of the rings and continued speaking in that deep, firm voice:

"I, Zion Holder, take Alena Farrel as my wife, my Star, and I promise to be faithful, to love her and respect her, in joy and in sorrow, in health and in sickness, every day of our lives."

Zion kissed my hand and slid a gold ring adorned with diamonds onto my finger; I couldn't help but notice the tiny star tips all over the jewelry.

I took a deep breath, trying to find my voice again. His tear-filled eyes swept me off my feet, and it was my turn to declare my love. I grabbed the microphone, my hands trembling, reverberating all the love, admiration, and passion I felt for that man.

"When I saw you for the first time, I was scared. You have no idea how much I regret that brief moment of panic, even though I didn't know who that silent, mysterious man was. Later, I would discover how loyal, respectful, admirable, and above all, protective you are. You took care of every one of my wounds, even those hidden deep in my heart. You taught me how a touch can make everything real." I lifted our intertwined hands. "And how there were still good people in the world. I am grateful that God sent me an angel like you just to care for me, and you've always been there. You took risks, protected me, saved me. You stood by my side even without knowing me. Zion, my bodyguard and owner of my world, when I was in despair, you sang to me, and I never forgot those words that were like sunlight chasing away the storm. I was scared, in a car without one of the windows, in the dark, cold night, in a deserted forest. And all I could hear was your voice calming me." I breathed and began to sing acapella, pouring all my love into the tones of "Don't Forget Me" by Nathan Wagner. A song that had become one of my favorites, I infused all my feelings into that melody.

I thought all my hope was gone
Until you arrived

"I, Alena Farrel, take Zion Holder as my husband, my Ghost," I sobbed, "and I promise to be faithful, to love him and respect him, in joy and in sorrow, in health and in sickness, every day of our lives." I placed the plain gold ring on his left hand.

"By the power vested in me, I declare you husband and wife. You may kiss the bride."

"Finally!" he whispered, wrapping his arms around my waist as laughter erupted behind us. "My wife..." he breathed, not letting me go, and Hope, our daughter, began to stir. I took his hand and placed it on my belly.

"She feels the same joy I do." He feigned nonchalance and looked away. The sleeve of his blazer brushed discreetly against his eyes, and he turned back to me with a huge smile.

"I love you. Damn, I love you so much!" he shouted, hugging me tightly.

"Oh my God, the priest, Zion!" I tapped his shoulder, cursing, which in the end wasn't so different from the foul-mouthed Alena I remembered.

"Oh, don't worry, I'm not a priest!" the man in the robe said with a shrug.

"What do you mean, you're not a priest?" Zion's eyes widened, and I mirrored his surprise.

"Don't worry, I'm authorized to officiate marriages. You're officially married." Both Zion and I looked at Snake, who was smirking at the altar. He had been responsible for hiring the priest.

I opened my mouth, about to question whether that marriage was even legal, but the question was overtaken by a sharp pain that made me grip Zion's shoulder tightly.

"Star?" he called, anxious, and more voices joined his. A cold wave coursed down my legs and spread across the fabric of my dress until a puddle formed around me.

"The bag..." I tried to say, but Jasmin was quicker than me and shouted to the heavens:

"Shit, the bag BURST!" My maid of honor tossed my bouquet into the bushes, lifted the folds of my dress, and ran toward me on her high heels.

"But it's not time yet!" Ghost shook his head, wrapping one arm around my waist and began to speak non-stop. "Hope's arrival isn't due until next month. What now? Damn it! How do you feel, love? Does it hurt? Of course it does, what kind of idiot asks that?!" And he lifted me off the ground as if I didn't weigh a good ten extra pounds, then shouted: "Let's go to the hospital. Wolf, call the doctor, she needs to be there when we arrive. Snake, you drive, Dad! DAD!"

"Calm down, son, I'm here. I'm right here." Reid touched his shoulder.

"Can you stop spinning and put me down?" I slapped his arm. "I'm already dizzy."

"No way, walking can be harmful. She's coming, our daughter is coming."

"Exactly, she's going to come out of me and slap you for making her nauseous in the womb, be quiet, Zion!" I shouted, panicked. "Jasmin!" I called for help.

"Stop!" She placed her hands on my husband's shoulders and held him firmly; her slender arms had conviction. "Put the pregnant woman on the ground, now," she growled.

Snake started laughing uncontrollably, like an agent of chaos; Wolf looked ready to shove his phone in his ears and drag me out by my hair. Reid stared at the priest with suspicion, and Shaw ran off, shouting a resonant "Mercy, prepare the carrrrrs!" toward the parking lot. It sounded like a siren, but he was the only one thinking of organizing the car exit to avoid delays, and before I knew it, everything had turned into a wild rush.

✴

"SNAKE, I ASKED FOR a priest!" Ghost growled, holding me in his arms in the back seat while Snake drove with Wolf beside him in the passenger seat.

"You asked for someone to officiate a ceremony. I thought you were open to all options," he shot back, laughing.

"In the end, you're married, and my niece is being born, so can we focus on this damn road?" Jasmin interrupted. Hope's maid of honor looked disheveled and flushed but insisted on sitting in the back with us in case of any unforeseen events.

"Oh, shit!" I groaned loudly as a sharp pain pierced the base of my belly, like a strong cramp.

"My God, breathe, breathe, one, two, three, puppy, Jesus, I don't know how to breathe like a puppy. I can't even swim like a dog!" Jasmin pressed her hand to her forehead, panicking.

"How does a dog breathe? Someone has to know!" Ghost shouted, waving his hand in front of my face as if he'd suddenly transformed into a human fan.

"I told our dad we needed a dog, but he didn't listen." Wolf's eyes were wide and mismatched. "Get out of the way, damn it, there's a baby being born here!" He cursed at someone on the highway, and Ghost's hand kept waving in my face. Another pang made me double over.

"Get that hand away from me!" I pushed him away, irritated, starting to understand what Aunt Ava meant when she said pregnant women could get aggressive.

It wasn't the pregnant women's fault. The men provoked it!

Ghost

"NO, I WON'T ENDURE another thrilling afternoon of your family causing a ruckus in this hospital corridor. Either everyone stays quiet, or I'll have to throw you out," Dr. Audra said firmly as we passed through the hospital entrance.

Star had already cursed a long list of swear words on the way to the hospital, some of which I swore I'd never heard before in my life, but now she was just pain and worry, which left me desperate. I preferred when she was cursing me out.

"Yes, doctor, they'll behave, you have my word," my dad promised.

"Great, then the water has broken." She turned to two nurses and instructed them to head to the delivery room, which was already prepared thanks to Wolf's call. "Will you be able to witness the arrival of our Hope, Dad?" the doctor asked me.

"Y-yes, of course I will," I stammered.

My dad placed a hand on my shoulder, and I looked at him uncertainly just moments before entering.

"We'll be here, son, waiting to meet the new member of our family, and you better get ready, because once you go through that door, your life will change." He smiled, and there was so much love in his gray eyes that I wrapped him in a tight hug, scanning each person present.

Lyon, Ray, and Shaw, our best friends. Wolf, Snake, and my dad, who were my support alongside Jasmin, my sister-in-law, my friend, and our daughter's godmother, whose big blue eyes were misty. Star's uncles beamed with joy, and Deloris and Bertha looked more anxious than I felt, while the priest who wasn't a priest stood there.

I narrowed my eyes at him, but I didn't have time to try to figure out what series of events brought him to the hospital.

I entered the delivery room and received the clothes I was supposed to wear. After cleaning up, I joined Star, who had already changed out of her wedding dress and was lying on the bed. Her golden eyes shone like two beacons, accentuated by makeup. Drops of sweat clung to her forehead as she twisted the sheets between her fingers, anxious.

"Everything will be fine, love," I tried to soothe her.

"I knew it... from the beginning."

"Knew what?"

"That a Holder would cause some chaos at our wedding." She laughed and started to cry. "I didn't imagine it would be my Holder."

"Don't cry, sweetheart." I wiped her tears with the back of my hand.

"I'm scared."

"I won't leave you, not for a second. Soon we'll be holding our daughter, right, doctor?" I glanced at the doctor checking some exams.

"Although this isn't the date we had in mind, Hope is healthy and weighs enough for a smooth arrival. So don't worry, Star. Just do what we ask, okay?" Another doctor and two more nurses entered the room. The contractions intensified, and according to the doctor, Hope was ready to come.

I could barely breathe. I felt every scream from Star in my heart, as if they were splitting me in two, each crease that appeared on her face as she strained. Her slender fingers almost crushed my hand, and occasionally she cursed strange words.

And then it happened. My wife was strong and courageous once more and gave birth to our Hope, who came into the world crying at the top of her lungs.

I stood frozen watching that little pink creature waving her hands and feet nonstop, crying loudly. My heart skipped a beat, and I was filled with the deepest, truest love, as if life and death merged into one, without time, without the world; all there was was the incessant sound of my daughter's cries.

For a moment, nothing else made sense besides those tiny wrinkled fingers and round little face. That's when I realized Reid was right. I had become a father. My life would never be the same, and I was about to drown in that wave of joy.

"She's beautiful." The doctor placed the bundle in Star's arms as she cried continuously, her hair matted with sweat, but I had never seen her more beautiful. It took me a moment to realize that I was also crying.

"Hi, Hope, I'm your mommy." She cradled our daughter, who immediately recognized her and sought her breast. I touched her with my hand, my whole world right there in the small inches of her tiny body. "And that big guy over there is your daddy."

"It's me, baby, your dad." I leaned in toward them and kissed Star, crazy with love, overwhelmed by so much happiness.

I had become so much more than Ghost, the marked and silent man. Now I was the husband of an indescribable and perfect woman, owner of starry eyes and a heart of gold. I was Alena's husband and the father of the most beautiful baby in the universe, our Hope.

I had rewritten my story, and I liked it so much more now.

EPILOGUE TWO

Ghost

"Can you remind me why I'm here?" Snake complained as we entered the pediatric clinic where Hope was having her routine check-up.

"You're one of the godfathers," I reminded him.

"I never agreed to watch my niece get tortured. Just look at her, she's too small for such cruelty." His hard eyes softened as they landed on the little pink bundle in my arms.

Hope was the most beautiful, adorable, and calm baby in the universe. Her big golden eyes, just like her mother's, smiled all the time. Even Snake couldn't keep his tough exterior for long.

"Where are Star and Jasmin?" Wolf asked beside me, his funny expression sweeping over every corner of the exam room.

"Jasmin is with Star checking out a warehouse downtown."

We were enjoying one of the few mornings when we weren't buried in back-to-back meetings. With the planning for the new Holder offices, I was swamped with work alongside my brothers and came home exhausted almost every night. Being able to hold my daughter and my wife had become the highlight of my day, and I knew all the effort and exhaustion would be worth it when I officially opened and took over the presidency of Holder Family. Until then, fatigue was my last name, and Star was just as overwhelmed as I was.

My wife was caught in a busy routine with her friend who supported her in everything, always with Hope and the babysitters nearby to help, a requirement of mine while she studied. Star had also started working on a project she intended to launch that year: opening a pub in downtown

Chicago. An interesting opportunity had come up that morning and required her evaluation. It was her dream, but she didn't want Hope to go to the clinic with anyone but her parents, so I took on the responsibility and dragged her godfathers with me. I wasn't going through this alone.

"They should be here. Women are naturally more resilient to pain." Wolf flinched when Hope's pediatrician appeared before him.

"Should I remind you that the one getting the shot is her?" the doctor said with a smile, looking at Hope with affection.

"How absurd!" Snake growled. "How can you smile?"

"All babies go through this. You survived."

"I'm not sure Snake was vaccinated," Wolf teased, earning an elbow to the ribs from our older brother.

"Take Hope to the end of the hall; the nurse will give the vaccinations," she instructed, still smiling and playing with my daughter before returning to her office.

"Hope Holder?" The nurse wanted to confirm, and I stammered a yes that sounded more like a croak. "Alright, wait for a moment." She picked up a syringe with a needle, and my eyes widened.

"For the love of God, there must be a smaller needle!" Snake began to get agitated.

"It's the right size for vaccinations. Don't worry." The young nurse tried to calm us and turned her back to grab the medication.

"Maybe you should hold her, Snake. You're the biggest of us three," I suggested, already shaking from head to toe.

"No way, remember what happened the last time I held her?"

My brother had tried to hold Hope during her first week after birth. It was hilarious to see a man his size trying to find the right way to hold a baby.

She cried the moment he closed his arms around her tiny body, and Snake panicked. His soul seemed to leave his body, leaving only the tattoos behind, and he turned very pale, truly believing he had hurt Hope in some way. It took us a while to calm him down; she cried every time she was handed from one person to another until she got used to it. At first, she only didn't cry in the arms of Star, Jasmin, and Shaw. And in mine, of course, and it took about fifteen days for her to accept a new hold without bursting into tears. But Snake wasn't going to risk trying again. He was scared, but the love he felt for his niece was real and shone in his very blue eyes.

"She's so tiny, how can they do this to her?" He was anxious, not more than I was.

"Let's be honest, none of us will be able to vaccinate her," Wolf whispered.

"I would have hung up on you if I knew you intended to drag me into this abomination," Snake retorted.

"Let's run away," Wolf suggested.

"But she needs to be vaccinated." I tried to act like an adult.

"Are you going to hold her?" I swallowed hard, remembering the huge needle, and looked at my daughter, calm in my arms, assured of her safety. Her little eyes roamed curiously around, she was so beautiful, so tiny.

"If we're going to do this, we need to know there will be consequences," I warned, looking at Wolf.

"Knowing Jasmin, we're going to suffer retaliation."

"All three of us," Snake added.

"Are we going to take the risk?" I asked, already backing away from the vaccination room door.

"Isn't that what we do all the time?" Wolf glanced down the hallway.

"Let's go!" Snake commanded.

I wrapped Hope in a hug, covering her little face as if hiding a puppy on a bus, and we hurried back down the hallway.

"Sir?" the nurse called, and we quickened our steps. "Sir! Come back here, sir. She needs to be vaccinated!"

"Go, go, go!" I urged hastily.

"Run and scatter, she doesn't know who she's dealing with. I mean, my niece!" Snake directed our escape.

"Gentlemen, come back here!"

I felt completely capable of participating in a car chase, entering a shootout, or storming a house with an armed psychopath. But all my courage dissolved when I had to vaccinate my daughter.

We ran, like the three cowards we were.

Wolf

Some time later

"WILL YOU MARRY ME?"

"No!" Jasmin replied, biting her lip in that mischievous way. "I already told you, we'll get married when I officially become CEO."

"What do I have to do to convince you to be my wife already? You can still be CEO; it's in your blood, nothing would stop you." I pulled her by the waist and made her sit on my lap on the sofa, under the hard erection she provoked with that indecent lingerie. I bit her nipple through the fabric and heard her softly moan, surrendering. "Shouldn't we get married and think about having a Hope for us?"

"A Hope?" Her eyes sparkled with lust, and I was sure that the same warm fervor that embraced my heart had enveloped hers at the thought.

It was always like this when we talked about our niece, who was also our goddaughter. The child seemed like a being of light. She had the same cinnamon-colored eyes as Star, but she was an absolute Xerox of Ghost, with the same brown, straight hair and that little upturned nose that made me laugh.

Hope brightened each day of our family but almost caused the deaths of Ghost, Snake, and me after Jasmin and Star discovered our little escape on vaccination day. It took them months to forget the incident, but Star's indignant expression when she laid eyes on my youngest brother and realized Hope hadn't been vaccinated would be etched deeply in my memories. I thought she was going to rip his head off, while the blonde who was his partner in crime was already plotting where to bury our bodies.

The memory made me smile.

"Maybe I'll think about your proposal if you stop torturing me." Jasmin's hands slid down to my shorts' zipper, but before she could fully open it, the apartment doorbell rang, interrupting the game. "Are you expecting someone?" She grabbed a robe and put it on.

"No. And the doorman didn't buzz." I went to the door and looked through the peephole. Well, I looked at the clock, and it was almost one in the morning. "What are you doing here?" I opened the door.

Snake was leaning against the doorframe, as if he could barely stand. I immediately caught the strong smell of alcohol.

"Eltáfilh..." he mumbled something unintelligible and swayed.

"What language is that?" Jasmin laughed behind me as I went to my brother, supporting his waist and bringing him inside.

"The language of alcohol. I'm fluent in it too." I chuckled. "What happened for you to drink so much?" I helped him sit on the sofa, and he buried his head in his hands.

"I'm going to..."

"Going where?" I tried to encourage him, and suddenly he grabbed me by the collar and pressed his face close to mine. He looked desperate, out of his mind. His very blue eyes were cold and somewhat lost. "Snake, you better say something; I'm starting to get worried."

"I'm going to be a dad." And he shook me.

"What?" Jasmin and I screamed in unison.

"I'm going to be a dad, damn it!" He ran his hands through his hair and collapsed onto the sofa.

"God, why me?" I pointed at a half-unconscious Snake. "You guys are going to give me a heart attack, you idiots."

Did you love *Dark Instinct*? Then you should read *The Commander's Weakness* by Amara Holt!

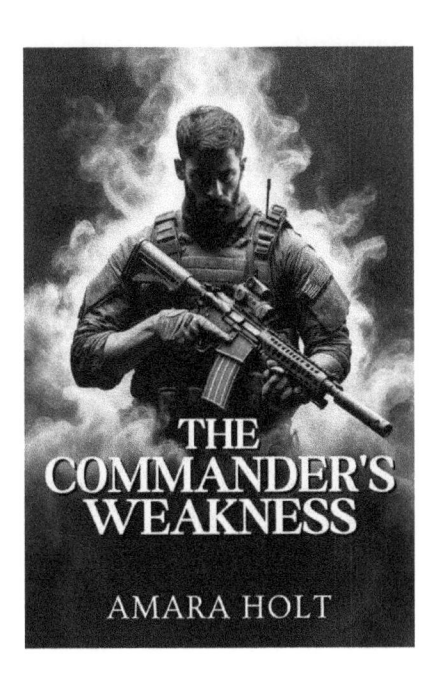

The Commander's Weakness: A Gripping Tale of **Love**, **Loss**, and **Revenge** in a World of Secrets

Kimberly thought she had a **normal life**—until everything shattered. Raised by **undercover agents** working for a secret government organization, her world is flipped upside down when an ambush takes her mother's life and her father vanishes without a trace. In the aftermath, Kimberly is thrust into the highly secured **Military Zone**, a mysterious and dangerous place created to protect the children of secret agents.

Under the command of the cold and ruthless **Commander First**, Kimberly quickly learns that survival in this world requires **obedience**, **strength**, and a resolve like no other. But as she navigates this new life, questions linger: What drove this hardened young commander to power? And why is he **feared** by so many?

Driven by **vengeance** and hardened by loss, Commander First had long believed he was **invincible**—until one fateful encounter changed everything. Kimberly's arrival stirs emotions he thought he'd buried forever, unveiling a **vulnerability** with a name and a face: Kimberly.

In a world where trust is a luxury and enemies are lurking everywhere, **The Commander's Weakness** tells the thrilling story of two lives intertwined by fate, forced to confront their deepest **fears** and **desires**. Will they rise above their pasts, or will their weaknesses become their downfall?

This **page-turning** novel is perfect for fans of military romance, action-packed thrillers, and stories of **unexpected love** set against the backdrop of a **secretive world** where danger lurks around every corner.

Discover **The Commander's Weakness**—a gripping blend of **intrigue**, **passion**, and the fight for **survival**.

About the Author

Amara Holt is a storyteller whose novels immerse readers in a whirlwind of suspense, action, romance and adventure. With a keen eye for detail and a talent for crafting intricate plots, Amara captivates her audience with every twist and turn. Her compelling characters and atmospheric settings transport readers to thrilling worlds where danger lurks around every corner.